Virginia Woolf

and the European Avant-Garde:

London, Painting, Film and Photography

• Allison Tzu Yu Lin

To My Parents

PREFACE

This work aims to situate Virginia Woolf's writing among modernisms. Through her response to modernism's diversity of genres, range of philosophies, visual arts and art criticism, Woolf creates her own way of narrating the city of London. I take the issue of gendered gaze as a critical focus and to synthesise this with the depiction of the visual and urban space in Woolf's novels. I want to pursue the answer to this question: how do Woolf's modes of vision work in the formation of her London? By answering this question, I hope to understand and analyse Woolf's aesthetics of urban vision.

I select some of Woolf's writings about London, looking at the way in which Woolf's writing strategies have evolved as a result of her engagement with painting, film and photography; through which Woolf has the Post-Impressionist painters' expression of the streets of London as maps of emotions. Woolf also makes abstract forms, colours and shapes of the inner time through the Cubist cinematic juxtaposition of the gaze, and finally using Surrealist photographic perspective to explore desire, and also to objectify a series of photographic images into a form of criticism and knowledge.

First of all, I will analyse the aesthetics of the Bloomsbury Group, looking at the historical context and artistic tradition from which Woolf begins. It shows that Woolf's work is informed and shaped by the Post-Impressionist movement. I also use Woolf's reading of Proust to illuminate her 'dual vision', a concept which is similar to Walter Benjamin's view of the flâneur. Secondly, in the next chapter, I will examine *Night and Day* (1919) in relation to William James's notion of the stream of consciousness and Henry James's concern with psychological realism and the painter's eye. Thirdly, I will discuss *Mrs Dalloway* (1925), looking at the dialectic of time in Bergson's pure duration and Deleuze's cinematic sense, as well as Eisenstein's montage. Finally, I will discuss *The Years* (1937) and *Three Guineas* (1938), to see how photography informs Woolf's gendered way of seeing and Roland Barthes's life-death game.

ACKNOWLEDGEMENTS

Virginia Woolf has lived again in my mind while I was writing this work in London. The idea of connecting Henry James and Virginia Woolf's writing came in the year 2000, when I saw the paintings of the Bloomsbury Group in the Centre of British Arts at Yale University. Four years of London life, for me, is a treasure, a once-for-a-life-time experience. It is a duration, for I have lived and visualised Yale's New Haven in Woolf's Bloomsbury, Monk House and Bell's Charleston in Newhaven, Sussex.

While I was studying Woolf's work, art sources and journals, I turned to libraries and archives for research. Particularly I want to thank Goldsmiths Library (Goldsmiths College, University of London), Senate House Library (University of London), British Library, British Film Institute (BFI) and Hyman Kreitman Research Centre for the Tate Library and Archive, Tate Britain, London.

I am extremely grateful to my editor, Mr. Maurice Lai, for his advice and help. A section of my third chapter of this work has been presented as a paper, 'The Dialectic of Time in Film Form: Mrs Dalloway', in the 17th Annual International Conference on Virginia Woolf (June 2007, University of Miami, Ohio, U.S.A.). A section in my second chapter of this work has been presented as a paper, 'Painting Psychological Realism: London and Art in Night and Day', in the 16th Annual International Conference on Virginia Woolf (June 2006, University of Birmingham, UK). My conference papers, 'The Aesthetics of Urban Viison: Reading Benjamin and Woolf' (presented in July 2005, Literary London International Conference, Kingston University, London) and 'The Flâneur's Gaze, Ideology and the Dialectical Representation of London' (presented in July 2004, University of Wales, Aberystwyth, Wales), both construct the framework of the Introduction of this work.

Finally I want to thank my parents and Ali Tolga Bozdana, for their endless love.

Allison Tzu-yu Lin

2008 London

LIST OF ABBREVIATIONS

D – *The Diary of Virginia Woolf*. Eds. Anne Oliver Bell and Andrew McNeillie. London: The Hogarth Press, 1977 – 1984, 5 volumes.

L – *The Letters of Virginia Woolf*. Eds. Nigel Nicolson and Joanne Trautmann. London: The Hogarth Press, 1975 – 1980, 6 volumes.

CH – *Virginia Woolf: The Critical Heritage*. Eds. Robin Majumdar and Allen McLaurin. London: Routledge and Kegan Paul, 1975.

E – *The Essays of Virginia Woolf*. Ed. Andrew McNeillie. London: The Hogarth Press, 1986 – 1994, 4 volumes.

ND – *Night and Day* (1919). Ed. J. H. Stape. Oxford: Blackwell, 1994.

MD – *Mrs Dalloway* (1925). Ed. Elaine Showalter. London: Penguin, 1992.

TY – *The Years* (1937). London: The Hogarth Press.

TG – *Three Guineas* (1938). London: The Hogarth Press.

CONTENTS

PROLOGUE

Androgynous Woolf

My central research interest is in the relation between the visual and the verbal in the writings of Virginia Woolf. The work of existing critics lays a foundation for an extensive understanding of Woolf, the city and visual cultures. I want to re-discover and re-consider Woolf's writing as an androgynous textuality. I focus my research interest on Woolf's narrative style, her life-long engagement with philosophy and fine arts.

Re-discovering Woolf: an Androgynous Textuality

The idea of androgyny is a solution for Woolf to the problem of what Herbert Marder called 'the opposites'[1] – namely, femininity and masculinity,[2] experimentation and tradition, inner and outer spheres, home and abroad,[3]

---

[1] Herbert Marder, *Feminism and Art: A Study of Virginia Woolf.* Chicago: The University of Chicago Press, 1968, p.128.

[2] As Jane Goldman points out, Woolf's androgyny 'has been understood as both synthesising and perpetuating gender difference'. See *The Cambridge Introduction to Virginia Woolf* (Cambridge: Cambridge University Press, 2006), p.130.

[3] As Maria DiBattista points out, Woolf's artistic identity depends on the 'soul-dislocating experience of exile to bring it to independent maturity', for her voyages are primarily imaginative ones, and while that made her 'more stay-at-home' than Henry James, Conrad, or Joyce, she was as much 'an international modernist' as they. As one can see in *A Room of One's Own*, Woolf takes the position of an outsider, in order to satirise British institutions such as the Army, the Judiciary, the Church, even the University. See 'An Improper Englishwoman: Woolf as a World Writer'. *Woolf Across Cultures*. Ed. Natalya Reinhold. New York: Pace University Press, 2004, p.18.

visual and verbal arts. For me, Woolf's androgynous mind goes beyond any biological or literal opposition of male and female sexual identities. It is a metaphor for a hybrid textuality, a mixture of literary genres (poetry, drama, essay and novel) and artistic forms (particularly painting, photography and film), in terms of her narrative technique.

Critics have discussed the significance of Woolf's idea of androgyny in the context of sexual difference, psychology and language. For instance, Toril Moi and Elaine Showalter highlight two different approaches to Woolf's work. Showalter, in her *A Literature of Their Own*, suggests that Woolf's 'flight' into androgyny does not express women's experience fully, because she reads Woolf's writing as a strategic escape from her troubles as a woman in a patriarchal society. According to Showalter, Woolf's suicide reveals the failure of her ideal emotional utopia – androgyny. A 'room' of one's own is actually a 'safe' remove, for women can express 'their own anger, rebellion, and sexuality' in this sanctuary and prison.[4] Showalter maintains that the Angel of the house is Woolf herself, and a room of one's own is one's own grave.

In Showalter's account, one can see her impatience with Woolf, for her ideal emotional utopia does not show enough anger. On the other hand, Moi takes a poststructuralist approach, separating the author and his / her works, in the light of the death of the author and the birth of the text, claimed by post-structuralists such as Roland Barthes. Consequently, the reader can see what Woolf tried to achieve in her writing, by considering how she uses language to de-construct the patriarchal myth and 'the death-dealing binary oppositions of masculinity and femininity'.[5] By doing that Moi puts herself in a position, from which it becomes possible to read Virginia Woolf as 'the progressive, feminist writer of genius she undoubtedly was'.[6]

---

[4]   Elaine Showalter, *A Literature of Their Own: British Women Novelists from Brontë to Lessing*. 1977. Princeton, NJ: Princeton University Press, 1999, p.264.

[5]   Toril Moi, *Sexual/Textual Politics: Feminist Literary Theory*. London: Routledge, 1985, p.13.

[6]   Moi, *Sexual/Textual Politics*, p.18.

Other critics have, like Moi, tried to see Woolf in a wider vision of feminist discourse and modernism. For instance, Makiko Minow-Pinkney synthesises Showalter and Moi's views, in order to re-define Woolf's symbolic 'androgynous mind' in the modernist context. By starting to question the 'utopian vision'[7] of undivided consciousness of the author and the text, sexuality and textuality, the subject and its symbolic, Minow-Pinkney shows two alternative approaches: first, Lacanian *méconnaissance* and second, feminist responses to Lacanian theory, particularly Kristeva and Cixous. Seeing Woolf's androgyny as a symbolic balance between two forces (patriarchy / the oppressed Other), Minow-Pinkney makes sense of Woolf's writing in terms of a modernist syntax, claiming the idea of androgyny is a symbol with subversive power, for its displacement of positions as "a challenge to the fixity of identity, as a challenge to the 'male' and 'female'," as a challenge of the "whole fix of 'sexuality'."[8]

In '1928-31: Androgyny and the End of the Novel', John Mepham argues that Woolf's vision of androgyny can be read as her 'modernist manifesto'.[9] By seeing her subsequent work as a series of 'anti-novels', Mepham suggests that Woolf's writing is a hybrid genre – for instance, the 'elegy' of *To the Lighthouse*, the anti-biography *Orlando*, and her A Room of One's Own in 1929 – a 'non-fiction work of history and theory, in the form of a series of lectures by a fictional character', the eyeless playpoem of *The Waves* and the 'Essay-Novel' of *The Pargiters*.[10] Catharine R. Stimpson, in 'Woolf's Room, Our Project: The Building of Feminist Criticism', also claims that in *A Room of One's Own*, one can see Woolf's feminist commitments

---

[7]   Makiko Minow-Pinkney, *Virginia Woolf and the Problem of the Subject*. Briton: Harvester, 1987, p.10.

[8]   Minow-Pinkney, *Virginia Woolf and the Subject*, p.15.

[9]   John Mepham, *Virginia Woolf: A Literary Life*. London: Macmillan, 1991, p.124.

[10]   Mepham, *Virginia Woolf*, p.125.

expressed by her narrative mode.[11] In her punning and playful style, Woolf maintains in her narrative practice a refusal to stick to one fixed position.

Woolf's Art and the Visual

Modernism offers a new way of expressing a rapid changing social and perceptual world. According to Sascha Bru, in 1906, the Futurist F. T. Marinetti, connected the term 'avant-garde' to an image of the future,[12] in which the picture of the artist's present is an allegory of a substantial future. The avant-garde, from the beginning, as Raymond Williams has pointed out, 'saw itself as the breakthrough to the future'.[13] The image of the future, as the modernist avant-garde depicted it through experimental modes of perception and expression, is an alternative to the here and now – the city, the machine, speed, time and space.

And yet, the creativity of the modernist avant-garde is not all about depicting external and physical movements. The conceptions of time and space are explored and conceived as the very essence of modernism. Time and space are experienced as an inner thinking process, as the semiotic, the imaginary and the metaphysical. The consciousness of time and space, when the viewing subject is situated in the modern urban milieu, is a combination of the internal and external elements. The modernist expression of time and space reveals modes of seeing, feeling and thinking.

---

[11] Catharine R. Stimpson, 'Woolf's Room, Our Project: The Building of Feminist Criticism'. *Virginia Woolf*. Ed. Rachel Bowlby. 1992. London: Longman, 1997, p.171.

[12] Sascha Bru, 'The Phantom League. The Centennial Debate on the Avant-Garde and Politics'. *The Invention of Politics in the European Avant-Garde*. Eds. Sascha Bru and Gunther Martens. Amsterdam: Rodopi, 2006, p.9.

[13] Raymond Williams, Introduction. *Vision and Blueprints: Avant-Garde Culture and Radical Politics in Early Twentieth-Century Europe*. Eds. Edward Timms and Peter Collier. Manchester: Manchester University Press, 1988, p.3.

The past, the present and the future can be experienced at one single moment and place, as one can see in the movement of time depicted on the space of one canvas in a Cubist painting. This non-linear psychology creates the unreal city of London, which T. S. Eliot evoked as his model of cultural decline and symbolic return. Virginia Woolf's hybrid textuality, for her part, challenges a fixed literary genre and a fixed gender definition. For Woolf, time and space are not objective facts, but the image of feeling and emotion, as it is created and constructed by the consciousness.

Woolf's narrative technique suggests her understanding and use of the visual arts. As I have mentioned, her writing illustrates a hybrid textuality, in which one can read a mixture of different genres and artistic media. Woolf's writing works through symbols and transforms scenes or solid visual objects into metaphors. This narrative form enables Woolf to join fragmentary visual elements in the process of thinking with 'the broad stream of life',[14] as Herbert Marder suggests. Fine arts create Woolf's own symbolism in her narrative technique, deepens her vision, revealing the psychological force beneath the practical affairs of daily life. Woolf's narrative method is to lead the reader into the consciousness of her characters, to show internal reality as the essence of lived experience, when emotion and feeling come from the entire stream of associated thoughts.

Woolf depicts the ways a character sees, feels and thinks, in which it shows how experiences of time and space have transformed from the external world to an expression of the psychological totality of the self. Visual objects are depicted as projections of the state of mind; emotions can be shown in an abstract form, a reverie, a dream-image. In a parallel manner, the inner world is externalised through the writing process, which concretises thinking, feeling and emotion into images, metaphors and symbols. Patterns of vision

---

[14] Herbert Marder, *Feminism and Art: A Study of Virginia Woolf.* Chicago: University of Chicago Press, 1968, p.154.

indicate different modes of time (past, present and future), the discontinuity of thoughts and visual impressions, and moments of perception. In Woolf's novels, the internal world is represented as a constant transformation, a synthetic experience of a constant state of change. This transformation reveals the flux of time and motion, thinking and walking. Her narrative technique makes me think of Henry James's major novel *The Ambassadors* (1903). I will discuss this point in detail in the second chapter of this work.

Woolf had significant connection with the visual arts, art criticism and philosophy. The friendship between Roger Fry and Woolf was critical for her creative works,[15] as Allen McLaurin points out. The problem involved in representation is central in both their arts. Fry's aesthetic theory illuminates the psychological element in Woolf's writing. According to Fry's theory of art, the artist should paint his own feeling in artistic forms, instead of slavishly presenting what things look like. In this light, the painter's perspective is a powerful influence on Woolf's writings. The paintings of Duncan Grant and Walter Sickert shaped and developed Woolf's narrative style, in terms of her use of colour to depict London as a significant form. Woolf's understanding of the painter's eye helps her to define the importance of visual elements, to show how this physical 'eye' is transformed into the mind's eye, into the desire of her characters, in which the external and the internal worlds can be synthesised in her narrative.

In *The London Mercury*, XIII, 73, November 1925, Charles Grinley, a reader of the magazine, had a letter addressed to the editor, saying that he had been subscribing to the magazine for three years, but he had never seen any article on film. For him, it is 'unfair' to imagine that film is 'unworthy of serious attention'.[16] Virginia Woolf, in 1925 and 1926, published the

---

[15] Allen McLaurin, *Virginia Woolf: The Echoes Enslaved*. Cambridge: Cambridge University Press, 1973, p.17.

[16] Charles Grinley, 'A Plea for the Cinema'. *The London Mercury* XIII, 73, November 1925, p.73.

novel *Mrs Dalloway* and the essay 'The Cinema', which in spite of her sense of the limitations of contemporary film, showed her awareness of the potential of cinematic technique, and her exploration and use of new cinematic visual language in her narrative style. Her narrative experiment comes close to Bergson's concept of the pure duration of time, which was later developed by Deleuze, as 'the time-image' in his *Cinema 2*.

Cinematic style drew from painting, and many of its themes have been explored in literature, music and the theatre. According to Standish D. Lawder, the cinema was discovered by modern painters, particularly the Italian Futurists in Milan (external / physical motion of a visual object), and the Parisian avant-garde (the Cubist multiple points of view). In 1913, in painting, poetry, music, theatre and the film, as Lawder noted that there appeared 'a deluge of new ideas, new experiments, and new theories'.[17] For example, Schönberg's experiments changed the sound of modern music; in French literature, it was an '*annus mirabilis*', with important work by Proust and Gide.[18] Jacques Copeau established the Vieux Colombier theatre, a decade later to be an important showcase for avant-garde films; in Berlin, according to Lawder, Expressionist drama was just emerging from the wings of the Deutsches Theatre.[19] However, the cinema still had its limitations at that moment. It was seen as the lowest of the arts, because it was considered only a mechanical toy which could never be dissociated from mechanics. From 1896 to 1914, it had its commercial development as an industry. After that, it began to be thought of as a form of art. In the early decades of the twentieth century, films were shown for entertainment, which attracted large and uncritical audiences.[20] At that time, everyone went to the

---

[17] Standish D. Lawder, *The Cubist Cinema*. New York: New York University Press, 1975, p.1.

[18] Lawder, *The Cubist Cinema*, p.2.

[19] Lawder, *The Cubist Cinema*, p.2.

[20] Lawder, *The Cubist Cinema*, p.2.

cinema, but not many artists or intellectuals took it very seriously. A typical evening at the movies in 1913, as Lawder points out, would consist of a number of 'photoplays' – that is, melodramas,[21] in which one does not need to use his brain to think what he sees in a sequence of images that move.

Cinematic language makes a city a metaphor after World War I. It is a change of style, which Deleuze defines as the shift from the movement-image to the time-image in his *Cinema 2*. French Futurist director Gaston Quiribet, in his *The Fugitive Futurist* (1924), gives his view and fantasy to London's future. The film shows a moment of prophecy, coming out from a mad man 'Napoleon', who claims that he has a magic camera. He is 'haunted' by a vision, which sees beyond the limitation of ordinary life. The images that he sees from the magic camera are his inventions, to name a few: Trafalgar Square flooded by the raising sea level, a spaceship on top of the Houses of Parliament, and electronic trains going through Tower Bridge. If in the Cubist era, the speed of future and the force of change come more substantial than the living present, then after the First World War, the image of the future is transformed to allegory. As Quiribet's curiosity shows in his film – is the image of the future only ironically, a delusion of a madman?

Virginia Woolf's awareness of the possibility of a new cinematic language comes long before Deleuze's theory. As I mentioned earlier, Woolf herself used cinematic techniques, such as montage and flashback, in her novel *Mrs Dalloway*, which she published before the essay 'The Cinema'. In *The Cabinet of Dr Caligari*, Woolf has noticed the black shadow on the wall, which symbolises the murder scene. The horror comes not from acting, but from the symbolic black shadow, which suggests what is actually to happen. In this light, the cinema, for Woolf, is not only a series of motion pictures which tires one's eyes. On the contrary, the new visual language of the cinema has the potential to depict something invisible: emotion and psychology.

---

[21]   Lawder, *The Cubist Cinema*, p.4.

Woolf had important relations with photography throughout her career as an innovative female writer. She was also conscious of the relation between photography and her family members, particularly Julia Margaret Cameron. Woolf's continuous attention to photography's visual effects impacts on her work, as on modernist aesthetics in general. The camera was invented by Fox Talbot in 1839; within thirty years, as John Berger points out, photography was being used for police filing, news reporting, documentation, family albums and so forth.[22] Woolf's use in *Three Guineas* of five published newspaper photographs shows a way in which a female gazer can exist to de-mystify a patriarchal world. The absent photographs of the dead bodies of women and children in the Spanish Civil War indicate that Woolf rejects the way of looking at the dead bodies as dead icons of patriarchy, making photography as propaganda which aestheticises politics.

For Woolf (and later for Barthes whose ideas in *Camera Lucida* come surprisingly close to Woolf), absence is a quality perceived and named, occupying the central place in her imagination, as when she is remembering and imagining herself with her mother, on a journey to St Ives or coming back to London. The visual image of her mother's dress, with black background and red, yellow and blue flowers, delicately evokes both her mother's presence (here and now in Woolf's mind) and absence (that-has-been). Barthes's peculiar search for his absent mother in his life, particularly looking at the Winter Garden Photograph, brings him a visual intoxication. It is one picture that activates the whole flood of feeling, emotion and memory. For Barthes, it is a photograph, a sign which is beyond any simple resemblance; it is the aura itself, without a reproduction, since the reader cannot find it in *Camera Lucida*. It exists only for Barthes. For a reader, as Barthes claims, 'it would be nothing but an indifferent picture'[23] – it would not hurt a

---

[22] John Berger, 'Uses of Photography'. *About Looking*. 1980. New York: Vintage, 1991, p.52.

[23] Roland Barthes, *Camera Lucida: Reflections on Photography*. Trans. Richard

reader's feelings. The Surrealist essence of photography locates in Barthes's reflection of the *punctum*, explaining the relation between the viewer and 'that-has-been'. Barthes's life-death game reinforces Benjamin's allegorical vision. In a photograph, the pictured object is liberated from its immediate material milieu. The image is allegorical in its effect on the viewer, for it shows nothing but the absence of the object – its 'there-has-been'. The image is the redemption of the (dead) visual object, as Benjamin's recognition, something would not die in the fish wife's eyes. Barthes's *Camera Lucida* does Sartre's *L'Imaginaire* homage, as Sartre has defined photography as a mode of perception. Sartre recognises his friend Pierre in the photograph because he knows Pierre deep in his mind. I use it as a theoretical metaphor that helps to demonstrate a significant aspect of *The Years*.

Woolf and Her London

Woolf's texts about London are significant, because they show how London should be understood in terms of human relations and human conditions. London is a labyrinth; the whole city is a symbol of the emotional and psychological condition of people. Woolf's Londoners walk the streets of London, to discover 'purpose or coherence'[24] in their city and in their lives. Woolf's narrative structure becomes a symbolic process that mimes a quest for meanings. In this 'eternal passing and flowing',[25] Woolf's novels move not to a comprehensive vision of society but to unify within her characters' imagination and perception.

Virginia Woolf was a Londoner. She loved to walk the city and observe the streets. Woolf admired the history, people and the charm of London of

---

Howard. 1980. London: Vintage, 1993, p.73.

[24] Sanford Schwartz, *The Matrix of Modernism: Pound, Eliot, and Early Twentieth-Century Thought*. Princeton, NJ: Princeton University Press, 1985, p.29.

[25] Schwarz, *Modern British and Irish Novel*, p.34.

her time. Her literary works are routes for readers to approach this complicated and inexhaustible city. London, for Woolf, is simply, as Jean Moorcroft Wilson points out, 'the centre of things'.[26] For Woolf, modernity is defined by her vision of London, in which her experience of walking, thinking and writing about the city are synthesised. There are a number of scholars who have analysed the relation between Woolf and the city. Among them, Susan Merrill Squier's scholarly contribution is a landmark in the field of women writers and the city. Dorothy Brewster focuses her criticism on the role of London in Woolf's writings. The critical studies of the city's role in the lives and works of women writers yield valuable insights to scholars and readers concerned with gender and class relations, artistic production, and the exercise of power relations in the urban space. The investigation of Woolf's idea of the city inevitably carries the reader beyond the physical frame into myriad aspects of life, society and culture. The city in Woolf's writing, as a text, a symbol, a theme, a setting, a character and a discourse, speaks fluently of her public and private life, of her experiences, of her struggle to gain freedom and find her own voice in literature.

Although these scholars have a common interest in London's role as a symbolic system and vehicle for the exploration of aspects of life in Woolf's works, their researches are different in methodology. Ranging from literary history and criticism to critical and feminist theory, they exemplify diverse approaches to literary texts from thematic, biographical and feminist aspects. Dorothy Brewster's *Virginia Woolf's London* (1959) analyses Woolf's London novels, arguing that Woolf's portraiture of London is not only significant in London essays such as 'Street Music' (1905) and 'Street Haunting: A London Adventure' (1927), but also in her diaries and in her novels such as *Night and Day* (1919), *Mrs Dalloway* (1925), and *The Years*

---

[26] Jean Moorcroft Wilson, *Virginia Woolf's London: A Guide to Bloomsbury and Beyond*. 1987. London: Tauris Parke, 2000, p.9.

(1937). According to Brewster, London for Woolf is not simply material and external. Her London has been transformed into a concept of life 'as a luminous halo'.[27] Woolf's London is not merely a city that can be mapped in a guide-book. London is abundant, yet ambiguous in Woolf's writings, because it is not only an external and physical setting, but also a mood, a deep feeling, a spirit of life, a psychological cityscape, an image.

Anna Snaith in her *Virginia Woolf: Public and Private Negotiations*, claims that Woolf's flâneuse develops her own experience in the city of London, which works around a politics of space in terms of 'gendered ideas of public and private'.[28] Her female character's walking the streets of London 'alone', can be read as a symbol of 'a regenerative power', as one can see in Clarissa Dalloway or Mary Datchet.[29] As Snaith argues, '[m]any women, like Woolf, would have seen themselves as strolling, observing, exercising their right to gaze on men and women'.[30] Snaith also reads Woolf's journey from city to country and back again as 'the ambivalence'[31] towards the city felt by many women in the late nineteenth century and early twentieth century. It is because, while a woman can be a gazer who exercises her right to gaze at the same time, she is also a gazee under the male gaze. According to Snaith, Virginia Woolf's life was interrupted by enforced rest at her stay in Monk's House, because London society was 'becoming too much for her'.[32] London 'at once allowed a literal enactment of increased rights and freedoms, and at the same time represented 'the very same institutions which had denied such freedoms'.[33]

---

[27] Dorothy Brewster, *Virginia Woolf's London*. London: George Allen, 1959, p.7.

[28] Anna Snaith, *Virginia Woolf: Public and Private Negotiations*. London: Macmillan, 2000, p.34.

[29] Snaith, *Public and Private Negotiations*, p.36.

[30] Snaith, *Public and Private Negotiations*, p.37.

[31] Snaith, *Public and Private Negotiations*, p.41.

[32] Snaith, *Public and Private Negotiations*, p.41.

[33] Snaith, *Public and Private Negotiations*, p.41.

Deborah L. Parsons, in her *Streetwalking the Metropolis: Women, the City, and Modernity*, explores the relation between women writers, the flâneur, the flâneuse, flânerie, and modernity. Looking at the gendered cartographies of urban space, Parsons reads the city as a text, which represents infinite versions, in the 'very structures of social and mental daily life'.[34] The urban writer is not only a figure within the city. He / she is also the producer of a city, who makes the 'interconnection' between body, mind, and space, 'myth, memory, fantasy and desire', 'the interplay of self / city identity'.[35] Parsons' study attempts 'to examine women's urban walking and writing from a perspective that looks at the gendered sites / sights of the city', but from a broader context than that of just the politics of power and marginalisation that emphasises the comparative experience of the male and female subject'.[36] In this light, a woman is not only a spectacle under the male gaze. A woman is a viewing subject, and she has a very different point of view from a man.

Woolf's outsider's position leads to her modernism, which according to Daniel R. Schwarz is 'more aesthetic than moral'.[37] For Schwarz, the order of Woolf's narrative, as a work of art, 'transform[s] the psychological process into a metaphor, a narrative form or a symbol'.[38] Schwarz's argument helps one to understand Woolf's gendered gaze in the context of the urban space. As Woolf herself claims in *A Room of One's Own* (1929), the experience of looking is gendered, because women and men see things differently. For Woolf, 'it is obvious that the values of women differ very often from the values which have been made by the other sex; naturally, this is so'.[39] Jane

---

[34] Deborah L. Parsons, *Streetwalking the Metropolis: Women, the City, and Modernity*. Oxford: Oxford University Press, 2000, p.1.

[35] Parsons, *Streetwalking the Metropolis*, p.1.

[36] Parsons, *Streetwalking the Metropolis*, p.2.

[37] Daniel R. Schwarz, *Reading the Modern British and Irish Novel, 1890 – 1930*. Oxford: Blackwell, 2005, p.33.

[38] Schwarz, *Modern British and Irish Novel*, p.32.

[39] Virginia Woolf, *A Room of One's Own* (1929). Oxford: Oxford University Press,

Austen and George Eliot, for Woolf, both 'wrote as women write, not as men write'.[40] A woman has a different vision, a different mind. A woman's writing explores these differences – the territories that a man had not been. George Eliot achieved the goal of depicting 'the ordinary tasks of womanhood' – 'the ancient consciousness of woman, charged with suffering and sensibility'.[41] There is no single state of mind, no single state of being: when Woolf describes Carlyle's house, she does not focus on the greatness of a great man, but thinks about what Mrs Carlyle has to face every day – the dust in the basement.

The Aesthetics of the Urban Gaze

The main body of this work will be divided into six parts, comprising 'Prologue'; Chapter One, 'Virginia Woolf and the Significance of the Eye'; Chapter Two, 'The Painter's Eye in Writing: the James Brothers and Woolf's Experimental Practices'; Chapter Three, "The Dialectic of Time in Film Form: *Mrs Dalloway* and 'The Cinema'"; Chapter Four, 'Photography in *The Years* and *Three Guineas*', and an Epilogue.

First of all, in Chapter One, 'Virginia Woolf and the Significance of the Eye', I will explore the relationship between Virginia Woolf's writing and the aesthetics of the Bloomsbury Group, from Cambridge to London; from 22 Hyde Park Gate to Bloomsbury. The starting point of my research is the question of how visual cultures and visual theories, particularly the aesthetics of the Bloomsbury Group defined, shaped and influenced Woolf's literary works and her gendered gaze in the context of the modern metropolis. Through reading works by Clive Bell and Roger Fry, I suggest that Woolf's

---

2000, pp.95 – 96.

[40] Woolf, *A Room of One's Own*, p.97.

[41] Virginia Woolf, 'George Eliot' (1919). *Women and Writing*. Ed. Barrett, Michèle. New York: Harcourt Brace, 1979, p.160.

work shows not only her affilations with them, but also that she finds her own narrative path by responding to them. Woolf's 'painter in writer' style is her own epistemological practice. Her narrative technique can be read as a process by which the writer selects visual impressions, translates them into words and composes them into fictional writings, to show the psychology of her characters in the modern metropolis.

In Chapter One I will also discuss the relation between the flâneur and the flâneuse in Walter Benjamin and Woolf. Woolf's flâneuse reveals her own gendered gaze – the 'dual vision' of the outsider. The 'dual vision' is a phrase that Woolf used in order to analyse the work of Proust in her 'Phases of Fiction' (1929), by which she means the combination of passionate looking and detached observation; poetic mystery and psychological detachment. In this chapter, I use this notion to reveal the significance of walking and looking in the portrayal of the consciousness of Woolf's flâneuse in the cityscape. I shall also argue in this chapter, that Woolf's female protagonists can be understood as flâneuses. I will develop the significance of the flâneuse and her gaze in new ways. Her female figures are walking through the streets with their passion for looking and observation in the city of London. London in Woolf's writing indicates the complexity of women's experience in the urban space. The female gaze is Woolf's aesthetic strategy, representing her struggle against male authority in her response to Victorian tradition. Woolf's gendered gaze indicates the way in which women and men look at London differently. Women are not simply designed to be objectified or to flatter men. Woolf subverts the myth of the male gaze, which no longer embodies the unchallenged power of patriarchy.

In Chapter Two, 'The Painter's Eye in Writing: the James Brothers and Woolf's Experimental Practices', I argue that Woolf's writing style draws on a painter's perspective. In order to pursue the relation between consciousness and visual impressions, I will trace William James's concept of 'the stream of consciousness', and look at Henry James's *The Ambassadors* and his London essays, to see the relation between the inner and outer worlds, and show how such ideas illuminate Woolf's dialectic of the inner and the outer in her narrative style, and the portrayal of the process of thinking of her characters, in particular Katharine Hilbery, Ralph Denham and Mary Datchet.

Woolf goes further in portraying the complexity of the visual sensations of London, moving from one consciousness to another. The streets of London symbolise patterns of states of mind throughout the novel. Through reading *Night and Day* (1919), I want to explore how her craft is established by the painter's eye, and how it shapes the form of this novel and her other short fictions. I aim to illuminate the way in which Woolf's narrative style and depiction of consciousness develop the form of psychological realism for which she aims. By studying Henry James's painterly perspective in literature, I suggest that Woolf transforms visual impressions into her own literary form. She portrays the psychology of her characters through the way they look at London.

In Chapter Three, "The Dialectic of Time in Film Form: *Mrs Dalloway* and 'The Cinema'", I will trace Henri Bergson's notion of *la durée* and Deleuze's theory of cinematography, to illustrate the way Woolf represents time and memory in her cinematographical narrative. Woolf develops her writing technique by using cinematic techniques. Her observation of cinema, as a form of modern art, focuses on how cinema can express human emotion, as one can see in her essay 'The Cinema' (1926). However, as I pointed out earlier, before she comments on the cinema in this particular essay, Woolf was using cinematic techniques in her narrative. Film offered Woolf a new visual aesthetics. By reading her short story, 'Mrs Dalloway in Bond Street' (1923) and her *The Hours* manuscript (1924), one can see that Woolf herself is making a film in words. Her novel *Mrs Dalloway* (1925) can also be read as a film. *Mrs Dalloway* synthesises multiple consciousness in the short story, developing Septimus and Clarissa as parallel as in *The Hours*. The intertextuality between versions of one complete literary text, one text within another, reveals Woolf's using cinematic visual language as symbols of human emotion, and techniques in film-making, such as close-up, flashback, and montage.

London gives *Mrs Dalloway* a coherent structure, in terms of the inner world of the characters, memory, time and space. The city has not only geographical significance but also a psychological and gendered one. The personalities of the characters are conveyed through their visions of London. The landmarks of the city, such as Big Ben, have symbolic meanings and can been seen as the outer form of the novel. The inner form of the novel, on the other hand, is the imaginary cityscape in each character's consciousness. Woolf creates a unified form of the novel by synthesising her vision of private and public spheres of London.

In Chapter Four, 'Photography in *The Years* and *Three Guineas*', I analyse the way in which the character's gendered gaze constructs the spatial and sexual politics of London through her narrative form. *The Years* covers the Pargiters' family saga from 1880 to 1937, and shows both a historically changing city and the transformation of female subjectivity. In this novel, her description of London reveals an awareness of the female experience and consciousness. Woolf grew up among photographs. Her family member Julia Margaret Cameron was a photographer, who took photographs of figures of her time. Woolf's understanding of and familiarity with photographic technique plays a significant role in her fictional writing. In *The Years*, Woolf's photographic syntax represents London through a number of gendered gazes. The camera's eye in Woolf's narrative makes minute details significant, suggesting a series of hidden messages. As Roland Barthes suggests, a photograph's *punctum* (Time, '*that-has-been*') pricks the viewer, breaks the *stadium* (the sovereign consciousness, signs, cultural interests). [42] The camera lens catches the unrevealed message

---

[42] Roland Barthes, *Camera Lucida: Reflections on Photography*. Trans. Richard

through photography. Barthers's viewer sees the photograph, making his own sense of it, in order to decode the message behind cultural signs. In *The Years*, Woolf's female gazers are also decoding messages behind the patriarchal society, in order to understand the role of a woman in her family and her society.

In *Three Guineas*, Woolf uses photographs of male figures to show the form of patriarchy. Her main concern is the social and cultural role of women within the patriarchal structure. Woolf read the coming to power of Hitler in 1933, the victory of Generalissimo Francisco Franco in the Spanish Civil War of 1936-1939, and the growth of Fascism as the apotheosis of patriarchal power. Woolf advocates a form of radical political action, in which women should use their position as outsiders to challenge the rise of Fascism. Woolf's gendered gaze is the outsider's critical vision; her use of photographs in *Three Guineas* is a powerful adjunct to her feminist arguments. The use of photography in this text shows a subversive power relation between the female gazer and male gazee. The photographs depict powerful figures: 'A General," "Heralds', 'A University Procession', 'A Judge' and 'An Archbishop', but are there to mock their self-importance. By using photographs of male authority to articulate her narrative frame, Woolf deconstructs the myth of masculinity as the embodiment of authority, offering instead her own illustration of female subjectivity and arguing for world peace.

To conclude, Woolf's dual vision draws together vision and design, visual and verbal representations, intellect and imagination, sane and insane, consciousness and subconsciousness, inter-gaze and inner gaze, imagery and visual object, mind pictures and the outside world. Woolf's modes of looking explore mental processes, in which the mind translates external visual objects into subjective vision: an epiphanic insight into the heart of things, an atmosphere, a mood, an emotion, a passion and a sensory

---

Howard. 1980. London: Vintage, 1993, pp.26 – 27, 94 – 96.

awareness of the most minute nuances of feeling. Avoiding the description of the appearance of things and details of conventional realism, Woolf's depiction of human consciousness and the imaginary cityscape illuminates her ways of seeing.

CHAPTER ONE

Virginia Woolf and the Significance of the Eye

After all, the arts are all the same; you can write a picture in words just as you can paint sensations in a poem.

-Picasso, *Picasso on Art*[1]

Your footsteps follow not what is outside the eyes, but what is within, buried, erased. If, of two arcades, one continues to seem more joyous, it is because thirty years ago a girl went by there, with broad, embroidered sleeves, or else it is only because that arcade catches the light at a certain hour like that other arcade, you cannot recall where.

-Italo Calvino, *Invisible Cities*[2]

Introduction

This chapter establishes the historical, literary, philosophical and aesthetic context, within which I situate my study of Virginia Woolf's writings. Beginning with Roger Fry at the very start of the development of the aesthetics associated with the Bloomsbury Group, and with his efforts to theorise aesthetic emotion and the relation between vision and design, form and colour, I trace his analysis of Post-Impressionism and Clive Bell's theory of significant form, examining their relations to Woolf's aesthetics of the visual, her gendered gaze and the

---

[1] Pablo Picasso, *Picasso on Art*. Ed. Dore Ashton. New York: Da Capo, 1972, p.131.
[2] Italo Calvino, *Invisible Cities*. Trans. William Weaver. 1974. London: Vintage, 1997, p.91.

construction of a female subjective viewer in her novels. The philosophical and aesthetic theories of the Bloomsbury Group and Post-Impressionism are important for a consideration of Woolf's aesthetics in her writing. Moving on from Fry and Bell's aesthetic concerns with the abstraction of emotions through colours, shapes and lines, Woolf discovered a form for her writing through the visual, establishing her dual vision through her reading of Proust and Henry James, writers who were both important to the Bloomsbury Group. As I will argue in the second part of this chapter, Woolf's dual vision combines the naked eye and the mind's eye, the inner and the outer worlds of the city of London, through the flâneuse's walking, looking and thinking.

Reading Virginia Woolf and the Visual

Before I discuss Woolf's gendered gaze, I want to comment on the philosophical tradition of vision to demonstrate the importance of the eye. In his 'Optics', Descartes claims that light is the link between the eye and the visible world. The physical eye receives 'all sorts of colours' through reflection and refraction of light.[3] As Martin Jay suggests, the Cartesian world is a 'thoroughly visual' one, in which the relation between viewing subjectivity and visual objects is established.[4]

However, when Jacques Lacan refers to the Cartesian *cogito* in his discussion of the gaze, he starts with a reading of Maurice Merleau-Ponty's *Le Visible et l'invisible*, situating the visible world in invisible thought. Lacan's meditation on this sentence, '*I see myself seeing myself*',[5] reveals

---

[3]   René Descartes, *The Philosophical Writings of Descartes, Volume I*. Trans. John Cottingham. Cambridge: Cambridge University Press, 1998, p.153.

[4]   Martin Jay, *Downcast Eyes: The Denigration of Vision in Twentieth-Century French Thought*. Berkley: University of California Press, 1994, p.70.

[5]   Jacques Lacan, 'Anamorphosis'. *The Four Fundamental Concepts of Psycho-analysis*. 1973. Ed. Jacques-Alain Miller. Trans. Alan Sheridan. London: Penguin, 1994, p.80.

the dialectic relation between the viewing subjectivity and his apprehension of himself as thought. The viewing self, therefore, is located by his own inner world. His gaze sees his own thought, which is a perception of the external visual world in his own consciousness. This thought is a representation of the visible world, which belongs to the viewing self, as soon as he perceives. In other words, the reflection of the visible world, such as the image in the mirror, is 'the original point of vision', from which emerges the 'eye' as the subjectivity of the seer 'I'.[6] To Lacan, the function of '*seeingness*' is to construct the gaze of the subjectivity – 'consciousness, in its illusion of *seeing itself seeing itself,* finds its basis in the inside-out structure of the gaze',[7] from the naked eye (the visible world) to the mind's eye (the inner world). The viewing subject does not only 'look' at (see) himself in the mirror, but also 'perceive' and 'recognise' (seeing / knowing) that self in his consciousness. For me, Lacan's concept of the gaze reinforces the importance of the visual, or, the visualisation of the invisible (thought, emotion) in literature and psychoanalysis. The Cartesian tradition is significant in terms of the discovery of light, the eye and consciousness; Lacan's reading of the physical eye and the mind's eye, on the other hand, indicates a complex subject-object relation, which not only stimulates a feminist thinker such as Irigaray to establish a female viewing subjectivity, but which is also useful for reading Woolf's texts through the visible and the invisible. At this point, the relation between looking and thinking is significant, for the Cartesian *cogito* is a 'synthetic notion'[8] of being, seeing, observing and perception, as Descartes himself claims, '*I think, therefore I am*'.[9] This who I 'am' refers to an inner being, a consciousness in a thinking process.

---

[6] Lacan, 'Anamorphosis', p.82.

[7] Lacan, 'Anamorphosis', p.82.

[8] Dalia Judovitz, *Subjectivity and Representation in Descartes: the Origins of Modernity.* Cambridge: Cambridge University Press, 1998, p.153.

[9] Descartes, *Discourse on Method and the Meditations.* 1637. Trans. F. E. Sutcliffe. London: Penguin, 1968, p.53.

In Luce Irigaray's meditations on sight, modes of seeing are gendered. Irigaray has criticised the privileging of the visual as the representation of a monological masculine subjectivity in Western culture. For her, women's relationship to vision is not as privileged in women as in men. While she claims that women tend to use other senses rather than sight, Irigaray's criticism ignores the importance of smell, taste, touch and hearing in Proust's novels. Irigaray does not take Lacan's discussion of the gaze into account. Lacan's thought about the split subjectivity (visible and invisible) is about the relation between the subject and his/her desire in terms of spectatorship, and does not necessarily reduce women to a position of the passive gazee.

Irigaray's account is useful to a female gazer, since the sight is not necessarily male-privileged. Woolf's demonstration of the female gaze in *Three Guineas* (in which no women's photographs had been shown) reinforces the role of a female gazer, who is capable of looking at photographs of male authority with an outsider's objective point of view. I find Irigaray's curved mirror metaphor is useful to demonstrate that the gaze in Woolf's writing is not a privileged but a gendered experience and phenomenon, by which she develops a way to show how a woman can depict men through her photographic vision, particularly in *The Years*.

I read a range of Virginia Woolf's literary texts, as well as the visual arts, writing new features of her dual vision, her gendered gaze and her depiction of female subjectivity. The visual in Woolf's writings can be understood from two aspects: in one through the aesthetics of the Bloomsbury Group and in another through the Baudelairian flâneur. The former illustrates the painter's perspective in her writings, the latter makes it possible to understand the development of Woolf's gendered urban gaze in London. My attempt to read Woolf through the visual is in line with an increasing critical attention to the importance of vision in literature. For instance, Arnold L. Weinstein uses 'vision' and 'response' to demonstrate different modes of narration in writers, particularly Henry James. The theme of vision and awareness is essential to Jamesian perception and narrative strategy. His portrayal of the centre of consciousness forms the cornerstone of modern fiction. *The Ambassadors* can be read as his richest and fullest expression of the modern treatment of perception, such as the process of Strether's observation and his growing awareness as a foreigner in Paris. Strether's perception reveals places, people and things, opening the reader's eye to the beauties and delights of the visible world: Paris itself, and also the secret behind it. As Weinstein maintains, vision in James's novels serves as the very narrative structure, which builds around solid events.[10] James's visual logic constructs an enclosed narrative world. For me, Woolf's way of writing can be read as a continuation of James's work, in which Woolf makes the modern British novel a form of fine arts. As Harvena Richter explains, Woolf 'achieves perspective, and that is through the *angle of vision*, the physical or psychological position or angle from which an object is viewed'.[11] Richter's angle of vision comes close to Woolf's dialectic of the inner and the outer – her dual vision, in which she depicts the way her characters see London as the way to express their emotion. The depiction of human emotion is Woolf's way of narrating the city, as one can see in *Night and Day*.

My interest in Virginia Woolf is to write the unexplored territories of Woolf's ways of seeing London. The attraction of reading Woolf's work in this way is in discovering both visual and verbal expressions at the same time. Woolf's perception is in her gendered gaze. She had managed to put into practice what critics formulated as a theory half a century after her, as I hope to show. It is not an easy task to trace the transformation of perception in Woolf's texts, as no simple visual imagery is to be found, but only diverse, changeable images spread here and there. Toril Moi also points out

---

[10] Arnold L. Weinstein, *Vision and Response in Modern Fiction*. Ithaca: Cornell University Press, 1974, p.73.

[11] Harvena Richter, *Virginia Woolf: The Inward Voyage*. Princeton: Princeton University Press, 1970, p.83.

that Woolf's writing presents an 'endless deferral of meanings', because of the multiplicity of perspectives, '[t]here is no final element'.[12] And yet, how from the fragmentation and dismembered visual images in the earlier novels, does Woolf move toward the construction of a new way of seeing, which in the later stages of her writing career at many points converges with a woman as a viewing subjectivity?

Woolf's *Roger Fry* and Post-Impressionist Psychology

The origin of the Bloomsbury Group was at the University of Cambridge and more specifically at King's College and Trinity College. Most of the men belonged to the Cambridge Conversazione Society, 'whose elected members were known as the Apostles',[13] as Ulysses L. D'Aquila points out. The society was formed for discussions of philosophy, politics, aesthetics and literature.[14] Leonard Woolf recorded his Trinity years in his *Sowing: An Autobiography of the Years 1880 – 1904*:

> During the years we were at Trinity, Henry James was at the height of his powers, writing those strange, involved, elusive novels of his last period. We read *The Sacred Fount*, *The Wings of the Dove*, and *The Golden Bowl* as they came out. Lytton Strachey, Saxon, and I were fascinated by them – entranced and almost hypnotised.[15]

[12] Toril Moi, *Sexual / Texual Politics*. London: Routledge, 1985, p.9.

[13] Ulysses L. D'Aquila, *Bloomsbury and Modernism*. New York: Peter Lang, 1989, p.5.

[14] Nigel Nicolson, 'Bloomsbury: the Myth and the Reality'. *Virginia Woolf and Bloomsbury: A Centenary Celebration*. Ed. Jane Marcus. London: Macmillan, 1987, p.12.

[15] Leonard Woolf, *Sowing: An Autobiography of the Years 1880 to 1904*. London: Hogarth Press, 1967, p.106.

After the Cambridge years, Leonard Woolf, Clive Bell, Lytton Strachey, Maynard Keynes and Thoby Stephen built a 'little Cambridge' in 46 Gordon Square, Bloomsbury, where 'they would turn back the calendar; repeat old stories; read poetry; laugh with the old laughter'.[16] The Thursday evenings were well established by the summer of 1905. The pipe-smoking young men came into Bloomsbury expecting a drawing room that would melt into Thoby or Lytton's Cambridge rooms. The Stephen sisters, Vanessa and Virginia, also 'sat up talking to young men till all hours of the night'.[17]

Hermione Lee in her biography, *Virginia Woolf*, notes that when Woolf describes the Bloomsbury Group, she often refers to 'conversation'.[18] As one can see in Woolf's diaries, through the conversation with other group members, Woolf could talk about Proust and James, exchanging ideas with them. Woolf herself in 'Old Bloomsbury' (1921-2) comments that

> These Thursday evening parties were, as far as I am concerned, the germ from which sprang all that has since come to be called – in newspapers, in novels, in Germany, in France – even, I daresay, in Turkey and Timbuktu – by the name of Bloomsbury. They deserve to be recorded and described. Yet how difficult – how impossible. Talk – even the talk which had such tremendous results upon the lives and characters of the two Miss Stephens – even talk of this interest and importance is as elusive as smoke.[19]

---

[16] Leonard Woolf, *Sowing*, p.123.

[17] Leonard Woolf, *Sowing*, p.126.

[18] As Lee points out, the pleasure and excitement of talk gets into Woolf's writing – "[s]ome of her best non-fiction, like *A Room of One's Own*, or the essays on Sickert, takes the form or has the air of conversation. This is what 'Bloomsbury' meant to her". See *Virginia Woolf* (London: Chatto & Windus, 1996), p.269.

[19] Virginia Woolf, 'Old Bloomsbury'. *Moments of Being*. Ed. Jeanne Schulkind. Sussex: Sussex University Press, 1976, pp.164 – 165.

The evening talk was filled with passionate intellectual exchange, as if conversation were simultaneously a union of their knowledge and spirit. The original members of the Memoir Club in 1920 were: Clive and Vanessa Bell, Lytton Strachey, Leonard and Virginia Woolf, Desmond and Molly MacCarthy, Roger Fry, E. M. Forster, Duncan Grant, Maynard Keynes, Bertrand Russell and G. E. Moore.[20] According to Raymond Williams, the aesthetics of the Bloomsbury Group indicate a particular way of seeing the visual and verbal arts, which placed great value on liberation, freedom of thought, modernisation, aesthetic enjoyment and intellectual openness.[21] Artists in the Bloomsbury Group aimed to make their works of art a harmonious unity of vision and design, a balance between emotion and intelligence.

In Woolf's *Roger Fry*, Woolf depicts the transformation of Fry's aesthetic theory and his own paintings through his discovery of French Post-Impressionist paintings. Post-Impressionist paintings exemplified the aesthetics of the art critics of the Bloomsbury Group – Roger Fry and Clive Bell. According to Desmond MacCarthy, the term 'Post-Impressionism' was invented by a journalist (Frances Spalding, in her *Duncan Grant: A Biography*, points out that this was Robert Dell) while he was working with Roger Fry to put on *Manet and the Post-Impressionists* (the official title of the First Post-Impressionist Exhibition) in the Grafton Galleries off Bond Street in London, which opened on Tuesday 8 November 1910,[22] running until 15 January of the following year. The press day was Saturday 5 November. Eight of the eleven daily newspapers reviewed the exhibition on

[20] Quentin Bell, *Bloomsbury*. London: Weidenfeld and Nicolson, 1968, p.14.
[21] Raymond Williams, "The Significance of 'Bloomsbury' as a Social and Cultural Group". *Keynes and the Bloomsbury Group.*Eds. Derek Crabtree and A. P.Thirlwall. London: Macmillian, 1980, p.59.
[22] Desmond MacCarthy, 'The Post-Impressionist Exhibition of 1910'. *The Bloomsbury Group: A Collection of Memoirs, Commentary and Criticism*. Ed. S. P.Rosenbaum. London: University of Toronto Press, (Croom Helm Ltd.), 1975, p.71.

either the 7th or the 8th, so that a substantial amount of press reaction was available to viewers before they saw the show themselves.[23] As Spalding points out, to those who love Edwardian 'tonal gradations, elegance, naturalism, sentimental anecdotalism and mimetic veracity, Post-Impressionism seemed crude, unskilled and unreal'.[24] Spalding also accounts for the anxious reaction of the British viewing public in 1910 by suggesting that the Post-Impressionist exhibition was interpreted as a symptom of 'social and political unrest'.[25] She claims that

> Britain might be enjoying a period of 'splendid isolation', but threats and anxieties were accumulating that made for an underlying nervousness. Industrial unrest had erupted in the Welsh coal-miners' strike, which was broken up that month by troops. The Irish were demanding Home Rule and the Suffragettes were gaining in strength. Only a few days after the show opened at the Grafton Galleries, the Suffragettes marched on the House of Commons while Asquith spoke on the question of Women's Rights: 117 arrests were made, the six-hour protest marking a 'Black Friday' that set off a programme of window-smashing, arson and bombs as the Suffragettes, denied political power through the normal democratic procedures, resorted to violence.[26]

Post-Impressionism was associated in the public's mind with Socialism and Women's Suffrage. These three movements shared an enthusiasm for changing an old order to a new. In addition to the mental shocks the pictures brought to the British public, the Post-Impressionist pictures, particularly the works of Gauguin, Cézanne, Matisse and Picasso, drew Fry and Bell's

---

[23] S. K. Tillyard. *The Impact of Modernism 1900 – 1920*. London: Routledge, 1988, p.81.

[24] Frances Spalding, *Duncan Grant: A Biography*. London: Pimlico, 1998, p.100.

[25] Spalding, *Duncan Grant*, p.100.

[26] Spalding, *Duncan Grant*, p.100.

attentions to a new aesthetic experience by their use of colour, primitive style and spatial arrangement of the canvas.

Leonard Woolf was the secretary of the second Post-Impressionist exhibition. The success of 'Manet and the Post-Impressionists' had prompted Fry to plan another Post-Impressionist show for two years on. It opened in the Grafton Galleries on 5 October 1912 in London and ran until the end of January 1913. The show was visited by twice as many people as the first one: the reaction, however, of the public was as negative as the 1910 exhibition, as Leonard Woolf recorded:

> Large numbers of people came to the exhibition, […]. Anything new in the arts, particularly if it is good, infuriates them and they condemn it as either immoral or ridiculous or both. As secretary I sat at my table in the large second room of the galleries prepared to deal with enquiries from possible purchasers or answer any questions about the pictures. […]. Hardly any of them made the slightest attempt to look at, let alone understand, the pictures, and the same inane questions or remarks were repeated to me all day long.[27]

The viewing public had little understanding of what the Post-Impressionists were trying to show. Leonard Woolf's comments reveal the moral shock of the viewing public and their negative attitude toward the controversial exhibition, particularly the themes (female nudity) and the technique (primitive way of constructing lines and shapes) of the Post-Impressionist pictures. As Jacqueline V. Falkenheim points out, the Post-Impressionist style is the 'absence of conventional modeling, and especially the intense colors and conspicuous outlines found in many of these works, were disagreeably unfamiliar to the viewing public'.[28] Frances Spalding also

[27] Leonard Woolf, *Beginning Again: An Autobiography of the Years 1911 – 1918*. London: Hogarth Press, 1964, p.94.
[28] Jacqueline V. Falkenheim. *Roger Fry and the Beginnings of Formalist Art*

describes the outrage of the viewing public: 'London was shocked to discover that one of its most distinguished critics had created a show in which Robert Ross detected 'the existence of a widespread plot to destroy the whole fabric of European painting'.[29]

In both Roger Fry and Clive Bell's art criticism, Post-Impressionist paintings represent a fresh emphasis on style, on line, colour, scale, interval and proportion, which for them has the impact of Byzantine art. As Fry's comment on Cézanne and Gauguin in 'The Last Phase of Impressionism' (1908), the Post-Impressionists

> are proto-Byzantines rather than Neo-Impressionists. They have already attained to the contour with wilfully simplified and unmodulated masses, and rely for their whole effect upon a well-considered coordination of the simplest elements. […]. The relations of every tone and colour are deliberately chosen and stated in unmistakable terms. In the placing of objects, in the relation of one form to another, in the values of colour which indicate mass, and in the purely decorative elements of design, Cézanne's work seems to me to betray a finer, more scrupulous artistic sense.[30]

The Post-Impressionists use simple colours and shapes to express emotions. The difference between Impressionism and Post-Impressionism lies in their way of dealing with light and shadow. C. J. Holmes claims in 'Notes on the Post-Impressionist Painters: Grafton Galleries, 1910 – 11' (for the exhibition *Manet & the Post-Impressionists*, London, 1910 – 11),

---

Criticism. Ann Arbor: UMI, 1980, p.14.

[29] Frances Spalding, *British Art Since 1900*. 1986. London: Thames and Hudson, 1996, p.37.

[30] Roger Fry, 'The Last Phase of Impressionism'. This is a letter to the editor of *The Burlington Magazine*, March 1908, pp.374 – 375, p.375.

> For the moment it is enough to recognise that in the first
> Post-Impressionist painters we have a reaction from the materialism
> which limited the original Impressionists to the rendering of natural
> effects of light and colour with the greatest attainable scientific truth.
> Within those iron limits art was bound to come to a standstill, and in
> setting up sincerity to personal vision as a guiding rule, in the place
> of sincerity to natural appearances, the Post-Impressionists were
> really only reverting to the principle which has inspired all the
> greatest art in the world.[31]

The Impressionists paint what they see; the Post-Impressionists paint what
they feel. The Impressionists

> were interested in analysing the play of light and shadow into a
> multiplicity of distinct colours; they refined upon what was already
> illusive in nature. […]. The Post-Impressionists on the other hand
> were not concerned with recording impressions of colour or light.
> They were interested in the discoveries of the Impressionists only so
> far as these discoveries helped them to express emotions which the
> object themselves evoked; their attitude towards nature was far more
> independent, not to say rebellious. […].[32]

The Impressionists capture the play of light and shadow in nature; the
Post-Impressionists personalise nature with emotion.

---

[31] C. J. Holmes, 'Notes on the Post-Impressionist Painters: Grafton Galleries,
1910 – 11' (for the exhibition, *Manet & the Post-Impressionists*, London, 1910 –
11), pp.7 – 17, p.10. Hyman Kreitman Research Centre for the Tate Library and
Archive, Tate Britain, London.

[32] Roger Fry, 'The Post-Impressionists'. Exhibition catalogue: *Manet & the
Post-Impressionists*, London, 1910 – 11, pp.7 – 13. See pp.8 – 9. Hyman Kreitman
Research Centre for the Tate Library and Archive, Tate Britain, London.

Both Fry's and Holmes's comments indicate what they saw as the fundamental difference between Impressionism and Post-Impressionism. When Cézanne died in 1906, according to James Beechey, he was 'barely noticed in England'.[33] However, his influence on modern painting style, English Post-Impressionism and the aesthetics of the Bloomsbury Group is demonstrated in Fry's and Bell's writings.[34] Frances Spalding points out that 'Roger Fry saw in Post-Impressionism two important developments: expression released from the tyranny of representation and, in the work of Picasso for example, a search for 'the intellectual abstract of form'.[35] The Post-Impressionist Exhibitions of 1910 and 1912 formed a historical moment for the visual arts in Britain, a new force broke in. For instance, Matisse's *La Danse (I)* 1909 (oil on canvas, 259.7 × 390.1 cm, The Museum of Modern Art, New York),[36] is a synthesis of the dual nature of painting, which contains not only the representation of the visual world (outer), but also the expression of the aesthetic emotion (inner) – suggestive 'psychological situations'[37] as Fry puts it. The plastic idiom, such as the flow of rhythmic lines, new use of colour, the gestures or expressions of the faces, and harmonious spatial relations, shows that an 'extreme poetic exaltation' has been achieved in 'a

---

[33] James Beechey. 'Defining Modernism: Roger Fry and Clive Bell in the 1920s'. *The Art of Bloomsbury: Roger Fry, Vanessa Bell and Duncan Grant.* Ed. Richard Shone. London: Tate Gallery, 1999, p.40.

[34] Simon Watney, *English Post-Impressionism.* London: Studio Vista, 1980, p.4.

[35] Frances Spalding, *Vanessa Bell.* London: George Weidenfeld and Nicolson, 1984, pp.114 – 115.

[36] Matisse made comment on this painting during a 1951 interview. The vivid expression of the flow of lines and spatial design comes from his emotion – the love of dance, expressive music and rhythmic movement. See Xavier Girard, *Matisse: The Sensuality of Colour.* Trans. I. Mark Paris. London: Thames and Hudson, 1994, pp.112 – 114.

[37] Roger Fry, 'The Double Nature of Painting', *Apollo*, May 1969, pp.362 – 371, p.367. According to the journal editor, it was delivered in French in Brussels during the autumn of 1933.

great plastic construction'.[38] 'In the work of Matisse, especially,' as Fry claims, 'this search for an abstract harmony of line, for rhythm, has been carried to lengths which often deprive the figure of all appearance of nature to primitive, even perhaps of a return to barbaric, art'.[39] Moments of vision are the key moments of aesthetic emotions and sensations which are contained in the simplest forms, such as 'a red poppy, a mother's reproof, a Quaker upbringing, sorrows, loves, humiliations'.[40]

Paul Smith explains emotion in Cézanne's landscape paintings. Cézanne's response to the landscape indicates "his love of his 'native' soil was grounded in deeply rooted experiences of his mother's body, [...], a real, expressive, psychological content in his landscape paintings that he intends them to express".[41] The landscape is a 'magnificent form', through which the painter expresses his emotion and his imagination, his desire to 'climb the slopes of her tremendous knees, and sometimes when the sickly mists of summer made her stretch out wearily across the fields, to slumber trustfully in the shadow of her breasts, like a quiet hamlet at some mountain's foot'.[42] I see the woman's brown face and arm evoke the brownness of the land, mother earth. Cézanne's maternalisation of landscape makes me think about Woolf and Barthes's spiritual journey of life and death intensity, in *The Years*, 'A Sketch of the Past' and *Camera Lucida*, as I will show in chapter four. Fry expressed his own emotion through the landscape of southern France, as he did not feel he could paint in England after the storm of criticism stirred up by the exhibition. His trip to Constantinople (Capital

---

[38] Fry, 'The Double Nature of Painting', p.371.

[39] Fry, 'The Post-Impressionists', p.11.

[40] Virginia Woolf, *Roger Fry: A Biography*. 1940. London: Vintage, 2003, p.161.

[41] Paul Smith, 'Cézanne's Maternal Landscape and its Gender'. *Gendering Landscape Art*. Eds. Steven Adams and Anna Gruetzner Robins. New Brunswick, NJ: Rutgers University Press, 2001, p.117.

[42] Smith, 'Cézanne's Maternal Landscape and its Gender'. *Gendering Landscape Art*, p.118.

of the Byzantine empire, now Istanbul), according to Woolf, confirmed his knowledge of Byzantine art, and his way of seeing emotion in the Post-Impressionist paintings, preparing his mood for organising the second Post-Impressionist exhibition.[43]

Fry's vision urged him away from the past and on to the future. 'It was not surprising', Fry wrote in the catalogue to the Second Post-Impressionist Exhibition,

> that a public which had come to admire above everything in a picture the skill with which an artist produced illusion should have resented an art in which such skill was completely subordinated to the direct expression of feeling. [...]. Now these artists do not seek to give what can, after all, be but a pale reflex of actual appearance, but to arouse the conviction of a new and definite reality. They do not seek to imitate form, but to create form, not to imitate life, but to find an equivalent for life.[44]

The purpose of art, for Fry, is not to imitate actual life, but to create imaginative life.[45] Fry's 'new and definite reality' means the portrayal of aesthetic emotion and sensation. According to Fry, psychological reality is the focus of the Post-Impressionists. They express aesthetic emotions with their use of colour, the logic of spatial relations and the rhythmic line. The artist's personal view of things is the most meaningful aspect of 'form'. For the Post-Impressionists, the emotional reality is the primitive essential reality, because the inner forces free a painter's mind and make a painter feel confident; he or she can paint whatever he or she wants, express his or her own aesthetic emotion and sensation. As Christopher Reed claims, the

---

[43] Woolf, *Roger Fry*, p.169.

[44] Roger Fry, 'The French Post-Impressionists', *Vision and Design*. Ed. J. B. Bullen. New York: Dover, 1981, p.167.

[45] Roger Fry, 'An Essay in Aesthetics', *Vision and Design*, p.13.

Post-Impressionists sought to 'present a mental image' rather than 'a direct impression of a real scene'.[46] David Summer also points out that a mental image 'is likened to a work of art made by the mind, and has a special status; [...]. So we say that paintings correspond not so much to things as to sensations, perceptions, and conceptions; or that they are, in equally mental terms, 'fantastic' or 'ideal''.[47] Reed and Summers's comments come close to Fry's aesthetics – an artistic vision reflects 'a unity of a metaphorical *psyche*'.[48]

Fry in his 'Expression and Representation in the Graphic Arts' (1908) explains that 'art is the means of communicating emotion from one human being to another'.[49] He sees art as the unity of artistic vision, emotion, and 'the mood'[50] of the artist. Post-Impressionist paintings are not representations but expressions of psychological conditions. The emotional effects are constructed by the alternation of light and shade.[51] In his "Introductory Note to Maurice Denis, 'Cézanne'" (1910), he goes further to argue that Post-Impressionism reveals a 'new ambition, a new conception of the purpose and methods of painting, [...]; a new hope too, and a new courage to attempt in painting that direct expression of imagined states of consciousness which has for long been relegated to music and poetry'.[52] The portrayal of psychological condition means the expression of the 'decorative unity'[53] of

---

[46] Christopher Reed, 'Forming Formalism: The Post-Impressionist Exhibitions'. *A Roger Fry Reader,* p.58.

[47] David Summers, 'Representation'. *Critical Terms for Art History.* Eds. Robert S. Nelson and Richard Shiff. Chicago: University of Chicago Press, 1996, p.3.

[48] Summers, 'Representation'. *Critical Terms for Art History*, p.14.

[49] Roger Fry, 'Expression and Representation in the Graphic Arts', *A Roger Fry Reader*, p.63 (unpublished lecture, written in 1908, made available by the Fry Estate from the Roger Fry Papers, King's College Library, Cambridge).

[50] Fry, 'Expression and Representation in the Graphic Arts', *A Roger Fry Reader*, p.70.

[51] Fry, 'Expression and Representation in the Graphic Arts', *A Roger Fry Reader*, p.68.

[52] Roger Fry, "Introductory Note to Maurice Denis, 'Cézanne'", *The Burlington Magazine*, January 1910, pp.207 – 219, p.207.

[53] Fry, 'Expression and Representation in the Graphic Arts', *A Roger Fry Reader*, p.70.

the Post-Impressionist paintings – colour, line, mass and spatial relation of a canvas. Cézanne is the painter who really started this movement, Fry argues, because he uses a pictorial language to appreciate 'the sensibilities of the modern outlook', a 'new manifestation of creative art'.[54]

Synthesis is a central idea in Fry's analysis of Cézanne's paintings. What Fry sees in Cézanne is the implied value of his work, which conceptualises the primitive, searching for an 'abstract harmony'[55] of line, colour and shape, as Christopher Butler points out. In 'An Essay in Aesthetics' (1909) and 'The Artist's Vision' (1919), Fry points out that a work of art is a 'harmonious'[56] expression of form and color which reveal the 'psychological and emotional aspects of life'.[57] The aesthetic vision does not mean the exact representation of the visual appearance of things. Rather, it is 'the expression of an idea in the artist's mind'.[58] In 'Paul Cézanne' (1917), Fry states that the significant form of Cézanne's paintings comes from 'a sensibility' affected by the smallest detail of daily life, which might produce at any moment a nervous explosion.[59] Cézanne is highly praised by Fry, because Cézanne expresses his own emotions in his paintings, as Fry does. Sensations are the most powerful inner force, which makes Cézanne's paintings 'the purest terms of structural design'.[60] The arrangements of form and colour aim to express the artist's aesthetic vision, to stimulate the viewer's aesthetic emotion, sensation and imagination. A work of art, in this light, is a 'balance between the emotions and the intellect, between Vision and Design', as Woolf concludes.[61]

---

[54] Roger Fry, 'The French Post-Impressionists', *Vision and Design*, p.167.

[55] Christopher Butler, *Early Modernism: Literature, Music and Painting in Europe, 1900 – 1916*. Oxford: Clarendon, 1994, p.215.

[56] Roger Fry, 'The Artist's Vision', *Vision and Design*, p.34.

[57] Roger Fry, 'An Essay in Aesthetics', *Vision and Design*, p.13.

[58] Fry, 'The Artist's Vision', *Vision and Design*, p.35.

[59] Roger Fry, 'Paul Cézanne', *Vision and Design*, p.180.

[60] Fry, 'Paul Cézanne', *Vision and Design*, p.185.

[61] Woolf, *Roger Fry*, p.245.

In comparison with Impressionism, the simplicity of Post-Impressionism has a primitive attraction, in terms of structure, form and the use of colour. According to Woolf, Fry's Omega Workshops "must be seen as an attempt to 'develop a definitely English tradition' of the decorative arts which would train the public eye to appreciate the beauty of mass, colour and form".[62] The art of Post-Impressionism brings the art of painting alive in terms of imagination, vision and design. It presents a subversive way of seeing, which aims to avoid the Impressionists' 'passive attitude towards the appearance of things'.[63]

An artistic form is unique because it conveys an emotion. The Post-Impressionists aim to search for 'abstract form' and to search for 'the permanent structure that underlies appearances';[64] they return to primitive-like forms, in order to convey emotional significance. As Woolf points out, for the British public, the paintings in Fry's two Post-Impressionist exhibitions were 'an insult', because they looked 'outrageous, anarchistic and childish'.[65] For Woolf, the criticism is like 'a storm of abuse', which expressed a mixed feeling of anxiety and excitement from the critics and the viewing public. Fry himself did not like to be called a 'pasticheur'.[66] He has to defend himself, because the French Post-Impressionist way of painting emotion comes close to the way he himself painted. The way Cézanne, Matisse and Picasso paint makes Fry see the tendency of the transformation of style – to express one's own 'petit sensation'[67] in painting. And yet, Fry's expression of one's petit

---

[62] See Rebecca Stott, "'Inevitable Relations': Aesthetic Revelations from Cézanne to Woolf". *The Politics of Pleasure: Aesthetics and Cultural Theory*. Ed. Stephen Regan. Buckingham: Open University Press, 1992, p.87.

[63] For instance, Monet painted snow in blue if it was under the shadow. See Jacqueline V. Falkenheim, *Roger Fry and the Beginnings of Formalist Art Criticism*, 1980, p.16.

[64] Falkenheim, *Roger Fry and the Beginnings of Formalist Art Criticism*, p.19.

[65] Woolf, *Roger Fry*, p.154.

[66] Woolf, *Roger Fry*, p.175.

[67] Woolf, *Roger Fry*, p.175.

sensation as psychological reality, at that moment, was not appreciated by many of the British critics and the general public.

With excitement, Fry feels that he can paint literary elements in Henry James on the canvas. Fry felt that he could almost *draw* James's psychological pattern, putting its elegant texture in visual terms. He also admired a visual poet like Coleridge, particularly his *Ancient Mariner*, for the rich colour of its literary images. His idea of seeing painterly elements in literature comes close to Woolf's creation of her own path of writing through the sensibility of the visual, to show a transformation from the Edwardian realism to the Georgian modernism, as she advocates in 'Mr Bennett and Mrs Brown' (1924). As Woolf saw it, literature 'was suffering from a plethora of old clothes. Cézanne and Picasso had shown the way; writers should fling representation to the winds and follow suit'.[68] For Woolf, English novelists should take their art seriously, detaching themselves from 'childish problems of photographic representation' [69] (Edwardian realism), and emphasise more the expression of emotion through abstract symbols, as two figures Woolf depicts in the opening of Fry's biography.

Bell's Significant Form and Woolf

Woolf would also learn from the theory of 'significant form',[70] the central notion of Clive Bell's aesthetics. In *Art* (1914), Bell claims that '[t]he starting point for all systems of aesthetics must be the personal experience of a peculiar emotion. The objects that provoke this emotion we call works of art'.[71] A work of art transforms the personal experience into an expression of emotion. The artist had his emotion expressed in a work of art,

---

[68] Julia Briggs, *Reading Virginia Woolf*. Edinburgh: Edinburgh University Press, 2006, p.97.

[69] Woolf, *Roger Fry*, p.164.

[70] Clive Bell. *Art*. London: Chatto and Windus, 1947, p.8.

[71] Bell. *Art*, p.6.

which evokes the viewer's emotion aesthetically. Every work of art provides different emotions. These emotions are recognisable – love, anger, sadness – anyone can feel them. The essential quality of a work of art is 'significant form'. This form refers to relations between shape, colour, line. As Beryl Lake argues, works of art are "significant ultimately of the reality of things, of 'that which gives to all things their individual significance, the thing in itself, the ultimate reality'".[72] For me, this reality, 'the thing in itself', is psychological and personal. That is the reason why the form is 'significant'.[73] In significant form, one can see the artist's feeling and emotion, the real thing, instead of the physical appearance of the visual object.

The Post-Impressionists express emotion and personal psychological condition, as profound truth and real significance, evoked by visual objects. They push this idea further and further, at the same time, the style of their paintings reveals a return to primitive art. Modernist primitivism indicates the simplicity and purity of form. Bell finds 'significant form' in primitive art and Cézanne's paintings. These artistic creations contain a sense of simplicity and originality:

> The fact that significant form was the only common quality in the works that moved me, and that in the works that moved me most and seemed most to move the most sensitive people – in primitive art, that is to say – it was almost the only quality, had led me to my hypothesis before ever I became familiar with the works of Cézanne and his followers. Cézanne carried me off my feet before ever I noticed that his strongest characteristic was an insistence on the supremacy of significant form.[74]

---

[72] Beryl Lake, 'A Study of the Irrefutability of Two Aesthetic Theories'. *Modernism, Criticism, Realism*. Eds. Charles Harrison and Fred Orton. London: Harper & Row, 1984, p.31.

[73] Lake, 'A Study of the Irrefutability of Two Aesthetic Theories'. *Modernism, Criticism, Realism*, p.32.

[74] Bell, *Art*, pp.40 – 41.

That primitive inner force Fry and Bell are looking for is in Cézanne's expression of spiritual calmness, in his painting of Southern France landscape (particularly Provence). Bell defines the essential quality of 'significant form' as 'lines and colours combined in a particular way, certain forms and relations of forms, which stir our aesthetic emotions'.[75] According to Bell, significant form moves its viewer aesthetically. This aesthetic emotion is 'Beauty',[76] an 'aesthetic, universal and eternal ecstasy'.[77] 'Significant form', claims Bell,

> stands charged with the power to provoke aesthetic emotion in anyone capable of feeling it. [...]. To those who have and hold a sense of the significance of form what does it matter whether the forms that move them were created in Paris the day before yesterday or in Babylon fifty centuries ago? The forms of art are inexhaustible; but all lead by the same road of aesthetic emotion to the same world of aesthetic ecstasy.[78]

Works of art and artistic movements represent the 'spiritual condition of an age'.[79] In this light, artists are sensibilities of an era. To Bell, Post-Impressionists created 'purely imaginary forms' which contain the state of mind, synthesising vision and design. Bell's aesthetic theory defines the formal qualities of arts, in which arts can transform human activity into an 'aesthetic exaltation', a 'state of mind'. As Bell argues,

> Art transports us from the world of man's activity to a world of aesthetic exaltation. For a moment we are shut off from human interests; our anticipations and memories are arrested; we are lifted above the stream of life. The pure mathematician rapt in his studies knows a state of mind which I take to be similar, if not identical.[80]

---

[75] Bell, *Art*, p.8.
[76] Bell, *Art*, p.13.
[77] Bell, *Art*, p.36.
[78] Bell, *Art*, pp.36 – 37.
[79] Bell, *Art*, p.215.
[80] Bell, *Art*, p.25.

Significant form can give the viewer a lift above the routine of everyday life, the physical space and clock time. This abstract form has the pure mathematician quality, which leads Woolf to give Katherine Hilbery her passionate response both to mathematics and to the city of London in *Night and Day*, as I will show in Chapter Two.

In Woolf's essay 'The Cinema' (1926), she gives the reader her way of interpreting how one's aesthetic emotion gives one a lift. As Woolf claims, when people look at a work of art, they see the stream of life itself in the motion picture, even when they have no part in it. For example, as Woolf claims, 'the horse will not knock us down. The King will not grasp our hands. The wave will not wet our feet'.[81] As one looks and thinks, one seems to be removed from the physical existence of the visual object – its appearance. For Woolf, 'Beauty' is a 'queer sensation', because it will 'continue to be beautiful whether we behold it or not'.[82] In other words, the aesthetic emotion of a work of art is everlasting; 'Beauty' is in the significant form of a work of art itself, rather than in the eye of its beholder. Here Woolf seems to be drawing on both Fry's and Bell's 'Beauty' in a work of art. For Roger Fry, on the one hand, Beauty is something quite different from one's 'praise of a woman, a sunset or a horse as beautiful'.[83] It is 'a means of communication between human beings' through the 'language of emotion'.[84] By saying so, Fry again defines the fundamental element of art – both painterly elements in literature and literary elements in painting – as the language of an aesthetic emotion, something that for Bell is to be found strikingly in Duncan Grant's paintings.

Bell's comments on Duncan Grant reveal the literary element in a painting's significant form. Grant's paintings remind Bell of the Elizabethan poets who wrote 'something fantastic and whimsical and at the same time

[81] Virginia Woolf, 'The Cinema' (1926). *E IV*, p.349.
[82] Woolf, 'The Cinema', p.349.
[83] Roger Fry, 'Retrospect'. *Vision and Design*, p.205.
[84] Fry, 'Retrospect', p.205.

intensely lyrical'.[85] What Bell sees in Grant's paintings is mixed motif, as one
can see Woolf's comments on Walter Sickert, that Sickert has a literary overtone
in his use of colour and human gesture, in which one can feel the spatial and
psychological tension on the canvas. The literary element in Grant's paintings is
not a story or a moral doctrine. According to Bell, it is something 'left over' –
'a germ of a poem and by curious cultivation grows out of it a picture'.[86]

As Simon Watney points out, Duncan Grant's techniques have many
aspects of Post-Impressionist aesthetics, because he has

> mastered three complementary manners in his desire to establish a
> type of lyrical genre painting which would nonetheless be resolutely
> 'modern': the tight hatching techniques of Cézanne, a loose
> pointillisme which relates closely to Denis and early Matisse, and a
> highly personal technique which was referred to as 'mobbling,'
> which was the result of his own responses to Byzantine and
> Renaissance decorative art.[87]

Grant's *The Dancers*, 1910-11 (Shone, 1999, Cat. 10) and *The Dance*,
1937 (Birmingham Museums and Art Gallery, UK, Private Collection) are
good examples to show the relation of his painting to Byzantine and
Renaissance art. He was under the influence of Botticelli's *La Primavera*
(the dancers' facial expressions and gestures), as well as Gauguin's *Three
Tahitians* (the dancers' dresses and his use of colour). Grant's techniques
are held within the large pictorial space by his decorative form, which is
constructed by one mosaic within mosaic. His style puts emphasis on line,
elongation of the body, serene facial expression, gracefulness of pose and
composition, and delicate coloring. For him, Post-Impressionism offers a

---

[85] Clive Bell, 'Duncan Grant'. *Since Cézanne*. 1922. London: Chatto and Windus,
1929, p.111.
[86] Bell, 'Duncan Grant', *Since Cézanne,* p.112.
[87] Simon Watney, *English Post-Impressionism*. London: Studio Vista, 1980, p.87.

new perspective on decorative art, in which 'the aims of decoration and of painting were no longer felt to be mutually exclusive, being seen instead as two aspects of the same thing'.[88]

The Dancers is a 'highly personal piece', as Richard Shone points out. Grant's portrayal of the stately movement of the five figures against the sky 'establish[es] a mood that recurs throughout his work'.[89] Duncan's expression of the harmonious and peaceful mood comes close to Fry's aesthetic emotion, which is a synthesis of the artist's vision and Bell's significant form. For this reason, Grant is 'more of an artist than an Englishman,[90] in Clive Bell's eye. In *The Sisters' Arts: the Writing and Painting of Virginia Woolf and Vanessa Bell*, Diane Filby Gillespie points out that when Virginia Woolf accompanied her sister to look at Perugino's paintings in Italy in 1908, they talked about what they saw to compare to the creative process of painters and writers. Both aim to create beauty, but painting is silent, wordless, static, whereas writing documents 'the flight of mind', the very process by which that beauty is perceived and achieved.[91] Woolf treats her own written fragments as a kind of painting that attempts to communicate the very act of perception. As Gillespie claims, during these early travels, Woolf was aware of different subjects for her pen, like a painter. The beauty is what the writer puts down: 'her own state of mind'.[92] Woolf learnt to use her mind's eye from the painter's perspective, in addition to her physical eye, to make her own literary images complete, as harmonious narrative patterns out of ordinary activities. The 'literary overtone' Bell sees in Grant comes surprisingly close to the way in which Woolf sees Sickert as a

---

[88] Watney, *English Post-Impressionism*, p.91.
[89] Richard Shone, *The Art of Bloomsbury: Roger Fry, Vanessa Bell and Duncan Grant*. London: Tate Gallery, 1999, p.68.
[90] Bell, 'Duncan Grant', p.112.
[91] Diane Filby Gillespie, *The Sisters' Arts: the Writing and Painting of Virginia Woolf and Vanessa Bell*. New York: Syracuse University Press, 1988, p.41.
[92] Gillespie, *The Sisters' Arts*, p.42.

'writer in painter'. Woolf also recognises a painter's eye in Proust and Henry James. Through reading literature and painting, Woolf has her own hybrid approach in composing her writing, as I will show in the following section.

Woolf's Hybrid Approach

A close reading of Woolf's novels, essays, letters and diary should be enough to convince one of the importence of painting in her life. The aesthetic theories of Fry and Bell were central to Woolf, because they offered the analogy for her career and aspirations and developments as a writer. This section will establish her intimate connection with painters and art critics, and suggest some ways in which Woolf found their ideas useful for her own writing. For example, in 'Mr Bennett and Mrs Brown' (1924), Woolf claims that the Georgians do 'as painters do when they wish to reduce the innumerable details of a crowded landscape to simplicity – step back, half shut the eyes, gesticulate a little vaguely with the fingers, and reduce Edwardian fiction to a view'.[93] The literary voyage from Edwardian realistic representation to Georgian psychological abstraction, to Woolf, is the transformation from traditional Victorian academic painting to a freedom of expressing emotion.

Woolf's association with the Bloomsbury Group was crucial for her writing. For a young woman born and raised by the rules of Victorian England and excluded from university education, the group offered an extraordinary opportunity for intellectual expansion, and one can identify the influence of the Cambridge Apostles on her work. The intellectual and aesthetic journey from Cambridge Apostles to London Bloomsbury was, as Perry Meisel points out, a 'visionary escape' from traditional Victorianism to the pursuit of "passionately intense and immediate 'states of mind'".[94] Woolf's narrative

---

[93] Virginia Woolf, 'Mr Bennett and Mrs Brown' (1924). *E III*, p.385.

[94] Perry Meisel, *The Absent Father: Virginia Woolf and Walter Pater*. New Haven: Yale University Press, 1980, p.37.

form re-creates Post-Impressionist psychology, which made possible the development of her own writing principles, in terms of the unification of the dualism of 'the visible and the invisible, the eye and the eyeless'.[95]

Woolf's aesthetics were not developed in theoretical isolation but in Apostolic Bloomsbury, in which Fry's position was pivotal as an aesthetic guide. Woolf, indeed, wrote his biography after his death, showing that Fry's personal biography anticipated the Cambridge Apostle's development into Bloomsbury. His ideas about the visual arts enabled Woolf to move away from the material realistic nature of literature, which she saw as her previous generation's paradigm for the novel. Her milieu shows her particular awareness of the painter's perspective. Her writings can be read through Clive Bell and Roger Fry's art criticisms, in terms of her use of colours and shapes to express emotion, in order to search for significant form. As a consequence, some of the passages in Woolf's writings invite visualisation and pictorialism. For instance, as Marianna Torgovnick points out, the interludes of *The Waves* (1931) are like works of art. The interludes portray 'a beach scene and a room slightly before dawn to slightly after dark'.[96] Woolf's way of depicting the changing of light and shadow suggests 'the idea of a *series* of perspectives on the same scene or objects',[97] as one can see in Monet and Cézanne's paintings. Through Henry James, one can see that Woolf's *Night and Day* shows a development from Impressionism to Post-Impressionism, in terms of narrative form, as I will show in the next chapter.

Woolf loved painting.[98] In 'Pictures and Portraits' (1920), she describes her way of looking at paintings in the National Gallery and the National

---

[95] Ann Banfield, *The Phantom Table: Woolf, Fry, Russell and the Epistemology of Modernism.* Cambridge: Cambridge University Press, 2000, p.258.

[96] Marianna Torgovnick, *The Visual Arts, Pictorialism, and the Novel* (Princeton: Princeton University Press, 1985), p.130.

[97] Torgovnick, *The Visual Arts, Pictorialism, and the Novel*, p.130.

[98] David Dowling, *Bloomsbury Aesthetics and the Novels of Forster and Woolf.* London: Macmillan, 1985, p.96.

Portrait Gallery, by seeing paintings as a kind of silent language, visualising by colours:

> the pictures with the least of language about them – canvases taciturn and congealed like emerald or aquamarine – landscapes hollowed from transparent stone, green hillsides, skies in which the clouds are eternally at rest. Let us wash the roofs of our eyes in colour; let us dive till the deep seas close above our heads.[99]

Woolf tries out descriptions of landscape and stories designed to show up elements of colour and light in language and human character in her novels. Her use of colour has an intrinsic, inner logic – an expression of sensation and meaning, rather than simply being a representation of visual appearance. In this way, colors and shapes do not only mean what the painter or the writer sees. Rather, they are what he or she feels. Writing and painting could take on new responsibilities: both media needed to find new languages for subjective experience; new ways of depicting the rhythms of the inner life. As Cheryl Mares points out, Woolf's ideal novel

> would strike a balance between the two powers, between what Fry called a work's appeal to purely formal, 'plastic and spatial values' and its 'dramatic appeal to the emotions of actual life'. To strike this 'razor-edge of balance', Woolf attempts to create open-ended, nonconclusive designs that subvert themselves by incorporating their own antitheses or that call attention to their own limitations, their fictive or merely provisional status. The novel's purpose, as Woolf sees it, is to 'bring us into close touch with life', and life, as she sees it, is 'something of extreme reality' that 'rear[s] and kick[s]'. Therefore, if she is not to betray her sense of the purpose of her

---

[99] Virginia Woolf, 'Pictures and Portraits' (1920), *E III*, p.164.

medium, impressions of form in her fiction, however intense, must be, like the sense of immunity, elusive.[100]

Emotion brings one into close touch with the inner life. Particularly in Bloomsbury aesthetics, an art form brings out the significance of the inner life. Woolf's writings reveal the psychological implications of her experimentation with narrative form, her attempt to portray an inner life, constructed by emotion and perception. As E. M. Forster commented, Woolf takes a variety of sensations, 'passing them through her mind where they encountered theories and memories, and then bringing them out again, through a pen, on to a bit of paper'.[101] Sensations have to be combined, arranged, selected and emphasised to create a unified artistic form.

In *Walter Sickert: A Conversation* (1934), Woolf writes about the relation between the use of colour, visual objects, the environment and human psychology. As Woolf has noticed, 'how different people see colour differently; how painters are affected by their place of birth, whether in the blue South or the grey North; how colour blazes, unrelated to any object, in the eyes of children, how politicians and business men are blind, days spent in an office leading to atrophy of the eye'.[102] She praises Sickert's dramatic use of colour to depict emotions and sensations. At Sickert's exhibition, Woolf says, she became 'completely and solely an insect – all eye',[103] looking 'from colour to colour, from red to blue, from yellow to green'.[104] Woolf depicts her fantastic experience as a viewer of the show: '[c]olours went spirally through my body lighting a flare as if a rocket fell through the night and lit up greens and browns, grass and tress, and there in the grass a

---

[100] Cheryl Mares, 'Reading Proust: Woolf and the Painter's Perspective'. *The Multiple Muses of Virginia Woolf*, p.75.

[101] E. M. Forster, *Virginia Woolf*. Cambridge: Cambridge University Press, 1942, p.7.

[102] Virginia Woolf, *Walter Sickert: A Conversation*. London: Hogarth Press, 1934, p.7.

[103] Woolf, *Walter Sickert*, p.9.

[104] Woolf, *Walter Sickert*, p.9.

white bird. Colour warmed, thrilled, chafed, burnt, soothed, fed and finally exhausted me'.[105] Furthermore, she comments, Sickert's portraits of great men (Charles Bradlaugh at the Bar of the House of Commons, Winston Churchill) are not mechanical representations of the likeness of human faces. Rather, they are 'a summing-up, an epitome of a million acts, thoughts, statements and concealments'.[106] Woolf sees Sickert as a writer. Sickert is like a biographer in Woolf's eye, because in a portrait by him, one can read a life. He seems to be a novelist as well, because some pictures of his suggest stories, such as '*Rose et Marie*; *Christine buys a house*; *A difficult moment*'.[107] For Woolf, the awareness of 'one pink cloud riding down the bosom of the west', over the shoulders of the innkeeper in Sickert's painting, reminds of her 'the poets who haunt taverns and sea beaches where the fishermen are tumbling their silver catch into wicker baskets'.[108] The figures in paintings are motionless but have been seized in a moment of feeling, one in which the emotion was 'distinct, powerful and satisfactory',[109] conveyed with 'expressive quality'.[110] Woolf reads Sickert's hybrid approach as a combination of literary and visual patterns, one which she finds useful for an understanding of Sickert's biographic, novelistic and poetic vision.

Woolf shapes her own hybrid approach, seeing literary elements in painters like Sickert, and also painterly elements in writers like James and Proust. Woolf turned to works of Henry James and Marcel Proust,[111] when

---

[105] Woolf, *Walter Sickert*, p.9.

[106] Woolf, *Walter Sickert*, p.10.

[107] Woolf, *Walter Sickert*, p.13.

[108] Woolf, *Walter Sickert*, pp.19 – 21.

[109] Woolf, *Walter Sickert*, p.25.

[110] Woolf, *Walter Sickert*, p.17.

[111] Woolf mentioned Proust for the first time in her diary entry, Thursday 18 April 1918. She was having a conversation with Roger Fry. Proust's *Du Côté de chez Swann* had been published in Paris in November 1913. The conversation between

she was in the process of gaining her understanding of the relation between literary form and painting, or elements in the novel which could be seen as comparable to a visual work of art. In 'The Art of Fiction' (1927), Woolf argues that E. M. Forster's 'notably harsh judgment' upon Henry James's novel was unfair. According to Forster, James was going to 'perish' because his story-telling is too different from what Forster calls '[t]he Story, People, Plot, Fantasy, Prophecy, Pattern, and Rhythm'.[112] In other words, James's way of presenting life, in Forster's reading, is a failure because there is not enough connection to real life; it is too much an aesthetic view of fiction. For Woolf, on the contrary, James creates a literary pattern which has beauty in itself. A novel becomes a work of art, which has the aesthetic function of rousing 'a thousand ordinary human feelings in its progress'.[113]

Proust's writing shows the balance and fusion of an aesthetic vision of real life. According to Cheryl Mares, Proust's interest in the art of painting as the source of his writing, its psychological and dramatic appeal to the emotions of actual life, the personal and the trivial, attracted Woolf to his work.[114] Woolf sees the significance of the eye in Proust. 'It is the eye', as Woolf comments, 'that has [...] produced effects of extreme beauty and of a subtlety hitherto unknown'.[115] Proust conceives his literary world as the main character's reflection of the past, and the narrative takes the form of a series of pictures – he depicts the inner life (such as memory) in a pictorial way. His narrator evokes the transitory and elusive beauty of colours, textures, and atmosphere while providing an exhaustive analysis of his

---

Woolf and Fry shows their enthusiasm for Proust's novel. See *D I*, p.140.

[112] Virginia Woolf, 'The Art of Fiction' (1927). *Collected Essays by Virginia Woolf: Volume Two*. London: Hogarth Press, 1966, p.52.

[113] Woolf, 'The Art of Fiction' (1927), p.54.

[114] Cheryl Mares, 'Reading Proust: Woolf and the Painter's Perspective'. *The Multiple Muses of Virginia Woolf*, p.60.

[115] Virginia Woolf. 'Pictures' (1925). *E IV*, p.244.

emotions at the same time. There is always metaphor after metaphor, image after image which organises his perceptions and shapes his emotional responses to a particular moment of life in the external visible world. The narrator has moments of inner astonishing excitement and impression, a state of personal feeling, which has been liberated from the sequence of ordinary time and space, as a moment of psychological and emotional self. As Lee McKay Johnson points out, in this process of perception, a visual object loses its physical particularity and becomes a symbol:

> This sense of the instantaneous deepening of reality, of form flashing out, is not only similar to Bergson's intuition, but also close to Baudelaire's concept of the 'surnatural', to Hopkin's 'inscape', to Joyce's 'epiphanies', to the 'moments' of perception in which 'symbolic meaning descends' in Virginia Woolf, to the 'moments' of sensation in Proust and in Pater. All of these experiences of momentary revelation are characterized by 'wholeness', a metaphysical change in everything at once, and the model for this experience is visual transformation, a sudden new sight that makes the ordinary visionary.[116]

Woolf's essay 'Pictures' (1925) is a good example of how she conceptualises the importance of the eye and symbolises the visual in her fictional writing. Woolf uses a visually oriented style of writing; as she comments, 'writers have begun to use their eyes'.[117] Great novelists such as James and Proust learn from the visual arts to sharpen their eyes. Their works can be read as a starting point for her analysis of 'the precise spot',[118] to show how vision makes writers use their pens in a way they have never tried before: '[i]t is

---

[116] Lee McKay Johnson, *The Metaphor of Painting: Essays on Baudelaire, Ruskin, Proust and Pater*. Ann Arbor: UMI, 1980, p.111.

[117] Virginia Woolf. *The Moment and Other Essays*. London: Hogarth Press, 1947, p.141.

[118] Woolf. 'Pictures', *E IV*, p.243.

the eye that has fertilised their thought'.[119] Moreover, the following scene shows how Woolf sees Proust's use of the eye to depict a character's emotion:

> We have to understand the emotions of a young man for a lady in a box below. With an abundance of images and comparisons we are made to appreciate the forms, the colours, the very fibre and texture of the plush seats and the ladies' dresses and the dullness or glow, sparkle or colour, of the light. At the same time that our senses drink in all these our minds are tunneling, logically and intellectually, into the obscurity of the young man's emotions which, as they ramify and modulate and stretch further and further, at last penetrate so far, peter into such a shred of meaning, that we can scarcely follow any more, were it not that suddenly, in flash after flash, metaphor after metaphor, the eye lights up that cave of darkness, and we are shown the hard, tangible, material shapes of bodiless thoughts hanging like bats in the primeval darkness where light has never visited them before.[120]

According to Woolf, a depiction of the appearance of the visible and sensory, such as 'the very fibre and texture of the plush seats and the ladies' dresses' is not in itself a portrayal of consciousness. The above passage shows her account of the dynamic relation between the physical eye and the mind's eye, the visible world and the psychological reality – the invisible / bodyless emotion and thought. For Woolf, a novelist is only a second-rate story-teller, if he or she writes only the surface of the external world. On the other hand, the portrayal of emotion makes a writer a painter, who is able to paint visual impressions and the mental picture in words. Woolf's way of seeing painting in writing demonstrates the influence of the Post-Impressionist portrayal of psychology and emotion.

---

[119] Woolf. 'Pictures'. *E IV*, p.244.
[120] Woolf. 'Pictures'. *E IV*, p.244.

Woolf's use of colours and shapes to express emotion in writing is her achievement, in terms of the Post-Impressionist aesthetics. For Woolf, Fry and Bell, colours and shapes can materialise what one feels. One can see the tendency towards primitive instincts in Fry and Bell's praise of the Post-Impressionist art – the harmonious composition of colour, shape and line does not reflect 'a matter of technique', but a flash of insight with 'significant form'.[121] In Woolf's writing, emotions and sensations are 'prints of mind'. As Woolf claimed in 'Phases of Fiction' (1929), '[e]verything that can be felt can be said'.[122] Pamela L. Caughie pushes this argument further, by focusing her discussion on Woolf's view of the relation between art, life and truth. In Woolf's artistic figures, particularly Lily Briscoe in *To the Lighthouse* (1927), one can see that the artist is questing after the 'essence beneath or the truth beyond all surface manifestations and conventional forms',[123] searching for artistic freedom, originality and difference.

Woolf's attitude toward the Bloomsbury Group indicates the dialectic between literary and visual patterns. Lily's painting highlights a lesson learned in Woolf's novel by the painter, because Lily's way of representing Mrs. Ramsay is pure absraction. It reveals her 'vision' – her understanding and her acknowledgment that shows Mrs. Ramsay in significant aesthetic form – a stable purple pyramid. In Woolf and Bell's writings, one can see that Walter Sickert and Duncan Grant are 'writers' in painters. On the other hand, James, Proust and Woolf are 'painters' in writings. The modern period is rich in artists who give expression to different emotions and sensations through a fusion of artistic techniques. In Woolf's writings, one can see her intention of finding new ways to perceive the essential modernist vision of her own.

---

[121] Bell, *Art*, 1947, p.44.

[122] Virginia Woolf, 'Phases of Fiction' (1929). *Collected Essays: Vol. Two*, p.84.

[123] Pamela L. Caughie, 'The Artist Figure in Woolf's Writings: The Status and Function of Art'. *Virginia Woolf and Postmodernism: Literature in Quest and Question of Itself*. Urbana: University of Illinois Press, 1991, p.30.

Woolf's Dual Vision in the Urban Space

Woolf values the Proustian pictorial scenes which depict timeless moments of impression, sensation, memory, desire, and imagination.[124] The 'I' in *À la Recherche du Temps Perdu* (1922) indicates the 'synthesis' of the physical eye and the mind's eye, being together with visual impression. Clive Bell, in his *Proust* (1928), points out the motif of this novel is 'memory'. 'And Proust', Bell claims,

> at least, came to be able to bring these monsters up from the deep at will almost and by the simplest devices. A surprise, the taste of a Madeleine soaked in tea, the phrase of a sonata by Vinteuil, the click of a lift as it passes a floor, the untying of a shoe-lace, the unbuttoning of an overcoat, such were the jolts that for him provoked explosion. *À la recherché du temps perdu* is a series of carefully planned explosions by means of which the submerged past is brought into the present, the deep-sea monsters of memory to the surface.[125]

Proust's vision gives vivid expression to the 'throbbing moment when emotion has the force and reality of sensation',[126] because he was 'an observer who analysed his experience, his mind was full of abstractions; because he was a poet these abstractions were seeking ever to give themselves concrete forms'.[127] For Bell, Proust's memories in words look like one image after another, containing emotions. Through Proust's writing, Bell's significant form can be theorised as an artistic abstraction with emotional significance. Significant form makes bodiless emotions and memories as visible images. The shape and the taste of a Madeleine or the untying of a shoe-lace is an 'emotional experience' to Proust, at its most 'intense and vivid, at the

---

[124] Woolf, *The Moment and Other Essays*, p.142.
[125] Clive Bell, *Proust*. London: Hogarth Press, 1928, p.41.
[126] Bell, *Proust*, p.42.
[127] Bell, *Proust*, p.22.

moment of being experienced, is uncapturable'.[128] The whole novel is an expression of pursuit, capture and exhibition of these, in Clive Bell's words, "an ever-flowing stream, not a ball of string cut into neat lengths. Time overflows punctuation. [...] [H]ow is a style to be anything but complicated and prolix when an artist is trying to say four things at once – to give a bird's eye view and 'a close up' at once in time and space"?[129]

In *Swann's Way*, the first volume of *À la Recherche du Temps Perdu*, Proust shows the reader that the theme of his auto-biographic writing is memory itself. Memory, for Proust, can be visualised in a way, in which

> Perhaps the immobility of the things that surround us is forced upon them by our conviction that they are themselves and not anything else, and by the immobility of our conceptions of them. For it always happened that when I awake like this, and my mind struggled in an unsuccessful attempt to discover where I was, everything would be moving round me through the darkness: things, places, years. [...]. Its memory, the composite memory of its ribs, knees, and shoulder-blades offered it a whole series of rooms in which it had at one time or another slept; while the unseen walls kept changing, adapting themselves to the shape of each successive room that it remembered, whirling madly through the darkness.[130]

For Proust, the mind's eye sees the flow of memory, as a series of symbolic/invisible walls and rooms. The mind's eye looks through the darkness, while he was half awake and half asleep. There is a whole series of images – people, things and places with emotional significance. While the narrator is half-awake, the image of the 'symbolic room' keeps changing. Walter

---

[128] Bell, *Proust*, p.42.

[129] Bell, *Proust*, p.13.

[130] Marcel Proust, *Remembrance of Things Past: Volume I, Swann's Way, Part One*. Trans. C. K. Scott Moncrieff. 1922. London: Chatto & Windus, 1957, p.5.

Benjamin also use the symbol 'four-wall room' to depict the way the flâneur walks in the city of Paris, as if he walks into his own Berlin childhood memory.

Apart form the use of the painter's eye, Woolf also learned from Proust the expression of sensations through the 'dual vision', which she defines in 'Phases of Fiction' (1929), as 'the sympathy of a poet and the detachment of a scientist to everything that it has the power to feel'.[131] A mental picture is like a puzzle, which contains different shapes, including 'a thousand emotional veins'.[132] The complexity of emotions brings the pleasure of figuring out the puzzle of the mental picture. The 'central point' is the state of mind. Proust's perception made his characters rise 'like waves forming, then break and sink again into the moving sea of thought and comment and analysis which gave them birth'.[133] This 'dual vision' makes possible for Proust the depiction of complex characters. Woolf makes a comparison between Proust and James's writing style: James's fictional world is like an envelope, 'thin but elastic, which stretches wider and wider and serves not to enforce a view but to enclose a world'.[134] The Jamesian fictional universe is the whole progress of thoughts, emotions, sensations and memories at the centre of consciousness. His psychological novels project a drama of the mind, through what people think and what is thought about them.[135] Woolf's writing has James's psychological complexity and also Proust's dual vision. The combination of these two creates Woolf's own dialectic of the inner and the outer worlds.

Woolf's 'dual vision' comes from Proust; it also comes close to Benjamin's theorisation of the flâneur. The figure of the flâneur is used by Charles Baudelaire to represent the poet as a walker and a viewer of the nineteenth-century Paris. Baudelaire's flâneur represents the aesthetic

---

[131] Woolf, 'Phases of Fiction', p.84.
[132] Woolf, 'Phases of Fiction', p.82.
[133] Woolf, 'Phases of Fiction', p.85.
[134] Woolf, 'Phases of Fiction', p.83.
[135] Woolf, 'Phases of Fiction', p.88.

sensibility of urban life. In both Benjamin and Woolf, the flâneur's dual vision indicates a dialectical visual experience in an urban space: both detached observation and poetic mystery. Because of his dual vision, the flâneur is an ambiguous figure in the city. As David Frisby says, he is the stroller, the detective, and the decipherer.[136] Frisby also suggests that Benjamin sees the flâneur 'not merely as a historical figure in the urban context, but also as a contemporary illumination of his own methodology. In this sense, the flâneur/detective is a central, albeit often metaphorical, figure [...]'.[137]

In 'The Painter of Modern Life' (1863), Baudelaire introduces the figure of the flâneur to describe the modern artist. The genius of the painter of manners, according to Baudelaire,

> is of a mixed nature, by which I mean that it contains a strong literary element. Observer, philosopher, *flâneur* – call him what you will; [...]. Sometimes he is a poet; more often he comes closer to the novelist or the moralist; he is the painter of the passing moment and of all the suggestions of eternity that it contains.[138]

The flâneur is a strange man, with artistic creative power and originality. For instance, he is the painter, who catches the modernity – the spirit of his time, the manner of his present. The flâneur is a passionate lover of crowds. Baudelaire uses Constantin Guys's paintings (1802-92) as examples of the flâneur's artistic vision and poetic passion. The flâneur is '*a man of the world*'.[139] His interest is 'the whole world; he wants to know, understand and appreciate everything that happens on the surface of our globe' – the 'spiritual citizen of the universe'.[140] The writer's country is the world.

---

[136] David Frisby, *Cityscapes of Modernity: Critical Explorations*. Cambridge: Polity, 2001, p.28.

[137] Frisby, *Cityscapes of Modernity*, p.28.

[138] Charles Baudelaire, *The Painter of Modern Life and Other Essays*. Trans. Jonathan Mayne. 1964. London: Phaidon, 1995, pp.4 – 5.

[139] Baudelaire, *The Painter of Modern Life*, p.7.

[140] Baudelaire, *The Painter of Modern Life*, p.7.

The flâneur's passionate gaze at the crowd is both a matter of the eye and of the mind. Physically, he is surrounded by the crowd; mentally, by his own thought. 'The crowd is his element', as Baudelaire claims,

> as the air is that of birds and water of fishes. His passion and his profession are to become one flesh with the crowd. For the perfect *flâneur*, for the passionate spectator, it is an immense joy to set up house in the heart of the multitude, amid the ebb and flow of the movement, in the midst of the fugitive and the infinite. To be away from home and yet to feel oneself everywhere at home; to see the world, to be at the centre of the world, and yet to remain hidden from the world – such are a few of the slightest pleasures of those independent, passionate, impartial natures which the tongue can but clumsily define.[141]

The flâneur is an ambiguous figure, not only because of his dual vision but also brcause of his dialectical relation with the crowd. He gazes passionately at the crowd but also 'remain[s] hidden in the crowd', a psychologically detached observer. The flâneur begins as an observer of life, and later his task is to turn what he has passionately observed into a work of art, such as a painting, a poem or a novel. His eyes and memories are full of impressions of life which are fusions of sensuous, aesthetic and emotional moments. Baudelaire sees the city as an endlessly exciting and stimulating place. The dynamic character of urban phenomena is visually intoxicating. With the visual stimulation of the urban space, artists are able to embrace the spectacle of metropolitan life and give aesthetic forms to the cityscape with a new mode of perception and expression. In the labyrinthine structures of the metropolitan environment, one may wander for hours, and enchantment may wait around the corner. In Baudelaire's view, the city is the centre of modern life. To lose oneself in the crowd, to succumb to its delights and joys is the intoxication of modernity. The flâneur's vision presents the experience of urban modernity.

---

[141] Baudelaire, *The Painter of Modern Life*, p.9.

The flâneur is not only a collector of visual signs; rather, he is an interpreter of these signs. His vision transforms a cityscape (buildings, streets, arcades and so on) from a puzzle and labyrinth to a readable text, a puzzle, a labyrinth and a 'discourse'[142] as Roland Barthes has put it. Barthes constructs the semiology of Paris by reading its buildings as signs; for him, the Eiffel Tower is a sign of a 'complete object',[143] embodying the subject-object dualism and the inner/outer dialectic. The Tower is not just a physical object but contains one's own memory and imagination of the city, which forms the 'simulacrum' of Paris, and contains the 'duration' of the city, in itself becoming the complex, continuous image of Paris – a panoramic vision.[144]

Barthes's semiotic reading of Paris reveals the flâneur's way of seeing, a dialectic of inner and outer spheres, virtual image and the matter. The panoramic vision of Paris, for Barthes, is a duration which has four levels. The first, according to Barthes, is the prehistory of Paris, when the city was covered by a layer of water 'in foggy weather'.[145] One can see only 'a few solid points': the Pantheon, Montmartre, and two blue stakes in the distance, the towers of Notre-Dame.[146] The second history before the Tower's gaze is 'the Middle Ages', in which the Tower and Notre-Dame of the Left Bank articulate a symbol of the dialectic of 'the past and the present, of stone, old as the world, and metal, sign of modernity'.[147] The third is 'a broad history' from the Monarchy to the Empire, the history of France.[148] The final one, under the Tower's gaze, Paris is being made 'now', composing itself 'like

---

[142] Roland Barthes, 'Semiology and the Urban' (1967). *Rethinking Architecture: A Reader in Cultural Theory*. Ed. Neil Leach. 1997. London: Routledge, 2003, p.168.

[143] Roland Barthes, 'The Eiffel Tower'. *Rethinking Architecture*, p.173.

[144] Barthes, 'The Eiffel Tower', p.176.

[145] Barthes, 'The Eiffel Tower', p.177.

[146] Barthes, 'The Eiffel Tower', p.177.

[147] Barthes, 'The Eiffel Tower', p.177.

[148] Barthes, 'The Eiffel Tower', p.177.

an abstract canvas', which certain monuments are beginning to 'set signs of
the future' with glass and metal.[149]

What one sees struggles with what one perceives; the simulacrum of a
city is a co-operation of memory (the virtual) and visual impression (the real)
produced in the mind, as the Tower witnesses the geographical, historical
and social structure of Parisian space. By climbing the Tower, one conquers
Paris visually, reducing the city to a visual object. At the same time, the
Tower itself is an empty centre – there is nothing to see inside, not like the
Louvre. The Tower, for Barthes, is a 'paradoxical object', because its inside
emptiness defines the simulacrum of Paris (Barthes's imaginary Paris from
the top of the Tower).

I suggest that the observations and poetic visions of the flâneur turn the
external visual world (the cityscape) into the inwardness (his own consciousness).
This turning process is a passionate transformation of the city into Walter
Benjamin's symbolic private 'four walled room'[150] in which the city has
turned into a virtual image. For Benjamin, the flâneur's walk in the city takes
him into his own memory. His personal history offers a whole series of rooms,
constituting the unseen walls for him to walk in the city, adapting himself to
the shape of the city, which is the shape of emotion that he remembered.

Benjamin expresses the dialectical relation between the inner and outer
worlds, the viewing subject and the city. The process of mapping and
thinking is central to consciousness. As Benjamin claims, the city is the
'Promised Land' of *flâneurs*. 'Landscape –' Benjamin writes, is 'what the
city becomes for the *flâneur*. Or, more precisely, the city splits into its
dialectical poles. It becomes a landscape that opens up to him and a parlor
that encloses him'.[151] The flâneur follows his own mind's eye, which leads

---

[149] Barthes, 'The Eiffel Tower', p.177.
[150] Walter Benjamin. *Charles Baudelaire: A Lyric Poet in the Era of High
Capitalism.* Trans. Harry Zohn. London: NLB, 1973, p.37.
[151] Walter Benjamin, 'The Return of the *Flâneur*' (1929). *Walter Benjamin: Selected*

his footsteps. Benjamin's city portraits contain a dual sensibility; as Peter Szondi has said, they are both metaphorical and melancholic in a 'very precise sense, [...], as poetic writing'.[152] Graeme Gilloch also points out in *Myth and Metropolis: Walter Benjamin and the City*, Benjamin's Paris is 'the city of dreaming, the site of modern enchantment filled with the fantastic objects and fashions that new technologies have magically conjured up before our eyes'.[153] Deborah L. Parsons, in her *Streetwalking the Metropolis: Women, the City, and Modernity*, also notices the significance of the literary geography of the city in Benjamin's writing. Benjamin's urban literary geography 'is indeed marked by an obsessive attempt to know the city in its entirety, a surrealist desire to penetrate the fantasies of its phantasmagoria, and a determined project of reacquisition of its fragments'.[154]

The flâneur's dual identity makes him an ambiguous and suspicious figure in the cityscape. He is a viewing subject, who is also objectified by what he sees. In 'The Return of the *Flâneur*' (1929), Benjamin describes the gaze of the flâneur as the entrance into the 'chambers' of the city. 'As he walks, his steps create an astounding resonance on the asphalt. [...]. The city is a mnemonic for the lonely walker: it conjures up more than his childhood and youth, more than its own history'.[155] Benjamin's walk in Paris reminds him of his own childhood in Berlin, as Peter Szondi points out.[156] The walk of the

---

Writings, Volume 2, 1927-1934. Cambridge, MA: Harvard University Press, 1999, p.263.

[152] Peter Szondi, 'Walter Benjamin's City Portraits'. *On Walter Benjamin: Critical Essays and Recollections*. Cambridge, MA: MIT, 1991, p.26.

[153] Graeme Gilloch. *Myth and Metropolis: Walter Benjamin and the City*. Cambridge: Polity, 1996, p.123.

[154] Deborah L. Parsons, *Streetwalking the Metropolis: Women, the City, and Modernity*. Oxford: Oxford University Press, 2000, p.7.

[155] Benjamin, 'The Return of the *Flâneur*' (1929). *Selected Writings: Vol. 2*, p.262.

[156] Walking in the streets of Paris and translating Proust's work with Franz Hessel, Benjamin walks into his own Berlin childhood. See Peter Szondi, 'Hope in the Past: On Walter Benjamin'. Trans. Harvey Mendelsohn. *Berlin Childhood Around 1990*. Trans. Howard Eiland. Cambridge, MA: Harvard University Press,

flâneur leads the reader to step into his own past, seeing his surroundings in terms of his personal history, which is mapped into the city's own past – the arcades, the world exhibitions, Louis-Philippe, and Baudelaire's streets of Paris. For Benjamin, flânerie is an art, in which aesthetic emotion is aroused. The act of walking and looking in the city shows the viewer's love and appreciation. Benjamin recalls that Fritz Hessel encouraged Berliners to embrace Berlin: '[w]e Berliners must inhabit our city much more fully'.[157] In Benjamin's reading of Hessel, the phrase 'inhabit' indicates the whole knowledge of 'dwelling'.[158] In this light, the flâneur's philosophy is to 'learn' a city, to read the city as a great book when one is there 'for the duration'. This reading is an 'overriding love of the enduring' that 'carves the unique, the sensational, [...] that seeks out eternal sameness'.[159]

While looking at works of art, building sites, bridges, squares and people, the flâneur sees into the heart of the city and its rapid changing nature, as in Baudelaire's metaphorical depiction, 'the city changes faster than a human heart'.[160] Through his gaze, the flâneur interacts with the crowd and embraces the people and things he sees as part of his mental life. 'We see only what looked at us', claims Hessel.[161] His statement reveals the exchange of the gaze between the gazer and the gazee. Jacques Lacan has an explanation of the dialectic between the viewing subject and external visual objects, the subject-object dualism. This 'gaze' something that 'looks at us', is imagined by Lacan not only to come from the organ of sight, but also from the visible field of the Other, the world of objectivity, which indicates the symbolic lack in the phallic system. In the exchange of the gaze, the role of the viewing subject in the visible world is changed; the notion of 'viewing

---

2006, p.5.
[157] Benjamin, 'The Return of the *Flâneur*', pp.263 – 264.
[158] Benjamin, 'The Return of the *Flâneur*', p.264.
[159] Benjamin, 'The Return of the *Flâneur*', pp.265 – 266.
[160] Benjamin, 'The Return of the *Flâneur*', p.265.
[161] Benjamin, 'The Return of the *Flâneur*', p.265.

subject' and 'visual object' is subverted. 'This is the function that is found at the heart of the institution of the subject in the visible', claims Lacan,

> What determines me, at the most profound level, in the visible, is the gaze that is outside. It is through the gaze that I enter light and it is from the gaze that I receive its effects. Hence it comes about that the gaze is the instrument through which light is embodied and through which – if you will allow me to use a word, as I often do, in a fragmented form – I am *photo-graphed*.[162]

At the moment of the exchange of the gaze, the subject 'takes in his own split', the subjective vision and consciousness becomes 'a privileged object', the *objet a*.[163] Once when Hessel was walking through Paris, as Benjamin notes, he saw 'women concièrges sitting and sewing in the cool doorways in the afternoon, [and] he felt they looked at him like his nurse'.[164] The combination of seconds of microcosmic personal life (as *objet petit a*) and the macrocosm (the grand history of the city) happens at the moment of the exchange of the gaze. The city echoes the vision of the flâneur, as sculptures gaze back: 'Like quarry stones, they stood there decorously holding their ball or pencil, those that still had hands. Their white, stone eyes followed our footsteps, and the fact that these heathen girls gazed at us has become a part of our lives'.[165] The gaze demonstrates the inner/outer dialectic; through the gaze, the external world (people, places and things, the history of the city) combines with one's personal history and life.

The question of whether it is possible for a woman to be a flâneuse has been much debated by feminist critics. Drawing on Lacan's idea of the gaze,

---

[162] Lacan, 'What is a Picture'? *The Four Fundamental Concepts of Psycho-analysis*, p.106.
[163] Lacan, 'What is a Picture'?, p.83.
[164] Benjamin, 'The Return of the *Flâneur*', p.265.
[165] Benjamin, 'The Return of the *Flâneur*', p.265.

one could argue that women are not merely visual objects of male gaze. Women do gaze back and make the male subjective viewer an *object a*. Janet Wolff, however, in her 'The Invisible *Flâneuse*: Women and the Literature of Modernity', claims that women are invisible in the male literary canon. The literature of modernity, according to Wolff, 'describes the experience of men', a canon about 'transformations in the public world and in its associated consciousness'.[166] The urban characteristics of modernity are identified by male writers, all of whose accounts share a concern with the public sphere, from which women were excluded. The city was a masculine domain because of the ideology of "the 'separation of spheres'". Throughout the nineteenth century in England, the ideology of women's place in the domestic realm permeated the whole society. Women belonged to "the 'private' sphere of the home and the suburb".[167] What is missing in modern literature, according to Wolff, is an account of life "outside the public realm, of the experience of 'the modern' in its private manifestations, and also of the very different nature of the experience of those women who *did* appear in the public arena: a poem written by 'la femme passante' about her encounter with Baudelaire, perhaps".[168]

In *Feminist Destinations and Further Essays on Virginia Woolf*, Rachel Bowlby also comments on the vision of the flâneur and its relation to 'women and writing', 'art' and 'femininity'.[169] Bowlby quotes from Proust and Baudelaire to demonstrate how "a woman's image" is dominated by the male 'wandering gaze',[170] as a literary stereotype, a 'fragmentary and fugitive *passante*'.[171] For Bowlby, the flâneur is simply a figure who looks

---

[166] Janet Wolff, *Feminine Sentences: Essays on Women and Culture.* Cambridge: Polity, 1990, p.34.

[167] Wolff, *Feminine Sentences*, p.34.

[168] Wolff, *Feminine Sentences*, p.47.

[169] Rachel Bowlby, *Feminist Destinations and Further Essays on Virginia Woolf.* Edinburgh: Edinburgh University Press, 1997, p.193.

[170] Bowlby, *Feminist Destinations*, p.197.

[171] Bowlby, *Feminist Destinations*, p.202.

at women from a male perspective. The most famous example in Woolf's writing is Peter Walsh in *Mrs Dalloway* (1925). He has left Clarissa's house until the evening party. He finds his attention diverted by a classical *passante*, a young girl who symbolises Peter's fantasy and voyeuristic desires. Griselda Pollock also argues that the male gaze transforms the modern metropolis into a masculine sexual realm. A man enjoys the freedom of looking, consuming, and possessing women in action or in fantasy. His gaze reveals not only male sexuality, but also a power relation between the male gazer / voyeur (who is powerful, subjective) and the female gazee (who is only a symbol of passive visual or sexual object).[172] Pollock deconstructs the map of the Impressionist territory (from the new boulevards via Gare St Lazare out on the suburban train to La Grenouillère, or Argenteuil) by investigating class struggles, sexuality and the spectacle from a feminist point of view. The Impressionist practice reveals the 'erotic territories of modernity' – theatres, parks, cafés and brothels – where women are looked at as signs or fantastic Others by bourgeois men.[173]

On the other hand, other critics, such as Deborah Parsons, have argued that women can be seen as flâneuse. I would also argue that Woolf's narrator can be understood as a flâneuse, the female writing figure walking through the streets with her passion for looking, discovering and observation as she wrote in *Jacob's Room* (1922): 'the streets of London have their map; but our passions are uncharted'.[174] The dialectical gaze of the flâneur cannot be simply defined as the male wandering gaze, especially in Benjamin's writing. As Wolff, Bowlby and Pollock argue, the gaze of the flâneur represents the male gaze. For them, the 'flâneuse' simply does not exist in male writer's writings. The experience of modernity per se is an ambiguous phenomenon, which is filled with the fleeting, ephemeral and impressionistic

---

[172] Griselda Pollock, *Vision and Difference*. London: Routledge, 1988, p.73.

[173] Pollock, *Vision and Difference*, p.73.

[174] Virginia Woolf, *Jacob's Room*. 1922. London: Hogarth Press, 1965, p.90.

nature of encounters in the urban environment. According to Lacan, as I have mentioned, the subject-object relation can be subverted by the 'gaze', which turns the subject into an object, which is gazed by his desire, his lack.

The social psychology of city life is complicated, as one can see in Georg Simmel's 'The Metropolis and Mental Life' (1905). Simmel's account of the metropolitan personality reveals the metropolitan type of individuality 'in the *intensification of nervous stimulation* which results from the swift and uninterrupted change of outer and inner stimuli'.[175] The interaction between vision and visual objects constructs the psychological map of the city and undermines the boundary of the private and public spaces. Laura Marcus points out that for women, specifically, 'entry into the public spaces of the city was used to mark their liberation from enclosure in the private, domestic sphere'.[176] Also, as Anna Snaith argues in her *Virginia Woolf: Public and Private Negotiations,* many women, like Woolf, would have seen themselves as strolling, observing, exercising their right to gaze on men and women. For instance, in *Mrs Dalloway* (1925), the freedom of Clarissa's thoughts 'parallels her freedom in the city'. Her mind is wandering with her footsteps in the public space. Her thoughts do not indicate an 'anxiety about her safety or right to walk the streets'.[177] However, this does not suggest that Woolf was unaware of the difficulties and fears many women experienced walking in the city. The issue of women's entry into the public space comes up most strongly in *The Years* (1937). London, in Woolf's writing, reveals her experience of the dialectic of urban space, the inner and the outer worlds, which 'allowed a literal enactment of increased rights and freedoms, and at the same time inscribed the very same institutions which

---

[175] Georg Simmel, 'The Metropolis and Mental Life' (1905). *The Sociology of Georg Simmel*. Ed. Kurt H. Wolff. New York: Free Press, 1950, p.410.

[176] Laura Marcus, *Virginia Woolf.* 1997. Devon: Northcote House, 2004, p.61.

[177] Anna Snaith, *Virginia Woolf: Public and Private Negotiations*. London: Macmillan, 2000, pp.37 – 38.

had denied such freedoms'.[178] This freedom is under a shadow of patriarchy. This ambiguity reinforces the role of Woolf's character as a flâneuse, a term which embodies the complexity of women's experience in the urban space.

Laura Doan and Terry Brown claim the importance of recognising the significance of Woolf's portrayal of London '[b]y situating Woolf in a specifically London context'. As Doan and Brown argue, 'we hoped to induce a movement of reciprocity; that is, on the one hand, to see the city and English culture through the eyes – the pen – of Virginia Woolf and, on the other hand, to grapple with the English Woolf'.[179] Particularly in 'Street Haunting: A London Adventure' (1927), the narrator demonstrates her own gaze as the flâneuse. Through reading 'Street Haunting', I find the similarity between Benjamin and Woolf. In this essay, the narrator walks along the bank of the River Thames to buy a lead pencil. The essay follows her thinking process, as she walks into her own inner world and memories which create her vivid literary picture of London.

The narrator walks through the streets of London, on a winter's late afternoon, between tea and dinner. As she writes, London streets are beautiful at this hour, with their islands of light and long groves of darkness. Woolf digs deeper than the physical eye can see, because visual objects and people stir up memories. While walking on the street, the narrator also walks into her own memory, which has been bought back to the present, creating a sense of inner time and space – the 'true self' as Woolf phrases it. Furthermore, as Woolf depicts,

> The moment was stabilised, stamped like a coin indelibly, among a
> million that slipped by imperceptibly. There, too, was the melancholy

---

[178] Snaith, *Virginia Woolf: Public and Private Negotiations*, p.41.

[179] Laura Doan and Terry Brown, 'Being There: Woolf's London and the Politics of Location'. *Re:Reading, Re:Writing, Re:Teaching Virginia Woolf: Selected Papers from the Fourth Annual Conference on Virginia Woolf*. Eds. Eileen Barrett and Patricia Cramer. New York: Pace University Press, 1995, p.17.

> Englishman, who rose among the coffee cups and the little iron
> tables and revealed the secrets of his soul – as travellers do. All
> this – Italy, the windy morning, the vines laced about the pillars, the
> Englishman and the secrets of his soul – rise up in a cloud from the
> china bowl on the mantelpiece.[180]

Visual objects bring the narrator memories, just as the china bowl on the
mantelpiece reminds her of the trip to Italian countryside. Consciousness, as
Woolf puts it, is 'a central oyster of perceptiveness, an enormous eye'.[181]
The narrator left her room, a symbolic 'shell-like' protection in her mental
self, and stepped into the symbolic 'four-wall room' of the cityscape, to
explore the city with her dialectic eye (the physical eye and the mind's eye).
The gaze reveals one's own consciousness – what one thinks, as it flows
freely from one visual object to another, from a 'single mind' to 'the bodies
and minds of others',[182] from memory to memory with the rhythm of her
footsteps. The mind's eye makes the present London scene and her memory
'a mixture', a unique moment, a fusion of time and space. 'Is the true self
this which stands on the pavement in January', the narrator wonders, 'or
that which bends over the balcony in June? Am I here, or am I there? Or is
the true self neither this nor that, neither here nor there, but something so
varied and wandering that it is only when we give the rein to its wishes and
let it take its way unimpeded that we are indeed ourselves'?[183]

'Scene-making', according to Laura Marcus, is central to Woolf's
art.[184] In her *Virginia Woolf*, Marcus suggests that Woolf recorded and
dramatised London 'as spectacle and theatrical setting', as one can see the
changing of light ('the meeting of sun set & moon rise', "the man-made

---

[180] Virginia Woolf, 'Street Haunting: A London Adventure' (1927). *E IV*, p.481.

[181] Woolf, 'Street Haunting', p.481.

[182] Woolf, 'Street Haunting', p.490.

[183] Woolf, 'Street Haunting', p.486.

[184] Laura Marcus, *Virginia Woolf*. 1997. Devon: Northcote House, 2004, p.63.

searchlight and the 'natural' moon") and the colour of things, streets, people and houses in Woolf's novel *Night and Day*.[185] For me, scene-making is a significant way of linking the past and the present, a mode of perception and organisation of the visual description in her 'Street Haunting'. London streets are haunted by the walker's memory, imagination and emotion. Woolf emphasises the geographic and textual elements of the city as well as its visual and cinematic qualities. The physical eye is like a 'butterfly', which rests on the beautiful visual impressions of the shop windows on Oxford Street. 'Passing, glimpsing, everything seems accidentally but miraculously sprinkled with beauty, […]; the eye is sportive and generous; it creates; it adorns; it enhances'.[186] The narrator's physical eye leads her from visual objects in the shop windows on Oxford Street to her imaginary cityscape of Mayfair, Princess Mary's garden wall. The eye sees the aesthetic beauty of the modern city as a work of art. At the same time, the narrator's consciousness transforms the visual appearance into a mind picture, which is a more cinematic aestheticised scene: '[w]earing pearls, wearing silk, one steps out on to a balcony which overlooks the gardens of sleeping Mayfair. There are a few lights in the bedrooms of great peers returned from Court, of silk-stockinged footmen, of dowagers who have pressed the hands of statesmen. A cat creeps along the garden wall'.[187] The mind's eye sees not only the appearance of the visual object. In the process of thinking, the visual object brings the viewer's memory back to the present. At this very moment, the past comes to live in the present. In my third chapter, I will analyse in detail, to show how shop windows create a cinematic sense in Peter and Miss Kilman's gaze in *Mrs Dalloway*.

When the narrator stands by the bank of the River Thames, she reflects on the relation between the past, the present and the future with one's own physical and mind's eyes, in which

---

[185] Marcus, *Virginia Woolf*, p.62.

[186] Woolf, 'Street Haunting', p.485.

[187] Woolf, 'Street Haunting', p.485.

> The sight we see [...] now [has] none of the quality of the past; nor
> [has] we any share in the serenity of the person who, six months ago,
> stood precisely where we stand now. His is the happiness of death;
> ours the insecurity of life. He has no future; the future is even now
> invading our peace. It is only when we look at the past and take
> from it the element of uncertainty that we can enjoy perfect peace.[188]

The flow of clock time is like the restless water of the River Thames. And
yet, the inner time reveals the true self, combining one's own past, present
and future. London scenes bring one's own past into one's present being.
Through walking, thinking and writing, the narrator can enjoy the 'perfect
peace' of the present moment. When the narrator goes back home, she gazes
at the lead pencil she has bought, as this pencil reminds her of all the people
and things that she came across on the street of London – the dancing dwarf,
the blind men, the book shop and the couple in the stationary shop – all
these 'treasures of the city'[189] – things, streets and people are combined
with her imagination, and fuse to form her literary expression of London.

Gendering the Urban Gaze

I suggest that Woolf's 'enormous eye' reveals a relation between
subjective individual psychic life and visual objects, art and the external
world. In her narratives, the external world is evoked through the flow of
emotion and the stream of thought, illuminating the psychological process,
in mapping the intricate labyrinth of consciousness. The process of thinking
is a process of sorting out visual impressions, aesthetic emotions and
sensations. Perception is both subjective and objective, both part of the
inner life and a psychologically detached spectatorship and observation,

---

[188] Woolf, 'Street Haunting', p.489.
[189] Woolf, 'Street Haunting', p.491.

which ventures into the world from the secure shelter of a room, to gaze and gaze upon the city's life.

In 'Modern Fiction' (1919), Woolf claims the mind's eye negotiates the private and public spheres by receiving, selecting and recording 'a myriad impressions – trivial, fantastic, evanescent, or engraved with the sharpness of steel' in the cityscape, and also tracing and mapping the psychological pattern by looking within, no matter how 'disconnected and incoherent' those visual impressions appear to be.[190] Emily Dalgarno praises Woolf's optics, which can see 'beyond the horizon of ordinary perception into a larger world that is only partly available to verbal representation'[191] – a twist of the real and the imaginary; visual memory and dream images. By creating this new narrative technique, Woolf invents a new way of seeing; her texts can be seen as a 'juncture'[192] – a fusion, which synthesises visibility and the invisible, consciousness and the unconscious, vision and fantasy, visual appearance and psychological depth, the physical eye and the mind's eye.

The flâneur's dual vision synthesises poetic passionate vision and psychological detached observation. In this light, the flâneur's gaze should not be simply equated with the predatory 'male gaze'. Benjamin's urban critique moved beyond the portrait of the flâneur he drew from Baudelaire. The nineteenth-century flâneur was for Benjamin a methodology, a symbolic figure of the dialectic, the fusion of the inner and outer worlds, the physical and the mind's eye, and a way of seeing the relation between one's own personal history and the city itself.

The flâneur illuminates Woolf's way of seeing London. As Christine W. Sizemore points out, Clarissa's sense of being an 'outsider' in terms of

---

[190] Virginia Woolf, 'Modern Fiction' (1919). *Collected Essays by Virginia Woolf: Volume II*. London: Hogarth Press, 1966, pp.106 – 107.

[191] Emily Dalgarno, *Virginia Woolf and the Visible World*. Cambridge: Cambridge University Press, 2001, p.1.

[192] Dalgarno, *Virginia Woolf and the Visible World*, p.2.

gender and political power structure 'allows her the freedom to observe all the details of city life and to look around the city for a new community, one based not merely on class status but on a shared love for city life. The tone of the novel combines nostalgia for some of the people and places of the past whom Clarissa loved and celebration of the new promises of urban life'.[193] I would suggest that Woolf's flâneuse is the starting point for the formation of her gendered gaze – Katharine's quest for love and a sense of self comes to map an emotional London in *Night and Day*, Clarissa's duration and feminine space in *Mrs Dalloway*, and Eleanor's snapshots as an outsider's photographic vision in *The Years*. Woolf structures her novels through these characters' walks, as she portrays the 'mysterious process of the mind',[194] bringing the reader, as Julia Briggs has said, 'closer to everyday life, in all its confusion, mystery and uncertainty',[195] as my further discussion in the following chapters will demonstrate.

The cityscape is the space where the gendered gaze is produced. It is also experienced and looked at by both male and female gazers. The relationship between the urban environment, women and writing is significant. As Laura Marcus points out, Woolf's writing creates a "female literary tradition; 'realist' versus 'modernist' writing as the most effective vehicle for a feminist politics; the place of feminist radicalism or 'anger' in aesthetic practice".[196] Woolf's definition of gender was always in flux, never static. It functions as an integral part of the development of her aesthetics of vision and writing. In this light, it becomes possible to identify

---

[193] Christine W. Sizemore, "The 'Outsider-Within': Virginia Woolf and Doris Lessing As Urban Novelists in *Mrs Dalloway* and *The Four-Gated City*". *Woolf and Lessing: Breaking the Mold*. Ed. Ruth Saxton and Jean Tobin. New York: St Martin's, 1994, p.62.

[194] Virginia Woolf, 'An Introduction to *Mrs Dalloway*' (1925). *E* IV, pp.549 – 550.

[195] Julia Briggs, *Virginia Woolf: An Inner Life*. London: Allen Lane, 2005, p.130.

[196] Laura Marcus, 'Women and Writing: *A Room of One's Own*'. *Virginia Woolf*, p.41.

her feminist politics as her writing practice.[197] Within her writing practice, one can see how Woolf's thinking about gender defines her urban gendered gaze. As Makiko Minow-Pinkney argues, Woolf broke with representation to create a new form for the art of the novel: Woolf's account of this gender-specific 'New Realism', searches for truth behind the veil of masculine materialism,[198] achieving a de-centered and shifting point of view in line with the new experiments taking place in the realm of contemporary painting,[199] as I will show in the next chapter.

Woolf's aesthetic strategy represents her struggle against male authority in her break with realism and her construction of female subjectivity. In *A Room of One's Own* (1929), Woolf claims that a woman must have a room and money of her own to support herself for artistic creation or any other profession. The city per se is equally important to the modern woman writer, because it provides the experience of modernity. Modern female writer aims to find her own voice in the urban space by setting her own mind free to try new literary forms. Woolf herself says of her imaginary female writer,

> all the older forms of literature were hardened and set by the time she became a writer. The novel alone was young enough to be soft in her hands – another reason, perhaps, why she wrote novels. Yet who shall say that even now 'the novel' (I give it inverted commas to mark my sense of the word's inadequacy), who shall say that even this most pliable of all forms is rightly shaped for her use?

---

[197] Sue Roe, *Writing and Gender: Virginia Woolf's Writing Practice*. New York: St. Martin's, 1990, p.13.

[198] Makiko Minow-Pinkney. *Virginia Woolf & The Problem of the Subject*. New Brunswick: Rutgers University Press, 1987, p.1.

[199] Richard Pearce. 'Virginia Woolf's Struggle with *Author-ity*'. *Image and Ideology in Modern/Postmodern Discourse*. Eds. David B. Downing and Susan Bazargan. Albany: SUNY Press, 1991, p.69.

> […]. And I went on to ponder how a woman nowadays would write
> a poetic tragedy in five acts. Would she use verse? – would she not
> use prose rather?[200]

The novel is a new, modern and contemporary art form, which is 'soft'
enough with creative potential. Compared with other literary genres, it does
not have a long male-dominated literary history. Woolf encourages female
writers to try different ways of writing and to explore the freedom of being
a female writer. For her, the city streets, buildings, arcades, and women who
walk and work in them are rich subject-matter. The street scenes bear
witness to the diversity and the excitement of everyday life in London. The
urban space is not only a male territory, which is hostile to women; it also
embodies female experience, in terms of walking, looking and thinking.
Woolf deepens her vision of the city in her writing career, making London a
central part of her writing, as a context through which to explore and to
develop the personal, literary and cultural lives of women. The city also
offered particularly fertile possibilities to Woolf's creative imagination,
because of its historical and cultural resonances.

In Woolf's London, the relation between the personal and the cultural
dimensions of the city reflect the experience of the female writer, the urban
space she created, and the urban culture in which she lived. Woolf's London
is distinct from that of other writers. It is the London of the flâneuses,
Katharine Hilbery and Mary Datchet in *Night and Day* (1919), Clarissa
Dalloway in *Mrs Dalloway* (1925) and the Pargiter sisters in *The Years*
(1937). I suggest that modernity in Virginia Woolf's writing is a significant
and particular gendered set of practices in the context of urban space. In my
discussion of her work from 1919 to 1938, I aim to analyse the formation of
Woolf's gendered gaze.

---

[200] Virginia Woolf, *A Room of One's Own and Three Guineas*. Oxford: Oxford
University Press, 2000, pp.100 – 101.

The term 'gaze' often is used to refer to the authority and the power of patriarchy, particularly in the relation between male gazer and objectified female body. As John Berger points out, the presence of male gaze promises the power masculinity embodies – moral, physical, economic, social and sexual. On the other hand, a woman's presence implies a different way of seeing, not because "the feminine is different from the masculine – but because the 'ideal' spectator is always assumed to be male and the image of the woman is designed to flatter him".[201] Woolf's gendered gaze, for instance, is shown in her looking and use of photography. Woolf's use of male photographs as signs in *Three Guineas* reinforces her feminist argument, making the bodies of professional men visual objects and signs of women's knowledge, as Gillespie points out.[202] She indexes literary practice to a complex set of negotiations of the gender and class struggle in the society of the modern metropolitan axis. Modernity, in Woolf's texts, is presented as far more then a sense of being 'up-to-date', in terms of class, gender, the spectacle and power.

It is important, I would argue, to establish a coherent correspondence between the social/private spaces of the represented and the literary texts of the representation. My research endeavours to find out to what extent Woolf, in her writing career, begins with the metaphorical portraiture of the enclosed domestic space, such as a 'room' or a 'house'. And then, she moves away from the traditional egoistic 'centre of consciousness' narratology, towards a formation of feminist subjectivity in terms of her gaze, gender and space, to define her own voice as a woman writer, liberating women's vision, consciousness and ways of thinking. Woolf's literary space is not orchestrated for sight alone, but by means of visual clues which refer to other sensations and relations of external visual objects in a lived world: touch,

---

[201] John Berger, *Ways of Seeing* (London: Penguin, 1972), p.64.

[202] Diane F. Gillespie, "'Her Kodak Pointed at His Head': Virginia Woolf and Photography." *The Multiple Muses of Virginia Woolf*. Ed. Diane F. Gillespie. Columbia: University of Missouri Press, 1993, p.138.

smell, hearing and taste, as her literary imagery becomes susceptible to different ideological, historical, cultural as well as subjective inflections.

Elizabeth Wilson argues that in the nineteenth century 'the ideology of women's place in the domestic realm permeated the whole society. [...yet] in practice the private sphere was – and is – also a masculine domain; although the Victorians characterised it as feminine, it was organised for the convenience, rest and recreation of men, not women, and it has been an important part of feminism to argue that the private sphere is the *workplace* of woman'.[203] As one can see in Woolf's essay 'Great Men's Houses' (1931-2), her description of their spatial structure reveals her gendered gaze and her particular sense of space, in terms of her critique of gender and class lines. Woolf depicts number 5 Cheyne Row (Carlyle's house) as a 'battlefield' of gender and class struggle through looking at Mrs Carlyle's portrait:

> Mrs Carlyle sat, as we see from the picture, in a fine silk dress, in a chair pulled up to a blazing fire and had everything seemly and solid about her; but at what cost had she won it! Her cheeks are hollow; bitterness and suffering mingle in the half-tender, half-tortured expression of the eyes. Such is the effect of a pump in the basement and a yellow tin bath up three pairs of stairs. Both husband and wife had genius; they loved each other; but what can genius and love avail against bugs and tin baths and pumps in the basement?[204]

Mrs Carlyle's portrait reminds her of how the spatial arrangements of the house oppress an impoverished middle-class woman. The domestic space, such as the basement, the bathroom and the kitchen, represents how femininity is situated in social discourse and practice in relation to the power

---

[203] Elizabeth Wilson, 'The Invisible Flâneur'. *New Left Review* 191 (1992): 90-110, p.98.
[204] Virginia Woolf, 'Great Men's House' (1931-2). *The London Scenes*, London: Snowbooks, 1988, p.41.

struggle of seeing and being seen. It is the product of a lived experience in the social relations. She evokes the domestic objects which reveal her struggles as a housewife, and her fight against dirt and cold: '[t]he horsehair couch needed recovering; the drawing-room paper with its small, dark pattern needed cleaning; the yellow varnish on the panels was cracked and peeling – all must be stitched, cleansed, scoured with her own hands; [...]. Another day had dawned and the pumping and the scrubbing must begin again'.[205] Woolf's gendered gaze reveals the politics of looking; it demonstrates and questions a particular social organization, which works to secure a particular social ordering of gender difference. Feminine space is a production of this kind of social practice: men move freely between public and private spheres while women are supposed to take care of the domestic space alone.

The sharpness of Woolf's way of seeing decodes the mythic boundaries of gender differences, masculinity and femininity. It problematises women's relation to and their experience of the very definition of 'modernity' of her time: the freedom of going out alone, of looking at the shops, the crowd and the spectacular city, of walking on the urban street at night. Woolf's writing demonstrates different types of looking, representing the critical perspective of a female gazer, through which the notion of 'femininity' is reconstructed, appraised, experienced and constituted. The gendered gaze in Woolf's writing embodies a transformation in power relations. It seeks different ways to expose the gap between seeing and being seen in literary history.

As Woolf herself questioned the image and the social role of a woman, she actually constructed the image of a female writing subjectivity: "[t]he Angel [of the house] was dead; what then remained? You may say that what remained was a simple and common object – a young woman in a bedroom with an inkpot. In other words, now that she had rid herself of falsehood, that young woman had only to be herself. Ah, but what is 'herself'? I mean,

---

[205] Woolf, 'Great Men's Houses', p.40.

what is a woman"?[206] I shall look at Woolf's writing and visual modernism, particularly cinematography and photography, to see to what extent they construct female subjectivity in Woolf's writing, particularly in *Mrs Dalloway* (1925), *The Years* (1937) and *Three Guineas* (1938). I follow the ideas of feminist visual theories to reconstruct images of women, in order to reveal new angles of vision on space, gender and class. As Toril Moi argues of the early Anglo-American feminist literary critics, 'the feminists' insistence on the *political* nature of any critical discourse, and their will to take historical and sociological factors into account must have seemed both fresh and exciting; to a large extent those are precisely the qualities present-day feminist critics still strive to preserve'.[207]

Both *The Years* and *Three Guineas* powerfully express Woolf's feminist views. As Susan Squier points out, an examination of female image and experience in the city reveals 'both the process and the product of Woolf's vision of woman's experience'.[208] The city space indicates the underlying sexual politics – women's lack of sexual freedom is a result of the 'restrictive structure of their lives'.[209] From Rose Pargiter in *The Years*, we shall see that sexuality and anger are taboos for women in a patriarchal society. In 'Women and Fiction' (1929), for instance, Woolf depicts the gendered experience,[210] discouragement and difficulty in the life of a

---

[206] Virginia Woolf, 'Professions for Women' (1931), *Women and writing*. Ed. Michèle Barrett. New York: Harvest, 1979, p.60.

[207] Moi, *Sexual/Textual Politics*, p.49.

[208] Susan Squier, 'The Politics of City Space in *The Years*: Street Love, Pillar Boxes and Bridges'. *New Feminist Essays on Virginia Woolf.* Nebraska: University of Nebraska Press, 1981, p.218.

[209] Squier, 'The Politics of City Space in *The Years*: Street Love, Pillar Boxes and Bridges'. *New Feminist Essays on Virginia Woolf,* p.219.

[210] For instance, Woolf compared the gendered experiences between George Eliot and Tolstoi. According to Woolf, Eliot could only stay in 'a middle-class drawing room' to write because of the scandalization of public opinion. Tolstoi, at the same time, was 'living a free life as a soldier, with men and women of all classes'.

female writer in a patriarchal society. Female writers need a 'very powerful mind to resist the temptation to anger'.[211]

The image of a woman as 'the Other' in patriarchal society is also true in literature. As Simone de Beauvoir argues of D. H. Lawrence's novels,

> there is a god who speaks through [his male heros]: Lawrence himself. As for woman, it is for her to bow down before their divinity. In so far as man is a phallus and not a brain, the individual who has his share of virility keeps his advantages; woman is not evil, she is even good – but subordinated. It is once more the ideal of the 'true woman' that Lawrence has to offer is – that is, the woman who unreservedly accepts being defined as the Other.[212]

Women are represented as men's Other. A thinker such as Simone de Beauvoir seeks to oppose her society's definitions of femininity, feminine writing and the constitution of the female gender. De Beauvoir's gendered-consciousness as a writer comes close to Woolf's. Her writing shows a radical awareness of feminist issues, and that it takes up the question of 'what is a woman' from a perspective which aims to deconstruct masculine prejudice. To give voice to an intellectually unashamed female perspective meant giving voice to a new form of narrative.[213]

Three Guineas reveals Woolf's life-long interest in the role of women in a patriarchal society.[214] Her resistance to war and fascism is

---

See 'Women and Fiction' (1929). *Women and Writing*, pp.46 – 47.

[211] Woolf, 'Women and Fiction' (1929). *Women and Writing*, p.47.

[212] Simone de Beauvoir, 'D. H. Lawrence or Phallic Pride'. *The Second Sex*. Trans. H. M. Parshley. New York: Vintage, 1989, pp.223 – 224.

[213] Virginia Blain. 'Narrative Voice and the Female Perspective in Virginia Woolf's Early Novels'. *Virginia Woolf: New Critical Essays*. Eds. Patricia Clements and Isobel Grundy. London: Vision Press, 1983, p.117.

[214] Patricia Laurence, 'A Writing Couple: Shared Ideology in Virginia Woolf's *Three Guineas* and Leonard Woolf's *Quack, Quack*'! *Women in the Milieu of Leonard and Virginia Woolf: Peace, Politics, and Education*. New York: Pace University

affirmed in her way of seeing women's roles through education. As
Catherine F. Smith points out,

> *Three Guineas* models a way of seeing, a structure of imagining to
> underlie new moral choice and political action. Woolf's collective
> solution to cultural crisis is fearless women. Her prophetic task in
> *Three Guineas*, therefore, is to create them as readers, to raise women's
> collective consciousness of strength. This purpose and this audience
> determine her rhetorical form. *Three Guineas* is phenomenological
> narrative presenting a model of the subject being talked about, the
> fearless asymmetry of the mind of an outsider.[215]

A woman's role is an outsider, because she does not belong to the power
stream of masculinity. And yet, Woolf's gendered gaze reflects an outsider's
mind, which maintains a psychological detachment from and observant eye
upon the patriarchal system. I shall establish a theoretical framework in the
following chapters of this thesis for the analysis of Woolf's work, which
includes Jacques Lacan's theory of the gaze and the psychology of the Subject
and the Other, Hélène Cixous, Julia Kristeva and Luce Irigaray's accounts
of the role of the visual in the constitution of the poetic and psychological
feminist subject. The development of a variety of perspectives from which to
examine Woolf's work illuminates the importance of her gendered gaze as
radical critique of the modern myth of 'phallogocularcentrism',[216] and

---

Press, 1998, p.126.

[215] Catherine F. Smith, '*Three Guineas*: Virginia Woolf's Prophecy'. *Virginia Woolf
and Bloomsbury: A Centenary Celebration*. Ed. Jane Marcus. London: Macmillan,
1987, p.226.

[216] Martin Jay uses the term 'phallogocularcentrism' to appreciate the importance of
French feminist critiques of "the mutual implication of ocularcentrism,
phallocentrism and the role of vision in Western patriarchal culture. See
'Phallogocularcentrism: Derrida and Irigaray'. *Downcast Eyes: The Denigration
of Vision in Twentieth-Century French Thought*, p.493.

makes possible an analysis of the ways in which her gendered gaze strategy is not only formed by her feminine experiences as a writer in the male-dominated culture, but also contributes to the deconstruction and reconstruction of these experiences in modern metropolis, moving towards the formation of a feminist subjectivity.

Conclusion

Woolf continually experiments with features of vision, radically reframing the visible world in her literary imagery. She is engaging in highly articulate and self-conscious ways with new images of gendered epiphanies, external and internal worlds, cognition and the visual. Woolf's dialectic vision represents her poetic passion and observational critique, as well as her position as a leading female writer of the Bloomsbury Group, a woman with an outsider's mind, a figure who teaches for several years at an evening college for working-class men and women, who marries a Fabian socialist and attends Labour Party conferences, who presides at meetings of the Women's Co-operative Guide held in her own house, and who writes significant texts which inspire feminists.[217] Her works are not only portraits of sensation, emotion and visionary imagery, but also powerful political criticism. This gendered gaze leads the reader to see a route to women's liberation and the construction of feminist subjectivity, consciousness and the visionary mapping of feminist politics.

Woolf's vision synthesises the inner and the outer worlds, combining the physical and the mind's eye. It is Woolf's hybrid approach, in which one can see the interaction between literature and the arts, allowing one to read Woolf as a painter, a film maker, and a photographer. As Woolf herself

---

[217] Alex Zwerdling, *Virginia Woolf and the Real World*. Berkeley: University of California Press, 1986, p.29.

wants to show in *Roger Fry: A Biography*, that a modern biographer should aim to become 'an artist', rather than a mere 'chronicler'.[218] Her method of composing Fry's biography is based on her memories – her 'impressions' of him, which create Fry as a person she knows and as a character in her verbal portrait. As Fry's biographer, Woolf, in her 'The Post-Impressionists' chapter, starts with a picture of two figures on a lawn at Cambridge – a dignified couple identified as Roger and Helen Fry, leading Woolf to associate modern painters and the avant-garde with the wide diverse range of experimental art forms, particularly Post-Impressionism,[219] achieving Woolf's aim for making British novels a form of fine art. Woolf's dual vision is situated in the city of London, depicting her characters' gendered experience of seeing the city, as I will show in the following chapters.

---

[218] Quoted in Diane Gillespie, 'Introduction', in Virginia Woolf's *Roger Fry: A Series of Impressions*. London: Cecil Woolf, 1994, p.4.

[219] Jane Goldman. 'Modernist Studies'. *Palgrave Advances in Virginia Woolf Studies*. Ed. Anna Snaith. London: Macmillan, 2007, p.35.

CHAPTER TWO

The Painter's Eye in Writing: the James Brothers and Woolf's Experimental Practices

Thought of from sufficiently far, London offers to the mind's eye singularly little of a picture. It is essentially 'town', and yet how little a town, how much of an abstraction.

- Ford Madox Ford, *The Soul of London*[1]

Introduction

In this chapter, through reading Virginia Woolf's novel *Night and Day* (1919), I want to explore how her craft is established by her relation with philosophy and the visual arts, and how this relation shapes the narrative form of her novel. By examining William James's notion of 'the stream of consciousness' and Henry James's narrative style in his London writings and his novel *The Ambassadors* (1903), I aim to illuminate the way in which Woolf's narrative style and depiction of consciousness develop the form of psychological realism. By studying James's 'painter's eye' in literature, Woolf develops her own narrative technique as 'painter in writer', conveying the psychology of her characters by depicting their ways of seeing London. In both James and Woolf's works, the relation between inner and outer worlds is depicted through a painter's eye. James brings sunlight into his

---

[1] Ford Madox Ford, *The Soul of London: A Survey of a Modern City.* 1905. Ed. Alan G. Hill. London: Everyman, 1995, p.7.

writing, which makes Paris a bright city. In *The Ambassadors*, one can see James's literary impressionism, which illustrates a process of vision. This process of vision internalises the external world as an impression, by which the inner and outer worlds are fused into one. Strether's impression of Paris and suburban landscape brings his memory back to the present, which leads him to a moment of revelation. Woolf, on the other hand, takes a Post-Impressionist narrative form. She makes the reader aware of her characters' mood, emotion and feeling visible through abstract forms, such as colours and shapes. Woolf visualises London by externalising her characters' inner world, and their ways of seeing the city, as one can see in *Night and Day*.

William James's Stream of Thought

William James's way of seeing human psychology helps one to understand psychological realism as a style in Henry James and Virginia Woolf's narrative.In *William James on Consciousness beyond the Margin*, Eugene Taylor claims that James's idea of psychology is 'a person-centered science'.[2] In the history of American psychology, James was the first to take up the study of consciousness within the context of Darwin's theory of natural selection [3] and Charles Edourd Brown-Sequard's experimental neuropathology. The major developments in the understanding of

---

[2]   Eugene Taylor. 'Preface'. *William James on Consciousness beyond the Margin*. Princeton: Princeton University Press, 1996, xiii.

[3]   As Lisa Ruddick points out, James reveals indirectly his Darwinian emphasis on people's selection of impressions. The selective attention of human consciousness forms the continuum of impressions. This 'impression' indicates a way of perceiving the external world. Through human consciousness, the external world and its image is perceived as 'one'. See 'Fluid Symbols in American Modernism: William James, Gertrude Stein, George Santayana, and Wallace Stevens'. *Allegory, Myth, and Symbol*. Morton W. Bloomfield, ed. Cambridge, MA: Harvard University Press, 1981, p.338.

consciousness came from James's conceptual fusion of experimental psychology and the study of psychic phenomena. Brown-Sequard introduced the 'new physiology' to demonstrate the nervous system, seeing consciousness as an efficacious force in biological evolutionary survival. Brown-Sequard, the first professor of neurology at Harvard University, whose neuropathological lectures were given between 1867 and 1868, was the major influence on William James's interest in the experimental method. As a young medical student, James learned the techniques of experimental medicine from Brown-Sequard, coming to understand clinical problems important to the practicing physician.

In William James's laboratory experiments, he remained strongly influenced by French experimental and clinical medicine. However, in his *Principles of Psychology* (1890), one can see that his interest has moved from clinical physiology to a metaphysical approach, making an effort to understand the relation of the mind and the body. The mind-body issue, particularly the relation of specific brain sites to bodily functions, has a significant role in the experimental study of consciousness, which established the study of psychology as a science. The book was an 'instant classic' when it came out, because it shows a transformation of psychological studies from a clinical point of view to a hermeneutic approach. G. Stanley Hall, James's student, described him as 'an *impressionist* in psychology'.[4] What Hall meant by seeing James as 'an impressionist' indicates James's awareness of impressionist aesthetics. One can see this impact of psychology and art on his brother Henry James's work, as I will show in the following section.

---

[4]   As I mentioned in note three, James did not construct his phenomenological psychology through scientific experiments. Rather, he uses metaphors to depict how human consciousness works, such as how nerves connect senses, transferring sensory experiences to the brain. This process is fundamental to James's discourse of psychology. In other words, metaphysics is a method by which James solves clinical problems. See also Ruddick, ''Fluid Symbols in American Modernism', p.26.

Accoring to Lisa Ruddick, in William Dean Howells's comments, he had pointed out that William James's approach to psychology is a mixed pleasure, which comes from literature and fine arts. James had a 'poetic sense of his facts and an acute pleasure in their presentation'.[5] In other words, James's writing does not aim to make psychology a popular science. Rather, he defines psychology as a metaphysical discourse, in which the external world is an impression, a product of perception, a process of thinking.

William James's analysis of consciousness helped to build up a discourse about mental states: the stream of thought, the perception of time and space, memory, impression, imagination, and emotions. James argues that consciousness works through sensory experiences, by which the inner and outer worlds are related. Human consciousness is the nexus of James's metaphysical interpretation of subject-object dualism,[6] because consciousness

> does not appear to itself chopped up in bits. Such words as 'chain' or 'train' do not describe it fitly as it presents itself in the first instance. It is nothing joined; it flows. A 'river' or a 'stream' are the metaphors by which it is most naturally described. In *talking of it hereafter, let us call it the stream of thought, of consciousness, or of subjective life.*[7]

The subject perceives the external world by making sense of the visual objects. Impressions are pictures of the mind. They are products of human consciousness. James's use of the metaphor of the stream of consciousness reveals the significant relation between vision and consciousness, and shows how vision internalises external visual objects as impressions

---

[5]   Ruddick, 'Fluid Symbols in American Modernism', p.26.

[6]   The interplay of opposites (such as a subject and an object) indicates an intractable dualism of the thought and visual objects. See Stanley J. Scott, *Frontiers of Consciousness: Interdisciplinary Studies in American Philosophy and Poetry*. New York: Fordham University Press, 1991, p.74.

[7]   William James, *The Principles of Psychology: Volume I* (1890). Cambridge, MA: Harvard University Press, 1981, p.233.

through consciousness. This subject-object dualism illustrates a process of seeing, which unifies external visual objects and perceptions of them. The mind's process of thinking the visible world as the symbolic can be seen as an act, in which the mind practises[8] its way of making sense of visual objects in the external world. In *The Principles of Psychology*, William James's understanding of the process of seeing focuses a way in which the mind interacts with the external world, to see *'what the world means to us'*.[9] As in Henry James's *The Ambassadors*, Strether will find out what does Paris mean to him, through his memory of a landscape painting in Boston, and his revelation of Chad's love affair. According to William James, impression is the fundamental ontological fact which leads the viewer to a psychological level of reality. Thought is like a river, the stream, the free water that flows around the objective world; consciousness perceives the objective world newly and freshly, making it a subjective experience.

William James uses pictorial language to depict the way an outward reality is visualised by the mind's eye and perceived as a mental image. In the following passage, he demonstrates how a painterly perspective reveals the 'real sensational effect' of visual objects:

> The grass out of the window now looks to me of the same green in
> the sun as in the shade, and yet a painter would have to paint one
> part of it dark brown, another part bright yellow, to give its real

---

[8] James's metaphysical way of seeing how consciousness works to make sense of the external world, for Emily Fourmy Cutrer, is a 'pragmatic mode of seeing'. William James's 'stream of consciousness' is a process of mind acting, to perceive the external world. See 'A Pragmatic Mode of Seeing: James, Howells, and the Politics of Vision'. *American Iconology: New Approaches to Nineteenth-Century Art and Literature*. David C. Miller, ed. New Haven: Yale University Press, 1993, p.261.

[9] Bruce Wilshire, *William James and Phenomenology: a Study of 'The Principles of Psychology'*. Bloomington: Indiana University Press, 1968, p.9. See also George H. Roeder, 'But what Thousand Words?' *Reviews in American History* 23.2 (1995): 250 – 255, p.252.

> sensational effect. We take no heed, as a rule, of the different way in
> which the same things look and sound and smell at different
> distances and under different circumstances. [...].[10]

From the above passage, one can see that James is aware of the Impressionist
way of painting. The essence of an Impressionist painting is its play of light
and shadow on the canvas. The same visual object can have different
sensual effect to people, because of the changing of the light. According to
James, no single sensation repeats itself. Sunlight brings visual impressions
to the painter's retina. The painter's eye brings out the visual sensation of
the grass through the colours he sees (which are not the same green as in the
sun and in the shade). The above paragraph reveals James's observation of
the sensation that sunlight brings to the eye, the kind of effect as one can see
in the Impressionist paintings. And yet, in the following paragraph, James's
notion of sensation moves from the Impressionist visual sensations, the
'eye's sensibility' in his own term, to the Post-Impressionist portrayal of
moods and emotions:

> The difference of the sensibility is shown best by the difference of
> our emotion about the things from one age to another, or when we
> are in different organic moods. What was bright and exciting becomes
> weary, flat, and unprofitable. The bird's song is tedious, the breeze is
> mournful, the sky is sad.[11]

According to this paragraph, one's mood and emotion can define sensations
and impressions of the external world. In other words, visual sensations can
not only be internalised, perceived, and materialised by colour (as in
Impressionist paintings), but also can be expressed through what one feels,
according to one's own mood at one particular moment (as in

---

[10] James, *Principles I*, p.226.
[11] James, *Principles I*, p.226.

Post-Impressionist paintings). According to James, visual sensations are modified in the stream of consciousness, as a series of impressions. In this light, an impression can be seen as a synthesis of outer and inner worlds. The stream of consciousness is a process of vision, which produces a stream of impressions. James defines impressions as 'psychic transitions'[12] which are produced by the process of thinking.

In his quotation from Hippolyte Taine (1828 – 1893), a sensory depiction of araucarias, one can see how James develops his theory of visual sensation and its representation:

> Some years ago I saw in England, in Kew Gardens, for the first time, araucarias, [...], with their rigid bark, and compact, short, scaly leaves, of a somber green, [...]. If I now inquire what this experience has left in me, I find, first, the sensible representation of an araucaria; in fact, [...], there is a difference between this representation and the former sensations, of which it is the present echo.[13]

An impression is a 'representation', a reproduction, an 'echo' of the immediate visual sensation. From the above passage, one can see that for James, perception is defined by the selection of visual sensation. The stream of thought is a metaphorical process of selection and representation, as one can see in Taine's account, in which it depicts visual sensations of twenty or thirty araucarias. Perception gives meaning to visual sensation. Visual sensation, on the one hand, is a process by which light impinges on the retina and is received by the entire nervous apparatus. On the other hand, visual sensation is not static, because it is aroused and changed by the mind's reaction to the external world. The mind, in this respect, is a 'eccentric projection',[14] which recognises the external world and makes

---

[12] James, *Principles I*, p.244.
[13] James, *Principles II*, p.694.
[14] James, *Principles II*, p.678.

sense of it by perceiving its meaning. Perception is a response to visual sensation, a process of realisation between 'the *knower*' and 'the *known*'.[15]

Woolf also uses the halo metaphor to depict the way in which human psychology works. The metaphor of the 'original halo'[16], like an impression, is used by James to explain the relation between inner and outer spheres, perception and the materialisation of it. The stream of thought illustrates the obscure relation between visual objects, vision and perception:

> And if we wish to *feel* that idiosyncrasy we must reproduce the thought as it was uttered, with every word fringed and the whole sentence bathed in that original halo of obscure relations, which, like an horizon, then spread about its meaning. Our psychological duty is to cling as closely as possible to the actual constitution of the thought we are studying.[17]

For James, the external world is a pragmatic perception, but for Woolf, emotion is the world. As one can see in *Night and Day*, London is an expression of inner feelings. Thought, according to James, is the key to *feel* the external world, rather than an expression of the inwardness. The stream of thought makes a series of impressions like a 'sentence' in literary impressionism. This 'sentence' is shown in the 'original halo of obscure relations' of impressions. Through this 'sentence', James studies psychology in a metaphysical way.

James's 'original halo' is a metaphor that indicates his sense of the complex relation between vision, visual objects, and thought. For James, the halo metaphor indicates the subject-object dualism, the relation between thought and its object, subjective perception and the visual object in the external world. This halo metaphor is used by Virginia Woolf in her essay 'Modern Novels' (1919), when she writes about the relation between mind, impression, and daily life:

---

[15]   James, *Principles II*, p.675.

[16]   James, *Principles I*, p.266.

[17]   James, *Principles I*, p.266.

> The mind, exposed to the ordinary course of life, receives upon its surface a myriad impressions – trivial, fantastic, evanescent, or engraved with the sharpness of steel. From all sides they come, an incessant shower of innumerable atoms, composing in their sum what we might venture to call life itself; and to figure as the semi-transparent envelope, or luminous halo, surrounding us from the beginning of consciousness to the end.[18]

The mind 'receives' 'a myriad impressions' everyday. This myriad of impressions is like a semi-transparent envelope, or 'luminous halo', which surrounds one's own consciousness. William James's phenomenological interpretation of psychology and the relation between outer and inner worlds had significant impact on both Henry James (the mind receives impressions, and reproduces the impressions through words) and Virginia Woolf (expressing the character's mood through the way they see the external world). Henry James illustrates the way of depicting visual impressions, which attempts to come closer to the character's consciousness, the inner life of the character. In this respect, Henry James makes possible new ways of writing fiction through practicing William James's 'stream of consciousness' notion in his fictional writing. The observation and the depiction of sensational atoms are means to reproduce them through his narrative form, which makes fictional writing a work of fine art, as I will show in the following section.

Henry James's Impressionist Paris, Pictorial London, and Woolf's Response

William James's brother Henry James transforms narrative from a depiction of objective events to a portrayal of his characters' perception and

---

[18] Virginia Woolf, 'Modern Novels' (1919). *E III*, p.33.

interpretation of the visual through consciousness. His use of visual impressions does not simply express the stream of thought but also explore its complexity in the very process of its formation. From this point of view, human consciousness can be known through the process of vision and perception. Sensation can also be defined as 'the fundamental ontological fact',[19] because in both the James brothers' writings, it marks a phenomenon, in which the outer visible world and the inner stream of thought are presented as one world of pure experience in one's own impression.

William James's understanding of psychology, visual sensation and the process of seeing illuminates Henry James and Virginia Woolf's narrative technique, particularly in their depictions of a character's stream of thought, and the way in which it relates to the external world. In James's novels, the reader will not be able to realise what has happened, until he reaches the very last page, because James shows the plot not by description, but through depicting the character's complex response to the external world. In 'Mr Henry James's Latest Novel' (1905), Woolf comments that James's way of depicting a simple plot 'needs skill of the very highest to make novels out of such everyday material'.[20] *The Ambassadors*, I would argue, illustrates this art of fictional writing. In this novel, James's Paris is Impressionist, because it is bright, bathed in sunlight, as one can see in the Impressionists's paintings. The Impressionist way of depicting sunlight and visual impressions fulfill his aim of making fictional writing one of the *'fine* arts'.[21] Henry James's Impressionist Paris is remarkable in literary history, and it prepares the way for Woolf's Post-Impressionist London to come.

---

[19] Henry Adams, 'William James, Henry James, John La Farge and the Foundations of Radical Empiricism'. *American Art Journal* 17 (1985): 60-67, p.66.

[20] Virginia Woolf, 'Mr Henry James's Latest Novel' (1905). *The Essays of Virginia Woolf, Volume I: 1904 – 1912*. Ed. Andrew McNeillie. London: The Hogarth Press, 1986, p.22.

[21] Henry James, 'The Art of Fiction' (1884). *The Art of Fiction and Other Essays by Henry James*. New York: Oxford University Press, 1948, p.6.

James and Impressionism

The word 'Impressionism' indicates what was a new concept in the art of fiction in James's time.[22] Henry James develops his aesthetic theory about fictional writing in his 'The Art of Fiction' (1884), in which he highlights the Impressionist view of visual sensations, to support his aim of making the novel one of the *'fine* arts'.[23] This artistic faith creates a theory, a conviction, and a consciousness of fictional writing. For James, fictional writing is not a business, which after all only makes a novel a production of 'make-believe'[24] plots. Rather, the art of fiction is to 'represent life'.[25] This 'life' is not a life someone lives in. It is a life someone perceives in his own consciousness, an 'impression' of the external world. The process of fictional writing is to select 'a myriad forms'[26] of experience. The portrayal of impression makes a novel a form of fine arts. James aims to depict one's own impression, as the external world is perceived by one's own consciousness. This psychological approach, for James, is 'an object adorably pictorial'.[27] He sees the same attempt on the canvas of the Impressionists. In this respect, the painter and the writer can learn from each other; the 'analogy between the art of the painter and the art of the novelist is, [...], complete'.[28]

James sees the profound relation between the visual and verbal arts, and their depictions of life:

> The only reason for the existence of a novel is that it does attempt to represent life. When it relinquishes this attempt, the same attempt

---

[22] Herbert Muller. 'Impressionism in Fiction: Prism vs. Mirror'. *The American Scholar* 7.3 (1938): 355–367, p.361.

[23] James, 'The Art of Fiction', p.3.

[24] James, 'The Art of Fiction', p.4.

[25] James, 'The Art of Fiction', pp.4 – 5.

[26] James, 'The Art of Fiction', p.10.

[27] James, 'The Art of Fiction', p.19.

[28] James, 'The Art of Fiction', p.5.

that we see on the canvas of the painter, it will have arrived at a very
strange pass. It is not expected of the picture that it will make itself
humble in order to be forgiven; and the analogy between the art of
the painter and the art of the novelist is, so far as I am able to see,
complete. Their inspiration is the same, their process (allowing for
the different quality of the vehicle) is the same. They may learn from
each other, they may explain and sustain each other.[29]

According to James, the art of fiction and the art of painting complete each
other, because of their ways of evoking the impression of life. Novelists and
painters use different vehicles to represent what they perceive as the real
thing of life. They have the same mission – to use artistic creations as forms
to record the impressions that they receive from everyday life. As Hazel
Hutchison argues, James's method of perceiving and depicting visual
sensations are closely linked to his increasingly experimental narrative style,
in which he aims to make a portrait of the process of vision, in the centre of
consicousness. In other words, his portrayal of the process of vision is 'the
primary means of engaging with reality'.[30]

The aesthetics of Impressionism was an essential part of the European
cultural milieu in Henry James's time. By reading through Charles Baudelaire's
'The Painter of Modern life' (1863), Henry James's 'The Impressionists'
(1876), 'John S. Sargent' (1893), and Roger Fry's 'The Philosophy of
Impressionism' (1894), one can see how the philosophy of Impressionism
developed. Furthermore, following the logic of these four essays, one can
see how Impressionism was received and defined in both literature and art.
The Impressionists' task is to portray visual sensation sincerely, to paint as
what they see.

---

[29] James. 'The Art of Fiction', p.5.
[30] Hazal Hutchison, 'James's Spectacles: Distorted Vision in *The Ambassadors*'.
The Henry James Review 26 (2005): 39 – 51, p.39.

Baudelaire's 'The Painter of Modern Life' (1863) is fundamental to Impressionist aesthetics. In this essay, he claims that a true artistic genius can grasp creative ideas from modern life, and shape them into a form of fine arts. 'Modern life', for Baudelaire, is the most important subject matter for modern artists. An artist is a passionate spectator, who is eager to gain visual impressions and to transform them into works of art with his perception. For instance, Baudelaire praises Constantin Guys' paintings, because they depict the 'manners of the present'.[31] As Baudelaire points out, what he meant by 'modernity' is

> the ephemeral, the fugitive, the contingent, the half of art whose other half is the eternal and the immutable. Every old master has had his own modernity; the great majority of fine portraits that have come down to us from former generations are clothed in the costume of their own period.[32]

Modernity, for Baudelaire, means that the originality of the artistic style which comes from his milieu – 'the seal which Time imprints on [his] sensations'.[33] 'Being present'[34] in the metropolis, is the essence of the Impressionist paintings, because they seize a moment of immediate perception, in order to 'discern the variable elements of beauty within a unity of the impression'.[35] An artist needs to weave the fragmentary elements of modern life and the experience of everydayness into a unified and unique impression through artistic perception.

The Impressionist painters continued Baudelaire's emphasis on using the modern metropolis as inspiration for art. As Henry James claims in 'The

---

[31] Charles Baudelaire, 'The Painter of Modern Life' (1863). *The Painter of Modern Life and Other Essays*. Trans. Jonathan Mayne. London: Phaidon, 1995, p.1.
[32] Baudelaire, *The Painter of Modern Life*, p.12.
[33] Baudelaire, *The Painter of Modern Life*, p.14.
[34] Baudelaire, *The Painter of Modern Life*, p.2.
[35] Baudelaire, *The Painter of Modern Life*, p.3.

Impressionists' (1876), the mission of the Impressionists is to 'give a vivid impression of how a thing happens to look, at a particular moment'.[36] That particular moment is Beauty itself. They paint what they see on the street of the modern metropolis, rather than make copies of classic paintings in art galleries and museums. The Impressionists' free style and spontaneous visual sensations bring a sense of looseness and lack of finish – rough sketches, broken strokes, and objects not in clear shapes or outlines; they leave their subject matter in an undefined form, loosely treated, to give an effect of the general expression of a visual sensation as a vivid impression.

In 'John S. Sargent' (1893), James develops his concept of literary impressionism further. By observing the point of view and style in Sargent's paintings, James sees in it the essence of Impressionism: an Impressionist painting is a 'pure tact of vision',[37] which depicts the visual objects as they appear. The Impressionists record their visual impressions with quick broken strokes and juxtaposition of colours which convey the immediacy and vividness of their visual sensations. To portray one's own impression of a visual object, according to James, is the 'finest' artistic expression in the 'simplest form'.[38] In this light, the Impressionists' quick broken strokes indicate a 'quick perception'[39] and a simplification of style.

Roger Fry's 'The Philosophy of Impressionism' (1894) provides the reader with a theoretical basis for Impressionism in terms of its nature and aim.[40] According to Fry, the Impressionist use of colour concentrates on the

---

[36] Henry James. 'The Impressionists' (1876). *The Painter's Eye*. Ed. John L. Sweeney. Wisconsin: The University of Wisconsin Press. 1989, p.114.

[37] Henry James, 'John S. Sargent' (1893). *The Painter's Eye*, 1989, p.217.

[38] James, 'John S. Sargent', p.218.

[39] James, 'John S. Sargent', p.228.

[40] Roger Fry, 'The Philosophy of Impressionism' (1894). Unpublished article originally written for the *Fortnightly Review*, 1894, and made available by the Fry Estate from the Roger Fry Papers, King's College Library, Cambridge. See *A Roger Fry Reader*. Ed. Christopher Reed. Chicago: University of Chicago Press,

observation of the way sunlight conveys visual impressions. The aim of the Impressionists is to represent the truth of their perception of that visual impression.[41] For example, Monet paints the play of light and shadow, drawing snow in the shadow in dark blue as what he sees, rather than painting it in white as what he knows. The new approach to colour made possible a new understanding of the relation between visual sensations and sunlight, which brought visual pleasure to the viewer. The Impressionists concentrated on the observation of sunlight. For Fry, a typical Impressionist is a 'finer'[42] observer, whose eyes are sensitive films which can sense the alteration of sunlight at different moments of a day; whose paintings visual impressions of their perception.

Fry's analysis of Impressionism shows his understanding of visual sensations and the depiction of impressions. For the Impressionist, the physical eye is a medium between consciousness and the external world. Through vision and perception, visual objects can be synthesised as an impression. Visual sensations fall on the painter's retina, which forms an impression in consciousness. As Fry points out, two of the Impressionists' revolutionary breakthroughs were their treatment of colour and tone; their scheme of colour conveys the 'quality of the atmosphere at the particular moment'[43] that they choose to represent. The juxtaposition and interaction of colours create a harmonious unity of visual sensations on one canvas. The synthesis of their interacting colours is the result of the immediate impression, which is represented as an eternal moment on one's own canvas. The tone value, on the other hand, brings a synthesis between light and shadow. According to Fry, shadow does not represent the absence'[44] of

---

1996, p.20.

[41] Fry, 'The Philosophy of Impressionism', p.20.

[42] Fry, 'The Philosophy of Impressionism', p.16.

[43] Fry, 'The Philosophy of Impressionism', p.16.

[44] Fry, 'The Philosophy of Impressionism', p.18.

light but a weak source of light – a darker and deeper colour. The dancing of light and shadow is the truth of the Impressionists' sense of sight. Through Impressionism, Henry James sees the way in which he can depict process of vision through the centre of consciousness in his narrative.

James's Impressionist Paris

James's literary impressionism has two aspects. First of all, in *The Ambassadors*, pictorial elements are abundantly present in each section of the novel. They reveal that the complexity of James's development in writing style and narrative form. Secondly, his use of the 'centre of consciousness' as the other aspect of literary impressionism is achieved through his understanding of the Impressionists' method, which is to seize a momentary visual sensation in one's own consciousness, then materialise this 'impression' as an art form. James portrays Lambert Strether's process of vision as 'a forced energy'[45] of inner transformation. The interaction between vision, the external visual objects and consciousness constructs Strether's 'impression', which is a moment of revelation: the love affair between Chad and Madame de Vionnet. In other words, James adopts the Impressionists' visually oriented methodology to develop his own literary impressionism, to depict the relation between visual sensations and one's psychological reaction to them. Strether's overflowing complex visual impressions are arranged as pictorial images in James's narrative pattern.

In the outdoor scenes in *The Ambassadors*, there are close similarities between painterly Impressionism and literary impressionism. As H. Peter Stowell points out, an impression takes place in moments of heightened awareness 'when the character reacts to an object, an action, or another character in such a way that he achieves a gestalt synthesis. This kind of

---

[45] Ford Madox Ford, 'Henry James'. *Mightier Than the Sword: Memories and Criticisms*. London: George Allen & Unwin, 1838, p.33.

moment has been given many names in literature and is not solely the property of impressionism, but these privileged moments, impressions, *instantanés*, or *moments bienheureux* do form a crucial basis for the impressionistic vision'.[46] The impression is a synthesis of inner and outer worlds, as soon as the visible world is looked at by the eye and perceived by consciousness. The significance of James's literary impressionism lies in the way he narrates these open-air scenes, which included the brightness of Paris, the French countryside, and the pleasant visual impressions Strether receives while he is walking in the city. He has a double consciousness: as Mrs Newsome's ambassador and a foreigner in Paris. Strether begins to enjoy a totally different way of life from that he knew in Woollett. In Paris, he starts to see people and things, in a way which does not have moral judgment involved. By so doing, Strether's whole process of vision can be developed aesthetically.

And yet, a letter from Mrs Newsome reminds Strether the real purpose for him to be in Paris. The Luxembourg Gardens is where Strether reads Mrs Newsome's letters, which crucially reminds him that his original purpose for being an 'ambassador', to bring Chad home. The letter now feels like an imperial edict from 'Queen Elizabeth'.[47] He takes her letters with him, and finds himself a place to sit and read:

> In the Luxembourg Gardens he pulled up; here at last he found his nook, and here, on a penny chair from which terraces, alleys, vistas, fountains, little trees in green tubs, little women in white caps and shrill little girls at play all sunnily 'composed' together, he passed an hour in which the cup of his impressions seemed truly to overflow.[48]

---

[46] H. Peter Stowell, *Literary Impressionism: James and Chekhov.* Athens: University of Georgia Press, 1980, p.37.

[47] James, *The Ambassadors*, p.43.

[48] James, *The Ambassadors*, pp.58 –59.

James's depiction echoes the Impressionists' sunlight-dappled visual impressions and the harmonious atmosphere in the air, which bring the viewer a taste as of something mixed with art. The garden becomes a work of art through the play of sunlight, in which James's Impressionist vision is depicted. The Luxembourg Gardens now look like an Impressionist painting, "all sunnily 'composed' together", overflowing in Strether's perception and in his coffee cup – a synthesis of green, white, figures of women and girls, alleys, fountains, trees, light and shade. Like Woolf's English gentleman in Italy in 'Street Haunting', Strether now is a foreigner, a tourist, who is revealing his secret among coffee cups, terraces, and Parisian visual impression.

Strether's overflowing impressions make the garden a charming and pictorial place. Strether is a sensitive observer who compares the different cultural modes of Paris and Woollett. His observation contributes to James's depiction of the brightness of Paris as an instant impression, which is like 'the vast bright Babylon, [...], a jewel brilliant and hard, in which parts were not to be discriminated nor differences comfortably marked. It twinkled and trembled and melted together, and what seemed all surface one moment seemed all depth the next'.[49] Paris is like a jewel, 'brilliant and hard' in its brightness, which gives the viewer visual sensations. Paris's brightness comes from its high civilization, the richness of its art collections in the art galleries and museums, in the dynamic Parisian life in the street, the café, the theatre, gardens, parks, in all types of individuals – the light of 'dear old Paris'[50] which touches Strether's heart and overwhelms him.

The Ambassadors can also be read as the memory of a painting, as a pictorial remembrance of things past. When Strether sees the French countryside – the white house, the blue sky and the green field in the village within his imaginary 'oblong gilt frame'[51] – a small landscape painting

---

[49] James, *The Ambassadors*, p.64.

[50] James, *The Ambassadors*, p.88.

[51] James, *The Ambassadors*, p.307.

comes to his mind. It is a small landscape painting that he cannot afford to have, which had charmed him long years before at a Boston dealer's. The reflection of his memory establishes a significant relation between the inner and outer worlds, between the past and the present, between the Tremont Street art shop in Boston and the French countryside landscape in front of his eyes. At this very moment, Strether has his own revelation. He sees 'the right thing', the boat which contains 'a man who held the paddles and a lady, [...], with a pink parasol'.[52] The scene – the landscape, the boat, the man and the woman – is like an Impressionist painting. Strether, at this very moment, has his 'impression' of Chad and Madame de Vionnet, which is his awareness of their love affair.[53]

James's Pictorial London

The way James depict Paris is different from his portrayal of London. For James, Paris is the sunlight dazzling city, while London has an aesthetic light in its landscape and museums under the grey sky. In arranging his travel essays on England into the collection *English Hours* (1905), Henry James retained their chronological order with one major exception: he set two relatively late pieces on London at the beginning of the book, 'London' (1888) and 'Browning in Westminster Abbey' (1890). This ordering of the essays provides 'the defining context'[54] for other essays on London, and implying rest of the collection in both literary impressionist technique and the focal theme – people, things, events and places. The reader will see how James completes his pictorial London in words, by reading the following essays as a process like that of an Impressionist painter painting his four seasons: 'London Sights' (10 November 1875), 'An English Easter' (1877),

---

[52] James, *The Ambassadors*, p.309.

[53] James, *The Ambassadors*, p.313.

[54] Brigitte Bailey, 'Travel Writing and the Metropolis: James, London, and *English Hours*'. *American Literature* 67.2 (1995): 201 – 232, p.201.

'London at Midsummer' (1877), 'London in the Dead Season' (7 September 1878). Furthermore, by reading James, one can see how Woolf draws on him to develop her own Post-Impressionist art of walking, looking and writing London through her reading and responding to James's travel writings, particularly in her essays such as 'Henry James's Latest Novel' (1905), 'Portraits of Places' (1906), 'The Old Order' (1917), 'The Method of Henry James' (1918), 'Within the Rim' (1919), 'The Letters of Henry James' (1920), and also 'Great Men's Houses', 'Abbeys and Cathedrals' and 'Portrait of a Londoner' in her essay collection, *The London Scene* (1931 – 32).

James's walking experience gives him an opportunity to observe English people closely, which also allows him to present what he sees as an idea of plot and character in his fictional writing. For instance, in the Preface of *The Princess Casamassima* (1886), he states that the story of this novel came to him during 'the first year of a long residence in London, from the habit and the interest of walking the streets'.[55] James's walking on the streets of London, and visiting museums and art galleries, is a passionate pilgrimage to see people and things which 'interest and fascinate'[56] him. His feeling for the atmosphere and the aesthetic charm of London has a significant influence on his art criticism, fictional and travel writings. London is the place where he is both an impressionist travel sketcher in words and an analytical observer. As he says in *English Hours* himself, he loves the city 'aesthetically'[57] and feels the glorious 'light of heaven in which we labour to write articles and books for each other's candid perusal [...]'.[58]

For James, walking, looking and thinking are the best ways to appreciate visual impressions of London. His London landscape represents the

---

[55] Henry James, *The Art of the Novel: Critical Prefaces by Henry James*. 1934. New York: Charles Scribner's Sons, 1962, p.59.

[56] Henry James, 'London' (1888). *English Hours* (1905). London: Heinemann, 1960, p.24.

[57] James, 'London', p.23.

[58] James, 'London', p.23.

aesthetic pleasure of looking, which creates an interaction between the public and private realms in the enclosure of consciousness; his travel sketches are works of art of the aestheticised experiences of looking. James's London is like Benjamin's Paris. For both of them, the city itself is a landscape which has dialectical meanings. The city opens to one while he is foreign in the city; and yet, the city feels like home while it encloses him, by bringing one's own memory back to the present. As James walks in the streets of London, he walks into his own childhood memories of learning European art and history, as the past comes to live again, visualising his English present. As he walks through Green Park and St James Park on his way to Westminster Abbey:

> London is pictorial in spite of details – from its dark green, misty parks, the way the light comes down leaking and filtering from its cloud-ceiling, and the softness and richness of tone which objects put on in such an atmosphere as soon as they begin to recede. Nowhere is there such a play of light and shade, such a struggle of sun and smoke, such aerial gradations and confusions. [...]. What completes the effect of the place is its appeal to the feelings, made in so many ways, but made above all by agglomerated immensity.[59]

For James, London has an interior image, as his home, with dark green and misty colours and light 'comes down from the cloud-ceiling'. The way James depicts his London is Impressionist. By gazing fixedly at the landscape, James approaches the aesthetic dialectics of light and shadow, green and grey, geographic openness and psychological closure – a calm and peaceful feeling as at his home. His English impression visualises the beauty of Constable's nineteenth-century landscape paintings – the castle, the cloud, the river and the forest are James's realm of the delightful and 'subtle English beauty'.[60]

---

[59] Henry James, 'An English Easter' (1877). *Collected Travel Writings: Great Britain and America.* New York: The Library of America, 1993, p.114.

[60] Bonny MacDonald, 'Henry James's *English Hours*: Private Spaces and the

James was, throughout his life, learning how to see and to appreciate paintings. His concern with learning was always 'at its highest pitch when the subject or object which engaged him also engaged the question of art'.[61] Apart from his quest of the four seasons of pictorial London, James also depicts his visual experience of visiting art galleries, museums and exhibitions in the so-called 'picture season' in London. By reviewing works of art, James makes his passionate enjoyment of pictures into an impression of a personal world, where he turns the painter's eye into prose, as in his pictorial depiction of London, when the city itself becomes a charming and delightful landscape.

James perceives literature in paintings, as he perceives his pictorial London. For James, London, the 'murky Babylon', becomes a spot of 'a perceptible brightness' in the picture (exhibition) season, because the pictures he sees in London produced 'a general impression of brilliancy'.[62] In 'The Picture Season in London' (1877), James sees the art galleries and exhibitions of the streets in the West End on a 'fine, fresh day in June', which reminds him of the 'charming brightness' of the Champs-Élysées in Paris, on a fine Sunday in the late spring – the light associates with 'pleasure-taking', an atmosphere of a 'charming harmony'.[63] If the light of Paris was a light of spectacle, the light of London for James, on the other hand, was something 'more impressive'.[64] It is not Parisian dazzling sunlight, but a 'suggestive' light of artistic complexity. As James comments on London's picture season, its suggestive aesthetic light depicts '[s]uch a

---

Aesthetics of Enclosure'. *A Companion to Henry James Studies*. Ed. Daniel Mark Fogel. Westport, CT: Greenwood, 1993, p.399.

[61] John L. Sweeney, 'Introduction'. *The Painter's Eye: Notes and Essays on the Pictorial Arts by Henry James*. Ed. John L. Sweeney. London: Rupert Hart-Davis, 1956, p.25.

[62] James, 'The Picture Season in London' (1877). *The Painter's Eye*, p.130.

[63] James, 'The Picture Season in London', p.130.

[64] James, 'The Picture Season in London', p.131.

vast amount of human life, so complex a society, so powerful a body of custom and tradition stand behind them, that the spectacle becomes the most solidly brilliant, the most richly suggestive, of all great social shows'.[65] James portrays the aesthetic quality of London in words. The 'richly suggestive' light of London helps him to observe and to appreciate its social complexity, which is 'richly suggestive' for his literary impressionism. It also helps to develop his own sensibility, in order to depict the psychological depth of characters in his novels in the context of the metropolis.

Woolf's Response to James

Henry James, as a tourist with detached eyes, is privileged to depict his enjoyment of staying in London (the murky modern Babylon), in which he appreciated the depth of history, its architecture and people. His England is like a landscape painting. As Virginia Woolf comments that James strolled through English towns, while all visual impressions and sensory experiences were associated together as a 'significant'[66] occasion, which is presented as a picture in his mind. This American stranger's brain, to Woolf, is like a very sensitive 'photographic film',[67] which records the nature of a scene as something charming, though '[n]o English writer would have thought that scene worth recording'.[68] However, as Woolf claims, James's written portraits of places are not only about grace, urbanity and a 'picturesque attitude';[69] rather, his eye observes with the 'proper detachment', [70] which is not possible for an average native.

In Woolf's comments on James's later novels and travel writings, one can see her understanding of James's writing strategy, which showed her

---

[65] James, 'The Picture Season in London', p.132.
[66] Woolf, 'Portraits of Places' (1906), *E I*, p.125.
[67] Woolf, 'Portraits of Places', p.125.
[68] Woolf, 'Portraits of Places', p.126.
[69] Woolf, 'Portraits of Places', p.125.
[70] Woolf, 'Portraits of Places', p.126.

the possibility of portraying the 'psychology of the land'.[71] James's passion for painting a foreign land in words is associated with the eye, which observes and selects what he sees, presenting a spectacle of memories, emotions and experiences blending beneath something which may look simple and familiar to a native, such as 'a cottage with a date upon the door'.[72] In Woolf's comments, she highly praises James's writing about England as it illustrates his own 'individual gifts of perception',[73] allows him to portray a picture of the land that is 'both pleasant and perspicacious',[74] 'so charming and so true'.[75]

For Woolf, James is a writer who is 'sufficiently great to possess a point of view'.[76] This point of view, I would argue, reveals the painter's eye in a writer, which is not only the observation of the character's 'process of vision' as a metaphor of perceiving the external world, but also a literary Impressionist way 'to say what he means, to say all he means, to leave nothing unsaid that can by any possibility complete the picture',[77] as a way of suggesting Strether's moment of revelation. As Woolf points out, James's eyes see people's thoughts and emotions 'as they are',[78] which allows his pen to picture them in the 'marvelous accumulation of detail'.[79] James makes the reader see the process of vision of the character, and, as Woolf claims, 'with a sure knowledge of anatomy, paints every bone and muscle in the human frame',[80] without making his character speak or interact with other people, as one can see in James's Strether in *The Ambassadors*. However,

---

[71] Woolf, 'Portraits of Places', p.124.
[72] Woolf, 'Portraits of Places', p.125.
[73] Woolf, 'Portraits of Places', p.125.
[74] Woolf, 'Portraits of Places', p.125.
[75] Woolf, 'Portraits of Places', p.127.
[76] Woolf, 'Mr Henry James's Latest Novel' (1905), *E I*, p.22.
[77] Woolf, 'Mr Henry James's Latest Novel', p.22.
[78] Woolf, 'Mr Henry James's Latest Novel', p.22.
[79] Woolf, 'Mr Henry James's Latest Novel', p.23.
[80] Woolf, 'Mr Henry James's Latest Novel', p.23.

Woolf also claims that James's portrait of human consciousness 'would be greater as a work of art if he were content to say less and suggest more'.[81] For Woolf, the 'suggestiveness' in a novel is not the sunlight, or the depiction of the centre of consciousness. It is a mood, an emotion of a character, through which she creates the atmosphere of London, portraying an emotional/imaginary map of the city, as I aim to show in *Night and Day*.

Walking 'a Map of Emotions': Woolf's London in *Night and Day*

Woolf's London is emotional. Her second novel, *Night and* Day, published by Duckworth on 20 October 1919 in an edition of two thousand copies,[82] has often been seen as a traditional novel, and an unsuccessful one. Clive Bell, for instance, claimed this novel was 'her most definite failure'.[83] E. M. Forster also commented in 'The Novels of Virginia Woolf' (1926) that to him, *Night and Day* is a 'deliberate exercise in classicism. It contains all that has characterised English fiction for good or evil during the last hundred and fifty years – faith in personal relations, recourse to humorous side shows, insistence on petty social differences'.[84] In 'Tradition and Revision: the Classic City Novel and Woolf's *Night and Day*', Susan M. Squier argues that this novel is a 'classic' city novel, because of 'the customary town/country morality',[85] and says that because the style of this novel has been 'moralized [...] though the machinery is modern, the resultant form is as traditional as

---

[81] Woolf, 'Mr Henry James's Latest Novel', p.23.

[82] B. J. Kirkpatrick and Stuart N. Clarke. *A Bibliography of Virginia Woolf.* Oxford: Clarendon, 1997, pp.18 – 19.

[83] Robin Majumdar and Allen McLaurin, eds. *Virginia Woolf: The Critical Heritage.* London: Routledge and Kegan Paul, 1975, p.140.

[84] E. M. Forster, 'The Novel of Virginia Woolf'. First published in *New Criterion*, April 1926; reprinted on pp.171 – 178 in *CH*, p.173.

[85] Susan M. Squier, 'Tradition and Revision: the Classic City Novel and Woolf's *Night and Day*'. *Virginia Woolf and London: the Sexual Politics of the City.* Chapel Hill: University of North Carolina Press, 1985, p.78.

Emma'.[86] For many critics, *Night and Day* is a traditional novel of manners, simply because its plot is standard: lovers who have chosen inappropriate mates and discover their error by the end of the novel. And yet, I would argue that this is an over-simplified way of reading this novel.

Night and Day is not simply a 'traditional' novel. Woolf has certain elements of composition, which go beyond the traditional use of the urban space and narrative form. In the process of portraying her own psychological London, Woolf was actually in the process of recomposing her 'inner life'.[87] As she explained to Ethel Smyth:

> After being ill and suffering every form and variety of nightmare and extravagant intensity of perception …, when I came to, I was so tremblingly afraid of my own insanity that I wrote Night and Day mainly to prove to my own satisfaction that I could keep entirely off that dangerous ground. […]. Bad as the book is, it composed my mind, and I think taught me certain elements of composition which I should not have had the patience to learn had I been in full flush of health always.[88]

During the period of being ill, she wrote *Night and Day* to prove that she was able to write a novel and to find her own voice. Her imaginary map of London composed her mind during the period of her illness, as her city mapped the emotion and psychology of her characters, which composed her novel in abstract forms of shapes and colours.[89] Woolf discovers her characters' emotions, in a way which shows their points of view of seeing London.

---

[86] Forster, 'The Novel of Virginia Woolf', *CH*, p.173.

[87] H. Porter Abbott, 'Old Virginia and the Night Writer: The Origins of Woolf's Narrative Meander'. *Inscribing The Daily: Critical Essays on Women's Diaries*. Ed. Suzanne L. Bunkers and Cynthia A. Huff. Amherst: University of Massachusetts Press, 1996, p.249.

[88] Woolf, Letter to Ethel Smyth, 16th Oct 1930. *L IV*, p.231.

[89] Woolf discovers the 'shapes' to convey emotions better in her experimental short

One can see that the streets of London are Woolf's characters' emotional paths, as lines on the canvas. Like the Post-Impressionists, Woolf visualises her characters' emotions in abstract forms – such as a square (where Katharine is waiting for Ralph), an oval (in Katharine's family small room, she is looking at Ralph's eyes, as if he was a hero). Woolf's London composes her own narrative pattern, makes a psychological turn in the writing of fiction, from James's centre of consciousness which passively perceives the external world, to her own expression of emotion – the characters' emotion which subjectively maps the cityscape. Woolf's mode of seeing illustrates a mode of narration. This mode of seeing reveals a process of mapping a psychological London. In this respect, Woolf is able to define her own aesthetics of urban vision as a critique of the historical gendered setting of London within her Post-Impressionist narrative form, in which walking, looking and thinking are ways of illustrating maps of emotional London of her characters.

Talking of her own process of writing in a letter to Lady Ottoline Morrell, she said that 'I cant believe that any human being can get through Night and Day which I wrote chiefly in bed, half an hour at a time. But it taught me a great deal, or so I hoped, like a minute Academy drawing: what to leave out: by putting it all in'.[90] Woolf's London is not a precise tourist guide-book (which tells one where to go via which bus), as the exactness of a Victorian drawing (which shows wrinkles of a dress). On the contrary, she depicts the places not through minute details, but by putting all her characters' emotions in. By putting different emotional aspects of London, Woolf makes the reader see a complex of narrative form, which re-writes Victorian heritage and moves toward her own psychological realism. The city of London, in this light, has embraced all these dynamic aspects, from Victorian literary Chelsea (the home that

---

fictions such as 'Kew Gardens'. This narrative technique generally getting mature in *Mrs Dalloway*, as one can see the way she uses the heart shape, the diamond shape and the black shadow to convey emotions: love and fear.

[90] Virginia Woolf, letter to Lady Ottoline Morrell, 19 February 1938. *L VI*, p.216.

Katharine wants to escape) to business area Lincoln's Inn Fields in Holborn (Ralph's work place), to British Museum and Russell Square (Mary's love and work place), and to Highgate (Ralph's home and dream). Woolf rewrites Victorian literary tradition by including emotional significance in these places.

Herta Newman argues that Woolf has her attention shift 'from the broad concept of reality to the specific issue of character',[91] because she believes that '[t]he foundation of good fiction is character creating and nothing else'.[92] Also, as Jean Guiguet points out, Woolf's 'experimental character'[93] has attracted considerable critical attention. Woolf's characters are experimental, because they are in the quest for the meaning of love and life. For instance, Ford Madox Hueffer saw *Night and Day* as a novel which reminded him very much of late James.[94] Eric Warner, in a panel discussion of the Virginia Woolf Centenary Conference at Fitzwilliam College, Cambridge in 1982, said that he himself sees Woolf 'very much in the tradition of Henry James, [...], in the sense that she is clearly concerned with a drama of consciousness, a drama of perception, and [...] a quest'.[95] For Warner, Woolf's writing represents a quest for the meaning of life, which reminds him very much of late James, particularly in characters such as Strether and Mme de Vionnet in *The Ambassadors*, in that there is always a dark secret behind the 'artful beauty'.[96]

The influence of Henry James is evident in the way in which Woolf depicts the aesthetic experience of her characters;[97] and yet, she has a gift

[91] Herta Newman, *Virginia Woolf and Mrs Brown: Toward a Realism of Uncertainty.* New York: Garland, 1996, p.7.

[92] Virginia Woolf, 'Character in Fiction' (1924). *E III*, 1988, p.421.

[93] Jean Guiguet, *Virginia Woolf and her Works*. Trans. Jean Stewart. London: The Hogarth Press, 1965, p.19.

[94] Ford Madox Hueffer, "'Novel' and 'Romance'." *Piccadilly Review* 23 October 1919. Reprinted in *CH*, pp.72 – 75, p.73.

[95] Eric Warner, *Virginia Woolf: A Centenary Perspective*. Ed. Eric Warner. London: Macmillan, 1984, p.154.

[96] Warner, *Virginia Woolf: A Centenary Perspective*, p.155.

[97] For instance, Mary gazes at winged Assyrian bulls and the Elgin Marbles in the

of her own, which allows her to make a social critique in gender and class.[98] Phyllis Rose sees Woolf's way of writing as an 'inevitable struggle between tradition and the individual talent'.[99] In other words, Woolf was conscious of and had to rebel against traditional fictional form, in order to develop a distinctively personal way of writing, a difficult struggle, because she could not easily deny the paternal authority of the literary heritage. Jane Wheare uses the term 'experimental novel'[100] to describe Woolf's way of making sense of ordinary experience, the everydayness of life in the modern world, in order to examine the relationship between language, habit and experience in Woolf's works. However, taking these comments into account, it seems to me that there are still similarities and differences in terms of narrative technique in Woolf and James's works. Woolf's essays on James's writings suggest that it will make sense to read her early novels and short fictions in the light of James's use of 'the painter's eye',[101] of his observation of human

---

British Museum suggests her aesthetic emotion. Through her gaze, she turns works of art into an imaginary love relation with Ralph. She begins to think about Ralph, because the presence of the 'immense and enduring beauty' of works of art makes her 'alarmingly conscious of her desire', her love for Ralph. See Virginia Woolf, *Night and Day* (J. H. Stape, ed. Oxford: Blackwell, 1994, pp.62 – 63). As C. Lewis Hind described, when he saw the Assyrian Winged Bulls, his aesthetic sense was stirred. It is a feeling – that 'something more', both 'strange and stimulating', transforms 'mere technique into mysticism'. See *The Post-Impressionists* (London: Methuen, 1911, pp.88 – 91).

[98] In his travel sketches, James does not show the English society that much, in terms of gender and class. And yet, Woolf does show this in her essays. For instance, she does not see the greatness of the great man in Carlyle's house, but life-long struggle of Mrs Carlyle, as I have shown in my previous chapter.

[99] Phyllis Rose, *Woman of Letters: A Life of Virginia Woolf.* London: Routledge & Kegan Paul, 1978, p.94.

[100] Jane Wheare, *Virginia Woolf: Dramatic Novelist.* London: Macmillan, 1989, p.4.

[101] Woolf's interest in paintings and her reconsideration of the traditional ontology of the novel's literary realism help her to compose a series of visual sensations into psychological reality. W. L. George also points out that the Neo-Georgians 'can be described as painters rather than writers. It is thus permissible to say that *the*

consciousness in the metropolis in both his novels and travel sketches. Her use of revelation (Mary's two revelations in *Night and Day*) and works of art in her novel also remind the reader of Henry James (Mary's looking at works of art in the British Museum, thinking about Ralph). And yet, in *Night and Day*, Woolf does not merely portray a 'centre of consciousness' or the perception of that centre of consciousness. Rather, she depicts a complex of consciousness, through which she expresses her characters' paths of emotion and mood as her own experimental practice of narrative form.

Modes of seeing, feeling and emotion serve the symbolic and structural needs of Woolf's artistic design. Her psychological London, as a metaphor with symbolic meanings, goes beyond its physical existence such as buildings, and reinforces its cultural depth. As Janis M. Paul argues, this novel attempts to deal with the visible world that concerned people living in London, and it attempts to counter everyday life with a sense of that felt inner world which, for Woolf, 'was simultaneous and just as real'.[102] Woolf's use of revelation is 'the drama of visionary moment', as Paul Maltby phrases it. Woolf's depiction of the process of psychological change is compressed into precisely a transcendent moment, in which visual sensation and thought flow together into the stream of narrative as a symbolic energy of cohesiveness, dramatising the character's way of feeling.

Woolf's expression of London relates to Henry James's Impressionist Paris and pictorial London. And yet, Woolf's depiction of London reduces the

---

modern novel is becoming a painter's literature', because they paint emotions and feelings in words. See 'A Painter's Literature'. *English Review* March 1920, 223 – 234. Reprinted in *CH*, 82– 84, p.82. R. M. Underhill also points out that the 'eye' Woolf has can picture the process of the spectacle of the mind – '[t]he curious fabric of minute-by-minute daily life, compound of emotion, sensation, thoughts half sized, actions half intended' – which leads to a revelation, 'the approach of truth'. See 'Review'. *Bookman* (New York) August 1920, 685 – 686. Reprinted in *CH*, 85 – 86, p.85.

[102] Joan Bennett, *Virginia Woolf: Her Art as a Novelist*. Cambridge: Cambridge University Press, 1964, p.91.

visible appearance of the city to its minimal sense, in order to reveal a complex interaction between outer and inner worlds, in which the physical/visible London is transformed into an imaginary and psychological form of narrative with a sense of daily life. This narrative form reflects the mood and emotion of her characters', and turns from the portrayal of the external impressionist sunlight to an exploration of inwardness. For Woolf, human consciousness does not have the purpose of making sense of the external world, as in William James's phenomenological psychology. For William James, the visible world is meaningless unless the mind perceives it. It is a pragmatic mode of seeing. For Woolf, the external world is an expression of what her characters feel, through which the inner and outer worlds become one.

William James's notion of 'space' is as a synthesis of fragmentary sensations.[103] The form, or '*quale*' of spatiality, according to James, is an arrangement of sensation, from which the external objects are related in the field of vision. In Woolf's writing, time is not the clock time in a chronological sense, and space is not a physical existence, but a fusion of feeling and emotion, in which one can regain in memory, as one walks into one's own personal history in a city. The spatial form reveals memory, the mode of feeling, the way of seeing, and the rhetoric of emotion. Woolf's emotional map of London, in this light, is expressed in an abstract and a metaphorical way, and gives the reader 'an ineffaceable shape'.[104]

For Woolf, the inwardness is externalised in a form of spatiality. The essential spatial character of London in Woolf's novels is revealed by her use of revelations, works of art, and walking scenes, in order to reflect the map of thought, emotion and feeling of her characters. The imaginary space is constructed by one's own mode of feeling, emotion and vision, because

---

[103] James, *Principles II*, p.786.

[104] Virginia Woolf, 'Literary Geography' (1905), *E I*, p.32.

> A writer's country is a territory within his own brain; and we run the
> risk of disillusionment if we try to turn such phantom cities into
> tangible brick and mortar. We know our way there without signposts
> or policemen, and we can greet the passers-by without need of
> introduction. No city indeed is so real as this that we make for
> ourselves and people to our liking; and to insist that it has any
> counterpart in the cities of the earth is to rob it of half its charm.[105]

Woolf develops the psychological basis of the metropolitan type of
subjective modes of vision and feeling, to create her own literary London.
Her use of walking scenes conveys the essential spatial character of London,
constructs the map of thought, emotion and feeling of her characters, which
unifies the inner and outer worlds.

The main action of *Night and Day* centres on five places in London: the
Hilbery home in Cheyne Walk, Ralph's shabby, middle-class house in
Highgate, Mary Datchet's flat at the top of a block of offices off the Strand,
the suffragette office in Russell Square, and William Rodney's rooms in
King's Bench Walk.[106] Walking on the streets of central London, or walking
to rooms and places is significant. Walking is a metaphor, which reveals the
psychological state, mood and emotion of the character. Walking is not only
a symbol of quest, but also Woolf's experimental practice of expressing the
character's thought, when he or she walks, as a 'map of emotions' (*ND* 272)
of his or her own imaginary London. Visual objects become metaphors,
which indicate the characters' attitudes toward the city itself, and also the
gender, social and political differences among them, and most of all, their
inner worlds. Through portraying the mode of seeing and feeling as a
narrative form, Woolf successfully connects the inner and outer worlds,
imagination and reality, visible and imaginary London. Through visionary

---

[105] Woolf, 'Literary Geography', *E I*, p.35.
[106] Hermione Lee, *The Novels of Virginia Woolf*. London: Methuen, 1977, p.59.

intensity, daily life is transfigured into an abstract painting. This painting transcends the external visible world of London into pure, abstract forms in a myriad colours and shapes: squares (public spaces, rooms), lines (streets) in red, gold, white, green, blue, grey colours. The mode of feeling of Katharine Hilbery, Mary Datchet and Ralph Denham illustrates Woolf's experimental practice, transforming traditional themes of love and marriage common in romantic comedy into a psychological mapping of the urban scene. Moreover, the mode of seeing reveals how these characters fall in love, how their minds are trapped in a continuous process of self-interrogation, how private and public spheres overlap in the dualism of illusion and reality.

Night and Day questions social and literary convention, in terms of a woman's role in society. The London setting with tea gatherings and drawing-rooms is depicted with subversive codes. Mrs Hilbery's problems with her biography of Katharine's grandfather Richard Alardyce, buried in the Abbey at Poet's Corner,[107] suggest that his 'great age was dead' (*ND* 27). For Woolf, the worlds of Victorian literature, romance and family life were deeply linked as sources of melancholy and nostalgia, as one can see in Mrs Hilbery's struggle to write the great poet's biography, which remain unwritten at the end of the novel. She fails to write 'in imagination with the dead'.[108] Katharine searches for true love and the meaning of her life, as she is 'forced to make her experiment in living' (*ND* 27), and has an unwomanly interest in mathematics, which is 'directly opposed to literature' (*ND* 32).

Woolf aims to go beyond traditional realism to an expression of the visible world in a metaphorical way. While Chelsea becomes the very

---

[107] In the novel, two works of art, Richard Alardyce's portrait and the photograph of his tomb at Poet's Corner, show the greatness of a great man in Katharine's family, see *ND*, pp.6, 24 and 26.

[108] Mrs Hilbery feels the duty to write the poet's biography, in order to establish and to keep his image as a great man. In that case, she cannot write in a poetic, 'musing and romanticising' mood. See Woolf, *ND*, pp.27 – 28

symbol of what Woolf criticises in literary tradition, her mode of seeing indicates a transformation from her father's 22 Hyde Park Gate to 46 Gordon Square, Bloomsbury. This move shows a path, which allows her the possibility of going beyond Victorian tradition, in order to find a voice of her own. Duncan Grant's *Interior, 46 Gordon Square* (1914)[109] and *Interior at Gordon Square* (1914 – 5)[110] demonstrate a painterly version of the flat within a concentrated abstract visual form. Between 1914 and 1915, Grant was frequently painting in Vanessa Bell's studio, before they both went to Charleston because of the First World War. These two paintings express an essential view of the double-interior which formed Grant's inspiration: the front and back rooms on the first floor of the Bells' house. The geometric scheme of the work is analogous to Katharine's pursuit of her dream world of mathematical signs in *Night and Day*, as a halo of pure and abstract thought, which goes beyond the literary tradition of her family and the visible reality of London.

At the heart of the novel stands the house of Katharine's remarkable family, a shrine to the dead poet Richard Alardyce. Cheyne Walk faces the River Thames, beyond the Embankment, in Chelsea, a place filled with historical and literary associations. For instance, Thomas Carlyle, a friend of Anny Thackeray Ritchie (Leslie Stephen's sister-in-law), had lived round the corner at 24 Cheyne Row. As Jean Moorcroft Wilson points out in *Virginia Woolf's London: A Guide to Bloomsbury and Beyond*,

> Cheyne Walk is full of interest in itself. Starting at number 4, you will see that the novelist George Eliot died there in 1880. Dante Gabriel Rossetti lived at number 16 from 1862 to 1882, when his house became a meeting place for artists and writers. […]. [B]oth

---

[109] Richard Shone, *The Art of Bloomsbury: Roger Fry, Vanessa Bell and Duncan Grant*. London: Tate Gallery, 1999, Plate 74, p.152.

[110] Shone, *The Art of Bloomsbury*, Plate 75, p.152.

> James and T. S. Eliot lived at Carlyle Mansions at the end. [...].
> Alternatively, you might wander back, by way of Cheyne Row,
> where Carlyle lived at number 24, and other side streets, most of
> which have their own blue plaques and charm.[111]

Leslie Stephen had taken the young Woolf to see Carlyle's house there in 1897,
and she revisited it in 1898, and in 1909 and 1931.[112] Carlyle's house in
Cheyne Walk and all its literary associations was potentially threatening to
Woolf, since she was trying very hard to walk away from the 'dangerous
ground' of Victorian literary tradition. Chelsea had been the centre of literary
London, because it had been home to many eminent Victorian writers. In
Woolf's writing, Chelsea represents the ideology of the literary and artistic
tradition of the great men and the greatness of their gender, as one sees in
her depiction of the portrait of Katharine's grandfather in *Night and Day* and
Carlyle's house in 'Great Men's Houses' in *The London Scene*. Through this
particular house and its location, Woolf makes a counternarrative in her novel,
re-writing its literary heritage with an experimental form in the modern context.

Woolf depicts emotion through her characters while they walk.
Walking, as a metaphorical pilgrimage in the quest for love, shows that
Ralph finds his feeling for Katharine 'inwardly ironical' (*ND* 13), because
he knows that Katharine has a very different social class and background
from him. After visiting Katharine's family house, he feels something
'which he had determined not to feel, now possessed him wholly' (*ND* 14) –
his love for Katharine. From the traffic on the London street to Katharine's
house in Chelsea, Ralph feels peace in Katharine's house: '[w]ith the
omnibuses and cabs still running in his head, and his body still tingling with

---

[111] Jean Moorcroft Wilson, *Virginia Woolf's London: A Guide to Bloomsbury and Beyond*. 1988. London: Tauris, 2000, pp.210 – 211.

[112] Andrea P.Zemgulys, "'*Night and Day* Is Dead': Virginia Woolf in London 'Literary and Historic'". *Twentieth-Century Literature* 46.1 (2000): 56 – 77, p.57.

his quick walk along the streets and in and out of traffic and foot-passengers, this drawing-room seemed very remote and still [...]' (*ND* 2). In her Cheyne Walk setting, Woolf evokes two literary spaces: the drawing-room and the smaller room. These settings are subjects of the gendered gaze.

The best way of tackling this matter is through a close reading of the novel itself. In Katharine's parents' house in Chelsea, the drawing-room has a dreamy atmosphere, because of the family glory – the Victorian myth of the greatness of the great men. In Katharine's childhood consciousness, this myth is like '[a] fine mist, the etherealized essence of the fog, [which] hung visibly in the wide and rather empty space of the drawing-room. All silver where the candles were grouped on the tea-table, and ruby again in the firelight' (*ND* 2). The smaller room across the drawing-room 'was something like a chapel in a cathedral, or a grotto in a cave' (*ND* 6). It gives the impression of a religious temple, or a museum space, which is crowded with an impressive collection of relics, clearly marking a long history as part of the literary establishment. Items such as the mirror, a square mass of red-and-gold books, a long skirt in blue-and-white paint lustrous behind glass, a mahogany writing table, the pen and the old ink which the poet used, the original manuscript of the 'Ode to Winter,' the first edition of the poems, the picture of Katharine's great-grandmother in a blue dress, Katharine's uncle Sir Richard Warburton's walking stick, the bowl owned by the founder of the original Alardyce in 1697. All these items are sacred, and they sparkle in different colours in the firelight – red, gold, silver. In the picture, the great poet Richard Alardyce's eyes have an aura of divine friendliness, 'mellow pinks and yellows' (*ND* 6).

Ralph receives all these dazzling visual impressions, as these visual objects show him Katharine's family glory in pink, yellow, red, silver and gold – the glory of the great poet of the past. That family glory is the Victorian myth, which arouses Katharine's emotion when she gazes at Ralph (a young lawyer who writes for the *Critical Review*, coming from a different social class from her) behind a sheet of glass. Ralph looks like young Ruskin to her, because she imagines him as her hero, who has a singular face, thin and healthy cheeks, and a pair of masculine eyes with brown colour, which reveal emotions (*ND* 7). Katharine's gaze of Ralph romanticises her Victorian family glory. In that romantic atmosphere, Ralph, a middle class young man from Highgate, looks like one of the Victorian great men, who has a face 'built for swiftness and decision rather than for massive contemplation; the forehead broad, the nose long and formidable, the lips clean-shaven and at once dogged and sensitive, the cheeks lean, with a deeply running ride of red blood in them' (*ND* 7). Moreover, Ralph's eyes are brown, which express the 'usual masculine impersonality and authority', suggesting 'more subtle emotions under favourable circumstances' (*ND* 7). However, when Katharine moves closer and looks at Ralph, she finds Ralph's face is thin and healthy, with 'tokens of an angular and acrid soul' (*ND* 7). Katharine and Ralph's meeting in the mysterious atmosphere of the drawing-room and the small room pushes them to look deeper into their own consciousness and their own thoughts in the following chapters.

By using Victorian settings, Woolf suggests the class difference between Ralph and Katharine. Katharine is in a family with the Victorian poet's glory, while Ralph is a young lawyer, who writes articles for Katharine's father. After Katharine changes her dress,[113] Ralph leaves her house, 'walks up the street' (*ND* 13) to Knightsbridge, in order to catch a train towards the suburban street of Highgate. Ralph's walk (*ND* 2, 13 and 14) from Chelsea to Knightsbridge, towards the train to Highgate indicates their class differences. His family lives at The Apple Orchard, Mount Ararat Road, Highgate. The Denham family appears to be a socially isolated one,

---

[113] Woolf uses brackets to communicate with her readers, and also to deconstruct the social manner in Katharine's family – '(though she's wearing a very pretty one)'. See *ND*, p.11.

attempting to survive in a challenging modern world following the death of the father. As one can see in the novel, Ralph's room is a cheerless one. Woolf depicts the shabbiness of the room, where '[a] flattened sofa would, later in the evening, become a bed' (*ND* 15).

London is a 'shapeless mass' (*ND* 83), a constantly changing image in Katharine's mind, when she looks out of the window from the family house. She does not know what to do with her life, and she does not see a clear path to access a future of her own. She wants to find a career to define her individuality, and to marry someone she truly loves. However, she has to leave the house and walk on the streets, to visualise her own 'imaginary map of London, to follow the twists and turns of unnamed streets' (*ND* 365), in order to find the direction of her life. Katharine walks out of the house, because she wants to escape from that family drawing-room, that 'aptitude for literature', the household affairs (such as supporting her mother to order meals, direct servants, pay bills, *ND* 30). Moreover, Katharine wants to escape from the character of the house: 'an indifferent silence', which shows the place as 'an orderly place, sharply, controlled – a place where life had been trained to show to the best advantage […]' (*ND* 31). She finds her own way to rebel: her unwomanly passion for mathematics, her mathematical mind, and her way of seeing things with 'star-like impersonality' (*ND* 32). In other words, Katharine's passion for mathematics gives evidence that she wants to live 'unwomenly', to be different from the Victorian literary tradition of her family.

Katharine can be described as a flâneuse in the novel, because of the dualism of her vision: on the one hand, she is passionate and has a desperate desire to find the direction of her life; on the other hand, she is also a detached thinker. For instance, after she leaves Mary's office in Russell Square in Chapter VI, Katharine feels that what people do in Mary's office surprised and annoyed her. Katharine walks 'very fast down' the Tottenham Court Road with her thought. She compares 'Mrs. Seal, and Mary Datchet, and Mr.

Clacton to enchanted people in a bewitched tower, with the spiders' webs looping across the corners of the room' (*ND* 71). For Katharine, Mary's office is unreal and apart from the normal world, because it is 'the house of innumerable typewriters, murmuring their frail spiders' webs over the torrent of life which rushed down the streets outside' (*ND* 71). The 'spiders' webs' cover Katharine's stream of thought, so she needs to rush down to 'the crowded street' (*ND* 72), to think through everything she sees in that office. The men and women in the crowd, the lamps, and the lighted windows surround Katharine like a halo, which exhilarated her to such an extent that she very nearly forgets her companion Ralph. As Woolf depicts, Katharine walks 'very fast', to run away from 'a queer dizziness' in her head (*ND* 72).

In Chapter XI, Katharine's mode of seeing reveals her conception of life itself, as a 'process' of discovery of her inner self, when she walks under the archway into the wide space of King's Bench Walk: '[i]t's life that matters, nothing but life – the process of discovering, the everlasting and perpetual process, [...] not the discovery itself at all' (*ND* 108). Katharine's mental image of life is pure, flat, highly concentrated and simplified, like an abstract painting. Her way of perceiving life is indicated by her desire to escape from a family house, from a memorial to the past to a room of her own, in order to be free from a traditional gendered role and to develop her own interests, vision and subjectivity. Katharine's mode of seeing is also expressed by Woolf in Chapter XXIII, in the scene when she is walking with Ralph around Waterloo Bridge. Ralph tries to express his feeling to Katharine in 'an orderly way', while Katharine's mind is elsewhere:

> If Denham could have seen how visibly books of algebraic symbols pages all speckled with dots and dashes and twisted bars, came before her eyes as they trod the Embankment [...]; and all the time she was in fancy looking up through a telescope at white shadow-cleft disks which were other worlds, until she felt herself possessed two

bodies, one walking by the river with Denham, the other concentrated to a silver globe aloft in the fine blue space above the scum of vapours that was covering the visible world (*ND* 245 – 246).

Katharine's feeling of happiness is created by her own halo of thought, especially when she is looking at the night sky,[114] which is like a visualisation of 'books of algebraic symbols' liberating her from the constraint of the visible world. The juxtaposition of inner life and the external social circumstance reveals Katharine's mode of seeing.

Woolf depicts the scene in Chapter XXXI skillfully, to reflect Katharine's emotion, as she waits for Ralph to come out from his office in Lincoln's Inn Fields, Holborn. Once Katharine senses the intimate glance between William and Cassandra in her family house, she leaves the house, and walks 'rapidly along the street' (*ND* 360). The 'exact degree of intimacy' (*ND* 360) between William and Cassandra indicates that they may fix their wedding day. It awakes and encourages Katharine to walk out of the house and go to see Ralph. She reaches Lincoln's Inn Fields before Ralph leaves the office. She buys a 'large scale map of Norfolk' (*ND* 360), like the blueprint of her dream, which symbolises something she can hold on to, the place where her future house may be located.

---

[114] Jane Goldman points out that Katharine's mathematical reference in the night sky and the moon subverts the 'solar light of masculinity', and also shows the 'dark country of feminine experience'. See *The Feminist Aesthetics of Virginia Woolf: Modernism, Post-Impressionism and the Politics of the Visual* (Cambridge: Cambridge University Press, 1998, p.93). This helps the reader to understand why Woolf uses lamp light in the night time instead of sun light in the day time, to symbolise feminine power, as one can see the lamp light in Mary's room. Holly Henry also claims that for Katharine, the night symbolises her power, which helps her secretly working out equations in her bedroom. See *Virginia Woolf and the Discourse of Science* (Cambridge: Cambridge University Press, 2003, p.58).

While Katharine is waiting for Ralph, she begins to walk 'to and fro upon the pavement' (*ND* 360). Her mental state is shown not by a direct description, but by a visual depiction of how she sees London at that particular moment. The blend of daylight and lamplight makes her 'an invisible spectator' (*ND* 360 – 361). When she walks, her mind flows with people and things she sees around her. To Katharine, the crowd looks like William James's 'original halo' with 'a semi-transparent quality', which surrounds her physically and mentally like 'the great flow, the deep stream, the unquenchable tide' (*ND* 360). Katharine is amazed by the visual impressions which are created by light and her emotion. While she sees each male figure around her has a look of Ralph, with 'professional dress and quick step' (*ND* 360), she is actually fancying a different life with Ralph, to escape from Chelsea and be independent from her family, gaining her own space for her interest. It is Lincoln's Inn Fields rather than 'the domestic streets of Chelsea' (*ND* 361) which suits her feeling. The whole place speaks to her of Ralph as an independent young professional: the square itself, the immense houses, the atmosphere of industry and power, the grey sky and scarlet clouds 'reflected the serious intention of the city beneath it' (*ND* 361). Katharine's vision expresses the rapture that indicates a sense of freedom and happiness in her future with Ralph.

Katharine does not see Ralph in Lincoln's Inn Fields. Woolf depicts Katharine's anxiety vividly, when Katharine is writing a letter to Ralph in a coffee shop. She wants to communicate with Ralph, but she cannot find the exact words to express her thought and her stream of emotion, 'as if the whole torrent of Kingsway had to run down her pencil' (*ND* 362). Without finishing her letter, she leaves the coffee shop at closing time. Katharine finds herself 'once more in the street' (*ND* 362). She wants to find Ralph, to take a cab to Highgate, but she cannot remember his correct address. Katharine's London is her map of emotion and imagination. There is no exact road or street name on that map, because Ralph's address can be 'an

Orchard Something, or the street a Hill' (*ND* 362). The real London is shapeless for Katharine, because she walks on the street, follows her own emotion, without any exact purpose. Her indecision about an exact direction in life makes her walk rapidly along one street, and walk as impatiently and 'as rapidly in the other direction' (*ND* 363). The streets make her anxious, overwhelm her, because she is unable to cope with the strength of her own desperate desire, a 'wild, irrational, unexplained, resembling something felt in childhood' (*ND* 363). Her decision to go to see Mary in her flat is a 'goal', a 'rational excuse', something more like a 'solid object' (*ND* 363) for her. She needs something concrete which connects her own map of emotions to the real world, such as the map of Norfolk in her hand.

Ralph seeks his own ultimate vision, an 'orderly world' (*ND* 415). In Chapter V, after seeing Mary, Ralph walks to the Tube at Charing Cross. On his way, he realises that Mary is a smart woman, 'and there's an end of it' (*ND* 53), because he is not in love with her. His vision is split between his dreamy image and the object of his dream: Katharine. For Ralph, Katharine's real figure 'completely routed the phantom one' (*ND* 74). When he finds out that Katharine is engaged to William, Ralph takes a walk on the gravel path in Lincoln's Inn Fields. Mary catches him looking as if he was walking in his sleep, because he is frustrated (*ND* 128). In Ralph's mental image, Katharine is both an 'old view' of night light and a 'new view' in the day light.

The contradictory images of day light and night light worlds in his consciousness express two forms of image: visible and imaginary. Mary has her first revelation – her awareness of Ralph's love for Katharine as 'the light of truth' (*ND* 189) in Lincoln's Inn Fields in the day light. Mary is an observer, who has two revelations in this novel which bring Katharine and Ralph's visions together. Her first revelation is of Ralph's 'disorderly' vision, split between dream and reality. Ralph cannot express his love for Katharine, because she is engaged to William. Once he feels an urge to marry Mary, however, he also wants to disappear and never see her again, since he is in love with Katharine. Katharine's 'tall figure' is an object, which is 'detached from her surroundings' (*ND* 188), on which Ralph focuses his eyes and mind. His sudden recognition of Katharine's figure indicates the visualisation of his mental image of her, 'as if he had thought of her so intensely that his mind had formed the shape of her, rather than that he had seen her in the flesh outside the street' (*ND* 188). The visualisation of Ralph's imaginary Katharine maintains his orderly world. When he sees Katharine in person, he realises that real Katharine looks different from his imagination. As he says to Katharine, 'Yes, I thought I saw you – but it wasn't *you*' (*ND* 191, my italics). Ralph's split vision moves between disorderliness and order; between the dreamy image (*you*) and the recognition of the real figure of Katharine (you). Ralph's vision is ambivalent, which represents the complex outer and inner realities, the visible world in the day light and the mental image in the night light, as the title of the novel *Night and Day* suggests.

In Chapter XXV, Katharine and Ralph's emotions are revealed by their walking, conversation, and thinking. In this chapter, Woolf develops her image of thought, mood and emotion with 'degrees of liking or disliking' (*ND* 271), lingering between inner and outer spheres, detachment and intimacy, loneliness and love, which is independent of the thinking individual and creating 'a destiny' (*ND* 271). Sitting on the bank of the lake in Kew Gardens, at 'a quarter-past three' (*ND* 269), Ralph is gazing at the 'ticking seconds' (*ND* 269) on his watch with a calm determination, waiting for Katharine. Katharine, half an hour late, walks down the grass-walk toward the lake. Ralph is looking at Katharine, in the distance. Her figure is an 'indescribable height' (*ND* 270) with a romantic sense created by the light. A 'purple veil' (*ND* 270) is filled and curved from her shoulders. The visual impressions, the sound of the wind and the smell of flowers, the lake, the 'broad green space', the 'vista of trees with the ruffled gold of the

Thames in the distance and the Ducal castle standing in its meadows' (*ND* 270) create a peaceful scene, where there is not 'a single person' (*ND* 270) in sight, and the stir of the wind in the branches 'so seldom heard by Londoners' (*ND* 271). Katharine feels that she can walk into Kew Gardens happy and relaxed like 'a small child' (*ND* 270).

Ralph expresses his love to Katharine by walking along the tree vista and the glass house with her, talking about a little green plant in its 'Latin name, thus disguising some flower familiar even to Chelsea' (*ND* 271). In the romantic green-blue atmosphere, Katharine is amused by Ralph's explanation of the shape of flowers, their coloured petals, bulbs or seeds. Ralph imagines the utmost fullness of communication with Katharine at Kew Gardens, where he feels the unification of two souls which takes him to a stage of visual ecstasy and emotional sublime, as if he fulfiled his 'wildest dreams' (*ND* 275), when they walk together to the Rock Garden, and then to the Orchid House. In the Orchid House, Ralph gazes at Katharine, which is a 'far-away look entirely lacked self-consciousness' (*ND* 272). He sees her beauty by the orchids, feels his own passion to her among the orchids 'in that hot atmosphere' (*ND* 272). Both of them keep silent with their thoughts, which put them in imaginary positions as lovers upon their 'map of the emotions' (*ND* 272).

In Chapter XXVIII, Ralph has a revelation while he sits in his room. Ralph's mental image of Katharine illustrates his 'terrible extremes of emotion' (*ND* 315) and passionate love for Katharine. His passion makes a 'visionary' image of her beauty, while he possessed a book of photographs from the Greek statues (*ND* 316). Ralph's revelation reinforces his self-awareness of love for Katharine. Ralph explains his ambiguous feelings about falling in love with Katharine, saying 'Mary! I'm in torment! One moment I'm happy, next I'm miserable. I hate her for half an hour, then I'd give my whole life to be with her for ten minutes; all the time I don't know what I feel, or why I feel it; it's insanity, and yet it's perfectly reasonable' (*ND* 320). Mary's second revelation, as she realises that Katharine loves

Ralph, happens when she catches sight of Katharine's dreamy look in Mary's room: '[h]er look, passing beyond Mary, beyond the verge of the room and out beyond any words that came her way, wildly and passionately, convinced Mary that she, at any rate, could not follow such a glance to its end' (*ND* 365). Mary's two revelations reveal love between Ralph and Katharine.

Mary makes a decision to be the 'mistress of her own destiny' (*ND* 365). Her political commitment and her suffrage office in Russell Square indicate her role as 'New Woman' – a celebration of her profession, as the light from her window shines out like 'a sign of triumph shinning there for ever' (*ND* 415), a sign of feminine dignity and faith. As Clive Bell points out in *Old Friends*, Woolf's concern with feminism goes beyond that particular political movement. She has her vision of 'the way in which men, as she thought, patronised women, especially women who were attempting to create works of art or succeed in what were once considered manly professions. Assuredly Virginia did not wish to be a man, or to be treated as a man: she wished to be treated as an equal – [...]',[115] as one can see in *A Room of One's Own* (1929). Woolf demonstrates the gap between the world of elite culture (as in Katharine's family) and the world of suffrage (as in Mary's work). Mary fulfils Katharine's strong predominate desire in Woolf's narrative: to have it all her own way and 'an empty space' (*ND* 83) before her. This 'empty space' can be read as a metaphor, which illuminates a transformation of Katharine's consciousness, from a family drawing-room to a room of her own, in order to develop a profession. Mary is a key reference in the novel. She is an example, which Woolf shows to her readers of the goal a female writer can possibly achieve, if she can free herself from the inheritance of her grand literary predecessors to find a narrative path of her own.

---

[115] Clive Bell, 'Virginia Woolf'. *Old Friends: Personal Recollections*. London: Cassell, 1956, pp.101 – 102.

Painting in Writing: Woolf's Experimental Short Fictions

In *Night and Day*, one can see Woolf's expressing modes of vision, emotion and feeling as an experimental practice of narrative form. She also develops her 'painter in writer' technique in her short fictions. The text of Woolf's short fictions tends to be neglected in studies of her longer works. In contributing to a revaluation of Woolf's achievement, I take up two short fictions, 'A Mark on the Wall' (1917) and 'Kew Gardens' (1919), to explore how emotion and feeling can be expressed by colour in the narrative form. In this way, one can approach an estimate not only of their significant role in Woolf's writings but of their importance in the history of fictional writing, in terms of the relation between verbal and visual arts. For Roger Fry, literary painting is a Cubist way of seeing, as one can see in his comments on Survage's painting; for Virginia Woolf, I would suggest, painterly writing is a composition of colour, shape, thought and emotion through walking, which aims to portray a Post-Impressionist genuine psychology, a mood.

The place of Woolf's short stories within the modern literary history of the genre deserves a study of its own, in terms of a form for generic developments. As Lukács observes, '[t]he short story is the most purely artistic form; it expresses the ultimate meaning of all artistic creation as *mood,* as the very sense and content of the creative process, but it is rendered abstract for that very reason'.[116] For Lukács, this is because the hard/exact outline of matter, modern dailiness, is redeemed by abstract form of vision and mood. Avrom Fleishman also points out that modern short fiction articulates 'emotion'.[117] In Woolf's experimental short fictions, one

---

[116] Georg Lukács, *The Theory of the Novel: A Historico-philosophical Essay on the Forms of Great Epic Literature.* Trans. Anna Bostock. 1971. Cambridge, MA: MIT, 1996, p.51.

[117] Avrom Fleishman, 'Forms of the Woolfian Short Story'. *Virginia Woolf: Revaluation and Continuity.* Ed. Ralph Freeman. Berkeley: University of California Press, 1980, p.48.

can see Woolf's achievement in perspective through her depiction of perception, because vision is the narrative pattern which unifies emotion, the visual object and thought into the narrative form. As Nora Sellei points out, Woolf's use of the perspective of a snail in 'Kew Gardens' is a narrative strategy, which is different from her Victorian predecessors.[118] For Woolf, life does not only mean daily life in the modern metropolis, but also the characters' mental process of perception, which is like a halo surrounding the visual object, making it significant. This halo of thought surrounds the visible object, creates an ambiguous relation between vision and its object; it constructs time, space, memory and all sensorial associations of things into one's own imagination, as Woolf listens to the 'wordless voices',[119] the silence of "Kew Gardens' and the city of London 'murmured',[120] while she sees through the flower-bed, the green-blue atmosphere and 'the pattern of falling words'.[121] In this respect, Woolf's narrative shows the stream of thought and feeling like a vivid drama, in which historical, gender, political and cultural boundaries do not exist, because the halo of thought unifies the subjective vision and the external visual objects, people, things and events; it cancels the boundary which articulates inner and outer spaces, the visible world and the imaginary cityscape.

'A Mark on the Wall'

Woolf's narrative style shows her own characteristic modernism. First of all, the interaction of inner and outer worlds reveals the relation between vision, visible objects, mental image and the halo of thought. 'A Mark on the Wall' (1917) reveals Woolf's methodology for writing modern fiction.

---

[118] Nora Sellei, "The Snail and the Times: Three Stories 'Dancing in Unity'." *Hungarian Journal of English and American Studies*. 3.2 (1997): 189 – 198, p.190.

[119] Virginia Woolf, 'Kew Gardens'. London: Hogarth Press, 1919, p.21.

[120] Woolf, 'Kew Gardens', p.21.

[121] Woolf, 'Kew Gardens', p.13.

She claims that the importance of depicting inner life is a way of 'leaving the description of reality more and more out of [novelists'] stories'.[122] In so doing, the reader may feel shocked, because of modern novelists' discovery of 'half phantoms' of the appearance of these so-called 'realities' – Sunday luncheons, Sunday walks, country houses and tablecloths are 'not entirely real'.[123]

Woolf does not describe the events – walking or dining – rather, she aims to depict the way which her characters think, see and feel about them. Inner life questions and deconstructs the dead image in the photograph and the notion of real standard things, as Woolf pursues the freedom of a writer's imagination. Woolf invents an imaginary world, '[a] world not to be lived in',[124] but a world of free associations of visual emotion, sensations, time, space and memory. She leaves the description of events, makes external objects meaningful by depicting inner life of people in the metropolis. The city, in this light, is a complex of reality and imagination. As Desmond MacCarthy points out, Woolf's portrayal of sensory experience is 'vivid and real', like 'bubbles made of private thoughts and dreams' or '[a]uras, in the sense of temporary and shifting integuments of dreams and thoughts we all carry about with us while pursuing practical aims […]'.[125]

Woolf's experimental short fictions represent visual objects as symbols and metaphors, dismantling traditional structures of character and plot, to establish an ambiguous relation between the real and the imaginary.[126]

---

[122] Virginia Woolf, 'A Mark on the Wall' (1917). *Selected Short Stories by Virginia Woolf.* Ed, Sandra Kemp.1993. London: Penguin, 2000, p.56.

[123] Virginia Woolf, 'A Mark on the Wall'. *Selected Short Stories*, p.57.

[124] Woolf, 'A Mark on the Wall'. *Selected Short Stories*, p.56.

[125] Desmond MacCarthy (Affable Hawk), 'Review', *New Statesman* 9 April 1921, 18. Reprinted in *CH*, p.91.

[126] Woolf's writing shows the dialectic of reality and imagination of life in a coherent progression of thought. As Dean R. Baldwin points out, this process 'reenacts the experience it reports'. See *Virginia Woolf: A Study of the Short Fiction*. Boston: Twayne, 1989, p.14.

Woolf sees the visible world not as events but as relations, in which inner time is a fusion of emotion, mood and space. As Wayne Narey points out, '[Woolf] avoids the linear view of time, where one sees past, present, and future [...], in favor of time that cannot be fixed in duration or progression, a time relative to the beholder'.[127] In 'Kew Gardens', one can see Woolf's portrait of time with memory, space, and colour.

'Kew Gardens'

'Kew Gardens' is a portrait of time. Woolf depicts the garden in two division of time: daytime and inner time. First of all, Kew seems 'a garden blazing in the sun'[128] in Bell's phrase, such as one sees in Impressionist paintings. Secondly, Woolf paints the garden in words as three symbolic moments. Each one of them is a fusion of mood, emotion and memory. In this respect, Woolf's 'Kew Gardens' is a painting in writing, which brings new ways of defining the subject-object dualism. As someone said in an unsigned review in *Time Literary* Supplement, it is "a work of art, made, 'created', as we say, finished, four-square; a thing of original and therefore strange beauty, with its own 'atmosphere', its own vital force".[129]

Woolf's narrative technique is a mixture of the visual and psychological. Colour and shape in this short story suggest Woolf's expression of emotion and mood. E. M. Forster also approaches 'Kew Gardens' by using the idea of 'vision'. Vision, for Forster, means 'something that has been seen'[130] – people, 'coloured blobs' and the green blue atmosphere of Kew'.[131] I suggest

---

[127] Wayne Narey, "Virginia Woolf's 'The Mark on the Wall': An Einsteinian View of Art". *Studies in Short Fiction* 29.1 (1992): 35 – 42, p.37.

[128] Bell, 'Virginia Woolf'. *Old Friends*, p.114.

[129] 'Kew Gardens', unsigned review, *Time Literary Supplement* 29 May 1919. *CH*, pp.66 – 67.

[130] E. M. Forster, 'Visions'. *Daily News* 31 July 1919. *CH*, p.68.

[131] E. M. Forster, 'Visions', *CH*, p.69.

that this 'vision' is expressed by Woolf's 'light', which has two levels: one is visual ('spots of colour raised upon the surface'[132]), the other is psychological ('beneath the surface'[133]). The green earth and the blue sky construct the daytime green-blue atmosphere. Under the green trees, and above the green turf, there are different 'shapes' of colour which express a fusion of emotions: the oval-shaped flower-bed 'there rose perhaps a hundred stalks spreading into heart-shaped',[134] tongue-shaped leaves, man, woman, children, things in red, pink, yellow, brown and black.

Thought, emotion and mood are visualised by symbolic solid objects. The man, Simon, walks six inches in front of his wife 'purposely', for he wants to 'go on with his thoughts'.[135] The lake at Kew and the dragonfly in the garden make him think about a scene, fifteen years ago when he proposed to a woman called Lily. The dragonfly went round and round on Lily's shoe 'with the square silver buckle at the toe',[136] but it 'never settle anywhere'.[137] The moment of seeing the dragonfly and the square silver shoe-buckle is symbolic. Simon himself is like the dragonfly, his emotion makes him to go round and round, but he cannot settle down with Lily. She walks away with her shoes.

The conversation between Simon and his wife, Eleanor, makes her think about a kiss, twenty years ago by the side of a lake (not at Kew), when she was painting 'the first red water-lilies'[138] she had ever seen. As Eleanor walks, she remembers that it was a sudden kiss on the back of her neck, from 'an old grey-haired woman with a wart on her nose', who was to her 'the mother of all kisses' for Eleanor's life.[139] In this very moment,

---

[132] Woolf, 'Kew Gardens', p.2.

[133] Woolf, 'Kew Gardens', p.2.

[134] Woolf, 'Kew Gardens', p.1.

[135] Woolf, 'Kew Gardens', p.3.

[136] Woolf, 'Kew Gardens', p.4.

[137] Woolf, 'Kew Gardens', p.5.

[138] Woolf, 'Kew Gardens', p.6.

[139] Woolf, 'Kew Gardens', p.6.

Eleanor's watch and the snail's shell are Woolf's metaphors of the past and the present time, as she depicts Eleanor's memory – how Eleanor could not paint, how she took her watch by her shaky hands to think about the kiss for five minutes. At this 'time', this particular 'moment' when Eleanor is walking and thinking at Kew with her husband, Woolf's Kew is transferred from a visible/external 'garden' to a 'space' of mood, sensation and memory. A snail is crossing between one stalk to another, which is a parallel to Simon and Eleanor's walk. The snail's shell symbolises the visible Kew, which had been stained by the sunlight, with the flower-bed in red, blue, and yellow colours. Its slight movement for the 'space'[140] of two minutes or so echoes Eleanor's slow walking, with her memory of a kiss. At this moment, the inner and outer spaces, the mental and visual states are fusing together through the act of walking, looking and thinking.

Shape is something one can see, colour expresses the emotion one feels. For instance, when the young man and woman both go to a walk at Kew, eventually stand on the edge of the flower-bed, and together press the end of the young woman's parasol 'deep down into the soft earth', the young man starts to imagine a scene of having tea with her with excitement –

> little white tables, and waitress who looked first at her and then at him; and there was a bill that he would pay with a *real* two shilling piece, and it was *real*, all *real*, he assured himself, fingering the coin in his pocket, *real* to everyone except to him and to her; even to him it began to seem real; and then – but it was *too exciting* to stand and think any longer, […] (my italics).[141]

The scene is only real in the man's imagination, for his emotion for the young woman. The heat, the 'green-blue blue' atmosphere,[142] 'yellow

---

[140] Woolf, 'Kew Gardens', p.7.
[141] Woolf, 'Kew Gardens', p.17.
[142] Woolf, 'Kew Gardens', p.19.

and black, pink and snow white, shapes of all these colours, men, women
and children'[143] at Kew are not only 'visual statements'[144] in Fry's term;
rather, they are symbols of characters' states of mind. The blue and green
sensations create Woolf's painting in poetry: *Blue and Green* (1921), its
pictorial terms suggest the flux of visual experience and renders them
integral and distinct. Clive Bell defines Woolf's narrative form as 'pure',
'almost painterlike vision'.[145] Clive Bell pictured Woolf's passion for
writing in two ways: one through her 'genuine and ardent'[146] feminism at
the tea-table; the other through her 'painterlike'[147] vision in her writings.
Woolf's pure painterly vision, as Bell named it, is a detached 'cool sheet
of glass'.[148] This cool sheet of glass is Woolf's dual vision; through this
objective sheet, one can see the characters' emotion and feeling. It also
leads her pen with a painter's passion and design. This vision redeems the
shape of events to an abstract mood within the narrative form, by which
Woolf finds her own artistic unity. The cool sheet of glass can also be
read as a metaphor of Woolf's camera eye, for which she matures a
cinematographic narrative style in *Mrs Dalloway* (1925).

Roger Fry also comments on a painter's literary vision that he found in
Leopold Survage's paintings. In 'Modern French Art at the Mansard
Gallery' (1919), Fry claims that in Survage's painting, he sees a new kind of
literary painting, which reveals the break of two kinds of painterly visions:
one is the Naturalists' ordinary vision, in which the general structure of their
paintings are 'built on the appearances of our familiar three-dimensional

[143] Woolf, 'Kew Gardens', p.20.

[144] Roger Fry, 'Modern French Art at the Mansard Gallery'. *The Athenaeum* 8
August 1919, 723 – 724. *CH*, p.71.

[145] Clive Bell, 'Clive Bell on Virginia Woolf's Painterly Vision'. *Dial* December
1924, 451 – 465. *CH*, p.144.

[146] Bell, 'Virginia Woolf'. *Old Friends*, p.102.

[147] Bell, 'Virginia Woolf'. *Old Friends*, p.113.

[148] Bell, 'Clive Bell on Virginia Woolf's Painterly Vision'. *CH*, p.143.

space';[149] the other is the Cubists' 'picture vision *de novo*'.[150] Fry sees in him as 'almost precisely the same thing in paint that Mrs Virginia Woolf is in prose'.[151] The visual and psychological multiple angles of seeing an object helps me to see modes of seeing and feeling of Clarissa, Peter and Septimus in *Mrs Dalloway*, which will be the theme of my next chapter.

Conclusion

The association between William James, Henry James and Virginia Woolf indicates a similar, fortuitous perception in three intellectuals. To what extent had Woolf an understanding of William James's train of thought and Henry James's process of vision? C. Lewis Hind, in his *The Post-Impressionists*, quoted William James to show the artistic aim of Post-Impressionism:

> Suppose, for example, that the whole universe of material things –the furniture of earth and choir of heaven – should turn out to be a mere surface-veil of phenomena, hiding and keeping back the world of genuine realities. Such a supposition is foreign neither to common-sense nor to philosophy. Post-Impressionism, at its highest, in its purest, is the search for 'genuine realities'.[152]

Although Woolf's diaries and letters give no direct evidence of such an influence, in 'The Post-Impressionists' (1911), Woolf refers to C. Lewis Hind's 'art sense',[153] which interprets Post-Impressionism as a new form of

---

[149] Roger Fry, 'Modern French Art at the Mansard Gallery'. *The Athenaeum* 8 August 1919, 723 – 724. Reprinted in Allen McLaurin's *Virginia Woolf: The Echoes Enslaved*. Cambridge: Cambridge University Press, 1973, 207 – 209, p.207.

[150] Fry, 'Modern French Art at the Mansard Gallery'. *Virginia Woolf*, p.207.

[151] Fry, 'Modern French Art at the Mansard Gallery'. *Virginia Woolf*, p.208.

[152] C. Lewis Hind, *The Post-Impressionists*. London: Methuen, 1911, p.84.

[153] Hind, *The Post-Impressionist*, p.65.

expressing 'human nature' in art.[154] Her *Night and Day* and experimental short fictions give evidence of a familiarity with the metaphysical language of psychology, and in turning to her early novels and short fictions, I believe that the James brothers and Woolf association is difficult to ignore. Her work can be read as practical examples of her artistic vision, which can be viewed, as metaphorically implies, from several equally valid perspectives. What William James achieved is a new way of seeing psychology; what Woolf aspired to is a new narrative style of fiction. In this respect, Woolf may have used her understanding of phenomenological psychology, to make her writing different from that of her literary predecessors, from Henry James's central process of consciousness, to her own perspective openness and imaginary London, for it coincided with her own approach to fictional writing as a process of viewing the visual as the transmutation of the symbolic, to an expression of an alternate awareness not in a form of visual reality, but an 'emotion which you feel'.[155]

William James's theories of consciousness give one a way to understand Woolf's portrayal of sensuous impressions. Woolf's *Night and Day* shifts from a single centre of consciousness to perceptual openness, just as there is no single focal point in cubist painting. Woolf's multi-consciousness echoes the flux of visual impressions which constructs the complexity of psychological reality. Both William James's idea of psychology and Henry James's idea of fictional writing are close to Woolf, and can illuminate her work. Woolf's portrayal of sensory experience conveys the fusion of internal and external worlds that characterise the psychological turn of the modernist novel.

---

[154] Woolf, 'The Post-Impressionists', *E I*, p.380.
[155] Virginia Woolf, 'On Re-reading Novels' (1922), *E III*, p.340.

CHAPTER THREE

The Dialectic of Time in Film Form: *Mrs Dalloway* and 'The Cinema'

Our eyes, aided by memory, would carve out in space and fix in time the most inimitable of pictures.

-Henri Bergson, *Laughter*[1]

Introduction

The relation between Woolf and the cinema has been explored by a number of critics.[2] In the introduction of *Mrs Dalloway* (1992 Penguin Edition, reprinted in the year 2000), Elaine Showalter points out that the narrative technique of *Mrs Dalloway* is 'very cinematic'[3]. Woolf shared with the Parisian avant-garde an emphasis on the significance of multiple points of view. The Cubists paintings attempted to render a visual object from several perspectives at several different moments, combining the multiplicity of perspective with collage on the two-dimensional canvas. Rudolf E. Kuenzli points out that Léopold Survage's painting, such as *Le Rhythme Coloré*

---

[1] Henri Bergson, *Laughter: an Essay on the Meaning of the Comic*. Trans. Cloudesley Brereton and Fred Rothwell. London: Macmillan, 1911, p.150.

[2] See Michael H. Whitworth's *Virginia Woolf* (Oxford: Oxford UP, 2005) for an introduction to Woolf and cinematic adaptation. For the relation between the literary text *Mrs Dalloway* and the film *The Hours*, see Carol Iannone's "Woolf, Women, and 'The Hours'" in *Commentary* 115.4 (2003): 50 – 53, and Heather Levy's "Apothecary and Wild Child: What Lies Between the Acts of 'The Hours' and *Mrs Dalloway* (*Virginia Woolf Bulletin* 13 May 2003, 40 – 49).

[3] Elaine Showalter, 'Introduction'. *Mrs Dalloway* (1925). London: Penguin, 2000, xxi.

(1912), 'outlines the future direction of abstract art as cinema'.[4] Avant-garde cinema is an extension of painting, in which Cubist and Futurist painters captured the sensation of physical movement in their work. As Kuenzli suggests, avant-garde painters saw in film 'a means of overcoming the static nature of painting through moving pictures'.[5] And yet, the Cubist cinema does not only create pictures that move; it is an experimental visual language of signs, in which abstract shapes contain meanings.

I suggest that through reading Bergson, one can see Woolf's characters as sharply clear figures, for Woolf is using a Cubist perspective to show a character through the dialectical relation between the inner and outer, time and movement; depicting what Deleuze has called the time-image in her characters' consciousness as they move about London. I would argue that although Bergson does not attempt to connect his philosophy of *la durée* to the reading of motion pictures, Deleuze's writing on the cinema, in which he re-invented Bergson's idea of pure duration in the cinematic context, helps one to understand how Woolf's fictional writing explores the aesthetics and the philosophy of the cinema. Woolf wrote *Mrs Dalloway* through a movie camera. In this novel, she depicts 'the time-image', which according to Deleuze emerged at the turning point of the cinema, from the pre-war movement-image to the post-war time-image. Woolf's cinematic narrative technique is significant and unique, and can be usefully explicated through Deleuze's view of the time-image as the 'pure visual situation' in the cinema.

Several critics have discussed the cinematic reproduction of Woolf's *Mrs Dalloway* (1925). For example, Leslie Hankins discusses the way which the cinema could decode Woolf's aged Clarissa, for it has been 'carefully coded'.[6] For example, when Clarissa gazes into the mirror and

4   Rudolf E. Kuenzli, 'Introduction'. *Dada and Surrealist Film*. 1987. Ed. Rudolf E. Kuenzli. Cambridge, MA: MIT, 1996, p.1.
5   Kuenzli, 'Introduction'. *Dada and Surrealist Film*, p.1.
6   Leslie Hankins, '"To kindle and illuminate": Woolf's Hot Flashes Against

looks at her own body, this for Hankins, is the way that Woolf coded menopause, hinted at in the reference to Clarissa's illness. Hankins claims that one would direct Woolf's novel by using 'experimental cinematography, innovative techniques of rhythms and editing, and daring play with superimposition, lens distortion and visual emotion'.[7] Hankins's analysis of the text offers the possibility of imagining Woolf's *Mrs Dalloway* on the cinema screen. Diane F. Gillespie, on the other hand, demonstrates the possibility of using cinematic renditions in the classroom.[8] However, in this chapter, my focus is not on Woolf and cinematic adaptations, such as the film *Mrs Dalloway* (1998), or on how Woolf's literary text *Mrs Dalloway* happens to be an inspiration of other people's literary/cinematic works. I explore how Virginia Woolf develops her narrative style by using a new visual language. Her observation of the cinema, as a form of modern art, focuses on how the cinema could express human emotion, as one can see in her essay 'The Cinema' (1926). And yet, before she commented on the cinema in this particular essay, Woolf was using cinematic-like form in her narrative. The cinema offered Woolf a new visual aesthetics. In reading *Mrs Dalloway*, one can see how its cinematic narrative form synthesises multiple points of view, the past and the present, *la durée* and clock time through Woolf's use of cinematic language: shots and filmic techniques, such as close-up, flashback, montage. In addition, by examining Woolf's cinematic narrative style, one can see how memory functions in motion, constructing the time-image, as Deleuze phrases it. Woolf explores the temporality of her characters through memory. The character's experience of time is visualised in the process of

---

Ageism – Challenges for Cinema'. *Virginia Woolf and Her Influences: Selected Papers from the Seventh Annual Conference on Virginia Woolf*. New York: Pace University Press, 1998, p.26.

[7] Hankins, '"To kindle and illuminate": Woolf's Hot Flashes Against Ageism – Challenges for Cinema', p.31.

[8] Diane F. Gillespie, '*Mrs Dalloway* and Film'. *Virginia Woolf and Her Influences*, p.162.

reterritorialisation and reconfiguring of the gaze. For the sake of clarity I have kept these sections separate, detailing the theory first, before using *Mrs Dalloway* as illustration.

Part I:
The Art of the Cinema in Philosophy and Literature – Bergson, Deleuze and Woolf

Henri Bergson: Time in the Cinematic Sense

Henri Bergson's notion of time is crucial to the emergence of modernism. In this section, I aim to trace Bergson's pure duration within the moment of Cubism, in order to see how his philosophy of duration helps one to understand Woolf's cinematic narrative form. The relation between Bergson's notion of time and Woolf's stream of consciousness has been noticed by many critics, and yet, there is still room for further exploration of the relation between Bergson's notion of *la durée* and Woolf's cinematic way of writing. I would suggest that Woolf's narrative form demonstrates her use of 'the time-image' in a metaphorical way. As Mary Ann Gillies points out, although there is no direct evidence to show that Woolf had read Bergson's work, a survey of Woolf criticism illustrates that many critics have noted 'a Bergson strain'[9] in Woolf's work. As early as 1932, according to Gillies, it had been discussed in Floris Delattre's 'La durée bergsonienne dans le roman de Virginia Woolf' published in 1932, which suggested that Bergson's work had had 'an impact'[10] on Woolf. Both Winifrid Holtby, also in 1932, and David Daiches, in 1942, claimed that Bergson is a force in Woolf's writing. By the mid 1950s and early 1960s, critics like James

---

[9] Mary Ann Gillies, *Henri Bergson and British Modernism*. Montreal: McGill-Queen's University Press, 1996, p.107.

[10] Gillies, *Henri Bergson and British Modernism*, p.107.

Hafley and Jean Guiguet carefully charted where Bergson's philosophy and Woolf's writing met.

Margaret Church's *Time and Reality: Studies in Contemporary Fiction* (1949) was the first book which clearly stated that Woolf's perception of time enabled her to find a new way of expressing the inner life, memory and emotion.[11] According to Church, inner time makes possible unique moments, a 're-creation of time past in the present moment', as one can see in Bergson's *la durée*.[12] Shiv K. Kumar, in *Bergson and the Stream of Consciousness Novel* (1962), claims that a novel like *Mrs Dalloway* makes 'a positive affirmation of a view of experience which can be understood in terms of Bergson's durational flux'.[13] However, as I have demonstrated in my second chapter, William James's concept of 'the stream of consciousness' helps one to understand Woolf's psychological turn in terms of narrative style. In this chapter, I suggest that Bergson's notion of time will be helpful in understanding Woolf's writing style in the context of the cinema.

A. A. Mendilow, in *Time and the Novel* (1972), points out the importance of time in the novel, claiming that 'the problems of time, its treatment and values', have been 'applied to the medium, theme and form' of the arts, for 'time is central to all our thinking'.[14] The emphasis on the significance of time is shown in the novel in new narrative techniques. According to Mendilow, Bergson's *la durée* is not only a contribution to metaphysics, but also 'to many of the fundamental problems of fiction',[15] for his theory brings new conceptions of character, plot and structure to the novel form. In this respect, a character in the novel can be read 'in the light of its moment-by-moment

---

[11] Margaret Church, *Time and Reality: Studies in Contemporary Fiction*. Chapel Hill: University of North Carolina Press, 1949, p.70.

[12] Church, *Time and Reality*, p.76.

[13] Shiv K. Kumar, *Bergson and the Stream of Consciousness Novel*. London: Blackie & Son, 1962, p.6.

[14] A. A. Mendilow, *Time and the Novel*. New York: Humanities, 1972, p.15.

[15] Mendilow, *Time and the Novel*, p.149.

renewal, as the ever-present past, which changes as it increases with his moving time-field, pours into and through the formation we call a human being'.[16]

The nature of time, as Mary Ann Gillies points out, is Bergson's central concern.[17] Time is a metaphysical problem, which involves memory, and the nature of inner time is related to all forms of sensory experience. *La durée* is life itself, a past in a living present. In *Time and Free Will*, Bergson uses the concept of *la durée* to explain that the nature of inner time is a matter of its quality not quantity. A quotation from Bergson will make this point clearer:

> Pure duration is the form which the succession of our conscious states assumes when our ego lets itself *live*, when it refrains from separating its present state from its former states. [...]. Nor need it forget its former states: it is enough that, in recalling these states, it does not set them alongside its actual state as one point alongside another, but forms both the past and the present states into an organic whole, [...], a living being [...].[18]

Pure duration is a psychic state, a form of organic whole, in which both the past and the present are synthesised in a moment, a 'dynamic temporal flux',[19] as Schwartz puts it. This 'moment' is a metaphor for a particular state of mind. According to Arthur Szathmary, it is 'an aesthetic mode of apprehension, a grasp of the peculiar and unique qualities of concrete objects'.[20] Bergson explains pure duration by giving an example of how

---

[16] Mendilow, *Time and the Novel*, p.150.

[17] Mary Ann Gillies, "Bergsonism: 'Time out of Mind'." *A Concise Companion to Modernism*. Ed. David Bradshaw. Oxford: Blackwell, 2003, p.98.

[18] Henri Bergson, *Time and Free Will* (1889). Trans. F. L. Pogson. New York: Dover, 2001, p.100.

[19] Sanford Schwartz, *The Matrix of Modernism: Pound, Eliot, and Early Twentieth-Century Thought*. Princeton, NJ: Princeton University Press, 1985, p.27.

[20] Arthur Szathmary, *The Aesthetic Theory of Bergson*. Cambridge, MA: Harvard

one's consciousness can project past time and space, extending that time and space as a 'mental image'[21] into the present moment. In this respect, a two-second kiss (quantity of time, clock time) from the past will be recalled as an image by someone at a particular psychological/emotional moment (quality of time, inner time). This mental image is a virtual image, which is like a scene on the screen, a projection of emotion in the brain. Pure duration is a juxtaposition of different impressions and emotions, a montage of consciousness, in which the past lives. In Bergson's aesthetics, a novelist's task is to show pure duration as 'an infinite permeation of a thousand different impressions',[22] by depicting the moment when memory, past time and space invade the present psychic state. Pure duration sets one free, in which one approaches the flux as intuition, the movement of the inner and outer exchange as mental images in one's own consciousness.

Pure duration is the sign of inner life, the inner time. Memory can be stimulated by the external world, which is physically outside of the mind, but at the same time also regained by the mind. In this respect, the external world can be transformed by the consciousness into pure duration, in which the past (memory of a visual object, a smell, a taste) and the present are synthesised into one. In *Matter and Memory*, Bergson explains how memory is recalled as a virtual image by 'the internal movements'[23] of the brain. The brain reacts to external objects at the present time, meanwhile past matters are recalled as memories in the brain, 'regarded as images'.[24] For

---

University Press, 1937, p.37.

[21] Bergson, *Time and Free Will*, p.101. Mark Antliff also points out that pure duration is 'a synthesis of the temporal and spatial'. It presents a deeper / inner reality. See 'The Rhythms of Duration: Bergson and the Art of Matisse'. *The New Bergson*. Ed. John Mullarkey. Manchester: Manchester University Press, 1999, p.188.

[22] Bergson, *Time and Free Will*, p.133.

[23] Henri Bergson, *Matter and Memory* (1896). Trans. Nancy Margaret Paul and W. Scott Palmer. New York: Zone Books, 1991, p.23.

[24] Bergson, *Matter and Memory*, p.23.

Leszek Kolakowski, these images are 'signs' of time.[25] Images of memory can be read as a system of signs, as they continuously move in consciousness.[26] In the following paragraph, one can see the way Bergson depicts the relation between the external world, memory and being, in order to demonstrate a continuous form of becoming:

> Here is a system of images which I term my perception of the universe, and which may be entirely altered by a very slight change in a certain privileged image – *my body*. This image occupies the center; by it all the others are conditioned; at each of its movements everything changes, as though by a turn of a kaleidoscope.[27]

There are two systems of image: one is the system of images which we think of as our perception of the external world (matter), the other is the system of images which are those of our consciousness, dependant on 'a certain privileged image' (memory of the remembering body). The movement of the brain, our thought, is transformed into energy, kaleidoscoping the past through the present, by which one can see a visual object differently at different moments and from different perspectives. This is an organic process, through which the privileged image is associated with the universe, and the external world is 'within' a certain state of mind. Pure duration involves memory, which prolongs one past image into a plurality of living moments. In this respect, the past image and the present matter 'coexist' in the moment of duration. Memory associates one's present experience with the past, blurring the boundary between the past and the present.

In *An Introduction to Metaphysics*, Bergson shows the reader how pure duration can be communicated and expressed within the multiplicity of metaphysical forms, and distinguishes 'two profoundly different ways of

---

[25] Leszek Kolakowski, *Bergson*. Oxford: Oxford University Press, 1985, p.15.

[26] Kolakowski, *Bergson*, p.25.

[27] Bergson, *Matter and Memory*, p.25.

knowing a thing'.[28] The first way of knowing a thing, according to Bergson, is 'the *relative*',[29] which one felt by moving around the object. It depends on 'the point of view'[30] at which one is placed and on 'the symbols'[31] by which one expresses oneself. The second way of knowing a thing is 'the *absolute*', the essence of the known.[32] It does not rely on any symbol or point of view. Rather, it is a state of mind, in which one enters into the essence of a thing. Paul Douglass points out that on the one hand, Bergson 'damned the cinematographical mechanism of thought as the apotheosis of spatialisation',[33] as critics like F. C. T. Moore have also noted. And yet, Douglass also points out that Bergson, on the other hand, like Virginia Woolf, sees the potential of the cinema, because of its ability to unroll the past, finding its own language and symbols, as critics such as Georges-Michel, Emile Vuillermoz and Gilles Deleuze have argued.[34]

I suggest that Bergson's two ways of seeing a thing, moving around something externally, and looking within, illuminate the way in which Bergson's idea stimulated the artistic work of the Parisian Avant-Garde, such as Cubist painting and cinema. As Mark Antliff points out, Bergson's philosophy was important to the Cubists, the 'Parisian avant-garde' at a time when Bergson's philosophy 'was part of a cultural controversy that began around 1905 and reached its apex in the months preceding the First World War'.[35] In this respect, Antliff considers Bergson's theory as 'part of a larger cultural matrix'.[36] I believe this point of view helps one to

---

[28] Henri Bergson, *An Introduction to Metaphysics* (1903). Trans. T. E. Hulme. Indianapolis: Hackett, 1999, p.21.

[29] Bergson, *An Introduction to Metaphysics*, p.21.

[30] Bergson, *An Introduction to Metaphysics*, p.21.

[31] Bergson, *An Introduction to Metaphysics*, p.21.

[32] Bergson, *An Introduction to Metaphysics*, p.21.

[33] Paul Douglass, 'Bergson and Cinema: Friends or Foes'? *New Bergson*, p.209.

[34] Douglass, 'Bergson and Cinema', p.214.

[35] Antliff, *Inventing Bergson*, p.3.

[36] Antliff, *Inventing Bergson*, p.6.

understand the aesthetics of Bergson's 'movement' and 'time' in relation to avant-garde Cubism. The Cubists' vision of modern life incorporates the multiple dimensions of time. The Cubists used their canvases to create an organic, intuitive, rhythmic unity, which establishes the multiplicity of consciousness, gaze, and geometric forms.

The Cubists incorporated 'time' in their works by 'moving around' an object, in order to give 'a concrete representation of it'.[37] While the Impressionists had depicted the changing of sunlight at different moments of a day, on different canvases; the Cubists, on the other hand, portray what a visual object looks like from different angles, all on one canvas. In other words, the Cubists perceive time through movement. The time-image, in this respect, is a production of movement. Bergson takes a character in a novel as an example, to demonstrate the way a character can be portrayed and understood:

> Consider, again, a character whose adventures are related to me in a novel. The author may multiply the traits of his hero's character, may make him speak and act as he pleases, but all this can never be equivalent if I were able for an instant to identify myself with the person of the hero himself. Out of that indivisible feeling as from a spring, all the words, gestures, and actions of the man would appear to me to flow naturally. [...]. All the things I am told about the man provide me with so many points of view from which I can observe him. [...] Symbols and points of view, therefore, place me outside him; they give me only what he has in common with others, and not what belongs to him and to him alone.[38]

The *absolute* view (the character's feeling, the inward, an interior, the inner life, a state of mind) leads the reader to enter the heart of the character, to see the essential person. The *relative* ('all the words, gestures, and actions of the

---

[37] Antliff, *Inventing Bergson*, p.3.
[38] Bergson, *An Introduction to Metaphysics*, p.22.

men'), on the other hand, maintains a detached point of view, which places the reader outside of the character. For Bergson, the *absolute* gives the intuitive truth about the character, and he sees the relative as exterior and limited; but, as Antliff points out, the Cubists believed they were extending Bergson's insights in portraying a character or an object from multiple points of view, illuminating how different points of view and time can be juxtaposed on the same canvas, portraying Bergson's flux in visual ways.

In *Creative Evolution*, Bergson uses cinematic terms to define pure duration as 'the cinematographical instinct of our thought'.[39] According to Bergson, pure duration 'is the intuition that we have of mind when we draw aside the veil which is interposed between our consciousness and ourselves'.[40] The word 'cinematographical' is used by Bergson in a metaphorical way, which does not refer to the cinema per se (so does Irigaray's use of 'mirror' as a metaphor: there is no 'mirror' as such). It is a metaphor of the mechanism of the inner time as an 'instinct' of thought. Deleuze develops Bergson's philosophy of pure duration, re-inventing *la durée* as the synthesis of the movement-image and the time-image of the cinema, as I aim to show in the following section.

Re-imagining Bergson: Deleuze's Semiology of the Cinema and Woolf's Time-Image

Henri Bergson conceives the mind as a fusion of movement and continuity. Motion pictures similarly illustrate a stream of thought through images. According to Deleuze in *Bergsonism* (1966), a 'return to Bergson' means not just a 'renewed admiration for a great philosopher but a renewal or an extension of his project today'.[41] For Deleuze, the concept of

---

[39] Henri Bergson, *Creative Evolution* (1907). Trans. Arthur Mitchell. New York: Dover, 1998, p.316

[40] Bergson, *Creative Evolution*, p.272.

[41] Gilles Deleuze, *Bergsonism* (1966). New York: Zone Books, 1991, p.115.

movement is central, and critics have stressed the significance of motion in Deleuze's theory of the cinema. For example, Carolyn Abbs, in her 'Virginia Woolf and Gilles Deleuze: Cinematic e-motion and the Mobile Subject', argues that Woolf's cinematic writing expresses the speed of modern life, by depicting 'the technology of the time, the train, the motor-car, as a new perspective on life'.[42] Abbs explores the way Woolf's writing creates mobility, connecting it to Deleuze's theory of the movement-image. Based on an understanding of his concept, Abbs sees the mobility of the point of view as a moving camera in Woolf's writing. However, through my reading of Bergson in the previous section, I will suggest, in this section, that the Cubists' development of Bergson's ideas as a way of seeing has already offered a model for multiple points of view in seeing a character. Through reading Deleuze, I can see the importance of the Cubist perspective once again, in his discovery of the time-image in movement. In other words, the point of view has shifted from the external motion to the internal perspective; the image of thought is reinforced by the movement of the body in the process of instant becoming in Bergson's *Creative Evolution.*

By reading Bergson, Deleuze sees that the relation between the movement-image (the image of physical reality in the external world) and the time-image (psychological reality in one's consciousness) can no longer be opposed. Deleuze's semiology of the cinema is constructed in the Hegelian dialectical relation between the movement-image and the time-image. In *Cinema 1: the Movement-Image* (first published in France as *Cinema 1, l'Image-Movement*, 1983), Deleuze explores the way one can think with images, by which he introduces 'movement to thought'.[43]

---

[42] Carolyn Abbs, 'Virginia Woolf and Gilles Deleuze: Cinematic E-motion and the Mobile Subject'. *Interactive Media* 1 (2005): 1 – 20, p.6.

[43] Gilles Deleuze, 'The Brain Is the Screen: An Interview with Gilles Deleuze'. *The Brain Is the Screen: Deleuze and the Philosophy of Cinema.* Ed. Gregory

Deleuze tries to express a Cubist way of seeing in terms of the cinematic form, such as frame, shot, and multiple angles/points of view. He reads cinematic form as an expression of Cubist perception, such as one can see in Cubist paintings. For Deleuze, the Cubist perspective expresses pure movement, because "it decomposes and recomposes the set, and, it also relates to a fundamentally open whole, whose essence is constantly to 'become' or to change, to endure; and vice versa".[44] In the process of decomposing and recomposing, the viewer sees the essence of the cinematographic movement-image. A Cubist shot is a mobile section of movements; which constantly puts 'bodies, parts aspects, dimensions, distances and the respective positions of the bodies which make up a set in the image into variation'.[45] Deleuze quotes Jean Epstein's comparison between a camera shot and a Cubist painting: 'All the surfaces are divided', as he observes,

> truncated, decomposed, broken, as one imagines that they are in the thousand-faced eyes of the insect – descriptive geometry whose canvas is the limit shot. Instead of submitting to perspective, this painter splits it, enters it. ... For the perspective of the outside he thus substitutes the *perspective of the inside*, a multiple perspective [...].[46]

A Cubist shot presents multiple points of view. In order to pursue the essence of the object, a Cubist painter depicts the gesture of looking itself, the movement of the gazing body, in which one perceives time through multiple points of view. As when Monet depicted the changing of sunlight in different periods of a day on different canvas, Albert Gleizes painted *Chartres Cathedral* in 1912 to express the essence of the cathedral from

---

Flaxman. Minneapolis: University of Minnesota Press, 2000, p.366.

[44] Gilles Deleuze. *Cinema 1: The Movement-Image* (1983). Trans. Hugh Tomlinson and Barbara Habberjam. London: Continuum, 2005, p.24.

[45] Deleuze. *Cinema 1*, p.24.

[46] Deleuze. *Cinema 1*, pp.24 – 25.

multiple points of view on one canvas. Deleuze argues for the multiple perspective, to illustrate the Cubists' way of looking at a visual object. In the cinema, according to Deleuze, a Cubist perspective 'conveys a relief in time, a perspective in time; it expresses time itself as perspective or relief'.[47] The concept of a Cubist shot is to express changing points of view, which enable the cinematographic perception to work as *'a temporal perspective'*.[48] A Cubist shot is not 'a certain instant' or an immobile section, as one sees in photography. Rather, it constitutes a variable, continuous and temporal mould. It is the essence of the movement-image, which reveals a transition point where the cinema is aware, as André Bazin suggests, of 'the paradox of moulding itself on the time of the object and of taking the imprint of its duration as well'.[49] In this respect, a Cubist perspective is not only a representation of the speed of the motion; rather, it is an expression of the image of time in the act of looking.

Deleuze's argument helps one to understand Woolf's cinematic-like writing. In 'Evening over Sussex: Reflections in a Motor-car', Woolf depicts her physical experience of sitting in a motor-car, looking out of the window and most importantly, her image of thought at that particularly moment. The window of the motor-car is a piece of glass, like the camera lens. The looking eye/body in a moving motor-car is like a camera, which is shooting the landscape of Sussex. Woolf portrays the landscape from a Cubist perspective, in which the landscape looks like a fractioned medley of objects: all Eastbourne, the brown line of cliffs, the red villas on the coast, the pink clouds, the green fields, 'all seems blown to its fullest and tautest, with beauty and beauty and beauty, a pin bricks; it collapses'.[50] Woolf's multiple point

---

[47] Deleuze. *Cinema 1*, p.25.

[48] Deleuze. *Cinema 1*, p.25.

[49] Deleuze. *Cinema 1*, p.25.

[50] Virginia Woolf, 'Evening over Sussex: Reflections in a Motor-car'. *Collected Essays by Virginia Woolf: Volume Two*. London: Hogarth Press, 1966, p.290.

of view is shown not only by a Cubist fracturing of the external landscape, but also by a conversation among four 'I's – 'the self splits up'[51] to the physical, the mental 'I's, 'I' the third party, and 'myself',[52] by which Woolf observes multiple dimensions of the landscape and her own thought as the car speeds along, 'for the beauty [of the landscape] spread, at one's right hand, at one's left; [at one's front], at one's back too'.[53] Because of the motion of the motor-car, the beauty of the landscape 'was escaping all the time'.[54]

These four 'I's express not only the multiple dimensions of the landscape, but also the multiple dimensions of time: the past, the present, the future, and pure duration. The present time (when the car is in motion) is January, the first month of a year, but the mind has a feeling of melancholy. The mind is full of images of thought, which expresses time in motion when 'I' the third party said to 'myself': 'Gone, gone; over, over; past and done with, past and done with. I feel life left behind even as the road is left behind. We have been over that stretch, and are already forgotten'. The road past is like the life past, the time past – a second, a minute, an hour, a day, a month and a year. In Woolf's metaphor, sitting in a moving motor-car, for the 'I', is such a passive and nostalgic feeling, because one can only see the passing of the road, life and time, without any power to stop the motion of the universe. 'There, windows were lit by our lamps for a second; the light is out now'.[55] At this very moment, the fourth 'I' sees the light of the star. A star light is a light comes from the past, but for the fourth 'I', it is a sign of the future. The star light is the 'I''s past, but the gaze of the 'I' is the star's future.

As Eisenstein points out in his 'The Filmic Fourth Dimension' (1929), the method of montage is the juxtaposition and the combination of a

---

51 Woolf, 'Evening over Sussex: Reflections in a Motor-car', p.290.
52 Woolf, 'Evening over Sussex: Reflections in a Motor-car', p.291.
53 Woolf, 'Evening over Sussex: Reflections in a Motor-car', p.290.
54 Woolf, 'Evening over Sussex: Reflections in a Motor-car', p.290.
55 Woolf, 'Evening over Sussex: Reflections in a Motor-car', p.291.

sequence of shots, according to their dominating indications.[56] Woolf's four 'I's can be compared to four shots, which are dominated by different dimensions of time in movement. In this respect, a montage complex is a two-fold overtone, which is not merely within the physical movement of the camera eye (the shot); rather, it is in 'the physical process of a *higher nervous activity*',[57] when the viewer sees the inner movement (the image of thought) in the movement of the motor-car. Montage makes the cinema a medium of great potential, because its visual language is suggestive, in which 'I see' and 'I feel' form a dialectical process of cinematic aesthetic experience. The cinema creates a world of creative evolution in Bergson's sense (in response to Albert Einstein's relativity); one lives in a 'four-dimensional space-time continuum'.[58] The speed of thought (Bergson) is like the speed of light (Einstein). Theoretically one can move from one space/physical dimension to another, from the past and back to the future, when one achieves the speed of light. The flash of light, as a symbol of the speed of thought, makes the consciousness move from one image to another.

To return to Woolf, suddenly the eye/'I' and the star emerge into all kinds of lights, the 'I'

> Feel[s] that the light over the downs there emerging, dangles from the future. [...]. I feel suddenly attached not to the past but to the future. [...]. Draughts fan-blown by electric power will cleanse houses. Lights intense and firmly directed will go over the earth, doing the work. Looking at the moving light on that hill; it is the headlight of a car. By day and by night Sussex in five centuries will be full of charming thoughts, quick, effective beams.[59]

---

56 Sergei Eisenstein, ''The Filmic Forth Dimension' (1929). *Film Form: Essays in Film Theory*. Ed. Jay Leyda. New York: Harcourt, Brace and Company, 1949, p.64.
57 Eisenstein, *Film Form*, p.67.
58 Eisenstein, *Film Form*, p.70.
59 Woolf, 'Evening over Sussex: Reflections in a Motor-car', p.292.

The light synthesises the multiple points of view, which composes the movement of the motor-car, the landscape, the star, the looking eye/I; it also synthesises all different dimensions of time – the past, the present, and the future, into one moment of pure duration, in an image of thought as quick and effective as a flash of beam in a moment of perception. Woolf is using light in a symbolic way to synthesise her moment of vision. Frances Guerin in *A Culture of Light: Cinema and Technology in 1920s Germany* claims that the use of light in particular, in a number of 1920s German films, offers an 'insight into their unique representations of a new industrialized way of life',[60] which gives significant meaning to the films' structure. Film technology brings the possibility of manipulating light, in order to produce a unique filmic vision by interacting with the Expressionist sets, as one can see in *Caligari*. Lighting is the structure of that film, because different lights express the development of plot, suggesting different atmospheres and states of mind. The use of light, in this respect, connects the film aesthetic to film technology. Light is recognised in both daily life and works of art. On the one hand, light gives structure and psychological depth to the cinema; on the other hand, electrical light is one important aspect of film technology which came to define the intense industrial growth and social transformation of the 1920s. Developments in sound, transport, and communications technologies, for instance, all gathered forced in the 1920s. The cinema also interacts with sound, speed and telecommunications during this period.

One cannot understand the time-image without mastering the movement-image and Bergson's two systems of images, as I have mentioned in the previous section. In the context of a Cubist perception, one can express time in movement. In this respect, the movement-image is not only a representation of the motion of a visual object. The film is the montage of a series of shots, a machine assemblage of experiments on its

---

[60] Frances Guerin, Introduction. *A Culture of Light: Cinema and Technology in 1920s Germany*. Minneapolis: University of Minnesota Press, 2005, xvi.

own conditions in terms of the relation between movement and time. As Woolf claims in her essay 'The Cinema' (1926), the birth of the cinema is a strange thing. The cinema is the youngest art, which has been born 'fully-clothed' while other forms of art were 'born naked'.[61] Other arts begun with primitive tools: it begins with sophisticated technology, and it inherits all the devices of the other arts. It can say anything 'before it has anything to say',[62] because the so-called cinematic techniques such as flashback and close-up, have been used to explore the relation between movement and time, in theatre, literature and painting long before the birth of the cinema. Sergei Eisenstein has a similar argument in 'Dickens, Griffith, and the Film Today' (1944). He claims that the cinema today is not a 'virgin-birth', 'without parents and without pedigree, without a past, without the traditions and rich cultural heritage of the past epochs'.[63] Many of Eisenstein's articles on the cinema were published in the film journal *Close Up* (edited by Kenneth Macpherson). In the January 1929 issue of *Close Up*, the frontispiece displays a photograph of Eisenstein inscribed: 'To K. Macpherson – Editor of the Closest Up to what cinema should be'. *Close Up* published nine translations of Eisenstein's writing between May 1929 and June 1933, in addition to a number of occasional pieces about him and his work.[64]

Eisenstein's theory of montage helps one to understand Woolf's narrative technique in *Mrs Dalloway*. Montage synthesises the dialectical relation between the movement-image and the time-image, completing the depth of the cinematographic perception, where, as Deleuze says, 'the

---

[61] Virginia Woolf, 'The Cinema' (1926). *The Captain's Death Bed and Other Essays.* London: Hogarth Press, 1950, p.171.

[62] Woolf, 'The Cinema', p.171.

[63] Sergei Eisenstein, 'Dickens, Griffith, and the Film Today' (1944). *Film Form*, p.232.

[64] James Donald, Anne Friedberg and Laura Marcus, 'Preface'. *Close Up 1927 – 1933: Cinema and Modernism.* Eds. James Donald, Anne Friedberg and Laura Marcus. London: Cassell, 1998, viii.

image is in movement rather than being movement-image'.[65] As Gregory Flaxman points out, montage breaks down the chronological nature of story-telling in classical narrative, for it is always a 'mixed art', a practice of 'combining images and creating relations'.[66]

I want to address the significant relation between Woolf's writing and Deleuze's semiology of the cinema, to see how Woolf treats the time-image as a system of signs. Before I analyse Woolf's *Mrs Dalloway*, I want to go through Deleuze's notion of the time-image: how can an image crystallise time? How can spatialised/ quantitative time be transformed to qualitative time through the time-image? In *Cinema 2: the Time-Image* (originally published in France as *Cinema 2, l'Image-Temps*, 1985), Deleuze goes beyond the concept of the movement-image, to take his semiology of the cinema to another level – the time-image. According to Deleuze, the post-war cinema transforms the movement-image into the time-image, because '[t]ime is out of joint: [...] time is no longer subordinated to movement, but rather movement to time'.[67] This 'movement' here means a process of Becoming; a process from a character's gaze to a visual object, which turns the physical object into an imaginary one within a '*pure optical situation*'.[68] The construction of the time-image allows Deleuze to explore a number of important issues of modern thought, such as the dialectical relation between the outside and the inside, truth and falsity, body and brain. Deleuze reads the time-images as signs of the order of time, to see the inner time as signs of a series of thought images. Deleuze's way of seeing helps one to see Woolf's novel writing through the eyes of a film-maker, as I will show in the following section.

---

[65] Deleuze. *Cinema 1*, p.26.

[66] Gregory Flaxman, Introduction. *The Brain Is the Screen: Deleuze and the Philosophy of Cinema*. Minneapolis: University of Minnesota Press, 2000, p.27.

[67] Gilles Deleuze, Preface. *Cinema 2: The Time-Image* (1985). Trans. Hugh Tomlinson and Robert Galeta. London: Continuum, 2005, xi.

[68] Deleuze, *Cinema 2*, p.2.

For Deleuze, the time-image is where 'thought' appears through a number of cinematic forms, such as the re-linage of images by inter-cuts.[69] This cinematic form can express a complex of consciousness. For instance, a character can invest a setting through his or her imaginary gaze, to transform an image-action to an optical-image. In the cinema, a director like Antonioni can transform the movement-image (actions) into the time-image by flashback, which dislocates body, movement and action in time.[70] Fellini, on the other hand, uses the time-image to synthesise the external and internal worlds. The time-image is a formula, through which the physical/external world becomes 'spectacle' or 'spectacular', as if the action 'floats' in the pure optical situation, in order to achieve a visionary aestheticism.[71] The cinema, in this respect, is no longer a form of sensory-motor linkages; rather, it is primarily and fundamentally optical, in which time can be crystalised in different forms, such as recollection-images, dream-images, fantasies, and so forth.

According to Deleuze, the time-image is a virtual image, because he sees the time-image as the 'double'[72] of the actual image created through cinematic techniques, such as flashback. In flashback, Deleuze sees the 'coalescene'[73] between the real and its reflection, 'actual *and* virtual'.[74] The coalescene of these two is the dialectic, 'a double movement of liberation and capture'.[75] In the time-image, the world has become 'memory',[76] the brain itself has become 'consciousness',[77] projecting the duration of the past and the present, the inner and the outer spheres on the

---

[69] Deleuze, Preface. *Cinema 2*, xvii.
[70] Deleuze, *Cinema 2*, p.5.
[71] Deleuze, *Cinema 2*, pp.4 – 5.
[72] Deleuze, *Cinema 2*, p.66.
[73] Deleuze, *Cinema 2*, p.66.
[74] Deleuze, *Cinema 2*, p.67.
[75] Deleuze, *Cinema 2*, p.66.
[76] Deleuze, *Cinema 2*, p.121.
[77] Deleuze, *Cinema 2*, p.121.

screen. The image itself, for Deleuze, is no longer dominated by space and movement, but has its 'primary characteristics' of topology and time.[78]

After the crisis of the movement-image, the time-image is constituted in post-war modern cinema, with new signs and new implications. On one hand, the movement-image contains time in chronological order, so that 'the past is a former present, and the future a present to come'.[79] On the other hand, the movement-image transformed into the time-image after the war; in this respect, time is no longer measured by movement, but becames a metaphorical expression of the movement of the brain – the image of thought. In the image of thought, time does not imply the absence of movement; rather, it implies the 'reversal' of the subordination. It is no longer time which is subordinate to the physical movement, but it is the movement of consciousness which subordinates itself to time. The war brings the viewer to see the crisis of the movement-image. It comes to a point, the 'very break-up of the sensory-motor schema', in which one can only react with a pure optical situation, because it contains a pure form of time. Woolf's *Mrs Dalloway* presents the time-image. Woolf is ahead of her contemporaries, because she creates a direct presentation of time in words, as I aim to show in the next section.

Part II:
The Gaze, Montage and Time in *Mrs Dalloway*

In Woolf's 'A Sketch of the Past' (1939), childhood memory is bought alive in the narrative, as a pure visual situation, which connects to a present stimulus – the Roger Fry biography on which she is working. After considering 'the enormous number of things'[80] she can remember, and 'the

---

[78] Deleuze, *Cinema 2*, p.121.

[79] Deleuze, *Cinema 2*, p.259.

[80] Virginia Woolf, 'A Sketch of the Past' (1939). *Moments of Being*. Ed. Jeanne

number of different ways in which memoirs can be written',[81] she decides to begin with the memory of her mother, as a way to describe a moment of pure visual ecstasy. Woolf's childhood is evoked in cinematic terms, using cinematic techniques to depict her earliest memory of colour. She recalls the sight of the pattern of 'purple and red and blue'[82] flowers on her mother's black dress, as she sat on her knee while they travelled in a train or in an omnibus from St Ives to London. This, to Woolf, is like a trip in time, from the present back to the past; it is also like a film in her consciousness, which makes her see the image of her mother in the movement of a train or an omnibus. The feeling of this particular moment of being as a child encourages the reader to identify with the young Woolf's early sensations of rhythmic movement and visual awareness.

According to Woolf, this moment of looking seems to be her primary sensation – her 'first' memory, the 'most important' of all her memories, '[i]f life has a base that it stands upon, if it is a bowl that one fills and fills and fills – then my bowl without a doubt stands upon this memory'.[83] Sitting on her mother's lap, Woolf can see the anemones on her mother's dress with a close-up shot of the colours purple, red and blue against the black, conveying the visual sensation and emotion. Lying 'half asleep, half awake in bed in the nursery at St Ives',[84] hearing the waves breaking, seeing the light behind a yellow blind, Woolf depicts this seeing and hearing sensation as a feeling of 'purest ecstasy'.[85] Woolf's moment of being is an expression of her moment of vision, by which the external motions and clock time are transformed into timeless entities: moments of *la durée*.

Schulkind. London: Hogarth Press, 1985, p.64.

[81] Woolf, 'A Sketch of the Past', p.64.

[82] Woolf, 'A Sketch of the Past', p.64.

[83] Woolf, 'A Sketch of the Past', p.64.

[84] Woolf, 'A Sketch of the Past', p.64.

[85] Woolf, 'A Sketch of the Past', p.65.

The way Woolf depicts her childhood memory here is cinematic. The time-image is carefully structured as a montage image of colour, sensory experience and motion. In *Mrs Dalloway*, too, one can see how Woolf uses images of montage (moments of being, montage of consciousness) to construct the form of the novel, giving the quantity of clock time *'a qualitative leap'*.[86] By juxtaposing the past and the present, Woolf makes one see the dialectics of time and motion, in which the 'double consciousness'[87] of Clarissa and Septimus creates a new quality of the whole. The relation between clock time and inner time, the temporal experiences of each character, structure the form of the novel. And with this, the relation between the dualism of the tale of time (inner and outer time, past and present time) is presented through the montage method of Woolf's narrative style, which juxtaposes Septimus's and Clarissa's experience of time. *Mrs Dalloway* is a cinematic novel, which employs the method of cinematic montage, in which the arrangement of discrete frames creates a meaningful visual sensation. Each scene is designed within an individual frame, long takes, and deep focus.

In this section, the central focus will be on how Woolf's gendered gaze expresses London as a psychological/gendered cityscape in the time-image, through cinematic techniques such as irrational cuts, sequence shots and flashback. The cinema shapes, reflects and embodies a transformation of consciousness, that Woolf associated with modernism and with fictional writing. In 'The Cinematic Novel: Tracking a Concept', Steven G. Kellman argues that the term *'cinematic novel'* illustrates a bizarre hybrid born in the twentieth century, 'as if there were no question about what is meant by *cinema* and what is meant by *novel*'.[88]

---

[86] Eisenstein, *Film Form*, p.239.

[87] As Woolf explains in 'An Introduction to *Mrs Dalloway*' (1928), Septimus was created to be Clarissa's double. Mrs Dalloway 'was originally to kill herself, or perhaps merely to die at the end of the party'. See *E IV*, p.549.

[88] Steven G. Kellman, 'The Cinematic Novel: Tracking a Concept'. *Modern Fiction*

Technologies of film-making are adaptable to fiction, and can express the character's inner life through montage, flashback and close-up. In this respect, cinematic technique changes the concept of the novel. Furthermore, in 'Movie Novel' (1918), Woolf argues that cinematic narrative form does not show a novel as a form, in which 'one picture must follow another without stopping, for if it stopped and we had to look at it we should be bored'.[89] For Woolf, the cinema is nothing 'new', if it shows merely a series of motion pictures. The art of the cinema is not a straightforward transposition of a work from page to screen. In any case, simply because a film drew its plots and characters from a novel does not make the film 'novelistic', or a novel 'cinematic', as the multiple screen versions of *Anna Karenina* show. Because of the invention of technology, a cinematic narrative form is able to illuminate a sense of the continuity of the plot in a non-linear way. According to Jerzy Kosinski, cinematic techniques such as montage, flashback, close-up and long shots reflect 'the modern thought process'.[90] Woolf incorporates cinematic techniques to develop the possibilities of her writing style. The mood and emotion of Woolf's characters makes her novels read like aesthetically sophisticated scenarios, as one can see in *Mrs Dalloway*.

Woolf's dual vision of London is interwoven in her narrative style through the character's experience of clock time and inner time, as in the most fantastic of her own parallel montage sequences, which establish her filmic dynamic narrative. First of all, the inner and outer time scales form a dialectical image of London. The conflict between two shots is potential montage, the juxtaposition of the gaze. The intercut between the inner emotional line, memory and the present external physical action forms another montage method of parallel scenes, linking the separate episodes.

Studies 33.3 (1987): 467 – 477, p.468.

[89] Virginia Woolf, 'Movie Novel' (1918). *Contemporary Writers*. London: Hogarth, 1965, p.84.

[90] Jerzy Kosinski, *The Art of the Self*. Mew York: Scientia-Factum, 1968, p.15.

The form of the novel achieves a whole, is complete in the montage method of parallel scenes, synthesised by the stroke of Big Ben. The chime of Big Ben does not only clearly marks the quantity of time, but also the sensation of the chime, '[f]irst a warning, musical; then the hour, irrevocable' (*MD* 4), which shows what people see and think, while they are walking in different parts of London at the same time. In this respect, the structure of *Mrs Dalloway* with the repeated chime of Big Ben, indicates several 'montage units' as Eisenstein names it.[91]

In 'Dickens Griffith, and the Film Today', Eisenstein shows how Dickens's 'intricate montage complex'[92] is expressed by breaking down one episode and mixing it with another episode, as one can see in his novel *Oliver Twist*, or in Griffith's inter-cut technique in his film *Intolerance* (1916). However, as one can see in *Mrs Dalloway*, Woolf's method of montage is not crowded with external events (such as the back and forth cross-cutting of the gang's clutch and Oliver's escaping). There is no chapter division in *Mrs Dalloway*. Woolf's concept of cinematic form leads to a new conception of fictional narrative technique, a process of narrative technique, which suggests a process of narrowing the fictional duration (say, from ten years to one day), simplifying the plot (focusing on Clarissa's party, rather than depicting a series of events), and at the same time expanding the psychological duration of the characters. As I have shown in previous sections, the Cubist viewpoint is a way of expressing time in motion, seeing thought within movement and space. Montage, through this fusion of shots, is a method that shows how time is experienced. As one can see a Woolf character

---

[91] As Eisenstein himself claims, the nature of montage, for him, is a recognition of an 'unusual' and 'emotional' way of thinking. Eisenstein uses montage sequence as a method of film-making, to set out 'the unit of impression', creating 'attraction' in art. See *Notes of a Film Director* (London: Lawrence & Wishart, 1959), pp.11 and 16.

[92] Eisenstein, *Film Form*, p.222.

from within and without; the duality of the story line highlighted by the stroke of Big Ben, means we see an internal movement image of thought through the character's physical motion in 'the London day' (*MD* 177).

Déjà Vu: Clarissa

Woolf's time-image begins with Clarissa's walk. Clarissa loves to walk in London. She wants to buy the flowers herself for her party in the evening. Her walk out of the house in Westminster is a walk into her own past, her childhood memory at Bourton. The fresh morning air of London makes her feel as if she had 'burst open the French windows and plunged at Bourton into the open air' (*MD* 3) when she was eighteen. Walking in the London street but thinking about the past, Clarissa feels 'very young; at the same time unspeakably aged' (*MD* 8). Clarissa's walk reveals the dialectic of time, a fusion of the new, the already past, and the ever-same.[93] The streets of London serve as a mnemonic system, for Clarissa, bringing images of the past into the present. Clarissa has the dual vision (old and young, past and present) of the flâneuse, which is poetic and at the same time analytic, nostalgic and at the same time allegorical. In the 'soft mesh of the grey-blue morning air' (*MD* 5) in the middle of June, the smell and colour of flowers in London streets remind Clarissa of the feeling she had at Bourton: one early morning she was standing at the open window, looking at the flowers, at the trees 'with the smoke winding off them and the rooks rising, falling' (*MD* 3). 'What a lark! What a plunge!' (*MD* 3) – Clarissa has the rooks of Bourton in her mind while she is walking on the London streets, seeing a lark. As Woolf shows in 'Mrs Dalloway in Bond Street', for Clarissa June is fresh. Her walk on the streets of Westminster is

---

[93] As Adorno writes of Benjamin's *Pariser Passagen*, the concept of a dialectical image is a presentation 'of the modern as at once the new, the already past and the ever-same'. See *On Walter Benjamin* (Ed. Gary Smith. Cambridge, Mass: MIT, 1988), p.10.

her moment of duration: 'Only for Mrs Dalloway the moment was complete […]. A happy childhood […]; flowers at evening, smoke rising; the caw of rooks falling from ever so high, down down through the October air – there is nothing to take the place of childhood'.[94] Clarissa's rich sensory experience in London streets brings her childhood memories back to her present consciousness. Proust depicts how the taste of the Petit Madeline soaked in tea brings back his childhood in *A la recherché du temps perdu*: the memory is an image, in which he can see his Mamma reading a bed time story. 'A leaf of mint, or a cup with a blue ring'[95] also brings the image of Clarissa's father Justin Parry back to her. *La durée* is a moment when Clarissa is temporarily suspended between the passing present (walking, motion) and the preserved past (the virtual image), within the sensory-motor continuity.

In Clarissa's Bourton memory, Peter was there. She remembers 'million of things' (*MD* 3) about him: things he said, his eyes, his pocket-knife, his smile and his grumpiness. Clarissa remembers that Peter may come back from India 'one of these days' (*MD* 3). Woolf aims to depict Clarissa's whole life in a day, from different psychological perspectives. Woolf shows Clarissa in a Cubist way, looking at her from the inner and outer perspectives, namely, her own movement of thought, and how she is looked at by other people. While Clarissa is waiting on the kerb for Durtnall's van to pass, Woolf zooms her camera and depicts Clarissa from another point of view. Scrope Purvis knows her 'as one does know people who live next door to one in Westminster' (*MD* 4), illustrating how Clarissa is seen in London. There is something charming about Clarissa, 'a touch of the bird about her, of the jay, blue-green, light, vivacious' (*MD* 4). Clarissa looks as fresh and as free, as the bird which flies in the sky.

---

[94] Virginia Woolf, *Mrs Dalloway's Party: A Short Story Sequence* (1923). Ed. Stella McNichol. London: Hogarth Press, 1973, p.19.

[95] Woolf, *Mrs Dalloway's Party*, p.19.

Woolf uses different symbols to communicate the inner time-shift. Clock time, the hour on the clock, breaks into the moment of *la durée* through the chime of Big Ben. Clarissa's moment of *la durée* is Woolf's way of measuring existence, seeing 'the privacy of the soul' (*MD* 139) in the essence of time. Memory, as Leon Edel points out, is 'at the heart of Bergson's concept of time' – *la durée* – 'the invisible progress of the past, which gnaws into the future'.[96] Time is 'the supreme reality', for Bergson, as even Wyndham Lewis recognised.[97] *La durée*, in this respect, indicates a metaphysical fusion of the past and the present, combining opposite ways of seeing the 'truth'. For Woolf, the visualisation of *la durée* is

> the truth about our soul, [...], our self, who fish-like inhabits deep seas and plies among obscurities threading her way between the boles of giant weeds, over sun-flinkered spaces and on and on into gloom, cold, deep, inscrutable; suddenly she shoots to the surface and sports on the wind-wrinkled waves; that is, has a positive need to brush, scrape, kindle herself, gossiping (*MD* 176).

The stroke of Big Ben itself is a symbol of interrupting and breaking the inner ceaseless durational flux; and yet, it is also a moment of 'gossiping' between the past and the present, a moment when being synthesises with becoming; intellect with intuition. Clarissa physically also has to stop and wait, listening to the chime in the middle of the traffic. Her emotion is powerful and highly personal, stronger than the effect of external light or sound. Clarissa's love for London brings her pleasure as she walks on streets. The sudden flashes of the past bring images to the present, in Clarissa's thought. The physical time is crowded with events: buying the

---

[96] Leon Edel, *The Psychological Novel 1900 – 1950*. London: Rupert Hart-Davis, 1955, p.28.
[97] Wyndham Lewis, *Time and Western Man*. 1927. Santa Rosa: Black Sparrow, 1993, pp.208 – 209.

flowers, crossing the street, looking and listening. The movement of Clarissa's thought is interrupted by the clock time. Clarissa waits 'in the midst of the traffic' (*MD* 4) for Big Ben to strike. Here Woolf zooms her camera lens again, to the London street, depicting Clarissa's sensory experience of London. While listening to the chime of Big Ben, Clarissa is crossing Victoria Street: her moment is complete after Big Ben struck the eleventh stroke.[98] She has a positive feeling, a feeling of love and joy that she 'can't be dealt with' (*MD* 4), a visual ecstasy inspired by London, at this hour, in 'people's eyes, in the swing, tramp, and trudge; in the bellow and the uproar; the carriages, motor cars, omnibuses, vans, sandwich men shuffling and swinging; brass bands; barrel organs; in the triumph and the jingle and the strange high singing of some aeroplane overhand' (*MD* 4). All these are what Clarissa loves – the interaction of the past and the present, in this very moment of June.

The cinema highlights the experience of 'time-shifting': life and death, the actual ('a present which passes') and the virtual ('a past which is preserved').[99] As Clarissa walks in the street of London, one can see the actual image and the virtual image 'coexist and crystallize'[100] in a montage attraction, which for Deleuze serves to extend the actual images by succeeding them for a time, during a sequence of physical and mental movements. Woolf shows how the dialectic of time forms the structure of *Mrs Dalloway*, by depicting Clarissa's inner life via flashback, slow motion and freeze frame (while she is waiting to cross Victoria Street). Clarissa's flânerie provides a paradigmatic model for female subjectivity, constructing a form of spectatorship which fuses the past and the present, the real and the virtual. This spectatorship frees the outer world by fusing it '*in our field of*

---

[98] Woolf, *Mrs Dalloway's Party*, p.20.

[99] Anne Friedberg, *Window Shopping: Cinema and the Postmodern*. Berkeley: University of California Press, 1993, p.129.

[100] Deleuze, *Cinema 2*, p.81.

vision', just as it is '*brought together in our own consciousness*'.[101] According to Hugo Münsterberg, mental processes draw together contrasting situations and interchanging diverse experiences in the soul, which can never be embodied 'except in the photoplay'.[102] Bergson did not use the term 'cinematography' until 1907. In *Creative Evolution*, Bergson defines the representation of mental process as 'cinematography'. This point has been taken further by Deleuze, to define his notion of the time-image. The subjective experience of time highlights the significance of the cinema.

As Deleuze argues, the experience of time offers a historical explanation for the stylistic changes in the cinema. Woolf's time-image is a process of out-of-joint, a time-shifting between life and death, the actual and the virtual, in which time depends on movement. The time-image refers to the narrative structure. The brain becomes the confrontation between the past and the present. The dialectic of time begins with the walking/thinking process (thesis), interrupting by clock time, when Big Ben strikes the hours (anti-thesis). The time-image (*la durée*), finally, overcomes real space and movement, combining the past and the present and creating an organic whole (synthesis).

Woolf is developing her own feminine / feminist aesthetic in depicting this June day in Clarissa's life, exploring a fascination with the identification of femininity, with forms of interiority and of inner space. As Alison Light points out, in the interwar period, there was a recognition that 'insideness' and domesticity could be seen as a feminine achievement, reinforcing an idea of the femininity of 'intimacy, deep rooted emotionalities' and 'privacy', which 'domesticity itself implies'.[103] Woolf, like women novelists of the period, makes the house or the room one of the dominant metaphors and physical

---

[101] Hugo Münsterberg, *The Photoplay: A Psychological Study*. New York: D. Appleton, 1916, pp.106 – 107.

[102] Münsterberg, *The Photoplay*, p.107.

[103] Alison Light, *Forever England: Femininity, Literature and Conservatism Between the Wars*. London: Routledge, 1991, p.139.

settings in her novels, exploring the way feminine subjectivity can be identified with the interior. Clarissa's house is the vessel of her social position. She had married Richard to assume a high social position, and the house displays her husband's wealth. She is locked into the house, thereby gains a power within it. A domestic interior allows Clarissa to interact on more equal grounds. Even if Richard goes to Lady Bruton's for lunch, to discuss political issues; leaving her behind, he still comes home with red roses, showing his love for his wife.

Clarissa's house can be read as the interplay between space and gender. Architectural space contains characters' emotional experience. Interior decoration both defines and is defined by the inhabitants. Lucy tells Clarissa that Richard will not be home for lunch. Clarissa is rocked and shivered 'as a plant on the river-bed feels the shock of a passing oar and shivers' (*MD* 32), because Lady (Millicent) Bruton invites only Richard for lunch in Mayfair. Clarissa feels an 'emptiness' (*MD* 33) in her life in the middle of the day, for Richard is in another woman's place for lunch. She goes 'slowly upstairs, as if she had left a party' (*MD* 33). Without Richard, Clarissa loses all her feminine characteristics, feeling 'suddenly shriveled, aged, breastless, [...], [l]ike a nun withdrawing' to her attic room (*MD* 33). The attic room which Clarissa decorates is an expression of her character, and also the attic room in which she obliged to live creates that character. It is her bedroom. On the bed, 'the sheets [are] clean, tight stretched in a broad white band from side to side' (*MD* 33). The white clean bed sheet and a '[n]arrower and narrower' (*MD* 33) bed indicate the inactivity of Clarissa's sexual life. The candle is half burnt down, as Clarissa enters her middle age crisis. Baron Marbot's *Memoir* in the attic, which Clarissa reads late at night (for she sleeps 'badly', see *MD* 34), evokes her sense of depression and failure. Reading the *Memoir*, Clarissa can see what she lacked at this very moment: the 'charm' of a woman. It is not beauty or mind, but 'something warm which [breaks] up surfaces and rippled the cold contact of man and woman, or of women together' (*MD* 34). Without feeling like a charming woman,

Clarissa has 'a sudden revelation' (*MD* 34) as 'an illumination', for she feels
'what men felt' (*MD* 34) – impotent, weak and hopeless.

Clarissa's flashback to the past refers to a very cinematic moment in her
attic room, when memories of love and jealousy comes back to Clarissa's
present. Sally's kissing Clarissa in Bourton parallels Clarissa's kissing Peter
in London. Clarissa's longing for Richard's attention in her attic room, 'as
she could just hear the click of the handle released as gently as possible by
Richard' (*MD* 35), parallels Peter's longing for Clarissa's love. Clarissa's
kissing Peter in her drawing-room, again, indicates her own melancholy:
Richard has lunch with Lady Bruton, and she will be 'alone for ever' (*MD*
51). Meanwhile, in Mayfair with Lady Bruton and Hugh Whitbread, Richard
learns that Peter is back in London, and he remembers 'how passionately
Peter had been in love; been rejected; gone to India; come a cropper; made a
mess of things' (*MD* 117). After lunch, Richard walks in Conduit Street with
Hugh 'at the very moment that Millicent Bruton is lying on the sofa' (*MD*
123). They look in at a shop window in the middle of the day, with contrary
winds buffeting the street corner, and 'two forces meeting in a swirl, morning
and afternoon' (*MD* 123), Richard and Hugh stop. Woolf juxtaposes two
forces in a Cubist way, by which the morning and afternoon are two
dialectical forces, creating Richard's moment of *la durée*. Looking at the
show window, Richard's mind is like 'a single spider's thread after wavering
here and there attaches itself to the point of a leaf' (*MD* 125), 'recovering
from its lethargy, set now on his wife' (*MD* 125). Richard suddenly has a
vision of Clarissa there at luncheon with Peter, and their life together – he
draws the tray of old jewels towards him, taking up first the brooch and then
the ring, asking 'how much is that' (*MD* 125)? Richard is afraid that he will
lose Clarissa, so he wants to hold something, a present for Clarissa, as he
holds his love for her. He is eager to 'travel that spider's thread of
attachment between himself and Clarissa' (*MD* 126), to go straight to her in
Westminster, and to open the drawing-room door, to show his love for her.

Clarissa comes down to the drawing-room. Her drawing-room is the empowerment of female space, which reveals the very pink grace and charm of the family circle with Clarissa at its heart. Clarissa prepares for her party in her fifty-second year, as if she 'plunged into the very heart of the moment of this June morning' (*MD* 40). Clarissa empowers herself through looking at the glass, the dressing-table, for that very night she is the one who is giving a party. Looking at the glass, she sees her 'delicate pink face', which is her self – 'pointed; dartlike; definite' (*MD* 40), like 'one centre, one diamond, one woman who sat in her drawing-room and made a meeting-point, [...], a refuge for the lonely to come to, perhaps; she had helped young people, who were grateful to her; had tried to be the same always, never showing a sign of all the other sides of her – faults, jealousies, vanities, suspicions' (*MD* 40). The diamond shape of her face, the single person, is the very centre and the 'very temper' (*MD* 41) of Clarissa's house at that very moment. Although Lady Bruton does not ask her to lunch, looking at her drawing-room filled with visual objects: 'the chink of silver on a tray' (*MD* 41), 'giant candlesticks on the mantel piece' (*MD* 41), 'the silver casket in the middle' (*MD* 41), 'the crystal dolphin' (*MD* 41), she is proud having clean silver for the party.

Before Peter arrives at Clarissa's house for the party, he recognises Clarissa's feminine charm, along with the feminine charm of London. Peter thinks of the coming of the London evening when it just begins

> a woman who had slipped off her print dress and white apron to array herself in blue and pearls, the day [...], changed to evening, and with the same sign of exhilaration that a woman breathes, tumbling petticoats on the floor, it too shed dust, heat, colour, the traffic thinned; motor cars, tinkling, darting, succeeded the lumber of vans; and here and there among the thick foliage of the squares an intense light hung (*MD* 177).

Clarissa's party gives her feminine charm, which empowers her. On the way to Clarissa's party, Peter feels that the charm, which makes him see the charm of London: the evening is new, free, and hot within an atmosphere of 'the yellow-blue evening light' (*MD* 177), which makes Peter feel 'as young as ever' (*MD* 177). Clarissa's house reveals her social level and taste, which makes Peter think himself as a failure 'in the Dalloways' sense' (*MD* 47). Before Clarissa's marriage, it is her childhood home that gives her precious memories. After marriage, it is the house in Westminster that makes her the centre, defining her socially and spiritually, and giving her order to her life.

After learning about Septimus's death, Clarissa goes into the 'little room where the Prime Minister had gone with Lady Bruton' (*MD* 201). There is no one around. Woolf depicts how Clarissa feels in the little room:

> What business had the Bradshaws to talk of death at her party? A young man had killed himself. And they talked of it at her party – the Bradshaws talked of death. He had killed himself – but how? Always her body went through it first, when she was told, suddenly, of an accident; her dress flamed, her body burnt. He had thrown himself from a window (*MD* 201).

Clarissa's body and her dress are burned by her anger and anxiety, as a sign that the soul, the process of thinking, is transformed into *la durée*, going beyond mathematic time and the external world. In the depth of her heart, Clarissa has an 'awful fear' (*MD* 203), that her party may be a failure. The Bradshaws are talking about death in her party, as if 'it were now to die, it were now to be most happy' (*MD* 202). Death can bring a pleasure, which there is no pleasure could equal. Septimus's death, for Clarissa, brings 'the triumph of the youth' (*MD* 203) and the freedom of his soul. Clarissa walks to the window, parting the curtains and looking – but 'in the room opposite the old lady [is staring] straight at her' (*MD* 203) for the first time. She usually looks out of the window 'quite unconscious that she was being watched' (*MD* 139). Under the sky above Westminster, Clarissa looks at the old woman, who quietly goes to bed alone. Suddenly she is happy for Septimus, because 'he had done it' without fear, thrown it away while they went on living' (*MD* 204). With the interruption of the chime of Big Ben, Clarissa returns to her party with her vision.

Shop Windows: Peter and Miss Kilman

In this section, I want to address the analogy between the shop window and the cinema screen. Large sheets of cast glass, rolled and poured, are used as show windows, displaying fancy goods. The shop window contains commodities, virtualising the gaze as a cinema screen, making the act of looking a surreal experience. As Benjamin claims, the commodities that appear in the shop windows have a fortuitous and random arrangement, an unexpected juxtaposition of fancy goods. The montage of commodities is a model of the clutter of modern urban life, which provides an atmosphere, an image of visual intoxication and sensual pleasure. For Benjamin, the arcade itself means the city, even the world. The arcade opens to the spectator but also encloses him; it is a public interior with a glass roof, iron-structured market halls and display windows. The display of the commodities constructs a 'dream world': the arcades as an 'invention of industrial luxury', 'glass-roofed', 'marble-walled passages cut through whole blocks of houses'.[104] The arcades and elegant shops are like theatres, staging their goods offered for purchases. It is a theatre, 'a city, indeed, a world in miniature' with 'light from above' and 'gas lighting'.[105]

As Anne Friedberg points out, unlike eighteenth-century London – 'a city that had the Pall Mall and the Strand as broad open-air shopping streets,

---

[104] Walter Benjamin, 'Paris, Capital of the Nineteenth Century'. *Reflections*. Ed. Peter Demetz. Trans. Edmund Jephcott. New York: Schocken, 1978, p.146.

[105] Benjamin, 'Paris, Capital of the Nineteenth Century', p.147.

streets where one could stroll and gaze into shops', walking in
pre-Haussmann Paris 'was difficult due to narrow streets and the lack of
sidewalks'.[106] The arcade fulfills the desire for strolling and looking. The
major arcades of Paris, Passage des Panorama (1800), Galérie Vivienne (1826),
Galérie Véro-Dodat (1826), Galérie Colbert (1826), Passage L'Opera (1821 –
1823), and Passage Choiseul (1825 – 1827) were complete by 1830; Passage
Verdeau (1846) and Jouffroy (1847) followed.[107] There were, however, some
arcades built in London as well. As Jane Rendell points out, the first two
arcades constructed during the early decades of the nineteenth-century in
London were the Royal Opera Arcade (between 1815 and 1817) designed by
John Nash and G. S. Repton, and the Burlington Arcade (1818 – 1819)
designed by Samuel Ware. A Third London arcade, the Lowther Arcade, was
also part of an urban improvement scheme around Trafalgar Square. The
London arcades 'were part of plans to promote the fashionable and wealthy
residential areas of the West End around Piccadilly, Bond Street, Oxford
Street and Regent Street as a zone of luxury commodity consumption'.[108]

The department store as a building type 'emerged as a corollary to the
dramatic changes in urban retailing between 1840 and 1870',[109] for
displaying the mass production of standardised goods. Glass windows
transformed the department store, the capital of modern commerce, into a
space for new modes of perception and experience. Glass show windows
constructed the department store as a phantasmagoria of fetishism. The glass
window can be seen as the illusionistic screen that reflects the gas light and
display of commodities, making the department store a site for the conflation
of physical movement (flânerie) and the gaze. I want to address the analogy

---

[106] Friedberg, *Window Shopping*, p.68.

[107] Friedberg, *Window Shopping*, p.70.

[108] Jane Rendell, 'Thresholds, Passages and Surfaces: Touching, Passing and Seeing
in the Burlington Arcade'. *The Optic of Walter Benjamin*. Ed. Alex Coles.
London: Black Dog, 1999, pp.170 – 171.

[109] Friedberg, *Window Shopping*, p.77.

between the shop window and the cinema screen. The shop window is displaced and incorporated by the cinema screen through the mobility of the flâneur / flâneuse in a particular urban space. In the architectural passage, the virtualised gaze finds its mobility. Cinematic spectatorship, in this respect, can be read as a further instrumentalisation of this consumer gaze; the shop window, moreover, virtualises the gaze through the gazer's fantasy. The glass of the shop window does not only display of commodities, but also offers a mode of voyeuristic desire and fetishism, for the commodity is something one can see but not touch. Cinema spectatorship, on the other hand, replies equally on consumer contemplation – the contemplation of a pure pleasure of looking.

The shop window introduces a virtual mobility that is both spatial and temporal, as one walks through the arcade and the department store. The passages in the arcade and the department store produce a virtual gaze – a dream image – by the movement of the gazer. In this respect, flânerie finds its metaphoric embodiment in the passage, creating the vision of the new, the already passed, and the ever-same in a spatial and temporal sense. The arcade and the department store in the city define walking as a motion through time, via the virtualisation of gaze. One does not only see the commodity, but also the fantasy, the fetishism and the desire that the commodity implies. The gaze, in this respect, provides a perceptual sensation of time travel, as in Peter's gaze.

As no one knows he is in London, Peter Walsh feels the 'strangeness of standing alone, alive, unknown, at half-past eleven, walking from Victoria Street to Trafalgar Square' (*MD* 56 – 57). The stroke of Big Ben had earlier broken into his thought, confusing his past and his present: 'What is it? Where am I? And why, after all, does one do it?' (*MD* 57) Peter's strong emotion is like 'moonshine', which appears twice in his mind: while he was meeting Clarissa in her Westminster house (with romantic illusion); afterwards he walks alone in Trafalgar Square, thinking about the divorce. However, the stroke of Big Ben overcomes him, 'as if the result of others, an irrepressible, exquisite delights; as if inside his brain by another hand strings were pulled, shutters moved' (*MD* 57). He suddenly feels 'so young', like a child 'who runs out of doors' (*MD* 57); his mind is like 'an unguarded flame' (*MD* 57). The stroke of Big Ben makes him free from his moment – his memory of Clarissa's look, while she is mentioning the lake – '[s]he looked at Peter Walsh; her look, passing through all that time and that emotion, reached him doubtfully; settled on him tearfully; and rose and fluttered away, as a bird touches a branch and rises and flutters away' (*MD* 47).

Escaping from these emotions, Peter's eye is caught by a young attractive woman, who is walking across Trafalgar Square in the direction of the Haymarket. The street is transformed into an imaginary realm. As she is passing the statue, Peter falls into another visual situation of his mind, for the girl becomes the very woman that he had always had in mind: 'young, but stately; merry, but discreet; black, but enchanting' (*MD* 57). The way Woolf depicts Peter's visual situation is totally cinematic: with excitement, Peter is '[s]traightening himself and stealthily fingering his pocket-knife, which seemed even with its back turned to shed on him a light which connected them, which singled him out' (*MD* 57), as if there is no one in Trafalgar Square, except for Peter, his voyeuristic gaze as the symbolic light of his concentration, and the girl he is following. However, Woolf zooms her movie camera again to take a long shot, to depict the crowd in the street, changing Peter's look to a romantic buccaneer as he contrasts himself to by combining what he sees in the shop windows:

> But other people got between them in the street, obstructing him, blotting her out. He pursued; she changed. There was colour in her cheeks; mockery in her eyes; he was an adventurer, reckless, he thought, swift, daring, indeed [...] a romantic buccaneer, careless of all these damned proprieties, yellow dressing-gowns, pipes, fish-rods, in the shop windows; and respectability and evening parties and

spruce old men wearing white slips beneath their waistcoats. He was a buccaneer. On and on she went, across Piccadilly, and up Regent Street, ahead of him, her cloak, her gloves, her shoulders combining with the fringes and the laces and the feather boas in the windows to make the spirit of finery and whimsy which dwindled out of the shops on to the pavement, as the light of a lamp goes wavering at night over hedges in the darkness (*MD* 58 – 59).

Shop windows turn Peter into absorbed spectator, fulfill his voyeuristic pleasure in looking, which turns the young girl into the 'erotic object of the gaze'.[110] The shop window indicates Lacan's mirror at the original moment of recognising the more perfect, more complete, more powerful ideal ego. The beauty of the young girl, for Peter, is a new sign of seductive powers of the female image. Woolf's depiction of Peter's male gaze, the visual objects in the shop windows and his object of desire, the young girl, is purely cinematic. Peter's gaze at the young girl reflects his inner desire, the repressed sexuality, and his lack: '[n]o sons, no daughters, no wife' (*MD* 208). The commodities in the shop windows of Piccadilly and up to Regent Street also reflect his lack. By gazing at the commodities, Peter imagines himself in a pure visual situation, as a romantic and reckless buccaneer. The image of a romantic buccaneer is his ideal self; as he is getting excited, he plays with the blade of his pocket-knife, which symbolises his masculinity. However, through visually he possesses the commodities and the young girl, objectified her, turning them into his object of desire, Peter shows his ideal self, by imagining himself with the buccaneer look: 'yellow dressing-gowns, pipes, fish-rods, in the shop windows'. Peter's pure visual situation shows how Woolf's cinematic technique works, by Peter's visually consuming the young girl and the commodities in the shop windows as 'his fun' –

---

[110] Laura Mulvey, *Visual and Other Pleasures*. London: Macmillan, 1989, p.20.

something he makes up for his 'exquisite amusement' – which is odd but 'quite true' to him (*MD* 59).

The interplay between Peter's gaze, object of desire, memory and commodity in the shop windows reveals the politics of the male gaze. Peter's gaze depicts the sexual topology of London through the physical morphology of architectural space. London as a whole, under Peter's gaze, inscribes a particular moment when civilization 'seemed dear to him as a personal possession' (*MD* 60). The city for Peter is a territory, a market with sexual objects that he wants to consume. The path Peter follows the young girl identifying specific features of locations and sites of sexualities in the city – of desire and fantasy. And yet, Peter's sexual fantasy indicates his lack. As the young girl crosses Oxford Street and Great Portland Street and turns down one of the little streets, Peter's expectation of visual intoxication seems to come – the great moment is approaching, for now she stops, opens her bag, and 'with one look in his direction, but not at him, one look that bade farewell, summed up the whole situation and dismissed it triumphantly, for ever' (*MD* 59). The young girl eventually looks back in Peter's direction but not even at him, winning the battle of sexual topology through the gaze, with her gesture of entering her own house – 'one of those flat red houses with hanging flower-baskets of vague impropriety' (*MD* 59). Peter's virtual image is gone, by the gaze and the gesture of the young girl.

Miss Kilman is having tea and the chocolate éclair with Elizabeth Dalloway in the Army and Navy Stores (in Victoria Street) at half past three. Elizabeth guides Miss Kilman, this way and that, to buy the petticoats, 'as if she had been a great child' (*MD* 142). Miss Kilman asks Elizabeth for tea, as if it is a way to rouse and to collect herself. Miss Kilman is eating 'with intensity, then looking, again and again' (*MD* 142). Eating and looking, particularly eating, seems to her the 'only pure pleasure' (*MD* 142), though to the reader it suggests her desire to possess Elizabeth. She wants 'that cake – the pink one' (*MD* 142), as if the pink cake revealed her desire of being beautiful, young and adorable, like Elizabeth 'with her hair done in the fashionable way, in the pink dress' (*MD* 185), at Clarissa's party, with her 'oriental bearing, her inscrutable mystery' (*MD* 144) and her white gloves. The way Miss Kilman eats the chocolate éclair symbolises her way of possessing Elizabeth, as she 'open[s] her mouth, slightly project[s] her chin, swallow[s] down the last inches of the chocolate éclair' (*MD* 144). Miss Kilman's eating behavior underlines a relation between eating and sexuality in psychoanalytic theory.

According to Freud, 'a baby sinking back satiated from the breast and falling asleep with flushed checks and a blissful smile' can be seen as a 'prototype of the expression of sexual satisfaction' in adult life.[111] The act of consumption in the department store, as Freud suggests, is a symbol of desire, for the 'pleasure-ego wants an object of satisfaction for him'.[112] The world of consumption highlights the relation between adult sexuality and adult power. Feeding is established psychologically as the symbol of love, aggression, pleasure and desire to control. The chocolate éclair is the object that satisfies Miss Kilman. Eating the chocolate éclair is a symbolic gesture, taking the pleasure of eating the cake and possessing Elizabeth into her ego, to synthesise the subjective and the object. Miss Kilman does not want Elizabeth to go – this girl, this young, that is so beautiful, 'whom she genuinely love[s]' (*MD* 144). Miss Kilman's 'large hand' (*MD* 144) opens and shuts on the table, as if she could grasp Elizabeth at once. The opening and shutting of Miss Kilman's hand refers to the mechanical physical and psychological tension. And yet, this physical gesture is a sign of a state of

---

[111] Sigmund Freud, *The Standard Edition of the Complete Psychological Works of Sigmund Freud, Volume 7 (1901 – 1905): A Case of Hysteria; Three Essays on Sexuality and Other Works*. Eds/Trans. James Strachey and Anna Freud. London: Hogarth Press and the Institution of Psycho-analysis, 1953, p.182.

[112] Freud, *Standard Edition, Volume 19: The Ego and the Id and Other Works (1923 – 1925)*, p.237.

mind: is she letting Elizabeth go back to Clarissa or not? She eats the chocolate éclair as if she could grasp her, if she could clasp her, if she could make her hers absolutely and for ever and then die' (*MD* 144). Miss Kilman cannot stand Elizabeth's leaving her, going home and preparing for the party. She sees that as Clarissa's triumph, for Elizabeth goes and turns against her. Her fingers 'curled inwards' (*MD* 144).

Miss Kilman tries to persuade Elizabeth to stay with her. However, Elizabeth sits silent, with Miss Kilman's 'great hand' (*MD* 145) opening and shutting. Eventually Elizabeth leaves her. Woolf depicts Miss Kilman's losing her way in the labyrinth of the Army and Navy Stores:

> She got up, blundered off among the little tables, rocking slightly from side to side, and somebody came after her with her petticoat, and she lost her way, and was hemmed in by trunks specially prepared for taking to India; next got among the accouchement sets and baby linen; through all the commodities of the world, perishable and permanent, hams, drugs, flowers, stationary, variously smelling, now sweet, now sour, she lurched; saw herself thus lurching with her hat askew, very red in the face, full length in a looking-glass; and at last came out into the street (*MD* 145 – 146).

Cinematic space is a signifier with connotative meaning, which brings its subject and its desire together. Miss Kilman sees herself in a looking-glass, lurching with a red face. Losing the object of desire, beauty and youth, after Elizabeth's absence, Miss Kilman loses her way and her mind. Sensations of commodities from all over the world with all kinds of smell and colour, are like threats to her unguarded mind. Without Elizabeth's guide, the whole department store is like a chaotic space, which parallels her mind. The juxtaposition of the Army and Navy Stores and the Westminster Cathedral articulates the psychology, memory, anxiety and self-awareness of Miss Kilman. After Elizabeth left, Miss Kilman is trying to get rid of this memory-haunted space, to free her own soul, as if Elizabeth's soul was something 'haunting the same territory' (*MD* 147) – the territory of the department store and Miss Kilman's very own mind. She at last comes out of the Stores, into the street. She sees the tower of Westminster Cathedral, the Abbey, 'the habitation of God' (*MD* 146) in the middle of the traffic of the street of London. She comes into the Abbey, the shelter of her soul. She comes from the street, into the Cathedral. Through the image of the 'double darkness' (*MD* 146): the haunted Army and Navy Stores and the tomb of the Unknown Warrior, Miss Kilman sees a light in the Abbey, which is 'bodiless', aspiring above 'the vanities, the desires, the commodities', and freeing her from hatred, jealousy and love.

The Haunted Image of Death and Redemption: Septimus

As I have argued in this chapter, Woolf's method is cinematic: if in this novel the gaze can be seen as an individual shot, the juxtaposition of more than one gaze can be compared to the method of montage. The meaning of each shot is single and neutral in content, until it is placed in juxtaposition. The cinematic method of montage articulates a radical aesthetic synthesis, such as that provided by the juxtaposition of multiple points of view on one Cubist canvas. Although Woolf's diary entries give no avowed indication of familiarity with Eisenstein's 'Dialectic Approach to Film Form' (1929), it is as if *Mrs Dalloway* is an equally radical aesthetic synthesis: a text devoted to the juxtaposition of the gaze. The re-creation of the past renews the old world, bringing a new way of seeing post-war London.

Mrs Dalloway, I would argue, is a montage of various consciousnesses. The novel makes use of the cinematic technique of juxtaposing places, creating a multiplicity of gazes. As Laura Mulvey points out, in Soviet montage, the cinema screen would show someone 'walking through, say, the Kremlin Square and looking towards something, shown in the next shot such as, say, Big Ben'.[113] Woolf's shots in a similar way are juxtaposed through the characters' walking in different parts of London. As Eisenstein shows in his theory and use of montage, intercutting (a flashback within one's consciousness/gaze) can create further dimensions of meaning, as can the cross-cut (switching from one consciousness/gaze to another), in each case juxtaposing of different images.

Septimus's memory is expressed by indexical signs, marking the trauma that stored in the unconscious by an incident lost to consciousness. Septimus's haunted images are another and darker indication of the duration of time, and are again evoked through Woolf's cinematic technique is waiting to be noticed. To the reader, Septimus's haunted images render his unconscious trauma in visual shapes, in a way which is close to the notion of the techniques of the Surrealists. As Linda Williams points out, the Surrealists articulate new associations of objects, searching for the 'irrational knowledge of the object'[114] by separating them from their functional connections, juxtaposing them in new ways, in order to create new meanings.

Septimus's haunted images are signs of trauma. A visual object leaves a mark or a trace of its physical presence, the very object that inscribes its sign at a specific moment of time, as one can see in *Mrs Dalloway*: the aeroplane, the sky writing, the motor-car, the shadow of Evans and the close-up of Rezia's face. *Mrs Dalloway* combines two cinematic fascinations: one with the boundary between life and death, and the other with the mechanical animation of the sign. According to Laura Mulvey, the 'pensive spectator is more engaged with the reflection on the visibility of time', and on the other hand, 'the possessive spectator is more fetishistically absorbed by the image

---

[113] Laura Mulvey, 'Cinematic Space: Desiring and Deciphering'. *Desiring Practices: Architecture, Gender and the Interdisciplinary*. Eds. Katerina Rüedi, Sarah Wigglesworth, and Duncan McCorquodale. London: Black Dog, 1996, p.208.

[114] Linda Williams, *Figures of Desire: A Theory and Analysis of Surrealist Film*. Berkeley: University of California Press, 1981, p.12.

of the human body'.[115] In this respect, Clarissa and Septimus are pensive spectators; they are each other's double, and they both see the dialectic of time. Peter and Miss Kilman are possessive spectators. Both of them gaze fetishistically towards their object of desire, Clarissa or Elizabeth, as I have shown in my previous section.

Clarissa learns about Septimus's death in her party, at the end of the novel. However, the reader is aware of Septimus's death before her. Through Clarissa's simple question, 'but how' (*MD* 201), the shifting of perceptions is articulated in the flashback of passing time, evoking the dialectic of life and death, and also the psychological expression of the inter-relation of different view points.[116] The other temporal dimension, the narrative past of the early London day, suddenly emerges in the stillness of Clarissa in the small room, which brings the preserved past time into the passing present. In this single image, the morning and the afternoon, the past and the present of this Wednesday of London, in mid June 1923,[117] has been brought together.

The motor-car moves from Bond Street to Oxford Street, comes to a standstill precisely opposite Mulberry's shop window, when Clarissa looks out of the shop window while Septimus is gazing at the car, and moves towards Piccadilly. Clarissa's standstill image, at this moment, framed by the window, represents a moment extracted from the continuity of narrative time, the temporal dynamic which unflows within the aesthetic structure.

---

[115] Laura Mulvey, *Death 24 x a Second: Stillness and the Moving Image*. London: Reaktion, 2006, p.11.

[116] Eisenstein, 'A Dialectic Approach to Film Form', *Film Form*, p.53.

[117] In Woolf's letter to Gerald Brenan, 13th May, 1923, refers to the novel she was currently working on. The name of the novel, among other titles, called 'At Home', 'The Party', 'Mrs Dalloway', and 'The Hours'. As her work takes place, in one draft after another, 'The Hours' represents 'what might be termed the first full-length draft of *Mrs Dalloway* (1925)'. See Helen M. Wussow, Introduction. *The Hours: The British Museum Manuscript of Mrs Dalloway*. Ed. Helen M. Wussow. New York: Pace University Press, 1996, ix.

The window creates a freeze effect, like an individual moment in the filmic frame. The build-up to this final moment, the moment when Clarissa is thinking by herself in the small room, had been geared around the movement of time, the sequence of the haunted images of Septimus's death drive, on this one particular day of London.

The sequence had been prefigured by a shot of the Bradshaws' car, seen from the multiple points of view of the crowd in the street. This shot indicates the energy of the gaze, leading into the figure behind the dove-grey blind in the car. This accumulation of movement of the motor-car had carried forward the multiplicity of the gaze and of time itself. Whose car is it? Who is in the car? No one knows. Woolf depicts the figure in the motor-car in an Expressionist way, for everyone stops and stares at the motor-car on the side of the pavement but no one sees exactly who is in the car. The figure is like a symbol, as the black shadow in *Caligari*. The spectator can only see for a moment 'a face of the very greatest importance against the dove-grey upholstery' (*MD* 15). Then there is nothing to be seen 'expect a square of dove grey' (*MD* 15). This figure in the grey motor-car is indeed 'invisible, unseen and unknown' (*MD* 11), as Clarissa had felt when she walked up Bond Street. Woolf spends eight pages, shooting these 'thirty seconds' (*MD* 19) while the spectators are gazing at the motor-car. The motor-car blocks the traffic, suspends the crowd on one side of Bond Street. For Clarissa, it is the 'Queen herself' (*MD* 18) unable to pass, although Woolf gives the reader a clue, saying it is 'a male hand' (*MD* 15) which draws the blind in the motor-car. Is it the Prince of Wales's, the Queen's, the Prime Minister's? Whose face is it? Nobody knows. Woolf uses a series of question marks to depict the act of looking in a Cubist way, in which different spectators' points of view are juxtaposed at the same time on the canvas as in cinematic montage.

The dove grey shape of the motor-car is suspended in the middle of Bond Street to Oxford Street. Woolf uses this underlying illusion of stillness to create a freeze frame, a still frame which refers to a halt in time. The stillness of the motor-car evokes in Septimus a secret, hidden past which will find its way to the surface. The suspended motor-car is a hint of stillness within a sequence of movement; it indicates something enchanting, something threatening, as the 'mystery', the 'authority' and the 'spirit' (*MD* 15) of death is 'passing invisibly, inaudibly, like a cloud, swift, veil-like upon hills, falling indeed with something of a cloud's sudden sobriety and stillness upon faces which a second before had been utterly disorderly' (*MD* 15).

Septimus himself is 'unable to pass' (*MD* 15) the call of death. The chime of Big Ben tolls for him. He is thirty years old, 'pale-faced, beak-nosed, wearing brown shoes and a shabby overcoat, with hazel eyes which had that look of apprehension in them which makes complete strangers apprehensive too' (*MD* 15). The motionless motor-car, for Septimus, is a dove grey shadow of horror, 'as if some horror had come almost to the surface and was about to burst into flames, terrifying him' (*MD* 16), because everything is at a 'standstill' (*MD* 15), as the motor engine stops. Clarissa comes to Mulberry's shop window 'with her arms full of sweet peas' (*MD* 16), looking out with her little pink face, guarding the threshold of the present access to the past, indicating that shop window is not only spatial but temporal, a screen which Clarissa and Septimus's gazes meet. Septimus, the shell-shocked soldier, carries with him, in Benjamin's words, a past with a temporal index, by which it is referred to redemption. Septimus has a sense of a 'Messianic power, a power to which the past has a claim'.[118]

Haunted by the past, Septimus's London day is Judgment Day. He has 'a historical consciousness'[119] of the significance of passing time. He has been marked by the fullness of the country's past – the history of war. The repressed is about to return to the surface of consciousness. Edgar J. Watkiss

---

[118] Walter Benjamin, 'Theses on the Philosophy of History'. *Illuminations*. Trans. Harry Zohn. New York: Schocken, 1969, p.254.
[119] Benjamin, 'Theses on the Philosophy of History', p.262.

says 'The Proime Minister's kyar' (*MD* 15), and Septimus hears him. So far the face itself in the motor-car has been seen

> only once by three people for a few seconds. Even the sex was now in dispute. But there could be no doubt that greatness was seated within; greatness was passing, hidden, down Bond Street, removed only by a hand's-breadth from ordinary people who might now, for the first and last time, be within speaking distance of the majesty of England, of the enduring symbol of the state which will be known to curious antiquaries, sifting the ruins of time, when London is a grass-grown path [...] (*MD* 17).

For Woolf, the moment of standstill is a single instance, which cannot be measured by any 'mathematical instrument' (*MD* 19). Spectators 'in all the hat shops and tailors' shops' (*MD* 19) look at each other, for the face in the motor-car stimulates something profound, deep down in the unconscious, and they think of 'the dead, of the flag, of Empire' (*MD* 19). Mr Bowley looks at the motor-car, waiting for its passing, thinking of 'poor women waiting to see the Queen go past – poor women, nice little children, orphans, widows, the War' (*MD* 21) – he has tears in his eyes. The face in the motor-car, for Septimus, is a living monument of the past, the traumatic experience of the war, a thing that has roots in the past and reminds him the horror of the war, which is concealed from the surface of consciousness. On 'this Wednesday morning' (*MD* 18), the present time indicates the model of 'Messianic time',[120] for Septimus the solder will kill himself in the afternoon.

In the sky-writing scene, Woolf again depicts both multiple points of view and the experience of standstill. In Regent's Park, Septimus looks up, although he has 'not read the language yet', enjoying the pure pleasure of looking with a religious ecstasy while 'tears filled his eyes as he looked at the smoke words languishing and melting in the sky in their inexhaustible charity

---

[120] Benjamin, 'Theses on the Philosophy of History', p.263.

and laughing goodness one shape after another of unimaginable beauty, [...], for ever, for looking merely, with beauty, more beauty' (*MD* 23). At the same time, Septimus also sees the image of the dead Evans behind the tree – the man in grey, the shape of an iron-black figure (*MD* 76 – 77). Everyone looks up, seeing an aeroplane which 'bored ominously into the ears of the crowd' (*MD* 21), 'coming over the trees, letting out white smoke from behind' (*MD* 21). Oppression returns as a ghostly image of the dead, springing from the haunted unconscious of the spectator. Again, the flying aeroplane is 'a concentration', 'a ghostly symbol' (*MD* 30) for the repressed past. As in Mrs Dempster's gaze, the aeroplane goes 'fast and fading', away and away it shoots,

> soaring over Greenwich and all the masts; over the little island of grey churches, St. Paul's and the rest, till, on either side of London, fields spread out and dark brown woods where adventurous thrushes, hopping boldly, glancing quickly, snatched the snail and tapped him on a stone, once, twice, thrice (*MD* 30).

The sky-writing reminds the spectators of the smoke and the aeroplanes shooting away during the war, the symbol of a solder's determination to protect his country. While gazing at the aeroplane, Mr Bentley has a moment of standstill, in which '[n]ot a sound [is] to be heard' (*MD* 31). The soul is unguarded by means of thought, 'gets outside his body, beyond his house', beyond Einstein and mathematical time. Woolf gives this moment a long shot. The moment frees his soul, speeding away like the aeroplane by its own free will in ecstasy, in pure delight, as the white smoke of the aeroplane writes 'a T, an O, and F' (*MD* 31).

The moment of standstill is the time of Septimus's revelation. As Rezia says, it is 'time', by which she means time on the clock. Twelve o'clock is the time she will have to bring Septimus to see Sir William Bradshaw in Harley Street, where Bradshow's house is located 'with the grey motor car in front of it' (*MD* 103). The relation between Sir Bradshaw and Septimus seems to parallel Dr Caligari and his patient, as I will explain more in the next section. As Big Ben chimes a quarter to twelve, Septimus tells his wife Rezia, 'smiling mysteriously at the dead man in the grey suit' (*MD* 77), that 'I will tell you the time' (*MD* 77), by which he means the time of his death, as

> The word 'time' split its husk; poured its riches over him; and from his lips fell like shells, like shavings from a plane, without his making of them, hard, white, imperishable, words, and flew to attach themselves to their places in an old to Time; an immortal ode to Time. He sang. Evans answered from behind the tree. The dead were in Thessaly, Evans sang, among the orchids. There they waited till the War was over, and now the dead, now Evans himself [...] (*MD* 76).

The notion of time splits into two, one stands for Rezia's clock time, and the other stands for Septimus's Messianic time – the time of redemption. Before he throws himself out of the window, 'the large Bloomsbury lodging-house window' (*MD* 163) as 'the scapegoat' (*MD* 27), Woolf depicts Septimus's sight of Rezia in close-up, enlarging the size of her face, in order to capture her face in greater detail, to give the effect of Septimus's emotion. As Eisenstein points out, the simplest close-up is the most moving.[121]

Septimus's gaze gives the reader a detail of Rezia's face, as he shades his eyes

> so that he might see only a little of her face at a time, first the chin, then the nose, then the forehead, in case it were deformed, or had some terrible mark on it. But no, there she was, perfectly natural, sewing, with the pursed lips that women have, the set, the melancholy expression, when sewing. But there was nothing terrible about it, he

---

[121] Eisenstein, 'In Close-Up' (1945). *S. M. Eisenstein: Selected Works, Volume III, Writings, 1934 – 47*. Ed. Richard Taylor. Trans. William Powell. London: BFI, 1996, p.270.

assured himself, looking a second time, a third time at her face, her hands, […] (*MD* 156).

Rezia, in this close-up shot, is as natural as he saw her for the first time, no matter how many times he looks at her. They both try Mrs Peters's hat, making the moment the happiest one in each other's life. For the first time for days Septimus speaks as he used to be. 'Not for weeks had they laughed like this together, poking fun privately like married people' (*MD* 157). Rezia never again feels 'so happy! Never in her life' (*MD* 157)! Septimus, too, forgets about all his fear, never feels so wonderful, 'so proud', 'so real' and 'so substantial' (*MD* 158).

Part III:
The Caligari Connection in Clive Bell and Virginia Woolf

Clive Bell in his 'Art and the Cinema' (1922), points out that the cinema has the potential to be a new form of art in modernist aesthetic practice. Like Woolf, Bell's article confirms the significant role of *The Cabinet of Dr Caligari*,[122] by exploring the difference between 'Victorian melodrama'[123] and real cinematic art. In order to explain what 'real art' means to him, Bell gives examples of Cézanne and Picasso's paintings. Both painters represent a remarkable change in terms of how visual objects can be seen. Cézanne and Picasso's paintings are revolutionary, because they are not merely 'the faithful representation'[124] of visual objects. Rather,

---

[122] As Eisenstein points out, *Caligari* 'is the first experiment in Expressionist montage carried out by the artists'. See 'The Eighth Art. On Expressionism, America and, of course, Chaplin' (1922). *S. M. Eisenstein: Selected Works, Volume I, Writings, 1922 – 34*. Ed./Trans. Ricahrd Taylor. London: BFI, 1988, p.31.

[123] Clive Bell, 'Art and the Cinema' (1922). *Vanity Fair* November 1922, 39 – 41, p.39.

[124] Bell, 'Art and the Cinema', p.39.

they change the very conception of the nature of art; there is no faithful visual representation, but the expression of an artistic vision, as I pointed out in chapter one.

As Bell claims, although photography bought to an end the Victorian way of treating paintings as imitations of nature, it also enables 'the crudest Victorian melodrama' to happen in the year 1900.[125] According to Bell, Victorian melodrama is crude, because of its inability to express the subtleties of human nature through its characters. At this stage, the cinema still works like Victorian melodrama with its potential on the 'visual side' held back by its 'contempt of brain',[126] until *Caligari* came alone.

Bell argues that *Caligari* is significant in the development of cinematic form, because it connects the brain and the eye through the 'aesthetic intention'[127] of its visual arrangement. As Eisenstein points out, in his essay 'The English Art. On Expressionism, America and, of course, Chaplin' (1922), Caligari is 'the first experiment in Expressionist montage'.[128] It uses painterly settings to create visual novelties, such as an atmosphere which makes the viewer feel the psychological experience of the characters, 'the nightmare of a lunatic that can be perhaps better expressed by the cinema than by any other means'.[129] Furthermore, the Expressionist decorative settings in *Caligari* suggest a dramatic effect. Bell admires the settings, because they are 'dramatically correct', in the accent and emphasis imposed on characters at critical moments. The setting itself creates an abstract form of the cinema, like 'the highest mathematics'[130] which makes *Caligari* different from Victorian melodrama and changes the conception of the

---

[125] Bell, 'Art and the Cinema', p.39.

[126] Bell, 'Art and the Cinema', p.40.

[127] Bell, 'Art and the Cinema', p.40.

[128] Eisenstein, 'The English Art. On Expressionism. America and, of course, Chaplin' (1922). *Selected Works I*, p.31.

[129] Bell, 'Art and the Cinema', p.40.

[130] Bell, 'Art and the Cinema', p.40.

nature of film. In Woolf's essay 'The Cinema' (1926), one can see how Woolf develops Bell's conception of the cinematic abstract form by looking at literature, the cinema, and human emotion.

Virginia Woolf's essay 'The Cinema' was published in 1926 in different contexts; by *Arts* in New York in June of 1926, reprinted as 'Cinema' in the *Nation and Athenaeum* in July of 1926, and as 'The Movie and Reality' in the *New Republic* in August 1926.[131] 'The Cinema' is one of her the most significant pieces of criticism, developing her interdisciplinary aesthetics in the fields of literature and the cinema. Like Deleuze, Woolf notices the suggestive message hidden in the abstract form of German Expressionism. For Woolf, the contrast of light and shadow, of different tones of colours, illustrates not only the complex of human emotion, but also the interrelation between the visual and verbal arts. Woolf analysed *Caligari* with a critical distance. The film had first been produced in Germany in 1919. The London Film Society exhibited this film on Sunday, March the 14th, 1926, at 3:30 in the afternoon.[132] As Laura Marcus points out, *Caligari* has been mentioned in the Film Society programme (Sunday October 25th, 1925),[133] 'in the context of Virginia Woolf's likely viewing of the *Cabinet of Dr Caligari* at a Film Society screening, the programmes exhibited both the evolutionary dimensions of film and its history and a continuum of cinematic representations, past and present'.[134]

---

[131] Leslie Kathleen Hankins points out that this range of publications 'indicates film theory's place as an interdisciplinary site in the literary journal, political newspapers, art magazines, and trade publications of the twenties'. See "'Across the Screen of My Brain': Virginia Woolf's 'The Cinema' and Film Forums of the Twenties". *The Multiple Muses of Virginia Woolf*. Ed. Diane F. Gillespie. Columbia: University of Missouri Press, 1993, pp.151-152.

[132] *The Film Society Programmes, 1925 – 1939*. New York: Arno, 1972, p.22.

[133] *The Film Society Programmes*, pp.3 – 4.

[134] Laura Marcus, *The Tenth Muse: Writing About Cinema in the Modernist Period*. Oxford: Oxford University Press, 2007, p.266.

This essay conveys Woolf's astute analysis of the nature of film; in it she explores her concern with the relation between literature and the cinema, and reveals her multidisciplinary aesthetics. Gilbert Seldes reviewed Woolf's essay on 15 September 1926 in *New Republic*.[135] Seldes accused Woolf of 'writing without knowledge of the abstract films which have been made in Paris'. This comment is not fair to Woolf, because Woolf does show her awareness of the 'new cinematic visual language'[136] and her sense of the importance and the potential of the cinema in the context of modernist aesthetic, using it in her fictional writing, as I have demonstrated in the previous section. A colour image, in *Caligari*, is not only for the sake of colouring – it is necessary for evoking emotional / psychological intensity (for instance, purple indicates Jane's anxiety in her house; the evening scenes and the murder scene are cold blue, which evokes the mysterious atmosphere). Interestingly, although Gilbert Seldes criticised Woolf in his essay 'The Abstract Movie' (1926), he agreed with Woolf's way of seeing the expression of emotion in *Caligari*, in which there are moments of feelings and thoughts 'without always depending upon action'.[137] For example, *Caligari* uses 'expressionistic settings' – the 'shape' of an attic or of a window, the use of 'levels, inclines and curves' – all suggesting 'the intensity of emotion which the story was to call up'.[138]

The film of Tolstoy's *Anna Karenina*, for Woolf, does not connect with what Tolstoy wrote. Woolf sees Anna's mind through reading Tolstoy – her charm, her passion, her despair.[139] However, the film itself does not show Anna's emotions. The eye of the viewer recognises a 'voluptuous

---

[135] Gilbert Seldes, 'The Abstract Movie', *New Republic* 15 September 1926, pp.95 – 96.

[136] *Encyclopedia of British Women's Writing, 1900 – 1950*. Eds. Faye Hammill, Esme Miskimmin and Ashlie Sponenberg. London: Palgrave, 2006, p.49.

[137] Seldes, 'The Abstract Movie', p.96.

[138] Seldes, 'The Abstract Movie', p.96.

[139] Virginia Woolf, 'The Cinema' (1926). *E II*, p.270.

lady in black velvet wearing pearls'[140] on the screen, who, Woolf suggests, could be anyone, even Queen Victoria. What Anna wears, her pearls, her velvet, do not show who she is. Woolf obviously is not interested simply in things the eye can see, or something as simple as 'A kiss is love', 'A broken cup is jealousy', or 'A grin is happiness'.[141] Rather, she is looking for a particular 'moment' in the cinema.

In the film *Das Cabinet des Dr Caligari*, it is a moment, which 'seemed to embody some monstrous diseased imagination of the lunatic's brain'.[142] This 'moment' is a moment for the viewer too, for visualising his or her imagination and emotion; it can be expressed and materialised in a black shape, as the shadow in an immense size, which 'shaped like a tadpole suddenly appeared at one corner of the screen'.[143] It 'quivered, bulged, and sank back again'.[144] This shadow on the screen is one central visual symbol, which enables the viewer to imagine the murderer without seeing him. The shadow on the wall in Alan's attic is the shadow of Cesare raising his arm, holding a blade and stabbing that of Alan. For Woolf, it is a shape which stimulates the emotion 'fear'. This black tadpole shape stimulates the viewer's imagination, better than the statement in words, 'I am afraid'.[145]

The Cabinet of Dr Caligari was a film written by C. Mayer and H. Janowitz, directed by Robert Wiene, and released by Decla in February 1920 in the Berlin Marmorhaus. As Ian Roberts points out, this film was significant in terms of its political message and its expressionist style, in the first ten years after the end of First World War, before Germany's film industry began to be overshadowed by the 'familiar hegemony' of

---

[140] Woolf, 'The Cinema', p.269
[141] Woolf, 'The Cinema', p.270.
[142] Woolf, 'The Cinema', p.270.
[143] Woolf, 'The Cinema', p.270.
[144] Woolf, 'The Cinema', p.270.
[145] Woolf, 'The Cinema', p.270.

Hollywood. [146] According to Siegfried Kracauer, this most widely discussed film of the time represented the political reality of postwar Germany, which is a 'vision of horror'.[147] Dr Caligari himself stands for an authority that manipulates power and desire for domination. He stands on the top of the stairs in the lunatic asylum, as a symbol of his position at the top of the hierarchy. Dr Caligari is a very specific premonition of Hitler, in the sense that he uses hypnotic power to 'force his will upon his tool – a technique foreshadowing, in content and purpose, that manipulation of the soul which Hitler was the first to practice on a gigantic scale'.[148] *Caligari* conveys an atmosphere of horror, in which the soul is wavering between tyranny and chaos in a state of confusion.

The 'Caligari style',[149] as Kracauer phrases it, is a depiction of madness as a strategy by which to critique 'a state authority manifesting itself in universal conscription and declarations of war'.[150] The setting in the film presents a chaotic world, in terms of social structure and of the inner life of people. It transforms material objects into emotions through colour and shape. The play of light and shadow constructs the Caligari world, in which colour and shape develop a pattern of psychological movement. Abstract geometrical compositions in rhythmic movements are the frame of the film, the aesthetic form and the symbolic content, depicting a psychological experience like a madman's fantasy. The line and figure produce an 'optic music', by which it marks an 'utter withdrawal from the outer world'.[151] As Kracauer points

---

[146] Ian Roberts, 'Caligari Revisited: Circles, Cycles and Counter-Revolution in Robert Wiene's *Das Cabinet Des Dr Caligari'. German Life and Letters* 57.2 (2004): 175 – 187, p.176.

[147] Siegfried Kracauer, *From Caligari to Hitler: A Psychological History of the German Film.* Ed. Leonardo Quaresima. 1947. Princeton: Princeton University Press, 2004, p.61.

[148] Kracauer, *From Caligari to Hitler,* pp.72 – 73.

[149] Kracauer, *From Caligari to Hitler,* p.70.

[150] Kracauer, *From Caligari to Hitler,* p.64.

[151] Kracauer, *From Caligari to Hitler,* p.68.

out, German expressionism as an avant-garde movement soon spread to other countries. From about 1924, French artists such as Fernand Léger and René Clair, 'made films which […] showed an affinity for the formal beauty of machine parts, and molded all kinds of objects and motions into surrealistic dreams'.[152] As René Clair claims, an artist can create a surreal world, because he is 'less interested in what he [sees] than in transforming it into what he [imagines]'.[153] Clair's point illustrates a psychological reading of a film, by which one can see a film as visual symphonies of symbols.

As Kracauer points out, during the postwar years, Expressionism was frequently considered to aim at the shaping of primitive emotions and psychological experiences. This movement showed 'how the spontaneous manifestations of a profoundly agitated soul might best be formulated'.[154] The Expressionist sets were designed by three members of the *Sturm* group, namely, Hermann Warm, Walter Röhrig and Walter Reimann,[155] who had an important role in *Caligari* and the development of German cinema. Rooms, streets and buildings are not merely backgrounds; rather, they are symbols of the scenery of the soul in spatial terms. The Expressionist abstract setting has a gloomy and mysterious atmosphere; an emotion of fear and horror is created by twisted stairs and roads. Curves and slanting lines of the wall create the effect of claustrophobia. The handling of light highlights the inner illumination of the soul, which is another major contribution of this film. Dark shadows reinforce the Expressionist design of the film, which suggests the emotions of terror and fear through abstract visual symbols, without reproducing the exact look of the visual object.

---

[152] Kracauer, *From Caligari to Hitler*, p.68.

[153] René Clair, 'Foreword'. *Caligari's Cabinet and Other Grand Illusions: A History of Film Design*. Léon Barsacq. Ed. Elliott Stein. Boston: New York Graphic Society, 1976, vii.

[154] Kracauer, *From Caligari to Hitler*, p.70.

[155] Lotte H. Eisner, *The Haunted Screen*. 1952. Berkeley: University of California Press, 1965, p.19.

According to Woolf, the cinema is the youngest art form, but it has
been born 'fully-clothed'. [156] In *Caligari*, one can see that German
Expressionist film is a 'radical and revolutionary' [157] artistic form, as
Dietrich Scheunemann points out. However, for Woolf, the cinema was not
born naked, in the sense that it inherited traditions and techniques from
other art forms, and Expressionist painting had in fact seen its heyday
before the First World War. Furthermore, the central and uncanny motif of
Caligari, the split personalities of Dr Caligari (the showman and the
scientist), is a gothic tale. Such characters have their origin in
nineteenth-century Romantic literature, or even earlier. For instance, as Peter
Beicken points out, Dr Caligari is Faust in film. The Faustian theme and
motif, above all, is 'the concept of the divided self and [...] the search for
superior knowledge'. [158] Such characters, Scheunemann claims, 'are haunted
by their shadows and alter ego'. [159] As Woolf claims, cinematographic form
does not aim to represent life merely in a representative / realistic way; it is
not 'the simple photograph of real life'. [160] Emotions should be expressed
aesthetically, in an abstract way. The emotion 'anger' cannot only be
represented physically, such as by 'red faces and clenched fists'; [161] rather, it
can be expressed through something abstract and suggestive, 'the likeness
of the thought' [162] in Woolf's term, perhaps 'a black line wriggling upon a

---

[156] Woolf, 'The Cinema', p.272.

[157] Dietrich Scheunemann, 'The Double, the Décor, and the Framing Device: Once
    More on Robert Wiene's *The Cabinet of Dr Caligari*'. *Expressionist Film: New
    Perspectives*. Ed. Dietrich Scheunemann. New York: Camden House, 2003, p.139.

[158] Peter Beicken, 'Faust in Film: The Case of Dr Caligari'. *Doctor Faustus:
    Archetypal Subtext at the Millennium*. Eds. Armand E. Singer and Jürgen Schlunk.
    Morgantown: West Virginia University Press, 1999, p.43.

[159] Scheunemann, 'The Double, the Décor, and the Framing Device: Once More on
    Robert Wiene's *The Cabinet of Dr Caligari*', p.130.

[160] Woolf, 'The Cinema', p.268.

[161] Woolf, 'The Cinema', p.270.

[162] Woolf, 'The Cinema', p.271.

white sheet'.[163] The cinema must avoid forms of expression which are 'accessible to words and to words alone', even the simplest image such as 'My luve's like a red red rose'.[164] In other words, the cinema should not only represent emotion. It should evoke the viewer's feelings and emotions through its aesthetic expression. The cinema should not be 'the savage'[165] art, in which a series of images on the screen only reveals rapid and violent changes of emotion. Rather, it should allow the viewer's fantasy to grow, to become something which 'visits us in sleep or shapes itself in half-darkened rooms […]. The past could be unrolled, distances annihilated […]'.[166]

The cinema, as a form of modern art, has been born 'fully-clothed', because the discourse of film theory, as it began to be articulated at Woolf's time, crossed the boundaries of various disciplines. The discourse opens up a space (as a text or a screen) for the diversity of aesthetic theories and concepts which are more rigidly codified in the fields of art criticism and literature. In a short essay such as 'The Cinema', Woolf expresses her interest in the aesthetic, theoretic and experimental potential of the cinema as a new medium. Film itself stimulates her investigations into the potential of the techniques of the visual arts for literature. From this point of view, one can read Woolf's essay on the cinema as a contribution to her literary practice, which mapped interrelations between different versions of text, emotion, space, time, and memory.

Conclusion

A return to the literary text of *Mrs Dalloway* through the lens of a movie camera enables the reader to explore new ways of answering this central question: what is meant by cinema and what is meant by a novel, in

---

[163] Woolf, 'The Cinema', p.270.
[164] Woolf, 'The Cinema', p.271.
[165] Woolf, 'The Cinema', p.268.
[166] Woolf, 'The Cinema', p.272.

discussing the novel's complex relation to time. Woolf's use of montage in a psychological sense expresses inner time, through the juxtaposition of images of thought, and the emotional fusion of the inner and outer spheres, of the past and the present. In this chapter, I have uncovered Woolf's cinematic writing technique. Woolf's cinematic style brings a new way of seeing the significance of time, between 'now' and 'then', within the context of the passing present. The sense of continuum of Woolf's novel is re-established with its own temporal logic (even Mrs. Hilbery from *Night and Day* appears in Clarissa's party, *MD* 193). The experience of time constantly occurs in its own unfolding aesthetic structure.

Both the movement and the stillness of the gaze are used in this novel, to explore the experience of time and to develop a new narrative aesthetics drawing on the techniques of film and literature. Images in a sequence of shots carry meanings, as words in sentences. The French critic, Jean Mitry, compares an Eisenstein film to a poem, which can be 'divided into several cantos in which each canto has a different meaning and a different style'.[167] Woolf's novel also provides the vividness of visual metaphor in a cinematic sense, by using verbal language. By shooting *la durée* with a dual vision, the first seeing the experience of time in movement of the body and the mind, illuminating the brain as the screen; the other employing a still frame to express a halt in time, Woolf juxtaposes different gazes as shots from different angles, bringing the cinematic method of montage into her exploration of time, consciousness and the gaze in literature.

---

[167] John B. Kuiper, 'Cinematic Expression: A Look at Eisenstein's Silent Montage'. *Art Journal* 22.1 (1962): 34 – 39, p.34.

CHAPTER FOUR

Photography in *The Years and Three Guineas*

Oh, mystery of Beauty! Who can tell

Thy mighty influence? who can best descry

How secret, swift, and subtle is the spell

Wherein the music of thy voice doth lie?

-Julia Margaret Cameron, 'On A Portrait'[1]

Ultimately, Photography is subversive not when it frightens, repels, or even stigmatizes, but when it is *pensive*, when it thinks.

-Roland Barthes, *Camera Lucida*[2]

Introduction

In this chapter, I explore the image of women in Woolf's *The Years* (1937) and *Three Guineas* (1938), looking at how images of women are recast in *The Years* and *Three Guineas*, and considering their effects and contributions in the light of the aesthetics of photography. I will discuss Virginia Woolf's 'Ellen Terry' and Julia Margaret Cameron, to see the way in which theatre has inspired Cameron, for her using photography to

---

[1] Julia Margaret Cameron, 'On A Portrait' (September 1875). *Macmillan's Magazine*, February 1876. Reprinted in *Julia Margaret Cameron: Her Life and Photographic Work*. Helmut Gernsheim. London: Fountain, 1948, p.73.

[2] Roland Barthes, *Camera Lucida: Reflections on Photography*. Trans. Richard Howard. London: Vintage, 1993, p.38.

perform gender and womenhood. Looking at Cameron's photographic work, I aim to show how the photographic perspective demonstrates a moment of seeing one's own self-perception, rather than the exhibition of human figures as fragmented visual objects. Reading Walter Benjamin's discussion of Atget, one can understand the dialectic of image in Woolf's work in relation to the avant-garde. Reading Roland Barthes's *Camera Lucida*, one can see the way Woolf uses photographs of male authority as *punctum*, recalling the photo not shown – the fragmented female body in *Three Guineas*.

Part I:
Virginia Woolf and Victorian Aesthetics

Cameron and her Camera

According to Margaret Harker, Julia Margaret Cameron, Virginia Woolf's godmother, 'Aunt Julia', is 'photography's great eccentric'.[3] When she was fifty in 1865, Cameron became a photographer. Her daughter and her son-in-law gave her a camera as a birthday gift, with the words, 'It may amuse you, Mother, to try to photograph during your solitude at Freshwater'.[4] After that, according to Virginia Woolf, all her 'sensibility was expressed' through photography, into which she put all energies that 'she had dissipated in poetry and fiction and doing up houses and

---

[3] Margaret Harker, *Julia Margaret Cameron*. London: William Collins Sons, 1983, p.4.

[4] Julia Margaret Cameron, 'Annals of My Glass House' (1874), an unfinished autobiography written in 1874, is a record of Victorian photographer Julia Margaret Cameron's first ten years of work. It was first published by her youngest son, Henry Herschel Hay Cameron, in a catalogue to the exhibition, *Mrs. Cameron's Photographs*, at the Camera Gallery, London, in 1889. Reprinted in *Illuminations: Women Writing on Photography from the 1850s to the Present*. Eds. Liz Heron and Val Williams. London: I. B. Tauris, 1996, pp.8 – 13, p.8.

concocting curries and entertaining her friends'.[5] To show her control in this new born art to her family, as Cameron herself describes in 'Annals of My Glass House', she turned 'the coal-house into a dark room, and the fowl-house a glass-house'.[6] For Woolf, Cameron's photographs go beyond realism, in their 'diminishing just in the least degree the precision of the focus'.[7] The soft focus brings out Cameron's brilliant aesthetic sense, in which her longing to arrest 'all the beauty'[8] of a person was satisfied.

For Roger Fry, Cameron's photographs confirm the status of photography as an independent art, rather than simply being an imitation of nature, people or things. Photography, Fry claims, 'at least in Mrs. Cameron's hands, can give us something that only the greatest masters were capable of giving' – the 'universal and dateless world which this imagination created for us'.[9] Cameron's photographic portraits reveal the inner personality of her sitters/characters at a given moment.

According to Roger Fry, Cameron creates a 'wonderful perception of character as it is expressed in form, and of form as it is revealed or hidden by the incidence of light'.[10] Her portraits articulate a conception, a 'revelation'[11] of character, which one does not find 'Whistler or Watts come near'.[12] They are products of extraordinarily skilful manipulation, of such elements as the wet plates and the long exposure. Cameron's technique of photography contains both expression and form, unifying the revelation

---

[5] Virginia Woolf, 'Julia Margaret Cameron'. *Victorian Photographs of Famous Men & Fair Women by Julia Margaret Cameron*. Ed. Tristram Powell. 1926. London: Hogarth Press, 1973, p.18.

[6] Cameron, 'Annals of My Glass House', p.9.

[7] Woolf, 'Julia Margaret Cameron', p.18.

[8] Woolf, 'Julia Margaret Cameron', p.18.

[9] Foger Fry, 'Mrs. Cameron's Photographs'. *Victorian Photographs of Famous Men & Fair Women*, p.24.

[10] Fry, 'Mrs. Cameron's Photographs', p.26.

[11] Fry, 'Mrs. Cameron's Photographs', p.26.

[12] Fry, 'Mrs. Cameron's Photographs', p.26.

of character and artistic design – the light and shade effect of the lips of 'Mary Mother' (May Hillier), the unanalysable oval features of 'The Christ Kind' (Margie Thackeray), and the transitions of tone of 'Mrs. Leslie Stephen' (Virginia Woolf's mother) in the cheek and the delicate suggestions of reflected light, which are "no less than the beautiful 'drawing' of the profile".[13] Photography, for Fry, can be seen as a 'possible branch of visual art', because it 'seems capable of transmitting the artist's feeling to us',[14] which makes a portrait an artistic expression of divine, poetical and allegorical composition, as one can see in the general organization of the forms, the balance of movements throughout the whole structure, the feeling of intensity, and quality of the light.

In 'Annals of My Glass House' (1874), Cameron depicts her own passionate emotions through photographing her characters. She treats her camera lens 'as a living thing',[15] which she loves tenderly. She lets it open the secret chamber of her heart, flirting with her senses, memory and her soul, forming a moment of emotional overflow, in which she sees 'all beauty'[16] that came before her – the peasantry of Freshwater, the memory of a sweet little girl Annie, and her old true friend Sir Henry Taylor. Cameron's emotion and passion for her 'lovely subjects'[17] are transformed through her 'out-of-focus'[18] photographic technique. The light illuminates her characters in a truly graceful way that 'cannot be described'.[19] Cameron's photographs contain the complexion of her characters' minds. She does not aim to photograph the greatness of her intimate male friends such as Taylor and Carlyle. For instance, she does not dress them up in

---

[13] Fry, 'Mrs. Cameron's Photographs', p.27.
[14] Fry, 'Mrs. Cameron's Photographs', p.28.
[15] Cameron, 'Annals of My Glass House', p.9.
[16] Cameron, 'Annals of My Glass House', p.9.
[17] Cameron, 'Annals of My Glass House', p.9.
[18] Cameron, 'Annals of My Glass House', p.9.
[19] Cameron, 'Annals of My Glass House', p.10.

customs which symbolise male authority (such as the uniforms in Virginia
Woolf's *Three Guineas*). Rather, I would argue, Cameron uses her camera
lens for depicting their inner nature, so that Sir Henry Taylor was 'crowned
with tinsel',[20] and Alfred Tennyson was 'wrapped in rugs'[21] as the 'Dirty
Monk'.[22] For Cameron, it is a psychological drama that she aims to express
in her photographic form.

Julia Kristeva: Imagining the Maternal Body

Cameron's portraits of women continued to disturb me. On the one
hand, her out-of-focus perspective can be read as a radical departure from
traditional photographic technique,[23] which has led to her recognition as a
great portraitist and one of photography's pioneers. On the other hand, I
cannot help myself looking for what Cameron's portraits of women have
conveyed about their creator and her time. They seem different from
Cameron's photographs of men.

As I have suggested in the previous section, her portraits of men
convey an inner complexity, emotion and passion. And yet, I wonder if
there truly was a different quality to Cameron's portraits of women? If the
answer was yes, I also wonder how and why they are not merely imitations
of Pre-Raphaelite paintings, in which, as Griselda Pollock argues, the
feminine is located in an ideological formation, as 'the passive, beautiful or
erotic object of a creativity exclusively tied to the masculine'.[24] The
central question, for me, is: in Cameron's work, do women perform

---

[20] Woolf, 'Julia Margaret Cameron', p.18.

[21] Woolf, 'Julia Margaret Cameron', p.18.

[22] Cameron, Annals of My Glass House', p.13.

[23] John Tagg, *The Burden of Representation: Essays on Photographies and Histories*.
1988. London: Macmillan, 1993, p.48.

[24] Griselda Pollock, 'Woman as Sign in Pre-Raphaelite Literature: the Representation
of Elizabeth Siddall'. *Vision and Difference: Femininity, Feminism and Histories
of Art*. London: Routledge, 1988, p.91.

archetypal personae of the classics of male tradition – as Sylvia Wolf points out, the Old Testament, the New Testament, Greek mythology, Renaissance painting, and the classics of English literature (Shakespeare, Milton, Keats, Shelly, Byron and Coleridge)?

Woolf clearly criticises an ideal image of a woman. She aims to kill Coverntry Patmore's 'ideal wife'[25] who was evoked in Cameron's *The Angel in the House* (1871, the title is from Patmore's poem). For Woolf, Cameron's *The Angel in the House* represents an image of ideal womanhood, 'an ideal existence', 'a dream', 'a phantom' that is created 'by the imaginations of men and women at a certain stage of their pilgrimage to lure them across a very dusty stretch of the journey'[26] in Victorian aesthetics. According to Woolf, killing the Angel of the House is a 'professional experience'.[27] If she did not kill the Angel of the House, then the Angel will kill her potential as a writer. Whenever Woolf 'felt the shadow of her wings or the radiance of her halo upon the page', she 'took up the inkpot and flung it at her'.[28] The Angel's territory is the House, and for Woolf, the Angel's hands are full of blood, because she is the murderer of the potential female '[w]riter after writer, painter after painter and musicians',[29] especially those young and unmarried.

Women in Cameron's portraits are not examples of Victorian greatness. They are not as well known as her male sitters such as Lord Alfred Tennyson or Sir Henry Taylor. These women are family members (such as her niece Julia Jackson, Virginia Woolf's mother) or ordinary domestic servants. However, as Phyllis Rose argues, she sees eternal beauty in the

---

[25] Sylvia Wolf, ed. *Julia Margaret Cameron's Women*. New Haven: Yale UP, 1998, p.228.

[26] Virginia Woolf, 'Speech Before the London / National Society for Women's Service'. *The Pargiters: The Novel-Essay Portion of THE YEARS*'. Ed. Mitchell A. Leaska. London: Hogarth Press, 1978, xxx.

[27] Woolf, 'Speech of January 21 1931', xxxiii.

[28] Woolf, 'Speech of January 21 1931', xxxii.

[29] Woolf, 'Speech of January 21 1931', xxxii.

everyday; Madonna in the milkmaid. The costumes, shawls and turbans somehow eternalise the maid's beauty, as signs, symbols, and 'enduring patterns'[30] of the empowerment of the artist's imagination. Cameron often gives mythological or literary titles to these portraits, such as 'Pomona' (Alice Liddell, 1872)[31] or 'The Gardener's Daughter' (1867, a photographic practice of Tennyson's poem). It is one of Cameron's rare outdoor studies, illustrating a passage in Tennyson's 1842 poem of the same title.[32]

'Pomona' particularly amuses me. It is the photograph of Alice Liddell, who is the original 'Alice' in *Alice's Adventures in Wonderland* and *Through the Looking-Glass* by Lewis Carroll. Alice Pleasance Liddell (1852-1934) was the middle of three daughters of Dean Liddell (Dr Henry Liddell, former head of Westminster School, Dean of Christ Church, Oxford).[33] It is one of my favorite Cameron photographs. I can see that the inner characteristic Cameron saw in Alice clamoring for expression was exemplified by Pomona, the goddess of trees. From Roman mythology, as Sylvia Wolf points out, Pomona's name is linked with 'the growth cycles of the earth and with other female divinities who represent fertility'.[34] I suggest that 'Pomona' articulates female creativity and inner personality of the character, the name as title, which subverts the image of an ideal woman under male gaze. In this respect, Cameron sees and depicts the inner divine nature of femininity as individual creativity, rather than treating women as a 'facial type' or 'a lip has been kissed',[35] an isolated and fragmented body, a suggestive figure,

---

[30] Phyllis Rose, 'Milkmaid Madonnas: An Appreciation of Cameron's Portraits of Women'. *Julia Margaret Cameron's Women*, p.14.

[31] See Harker, *Julia Margaret Cameron*, p.44.

[32] See Julia Margaret Cameron's *The Herschel Album: An Album of Photographs by Julia Margaret Cameron, Presented to Sir John Herschel*. London: National Portrait Gallery, 1975, plate 18.

[33] Amanda Hopkinson, *Julia Margaret Cameron*. London: Virago, 1986, p.60.

[34] Sylvia Wolf, *Julia Cameron's Women*, p.232.

[35] Pollock, 'Woman as Sign: Psychological Readings'. *Vision and Difference*, p.132.

a sign or a flat image, that draws male sexual desire and gaze. Cameron's photographs capture the beauty in models themselves. It is not 'beauty' objectified for the male gaze, which is how Pollock interprets Rossetti's paintings. Cameron's work illustrates the power of creativity, which comes from her emotion and passion, making it possible for her to visualise the moment of Ideal beauty that she sees – writing (May Prinsep), Madonna, sisterhood, the changing seasons and fertility.

For Cameron, the female body is beauty itself, which expresses female inner divinity, as one can see in her photographs. And yet, Woolf has a rather negative way of seeing a female body, because of her own personal experience. The way Gerald Duckworth treated Woolf, as Madelyn Detloff argues, making her 'a person who [was] ashamed of her body',[36] of her sexuality; whose body was subject to the controlling forces of elder males in her Victorian family. Woolf was ashamed of her body, because it had been treated as a sexual object, when Gerald Duckworth lifted her onto a slab and explored her body. Woolf resented and disliked it, as one can see in 'A Sketch of the Past'.[37] She did not like to be touched in that way, and she felt that some parts of her body should not be touched like that at all. The very instinct proves, as Woolf herself suggests, that 'Virginia Stephen was not born on the 25th January 1882, but was born many thousand years ago; and had from the very first to encounter instincts already acquired by thousands of ancestresses in the past'.[38] At that particular moment, Woolf went

---

[36] Madelyn Detloff, "Imagined Communities of Criticism: 'Wounded Attachments' to the Icons of H. D., Gertrude Stein, and Virginia Woolf". *Virginia Woolf and Communities: Selected Papers from the Eighth Annual Conference on Virginia Woolf.* Eds. Jeanette Mcvicker and Laura Davis. New York: Pace University Press, 1999, p.55.

[37] Virginia Woolf, 'A Sketch of the Past' (1939). *Moments of Being: Unpublished Autobiographical Writings.* Ed. Jeanne Schulkind. Sussex: University of Sussex Press, 1976, p.69.

[38] Woolf, 'A Sketch of the Past', p.69.

through the feeling of shame, which many women had before or after her. As she looked at her own face in the mirror in the hall, she realised that her body was haunted by the male gaze of Gerald Duckworth, and saw in the mirror a 'horrible face – the face of an animal'.[39]

The face of an animal in the mirror, for Woolf, is that of 'the appearance of the phallic ghost'[40] in the Symbolic, as Lacan phrases it. Woolf is haunted by the phallic ghost, and photographed by the male gaze reflected in the mirror. What she sees in the mirror is beyond the appearance, the visible; the spectacle evokes a feeling of strangeness and uncanny. As Bracha Lichtenberg Ettinger points out, this uncanny anxiety is the return of the repressed – the origin of the '*matrixial/womb phantasy (-complex)*'.[41] For Julia Kristeva, the re-discovery of the maternal body in poetic language gives one a possible way, to re-think the paternal law at the level of semiotic itself – an unfixed, pre-oedipal maternal space.[42] She tries to show that the maternal body, as Judith Butler points out, is an '*effect* of culture rather than its secret and primary cause'.[43] As Madelon Sprengnether points out, Freud suggests that

---

[39] Woolf, 'A Sketch of the Past', p.69.

[40] Lacan, *The Four Fundamental Concepts of Psycho-Analysis*, p.88.

[41] Bracha Lichtenberg Ettinger, *The Matrixial Gaze*. Leeds: University of Leeds Press, 1995, p.7.

[42] As Elizabeth Grosz points out, when a little girl is unable to resolve her oedipal relation to her mother, as a female writer, she cannot recall or represent the maternal space without being consumed by it. This woman has the masculinity complex, which occurs when the woman disavows sexual difference. She disavows being a woman, because she thinks her genital is 'small', someday it will grow. Such a woman would not write as a woman, 'but as man'. She remains at the pre-oedipal 'masculine' phase. See *Sexual Subversions: Three French Feminists*. Sydney: Allen & Unwin, 1989, pp.64 – 65. See also Juliet Mitchell, *Psychoanalysis and Feminism*. 1974. London: Penguin, 1990, p.96.

[43] Judith Butler, *Gender Trouble*. 1990. London: Routledge, 2006, p.109.

the infant's relation to the feminine threatens the structure of masculine development, yet he cannot accept systems of explanation, such as those of Jung, Bachofen, or Rank, which rest on assumptions of female priority. As a result he locks femininity into a position of subordination and disruption. This structure, in turn, has had a significant impact on subsequent develpmmets of psychoanalytic theory.[44]

Culture in itself can be read as a paternal structure. The semiotic process is, rather, the continuity of the mother-infant relation.[45] As Terry Eagleton points out, the semiotic is the 'other' of language, 'which is nonetheless intimately entwined with it. Because the semiotic stems from the pre-Oedipal phase, it is bound up with the child's contact with the mother's body, whereas the symbolic, […], is associated with the Law of the father'.[46] For Woolf, to break through the threshold of sexual repression is to identify with motherhood, in which maternal jouissance is experienced, perceived and expressed. This search for jouissance in virginal images, as Kristeva points out in her *Desire in Language*, situated the mother beyond the Law, by which it shows 'the very *function* of jouissance'[47] that is explored and experienced through the Mother.

Woolf's *Freshwater: A Comedy*

Virginia Woolf found her own way of seeing female inner divinity – a woman's creativity in Ellen Terry. Woolf's *Freshwater: A Comedy* (1935) was staged in the mid-1930s in Vanessa Bell's London studio at 8 Fitzroy

---

[44] Madelon Sprengnether, 'Femininity as Subversion'. *The Spectral Mother: Freud, Feminism, and Psychoanalysis*. Ithaca: Cornell University Press, 1990, p.183.

[45] Terry Eagleton, *Literary Theory*. 1983. Oxford: Blackwell, 1995, p.188.

[46] Eagleton, *Literary Theory*, p.188.

[47] Julia Kristeva, *Desire in Language: A Semiotic Approach to Literature and Art*. Ed. Leon S. Roudiez. Trans. Thomas Gora, Alice Jardine, and Leon S. Roudiez. 1977. New York: Columbia University Press, 1980, p.248.

Street, on the evening of 18 January 1935. The event celebrated Angelica Bell's birthday, and the audience was 'in a party mood'.[48] According to Lucio P. Ruotolo, the play 'began at 9:30, was performed in an atmosphere of noise and levity. Clive Bell's booming voice and laughter in particular were heard throughout the performance'.[49] And yet, I would suggest, this play cannot be read only as a joyous farce. It shows what is real and beautiful for Cameron and Watts through Ellen Terry's posing for them.

As Victoria Olsen points out, when photography emerged from the amateur tradition in the 1840s and 1850s, becoming commercial and popular in the 1860s, though it was 'inevitably compared to painting', in addition, it was 'insistently compared to the theater'.[50] According to Olsen, the Victorian period was an age when the theatre included a broad range of professional and amateur shows, covering forms from Shakespeare's newly canonical high art to 'traveling vaudeville companies, circus performers, freak shows, and acrobats', and she argues that 'the theater touched many more Victorian lives than painting or sculpture'.[51] From the beginning, critics compared photographs to some kind of living sculpture or living picture, as if photography is thought to be second rate, without its own specific quality, when it comes to the categorisation of arts. And yet, I suggest that the interaction between different forms of art and the comparison between them – say, Cameron's photography, Tennyson's poetry and Watt's painting – does not necessarily construct a hierarchical relation between the arts. Issues such as which art influences which, or which artist is better than which, are not my focus. Victorian artists were searching for a form and a content to express what was

---

[48] Lucio P.Ruotolo, Preface. *Freshwater: A Comedy*. Ed. Lucio P.Ruotolo. London: Hogarth Press, 1976, viii.

[49] Ruotolo, Preface, viii.

[50] Victoria Olsen. *From Life: Julia Margaret Cameron & Victorian Photography*. London: Aururm, 2003, p.161.

[51] Olsen, *From Life*, p.161.

real to them. In this light, an actor can be inspiring for a painter, just as photography is as inspiring as theatre.

For Cameron and her friends, the theatre meant attending plays and meeting actors as well as a heightened form of self-expression that pervaded both public and private life, as Olsen points out.[52] The world of theatre makes room for fantasy, exploring a more playful and experimental world, for other possible selves and identities to exist. Cameron photographed people who were accustomed to posing and performing for each other. For example, behind her camera, she photographed and made studies of Holman Hunt in Eastern dress, Henry Taylor as Friar Lawrence.[53] She draped her models in cloaks and posed them with bows, arrows and turkey wings. I would suggest that Cameron's photography creates opportunities for her models to perform; her studio is like a stage in the theatre.

Cameron's originality also lies in the way her photography gives room for performing womanhood. Acting permitted flirtations, rebellions, and all sorts of exceptional behaviour under cover of a costume. A costume gives Cameron a sense of liberty – 'the more the merrier, the more melodramatic the better'.[54] Her love of theatre made her to build a studio near her house to stage plays. Cameron's photographs seem theatrical, coming to be her narrative tableaux of Beauty – the dramatic thing that Cameron sees in life. For instance, her most used models were her own housemaids, especially Mary Hillier, often known as 'Madonna Mary' after her best-known role. Hillier was born in Freshwater. Her sister and brother worked for Tennyson at Farringford. In 1861, at the age of fourteen, Hillier started serving Cameron.[55] Cameron does not see Hillier as a working-class woman. On the contrary, she sees Beauty in her. Cameron tries to represent inner as well

---

[52] Olsen, *From Life*, p.161.

[53] Olsen, *From Life*, p.162.

[54] Olsen, *From Life*, p.162.

[55] Stephanie Lipscomb. 'Sitters' Biographies'. *Julia Cameron's Women*, p.221.

as outer realities. Her relation with Hillier, founded on over ten years of modeling and shaped by the daily interactions within a household, is intimate. That intimacy comes to Cameron, making her believe that Hillier is the very person for role-playing her Virgin Mary – a strengthened faith in transformation, a symbolic reference to the miracle of divine intervention, which seems to answer Cameron's own divine calling and creative power.

Cameron's maternal vision seems to intend the creation of a matriarchal lineage for photography. Cameron's vision of the maternal let women into the photograph as actresses, performing motherhood. The Madonna and child images dramatises motherhood, which becomes the essence of Cameron's vision. Cameron uses her passionate studies of the Madonna and child to signify a new sensibility about psychological relations. As Mike Weaver points out, Cameron's photographs are revisions of the accepted interpretation of the Bible, as she plays with typological feminine roles, using female models (such as her niece Florence Fisher as well as Mary Hillier) to portray the child John the Baptist and *The Angel at the Tomb*, who were male in the Bible.[56] Through the costume, the inner and the outer are being transformed. Gender is performed through the costume, turning a woman into an allegorical portrait. Cameron's photograph shows a sense of playful abstractisation of gender, in which photography can represent the essence of this abstraction, by performing gender without using physical reality. This sense of bodiless abstraction makes photography an art, which is mortal 'and yet divine',[57] as Julian Cox and Colin Ford point out. The sense of divinity, as Weaver suggests, Cameron's 'light',[58] which reminds the viewer

---

[56] Mike Weaver, *Julia Margaret Cameron: 1815 – 1879*. London: Herbert, 1984, pp.23 – 24.

[57] Julian Cox and Colin Ford. *Julia Margaret Cameron: The Complete Photographs*. London: Thames & Hudson, 2003, p.56.

[58] Helmut Gernsheim. *Julia Margaret Cameron: Her Life and Photographic Work*. London: Gordon Fraser, 1975, p.66.

her close friend G. F. Watts's paintings. Woolf in her later works also explores the concept of bodiless abstraction, for instance, *A Room of One's Own*, in which a female writer can always perform and liberate her inner drama and emotion, without the limitation of her physical reality of being a woman.

Freshwater clearly pictures Ellen Terry as a triumphant heroine, a child 'born to the stage', as Woolf phrases it.[59] Terry was married at sixteen to the elderly famous painter, G. F. Watts. The marriage changed her life dramatically, as Woolf puts it in her essay, 'Ellen Terry' (1941): "[t]he theatre has gone; its lights are out and in its place is a quiet studio in a garden. In its place is a world full of pictures and 'gentle artistic people' with quiet voices and elegant manners".[60] It is a world of Victorian aesthetics, which belongs to Watts, Cameron and Tennyson. Terry sits for Watts, washes his brushes, and plays the piano while he paints; poses for Cameron, and walks with Tennyson as his muse. Terry posed for Cameron and Watts' ideal beauty, not for showing 'herself'.

Ellen Terry's marriage to Watts does not make her a housewife, but a muse and model. She constantly refers to her experience of posing for Watts. For instance, in *Choosing*, one of Watts's many paintings of his wife, Terry smells a camellia. Of all the portraits of done of her, it was Terry's favorite. The marriage of Watts and Terry did not work out. She returned to the stage, met the architect and critic Edward Godwin, who created a daring 'Greek *chiton*' for Terry's role as Titania in *A Midsummer Night's Dream*, drawing her attention to costume design. According to Veronica Franklin Gould, in 1856, it was the first time that Terry began to appreciate beauty, to 'observe, to feel the splendour of things, to *aspire*'![61] As

---

[59] Woolf, 'Ellen Terry' (1941), *Collected Essays by Virginia Woolf, Volume Four*. London: Hogarth Press, 1967, p.69.

[60] Woolf, 'Ellen Terry', p.69.

[61] Veronica Franklin Gould. *G. F. Watts: The Last Great Victorian*. New Haven: Yale University Press, 2004, p.65.

Marguerite Steen points out, Ellen Terry has the 'divine madness', which is 'an ingredient of genius'.[62] She was in love with 'Edward Godwin – for a while; she was in love with Henry Irving – for a while. Her true love was for her art – which, […], she called her *work*'.[63]

Woolf sees Terry's marriage with Watts as the blank pages in Terry's self-portrait; those pages symbolises her as an out-of-tune, an 'incongruous element'[64] in that Victorian world. She was doing everything to complete other people's art,[65] rather than create an art of her own. The blank pages in Terry's self-portrait are the gap between the two Ellen Terrys – 'Ellen the mother, and Ellen the actress'.[66]

For Woolf, the blank pages are something in Terry that she herself does not understand: 'the voice of her genius; the urgent call of something that she could not define, could not suppress, and must obey'.[67] So she followed the voice back to the stage, started again a long life of 'incessant toil, anguish, and glory',[68] as one can see in the full-length portrait of Ellen Terry that Sargent painted her as *Lady Macbeth* (1889), in a magnificent green and blue dress, holding the crown over her head.

Terry's performance, for Woolf, symbolise those 'bodyless'[69] moments of creative energy, when she is so 'close and critical a student of Shakespeare',[70] that she has studied 'every line, weighted the meaning of every word; experimented with every gesture'.[71] She lives her part 'until

---

[62] Marguerite Steen. *A Pride of Terrys: Family Saga.* London: Longmans, 1724, p.260.
[63] Steen, *A Pride of Terrys*, p.260.
[64] Woolf, 'Ellen Terry', p.69.
[65] Woolf, *Freshwater*, p.15.
[66] Woolf, 'Ellen Terry', p.70.
[67] Woolf, 'Ellen Terry', p.70.
[68] Woolf, 'Ellen Terry', p.70.
[69] Woolf, 'Ellen Terry', p.71.
[70] Woolf, 'Ellen Terry', p.71.
[71] Woolf, 'Ellen Terry', p.71.

she is it'.[72] Terry re-thinks, re-imagines and re-writes it, then every phrase is her own; every gesture spontaneous, comes out on to the stage as Imogen, Ophelia, or Desdemona. Something of Ellen Terry, her creativity, seems to Woolf that it came out of her physical body, overflowed every part 'and remained unacted. Shakespeare could not fit her; not Ibsen; nor Shaw'.[73] Ellen Terry is remembered because she acted a new part – Ellen Terry is not the signifier of the parts, but herself.

Ellen Terry was not only an inspiration of Cameron's photography, but she was also inspired by photography. As Roger Manvell points out, in London, Lewis Carroll had earlier been attracted by the Terry family ever since 'seeing Ellen as Mamillius in June 1856': a 'beautiful little creature', as Reverend Charles Dodgson had written, 'who played with remarkable ease and spirit'.[74] Carroll had done many studies of the Terry family, such as *Sarah and Benjamin Terry, Ellen (in the dark frock) Standing with Kate at the Window, Ellen Terry, Sarah and Ellen Terry.* Carroll's studies of the Terry family, especially of Ellen Terry, reveal a delightful photographing experience. He thought Ellen Terry 'lively and pleasant, almost childish in her fun, but perfectly ladylike'.[75] It was at Christmas – Ellen staying at the family home, appearing full of high spirits. Her fun seemed almost 'childish'[76] to Lewis Carroll, in which Carroll sees the creativity and imagination of an artist. Carroll sees the character in Terry herself, making her a subject, rather than an object as in Watts and Cameron's art, or a muse for Tennyson's poem (as in *Freshwater*). Carroll sees Terry as a work of art herself.

The ease and childishness Carroll sees in Terry – showing 'herself' in his photographs, making her see a Shakespearean heroine with her own

---

[72] Woolf, 'Ellen Terry', p.71.
[73] Woolf, 'Ellen Terry', p.71.
[74] Roger Manvell, *Ellen Terry*. London: Heron, 1968, p.54.
[75] Lewis Carroll, *The Diaries of Lewis Carroll: Volume I*. Ed. Roger Lancelyn Green. London: Cassell, 1953, p.225.
[76] Manvell, *Ellen Terry*, p.55.

vision. As Terry claims, a kissing scene in a church, for example, can throw 'such a flood of light on Beatrice's character that an actress has little excuse for not seeing clearly what kind of woman she has to impersonate'.[77] For Terry, the Shakespearean 'triumphant heroines'[78] are 'the real women'[79] who are intelligent, merry and honest. Shakespeare's plays reveal their 'nobility beyond possibility of mistake',[80] because these heroines 'have in them a simplicity, a naïve goodwill, a delicate good feeling that separate them from the arrogant assumptions or false noblesse', such as women in *The Merry Wives of Windsor*.[81] These triumphant heroines represent the Shakespearean concept of femininity bringing the audience 'Elizabethan fun',[82] which means 'whether Shakespeare's scene is Athens, Rome, Verona or Egypt, whether the period is classical or renaissance, his characters are all English and all Elizabethan'.[83]

Terry wonders how Shakespeare achieved that 'local colour',[84] such as representing Portia as a Venetian lady in *The Merchant of Venice*. According to Terry, there are many different ways of playing Portia. And yet, Terry's Portia has her independence of mind in 'the Italian way, the Renaissance way'.[85] For Terry, Portia's character represents the fruit of the Renaissance – a period of 'beautiful clothes, beautiful cities, beautiful houses, beautiful ideas. She speaks the beautiful language of inspired poetry'.[86] Terry sees

---

[77] Ellen Terry, *Four Lecturers on Shakespeare*. Ed. Christopher St. John. London: Martin Hopkinson, 1932, p.95.

[78] Terry, *Four Lecturers on Shakespeare*, p.111.

[79] Terry, *Four Lecturers on Shakespeare*, p.82.

[80] Terry, *Four Lecturers on Shakespeare*, p.97.

[81] Terry, *Four Lecturers on Shakespeare*, p.97.

[82] Terry, *Four Lecturers on Shakespeare*, p.115.

[83] Terry, *Four Lecturers on Shakespeare*, p.110.

[84] Terry, *Four Lecturers on Shakespeare*, p.115.

[85] Terry, *Four Lecturers on Shakespeare*, p.116.

[86] Terry, *Four Lecturers on Shakespeare*, p.117.

something 'independent, almost masculine in her attitude towards life'.[87] She retains generosity in her personality and an independence of thought and action. For Terry, this type of women has a 'living force'[88] in her heart.

As Woolf shows in *A Room of One's Own* (1929), a female writer ought to explore the territory that male writers have not explored yet. A female body with what is thought of as a masculine attitude (independent and active), is what Woolf meant by androgynous creative power, when she writes that 'Shakespeare's sister will put on the body which she has so often laid down. Drawing her life from the lives of the unknown who were her forerunners, as her brother did before her, she will be born'.[89] Woolf's androgynous writer is bodiless. The reader can only see the incarnation of her through the character she creates. Like Ellen Terry, she does perform through different make ups and costumes, through expressing herself in the lines and gestures of the characters she plays. Shakespeare's sister, for Woolf, is also capable of performing an inner life and emotion dramatically. Woolf's female writer, like Ellen Terry, becomes bodiless, putting on different 'bodies' of her characters, to imagine and to perform the inner drama in them in words.

For Woolf, Terry's acting is a moment of bodilessness. For Terry, it is a moment when she is not herself but a divine, creative energy – something 'comes upon' her, as she is 'always-in-the-air, light and bodiless'.[90] When the part was congenial, 'every word, every comma was consumed. Even her eyelashes acted. Her body lost its weight'.[91] Woolf again uses bodiless imaginary to reveal the process of artistic creation. This 'bodiless' moment, for Woolf, shows how Ellen Terry can be remembered, as a moment of

---

[87] Terry, *Four Lecturers on Shakespeare*, p.117.

[88] Terry, *Four Lecturers on Shakespeare*, p.122.

[89] Virginia Woolf, *A Room of One's Own and Three Guineas*. Oxford: Oxford University Press, 2000, p.149.

[90] Woolf, 'Ellen Terry', p.67.

[91] Woolf, 'Ellen Terry', p.67.

Being, while Terry and her character's personality come into One, as in the theatre 'all is real, warm and kind – we live a lovely spiritual life here'.[92] When Terry forgot what Lady Cicely said next, for instance, is a sign that 'Lady Cicely was not a part that suited her'.[93]

For Woolf, Ellen Terry's artistic creativity does not only make her a great actress but also a writer, although it never "occurred to her when she wrote her autobiography, or scribbled page after page to Bernard Shaw late at night, dead tired after a rehearsal, that she was 'writing'. The words in her beautiful rapid hand bubbled off her pen".[94] This creative power connects acting to writing, writing to painting, painting to photography, as of Terry has 'painted a self-portrait'[95] with her pen: her childhood, her marriage, her being a mother of two children, and the blank pages among them as intervals. Terry's self-portrait is not a 'framed, glazed or complete'[96] academic portrait which can be admired by the Victorians. It is rather a 'bundle of loose leaves'[97] with Post-Impressionist and Cubist sketches, which had been done 'in different moods, from different angles, sometimes contradict each other. The nose cannot belong to the eyes; the arm is out of all proportion to the foot. It is very difficult to assemble them. And there are some blank pages, too'.[98] The most important question is – who is she? Who is the real Ellen Terry? Woolf asks: 'Is she mother, wife, cook, critic, actress, or should she have been, after all, a painter'?[99]

In both *Freshwater* and 'Ellen Terry', one can see that Woolf is critical of Victorian aesthetics. Looking at Watts and Cameron, she criticises the

---

[92] Woolf, 'Ellen Terry', p.69.
[93] Woolf, 'Ellen Terry', p.67.
[94] Woolf, 'Ellen Terry', p.68.
[95] Woolf, 'Ellen Terry', p.68.
[96] Woolf, 'Ellen Terry', p.68.
[97] Woolf, 'Ellen Terry', p.68.
[98] Woolf, 'Ellen Terry', p.68.
[99] Woolf, 'Ellen Terry', p.71.

concept of idealising the female body, representing it as 'Beauty' (Watts) or 'An Angel in the House' (Cameron). As John Pultz argues, Cameron photographed friends and family members in costume, acting roles she had 'assigned' to them,[100] roles which encourage domestic virtue. As Laura Troubridge points out in her *Memories and Reflections*, Cameron treated her models with large and ominous power, as in Troubridge's childhood memory, that:

> Aunt Julia appeared as a terrifying elderly woman, […]. Dressed in dark clothes, stained with chemicals from her photography (and smelling of them too), […]. We were at once pressed into the service of the camera. Our roles were no less than those of two Angels of the Nativity, and to sustain them were scantily clad and each had a pair of heavy swan wings fastened to her narrow shoulders, while Aunt Julia, with ungentle hand, tousled our hair to get rid of its prim nursery look.[101]

Woolf clearly sees a power relation between the artist and his/her model. I would suggest that Woolf comes to a rather original conclusion, transforming this female body obsession that she sees in Watts and Cameron, from a representation of ideal Beauty to a demonstration of creative power, as one can see in Ellen Terry and Woolf's fictional 'Shakespeare's sister' in *A Room of One's Own*. Woolf's use of the bodilessness refers to feminine creative power, which comes close to Barthes's and Irigaray's maternal imaginary, as I will show in the following parts.

---

[100] John Pultz, *Photography and the Body*. London: The Everyman Art Library, 1995, p.40.

[101] Quoted in Carol Mavor, *Pleasures Taken: Performances of Sexuality and Loss in Victorian Photographs*. London: I. B. Tauris, 1996, pp.45 – 46.

Part II:
The Maternal Imaginary and the Gaze – Barthes and Irigaray

Roland Barthes's Life-Death Game

I want to theorise the maternal imaginary in terms of the gaze, in order to understand how photographic vision works in Woolf, particularly in *The Years*. The relation between memory, loss and desire helps to define the maternal imaginary moments in Woolf's writing.

Barthes defines photography in terms of lost time; in other words, in terms of memory, death and absence. The fundamental characteristic of photography is that the bond between the looking subjectivity and the looked object is broken. This break is primarily temporal (through death), but it is also re-connected through the visual image – the photograph itself. The gaze enables one to see not only the flat image of the thing 'that-has-been'[102] there, but also casts an uncanny gloom over the object that one knows – that has presented as a frozen and a fixed perception in the image.

This image is a fixed perception, in which the visual object 'yields itself wholly'[103] through photography, as one can see in Sartre's comments in Barthes's quotation. For Sartre, imagination is precisely the active function of consciousness that transcends the external world. As he pointed out in *The Imaginary* (first published in 1940 in French as *L'imaginaire*), the phenomenon of the 'mental image'[104] is an element in consciousness. A mental image 'makes present' a visual object, as Sartre finds when he 'regain[s]'[105] his friend Pierre through his mental image of him. A mental image also suggests human imagination and subjective consciousness.

---

[102] Barthes, *Camera Lucida*, p.107.

[103] Barthes, *Camera Lucida*, p.106.

[104] Jean-Paul Sartre. *The Imaginary: A Phenomenological Psychology of the Imagination*. Trans. Jonathan Webber. 1940 London: Routledge, 2004, p.17.

[105] Sartre, *The Imaginary*, p.17.

Therefore, Sartre identifies one's self with one's imagination, "challenging the ocularcentric tradition's equation of the 'I' and the 'eye'".[106] A mental image reveals 'this'[107] moment of being, as Sartre explains in his *Being and Nothingness* (first published in 1943 under the title *L'Etre et le Néant*). This moment of being refers to a temporal condition, a moment which links multiple temporal dimensions – the past, the present and the future. The photographic motionless world is a revelation, a moment which is grasped 'through and in a temporality which temporalizes itself'.[108] This moment is 'the real',[109] the 'duration'[110] and the 'now'[111] which combines being (time, 'in-itself'[112]) and nothingness (the 'non-temporality'[113] of being). Consciousness, as Sartre claims in *Truth and Existence* (originally published as *Vérité et existence*, 1989), is 'not knowledge but existence'[114] – the 'In-itself-For-itself'[115] pure type of *being*. Sartre's mental image of Pierre and Pierre himself in the photograph comes very close to Barthes's reflections on his mother: she exists both in the *Winter Gardens* photograph and in Barthes's mental image in *Camera Lucida*. As Barthes argues, one's vision of the visual object in the mental image may be 'contrary to the text or to other perceptions',[116] which gives one the visual object in a vague,

---

[106] Martin Jay, *Downcast Eyes*, p.284.

[107] Jean-Paul Sartre. *Being and Nothingness: An Essay on Phenomenological Ontology*. Trans. Hazel E. Barnes. 1943. London: Routledge, 1993, p.204.

[108] Sartre, *Being and Nothingness*, p.205.

[109] Jean-Paul Sartre. *The Philosophy of Existentialism*. Ed. Wade Baskin. New York: Philosophical Library, 1965, p.92.

[110] Sartre, *Being and Nothingness*, p.205.

[111] Sartre, *Being and Nothingness*, p.204.

[112] Sartre, *Being and Nothingness*, p.205.

[113] Sartre, *Being and Nothingness*, p.205.

[114] Jean-Paul Sartre. *Truth and Existence*. Trans. Adrian van den Hoven. 1989. Chicago: Chicago University Press, 1992, p.4.

[115] Sartre, *Truth and Existence*, p.3.

[116] Barthes, *Camera Lucida*, p.106.

arguable manner; and therefore, denies one's suspicion of what he thinks he is seeing. And yet, the photographic eye separates knowing from the known, and challenges what can be seen by the naked eye.

Photography is a mode of perception. Sartre recognises his friend Pierre in the photograph because he knows Pierre in his mind. Here I use Sartre's theoretical metaphor to demonstrate a significant aspect of *The Years*. Lacan's psychoanalytical way of seeing the return of the gaze, 'I am *photo-graphed*',[117] for me, is a rapid broken succession of different images of the same subject. This broken succession is the beginning of the dialectic, suspending the image which is beyond the subject. As in Lacan's own words, 'I am *photo-graphed*' is something that establishes a 'fracture, a bi-partition, a splitting of the being to which the being accommodates itself'.[118] The distance between the subject and the object, therefore, is also a metaphor of the distance that separates the subject from an image of him. The separation of the photographic image from the subject can be read as an unbridgeable distance that divides 'I' as referent from 'I' as reference;[119] 'I' as a signifier from 'I' as signified. For Barthes, this photographic image of his mother, the *Winter Gardens* photograph in itself, has 'nothing' which can be undone, because it proves nothing, but only 'that *this-has-been*' – the essence of a photograph. The photographic image, again, divides his mother as referent (the one that he knows) from herself as reference (who she is).

Barthes draws specific attention to the temporality of the photograph. Its importance recurs implicitly throughout *Camera Lucida*, and specifically as a characteristic of the photograph. A photograph, especially in a family

---

[117] For Lacan, the desire of the subject gazes back, reducing the subject to *object a*, 'at the level of the lack'. The subject is 'looked at' by his own desire, that is to say, he is a 'picture'. See *The Four Fundamental Concepts of Psycho-Analysis*, p.104.

[118] Lacan, *The Four Fundamental Concepts of Psycho-Analysis*, p.106.

[119] Mieke Bal, *The Mottled Screen: Reading Proust Visually*. Trans. Anna-Louise Milne. Stanford: Stanford University Press, 1997, p.203.

album, as André Bazin claims, is a 'disturbing presence of lives halted at a set moment in their duration, freed from their destiny [...] by the power of an impassive mechanical process: [...] it embalms time, rescuing it simply from its own proper corruption'.[120] As Laura Mulvey explains, once time is embalmed in the photograph, it 'persists, carrying the past across to innumerable futures as they become the present'.[121] For Barthes, a photographic image records 'absence' – 'what I see has been there'.[122] It does not show eternity but a fraction of time. In a photographic image, one can see that the object has been there, and immediately separated from its own space and time; it has been absolutely present, and yet already deferred.

The separation of the visible object and its image, the referent and the reference, for Barthes, means a paradoxical order in terms of what is 'true' to the viewing subject. As he claims, one verifies things before declaring them 'true', under the 'intensity' of new experience.[123] What Barthes means by 'true' is not merely an identification of the truth of the image, or the reality of its origin. Rather, Barthes identifies truth and reality 'in a unique emotion', in which he places 'the nature – the genius – of Photography'.[124] This 'unique emotion' is the dialectic relation between the *studium* and the *punctum*.

Barthes uses G. W. Wilson's photograph *Queen Victoria* (1863) to demonstrate what he meant by *studium* and *punctum*, and also how they create the spectator's unique emotion. For Barthes, the Queen on the horse back is the *studium – her majesty* – Victoria. The viewer can see her as an example of general political testimony or as a historical scene, for she is 'culturally' seducing Barthes's gaze: her face, her gesture, the setting of the

---

[120] André Bazin, 'The Ontology of the Photographic Image'. *What is Cinema?* Trans. Hugh Gray. Berkeley: University of California Press, 1967, p.15.

[121] Laura Mulvey, *Death 24 x a Second*, p.56.

[122] Barthes, *Camera Lucida*, p.77.

[123] Barthes, *Camera Lucida*, p.77.

[124] Barthes, *Camera Lucida*, p.77.

photograph.[125] And yet, the *punctum* – something disturbing, a mark, a sensitive point that breaks the knowledge zone of the motionless image – a code, a sign. According to Barthes, fantastically this *punctum* is the Scottish man, who was wearing a kirtle and supervising the horse's behavior, bringing out 'the Victorian nature', the 'erotic' element.[126]

The dialectic of *studium* and *punctum* is the union of the image and being, in the struggle of the life-death game. In other words, where the photographic image separates from its referent is where Barthes starts to visualise the truth of photography as a 'bizarre *medium*, a new form of hallucination: false on the level of perception, true on the level of time: a temporal hallucination, so to speak, a modest, *shared* hallucination (on the one hand "it is not there," on the other "but it has indeed been"): a mad image, chafed by reality'.[127]

As Lacan claims, it is through imagining masks (that is, photographic images) 'that the masculine and the feminine meet in the most acute, most intense way'.[128] The being gives (or receives from the other) an image, which is like 'a mask, a double, an envelope, a thrown-off skin'.[129] *Studium* and the *punctum* create a unique emotion, a 'painful and delicious' intensity, in one evening with some friends, when Barthes felt sad, saw Fellini's *Casanova*, when Casanova began dancing with the young automation. His sympathy, with 'a lover's sentiment' towards the young automation ('that painted yet individual, innocence face'),[130] overwhelms him. The intense emotion makes him pass 'beyond the unreality of the thing represented'[131] (a photograph is as unreal as a mask), entering 'crazily into the spectacle,

---

[125] Barthes, *Camera Lucida*, p.26.

[126] Barthes, *Camera Lucida*, p.26.

[127] Barthes, *Camera Lucida*, p.115.

[128] Lacan, *The Four Fundamental Concepts of Psycho-Analysis*, p.107.

[129] Lacan, *The Four Fundamental Concepts of Psycho-Analysis*, p.107.

[130] Barthes, *Camera Lucida*, p.116.

[131] Barthes, *Camera Lucida*, p.117.

into the image', to embrace 'what is dead, what is going to die'.[132] Through
the gaze, the emotion and imagination makes Barthes embrace the image of
his mother; imagining 'that-has-been', going deeper than the flat death of the
photographic image. Reaching the essence of the image, for Barthes, is to be
able to look at the model from the outside, without intimacy, as one draws an
object through a prism (it is *camera lucida*, 'anterior to Photography'[133]),
'and yet more inaccessible and mysterious than the thought of the inner-most
being'; 'unrevealed yet manifest', which is that 'absence-as-presence'.[134]

Barthes does not recognise his mother from the likeness of the photographic
image. In the 'Winter Gardens Photograph', he discovers her, as "a sudden
awakening, outside of 'likeness', a *satori* in which words fail".[135] He looks into
the flat death, trying to prove that photography "*authenticates* the existence of a
certain being, *i.e.,* in its essence, 'as into itself'".[136] The photograph in itself, at
this moment, is something beyond simple resemblance. Barthes sees something,
'the *air*'[137] of his mother's unanalysable face. The face in the photograph is
an expression of truth – 'a kind of intractable supplement of identity'.[138]
This 'air' is an 'ageless'[139] soul of the being, his mother, whom he used to
love and see, 'each day of her long life'.[140] The air that the photographic
image kept is the 'truth' for him, through his gaze and recognition.

Through the imaginary, Barthes is able to think about life and death,
Being and nothingness in *Camera Lucida*. Looking straight at his mother's
eyes in the photograph, Barthes feels the potential craziness of the Look: a

---

[132] Barthes, *Camera Lucida*, p.117.
[133] Barthes, *Camera Lucida*, p.106.
[134] Barthes, *Camera Lucida*, p.106.
[135] Barthes, *Camera Lucida*, p.109.
[136] Barthes, *Camera Lucida*, p.107.
[137] Barthes, *Camera Lucida*, p.107.
[138] Barthes, *Camera Lucida*, p.109.
[139] Barthes, *Camera Lucida*, p.109.
[140] Barthes, *Camera Lucida*, p.110.

crazy point 'where affect (love, compassion, enthusiasm, desire) is a guarantee of Being'.[141] The look leads Barthes to reach a dialectical point, which accomplishes the 'unheard-of identification of reality ("*that-has-been*") with truth ("there-she-is!").[142] This point is what Kristeva called '*la vérité folle*'.[143] Barthes defines the paradoxical nature of Photography – mad and tame. Photography can be one or the other. When it remains relative, 'tempered by aesthetic or empirical habits', photography is tame. It is mad, according to Barthes, when the photograph is 'absolute', 'original', 'obliging the loving and terrified consciousness to return to the very letter of Time: a strictly revulsive movement which reverses the course of the thing' – 'the photographic ecstasy'.[144]

At this moment I suddenly remember the ending of *Mrs Dalloway*. After all those cinematic techniques that Woolf demonstrates, one finds a shock technique Woolf uses to depict the sudden reverse of the past and the present, the ending and the beginning. Peter Walsh goes through the same terror, excitement and photographic ecstasy that Barthes did, when he looks at Clarissa in her party. What fills him with the 'extraordinary excitement' (*MD* 213) is the sudden return of the very letter of Time, which reverses the past and the present of the thing:

> It is Clarissa, he said.
> For there she was.

The ending of *Mrs Dalloway* is a photographic perception, in which Peter Walsh re-discovers Clarissa's 'air' – the truth of who Clarissa is – the being he used to, and will always know and love. Peter Walsh's mental image of Clarissa is a photographic perception, which represents 'the real' in Sartre's

---

[141] Barthes, *Camera Lucida*, p.113.
[142] Barthes, *Camera Lucida*, p.113.
[143] Barthes, *Camera Lucida*, p.113.
[144] Barthes, *Camera Lucida*, p.119.

phrase, combining the passing present (the fact of seeing Clarissa's figure in the party) and the one that he always knows in his mind.

Luce Irigaray's Curved Looking Glass

Luce Irigaray also contributes to the theory of the visual and the imaginary. According to Martin Jay, Irigaray deconstructs the myth of 'vision' (the eye) as a privilege of phallogocentric culture, and constructs the female gazer on the other hand, who is not 'the passive object'[145] of the male gaze. Irigaray's definition of the gendered gaze makes one see that not only do men and women have biological differences, but also that they see things differently. She explores the gendered dimension of the visual experience, confronting the implications of Lacan's influential argument about the mirror stage. My analysis of Irigaray's feminist theory will centre on the two texts in which she develops her central arguments about the gendered gaze: firstly, *Speculum of the Other Woman* (1974); secondly, *The Sex Which Is Not One* (1977).

Speculum of the Other Woman can be divided in three main parts. The first part, 'The Blind Spot of an Old Dream of Symmetry' contains an abrasive critique of Freud's way of theorising femininity. It is precisely a critique that consists in showing how women are described as the unknown, the lack. Through re-reading Freud in the first part, Irigaray is able to find her own way of defining sexual difference and the development of female sexuality in the second part: 'Speculum'. The second part contains a series of readings of philosophical texts from Plato to Hegel, through which Irigaray presents her own theoretical position. The third part, 'Plato's *Hystera*', is a close reading of Plato's cave parable in terms of light and vision – the two elements that construct Western philosophy as a male-centered discourse. For Irigaray, this male-dominated discourse ignores women's desire. It is

---

[145] Jay, *Downcast Eyes*, p.525.

'forbidden by the law of the father, of all fathers: fathers of families, fathers of nations, religious fathers, professor – fathers doctor – fathers, lover – fathers, ect.'.[146] Irigaray's idea comes close to Woolf's critique of the male-centered discourse (in which a female body is objectified or idealised as 'The Angel in the House', as Woolf suggests), when she objectifies men in the photographs in *Three Guineas*, as I will show in the following sections.

Irigaray's feminist deconstruction and critique of patriarchal discourse can be read as women's empowerment in their role of outsiders, which comes close to Woolf's strategy in *Three Guineas*. I will come back to this point in the following sections. 'Speculum' has its original Latin meaning: a mirror. The word itself is a key to read Irigaray's analysis, which contains several main themes. Irigaray's mirror is curved; it is a concave mirror which used to be a male instrument for exploring the female body. To make her point, Irigaray looks at the cavities of the female body itself. For Irigaray, women are 'turned into an excess of power, into an all-powerful *matrix* that makes [the man] lucidly reconsider to what and to whom he owed his life'.[147] Through the curved mirror, Irigaray is able to turn the objectified / marginalised female body into a subversive power, demonstrating a different description of the Imaginary, which comes to challenge Lacan's mirror stage. Lacan's mirror stage imaginary, as Margaret Whitford points out, 'has its origins in Freud's theories of the Ego and of narcissism.[148] Lacan's article entitled 'The Mirror Stage as Formative of the Function of the I as Revealed in Psychoanalytic Experience' in *Ecrits* reveals the 'imaginary' as "a moment in the formation of the Ego or 'I': the baby, whose experience of its body until then had been fragmented and

---

[146] Luce Irigaray. 'The Bodily Encounter with the Mother'. *The Irigaray Reader*. Ed. Margaret Whitford. Oxford: Blackwell, 1991, p.34.

[147] Luce Irigaray, *Speculum of the Other Woman*. Trans. Gillian C. Gill. Ithaca: Cornell University Press, 1985, p.185.

[148] Margaret Whitford. *Luce Irigaray: Philosophy in the Feminine*. London: Routledge, 1991, p.63.

incoherent'.[149] The reflection in the mirror gives the baby an imaginary coherence. This imaginary coherence is necessary, according to Lacan, to enable a split between the baby and the mother, the subject and the object.

For Irigaray, the male gaze is drowned in the womb. The male gazer cannot transform the woman into an '*object of use*'.[150] Rather, Irigaray uses the 'sea' as a metaphor, which drives the male gazer away from his position as a 'surveyor-subject',[151] making the '*mother*' an 'extension' of him instead of his lack.[152] At this point, for Irigaray, the constitution of subjectivity is more than recognising one's own mirror image. I suggest that the self does not have to be united with '*an image in a mirror*' (as Lacan suggests), in order to construct one's own subjectivity. As Margaret Whitford claims, in *Speculum*, Irigaray 'takes the Lacanian term imaginary, and applies it to what psychoanalysis had previously called unconscious phantasy'.[153] Irigaray helps one to see the relation between the subject and his mother, seeing his mother as an imaginary extension of himself (rather than having a mirror image as an imaginary subjectivity), which reinforces the status of the claim that Irigaray makes, 'I exist' (to live), or 'I am' (to be).[154]

Irigaray sees the politics of the imaginary. As Margaret Whitford points out,

> the question of women's position in relation to society as a whole, at what points they are 'inside' and at what points they are 'outside', seems to be a crucial question for thinking about equality and difference'. In Irigaray's account women are positioned *outside* the

---

[149] Lacan, 'The Mirror Stage as Formative of the Fuction of the I as Revealed in Psychoanalytic Experience'. *Ecrits: A Selection*. Trans. Alan Sheridan. London: Tavistock, 1977, p.4.

[150] Irigaray, *Speculum*, p.185.

[151] Irigaray, *Speculum*, p.186.

[152] Irigaray, *Speculum*, p.186.

[153] Whitford, *Luce Irigaray*, p.65.

[154] Irigaray, *Speculum*, p.182.

social contract, [...], while, from women's point of view, it is *patriarchy* that is deadly.[155]

In *The Sex Which Is Not One*, Irigaray tries to theorise the female gaze from the 'other' side of the mirror, behind the screen of the male gaze. The glass in the house represents Alice and her reflection. She is alone in the house. '*And [her mother is] the only one who seems to know who Alice is*'.[156] The male surveyor, Lucien, looks at the glass, and his question is: '*She ... She? She who? Who's she? She {is} an other ... looking for a light. Where's a light*?'[157] For Irigaray, the male surveyor's anxiety is that he cannot prove who Alice is, using his own logic such as '*a + b, or 1 + 1, that is, an element that repeats itself, one that stays the same and yet produces a displacement in the sum*'.[158] He needs to light up a cigarette, to cover his sense of confusion, ambiguity and anxiety – "*She's been 'in wonderland*",[159] but there is no trace of such an adventure in the male surveyor's eyes. Irigaray's looking from the 'other' side of the glass indicates her aim to demonstrate the anxiety of the male gaze, subverting the patriarchal myth (in which Lacan defines subjectivity by looking into his image mirror, the act of looking which separates the subject and the object, before the subject enters into the Law, the Phallic) and giving an alternative to the passive role of women in phallocratic discourse.[160]

---

[155] Margaret Whitford. 'Irigaray, Utopia, and the Death Drive'. *Engaging with Irigaray: Feminist Philosophy and Modern European Thought*. Eds. Carolyn Burke, Naomi Schor, and Margaret Whitford. New York: Columbia University Press, 1994, p.381.

[156] Luce Irigaray, *This Sex Which Is Not One*. Trans. Catherine Porter with Carolyne Burke. Ithaca: Cornell University Press, 1985, p.10.

[157] Irigaray, *The Sex Which Is Not One*, p.12.

[158] Irigaray, *The Sex Which Is Not One*, p.12.

[159] Irigaray, *The Sex Which Is Not One*, p.12.

[160] Toril Moi, *Sexual/Textual Politics*, p.127.

It is clear that Irigaray's criticism is directed at the privileging of the visual in Western philosophy, which she argues is tied to the 'perpetuation of a monological masculine subjectivity'.[161] However, what I am interested in Irigaray, is that: is she anti-visual? What is a woman's position in the discourse of the visual (apart from being a passive gazee of men)? Irigaray challenges Lacan's theory of the mirror stage, proposing a non-visual way of constructing subjectivity. And yet, she does not address Lacan's theory of the Eye and the Gaze, in which he clearly defines a situation when the subject can be objectified by his own desire ('I am *photographed*'). In Kristeva's writing, one can also see the semiotic depth of looking and the imaginary, which does not relate to the gender of the subjectivity. Is Irigaray running away from the visual discourse because it is just for men (according to her)? What is her way of defining the gendered gaze?

Irigaray does in fact show a theorisation of the visual rather than only considering the privileged male gaze in a phallocentric discourse. And yet, her attitude toward the visual is ambivalent, because she seems to try to deconstruct Lacan's visual theory, but still, her view of the gendered gaze is not clear. Irigaray's conception, as Cathryn Vasseleu argues, is not set against visual theory as a part of phallocentric discourse, but instead extends the significance of the visual in a way that men do not consider.[162] Irigaray is right to say that a woman's development is to 'liberate woman's desire',[163] which may include visual, sexual, sensual desires. As Vasseleu claims, Irigaray's critique of women's relation to vision is always set at a 'distance', because for her, other senses such as smell, taste, touch and hearing should have the same importance, in terms of how culture has

---

[161] Cathryn Vasseleu, 'Illuminating Passion: Irigaray's Transfiguration of Night'. *Vision in Context: Historical and Contemporary Perspectives on Sight.* Eds. Teresa Brennan and Martin Jay. London: Routledge, 1996, p.129.

[162] Vasseleu, 'Illuminating Passion: Irigaray's Transfiguration of Night', p.132.

[163] Irigaray, *This Sex Which Is Not One*, p.32.

been constructed in 'bodily relations'.[164] However, I argue that Irigaray's curved mirror in her 'Alice in the Underground' in the first chapter of *The Sex Which Is Not One* suggests an unfixed, unstable body which subverts the phallocentric view (the fixed and the stable subject, after his separation from the Other). This concept of the unfixed and unstable body, like the skull in Hans Holbein's *The Ambassadors* (1533), deconstructs a single and fixed vanish point, as in Lacan's term, 'escap[ing] from vision'[165] – the lack, the phallic ghost.[166] According to Lacan, the skull appears from some angles, 'flying through the air'[167] as 'a trap for the gaze'.[168] This trap deconstructs the two frozen human figures and between them a series of objects – vanity, the realistic appearance of objects which represents 'the sciences and arts'.[169] Surrealism, as one can see in Dali's soft watches, in this sense, is 'less phallic'.[170] Here, Lacan's use of 'phallic' is metaphorical, suggesting something which is authoritative and fixed. Woolf also demonstrates a critical view of that phallocentric gaze, a critique made through the outsider's point of view in *The Years and Three Guineas*.

---

[164] Cathryn Vasseleu, *Textures of Light: Vision and Touch in Irigaray, Levinas and Merleau-Ponty*. London: Routledge, 1998, p.15.

[165] Lacan, *Four Fundamental Concepts of Psycho-Analysis*, p.87.

[166] Lacan, *Four Fundamental Concepts of Psycho-Analysis*, p.88.

[167] Lacan, *Four Fundamental Concepts of Psycho-Analysis*, p.88.

[168] Lacan, *Four Fundamental Concepts of Psycho-Analysis*, p.89.

[169] Lacan, *Four Fundamental Concepts of Psycho-Analysis*, p.88.

[170] Lacan, *Four Fundamental Concepts of Psycho-Analysis*, p.88.

Part III:
Photography in *The Years* and *Three Guineas*

'Her mind is like a family album':[171] Photographic Vision and the Self in *The Years*

The Years (1937) is commonly recognised as a 'family saga'.[172] As Jeri Johnson points out, this novel follows the lives of three generations of the Pargiter family from '1880' to the 'Present Day'.[173] This novel reveals Woolf's 'true fear',[174] for its writing process was like a long and painful childbirth. In her diary entry, 21 June 1936, one can see that Woolf's fear is a feeling of 'complete despair & failure'.[175] Coming from her own uncertainty about her ability to create a new literary form, Woolf aims to make *The Years* a 'Novel-Essay'.[176] At the first glance, the novel does look like a heritage, rather than a re-creation of Victorian tradition. It is very long, very historical and realistic, with exact years as separate titles for each chapter. And yet, I would argue, Woolf's hermeneutic struggle with Victorian generic conventions can be read in her use of photographic vision, which serves as 'punctum' of the cultural and historical 'studium', revealing loss, death, and the inner desire of her characters.

In *The Years*, a photographic vision reveals the revelational moment, where emotion and cognition, the self and the other, the near and the far, the internal and the external, are inextricably mixed. Thus one can see that this

---

[171]Hermione Lee points out that Woolf made a fictional description of Sophie Farrell, the family cook, with a connection to photography – 'Her room is hung with photographs. Her mind is like a family album. You turn up Uncle George you turn up Aunt Maria. She has a story about each of them'. See *Virginia Woolf*, p.49.

[172] Jeri Johnson. Introduction. *The Years*. London: Penguin, 1998, xi.

[173] Johnson, Introduction, xi.

[174] Johnson, Introduction, xi.

[175] Virginia Woolf, *D V*, p.24.

[176] Johnson, Introduction, x.

novel-essay consists in an interweaving of the external and the internal mental image, 'true' (it has been there). The naked eye and the camera lens refer to a visible fact – the essence of photography, 'there has been'. As Barthes's comment on looking at a photograph of Napoleon's youngest brother Jerome (taken in 1852) shows, he is 'looking at eyes that looked at the Emperor'. Here Barthes's look refers to a double ça-a-été: the existence of Jerome (who has been photographed) and his eldest brother Napoleon (who exists in the pre-history of photography).[177] Photographic vision and the photograph of the mother are central. The photograph of the mother is combined with the imaginary of life and death, through the dialectic of *studium* and *punctum*.

Eleanor's London: A Series of Snapshots

Woolf's London in *The Years* is dialectical, for it is a combination of the inner and the outer worlds, the material world and the imaginary. The city itself is an essential imaginary space in her narrative, which represents something 'other' than itself. London carries symbolic meanings, in which Woolf maps the movement of her characters in the space of time. The mental lives of Woolf's characters are fully drawn through her photographic vision of London streets. Through photographic vision, Woolf's characters see both the past and the present, the public and the private worlds, creating a dialectical combination of unexpected juxtapositions, which suggests symbolic meanings. Woolf depicts the interlocked, interwoven relation between the public and the private worlds through the mental life's confrontation and interaction with the public sphere, and she does this through a photographic vision. Eleanor's inner feeling is revealed in her way of seeing London.

In Woolf's chapter, titled '1891', after lunch with her father, Eleanor takes a cab to the Law Courts, where her brother Morris is to argue a case

---

[177] Barthes, *Camera Lucida*, p.3.

that afternoon. As they are held up by the traffic at Marble Arch, Eleanor
looks out of the cab window, and the glass window becomes the camera
lens and the window frames a succession of photographic images. Eleanor
reads a letter from Martin in India, about his experience of lighting a fire in
the jungle. Stuck in London traffic, Eleanor's moment in the cab becomes a
frozen moment, envisioning Martin's face in her mind, mixing up the
London scene with her brother's story. Eleanor reads Martin's letter, it says:

> 'I found myself alone in the middle of the jungle. ...'[...].

> She saw her brother; his red hair; his round face; and the rather
> pugnacious expression which always made her afraid that he would
> get himself into trouble one of these days. [...].

> 'I had lost my way; and the sun was sinking', she read.

> 'The sun was sinking ...' Eleanor repeated, glancing ahead of
> herdown Oxford Street. The sun shone on dresses in a window. A
> jungle was a very thick wood, she supposed; made of stunted little
> trees; dark green in colour. [...]. The street before her lost its detail.
> [...].She read again. He had to make a fire. [...]. She saw a heap of
> dry sticks and Martin alone watching the match go out. [...]. They
> had stopped at Chancery Lane. An old woman was being helped
> across the road by a policeman; but the road was a jungle. [...].

> The cab was stopped. For a moment Eleanor sat still. She saw
> nothing but stunted little trees, and her brother looking at the sun
> rising over the jungle (*TY* 114 – 115).

Martin is in the jungle alone, as Eleanor is alone in the cab, gazing at the
dresses in the shop windows in Oxford Street – everything loses its detail,
having an atmosphere of dark green colour as in the jungle. In Chancery
Lane, in Eleanor's eyes, the London road and traffic become a jungle scene.

Martin's first match in India goes out; Eleanor can feel the anxiety to see the match reaches the end. Then she sees the flame of Martin's second match, 'for a moment danced over the vast funereal mass of the Law Courts' (*TY* 115). Eleanor's photographic vision in the taxi sees both inner and outer lights, Martin's flame of life in the letter in her hand and the heavy mass of the Law Courts. Woolf juxtaposes the inner and the outer worlds, consciousness and unconsciousness, as Martin's flame of life in India and Eleanor's seeing death in front of the Law Court become one. Eleanor's photographic vision is a snapshot, an instantaneous crystallisation of the invisible movement of thought and emotion, which wrested from the linear continuum of time and traffic (movement), as a 'specific constellation is made visible'.[178]

The dialectic is a way of conceptulising the signifying process – the mode of articulating the semiotic *chora*. As Leon S. Roudiez points out, the semiotic process relates to the *chora*, a term that Kristeva borrowed from Plato, who describes it as 'an invisible and formless being which receives all things and in some mysterious way partakes of the intelligible, and is most incomprehensible'.[179] The semiotic *chora* belongs to the pre-Oedipal phase, which is characterised by a relation to the mother, to be understood as a condition before the subject's entry into the symbolic / language. In Eleanor's snapshot, one can see Woolf's juxtaposition of life (Martin in the jungle) and death (the darkness of the Law Court) in the image of the flame of a burning match, articulating an ecstasy of rebirth for Eleanor as a subversive power, making her able to objectify figures of male authority, such as the Judge in the Law Court, with her photographic vision.

The Law Court seems 'dark and crowded' (*TY* 115). There are men 'in wigs and gowns', 'getting up and sitting down and coming in and going out

---

[178] Sigrid Weigel, *Body-and Image-Space: Re-reading Walter Benjamin*. Trans. Georgina Paul with Rachel McNicholl and Jeremy Gaines. London: Routledge, 1996, p.69.

[179] Leon S. Roudiez, Introduction. *Desire in Language*. Julia Kristeva, p.6.

like a flock of birds setting here and there on a field' (*TY* 115). Eleanor
looks around with a detached eye. People all look unfamiliar – even Morris.
For example, she sees Morris, but at the same time she feels how odd he
looks 'in his yellow wig! His glance

> passed over them without any sign of recognition. Nor did she smile
> at him; the solemn sallow atmosphere forbade personalities; there
> was something ceremonial about it all. From where she sat she could
> see his face in profile; the wig squared his forehead, and gave him a
> framed look, like a picture. Never had she seen him to such
> advantage; with such a brow, with such a nose. She glanced round.
> They all looked like pictures; […] hung upon a wall (*TY* 116).

Eleanor's vision frames Morris as a profile, as the Judge in his robes, not as the
Morris that she knows. Eleanor feels 'a little thrill of awe run through her',
when she sees the Judge comes in and takes his seat under the Lion and the
Unicorn (*TY* 116). Eleanor remembers Morris's passion for the Bar as a boy.
She fixes her eyes on Morris, as if focusing her camera lens on him, preparing
to take a snapshot of him. Morris stands up, getting ready to argue. For Eleanor,
he looks 'very tall', and 'very black and white' (*TY* 117). She feels very
unfamiliar with this picture of Morris. The black and white robe, for Eleanor,
makes Morris a visual object in the Court, rather than her own brother. Eleanor
tries to see in this picture the Morris she knows – for a moment a familiar
gesture makes her see 'the white scar' (*TY* 117) under that black and white
robe, where Morris had cut himself bathing – 'How like Morris!' (*TY* 117).

As W. J. T. Mitchell points out in his *Picture Theory*, the dialectical
image reveals a double cross of the bodily eye and the mind's eye, as a
spectatorial model which is based in photography. The eye

> may be compared to a photographic camera, with its eyelid cap, its
> iris shutter, its lens, and its sensitive plate, – the retina'. This model

of the eye then generates a familiar model of the mind: 'The pictures that are developed are stacked up, like the negatives in the photographer's shop, in the pigeon-holes of our mental storerooms'. The Duck-Rabbit, [...], reveal the presence of a 'mind's eye' roving around this storeroom, interpreting the pictures, seeing different aspects in them.[180]

The physical eye provides a photographic vision, generating 'a familiar model of the mind'. According to Mitchell, when the viewer eye sees the duck, the mind's eye interprets the Duck-Rabbit as a duck; when the viewer sees a rabbit, the mind's eye interprets it as a rabbit. When Eleanor sees Morris as a lawyer, her mind's eye interprets this Lawyer-Boy image as a tall, black and white figure. When Eleanor sees Morris as a little boy, her own brother, her mind's eye interprets him as someone in her family, with whom she is familiar. Her bodily eye simply transmits information (the tall, black and white figure), but her mental eye reflects her cognition, as she recognises Morris's white scar, which serves as an inner picture, symbolising a particular memory of a family member.

Eleanor finds the little boy she knows in Morris's gesture and his white scar. After that she gazes at the Judge himself. He is now lying back in his great carved chair under the Lion and the Unicorn. He looks 'sad and wise, as if words had been beating upon him for centuries' (*TY* 118). His eyes are half-shut, in his 'eternal vigil over the strife of unhappy human beings' (*TY* 118). When Eleanor is half asleep and half awake, her mind is wandering and scenes from her morning 'began to form themselves; to obtrude themselves' (*TY* 118). 'Judd at the Committee; her father reading the paper; the old woman plucking at her hand; the parlourmaid sweeping the silver over the table; and Martin lighting his second match in the jungle ...' (*TY*

---

[180] W. J. T. Mitchell. *Picture Theory: Essays on Verbal and Visual Representations.* Chicago: University of Chicago Press, 1994, p.51.

118). The relation between image and reality has been a constant central focus for Woolf in *The Years*. When Eleanor's mind is half asleep and half awake, the images that she has seen in that morning become a set of appearances, which have been detached from the place and time in which they first made their appearances and preserved, as Woolf had made Eleanor's series of images in the Law Court.

As Azade Seyhan points out, for Benjamin, it is not the "captured 'reality' but the telltale signs that signify contingency and link the photographic image dialectically to the beholder's present".[181] Benjamin's allegory consistently points to hidden meanings that demand to be seen from the gap between reality and the imaginary. Historical sites are evoked as images. As Susan Buck-Morss points out, historical memory (represented as images) is the operative force which 'affects decisively the collective, political will for change'.[182] Reading historical memory is an allegorical process, in which historical consciousness is captured in dialectical images, myths can be demystified, and thus the dialectical image can release its reformative and revolutionary power, as one can see in Eleanor's photographic vision and Woolf's *Three Guineas*.

Eleanor feels tired, walks out of the dark Law Court and into the street. She feels herself expand and come alive in the daylight on the street of London. She wanders around Strand, looking with pleasure at 'the racing street; at the shops full of bright chains and leather cases; at the white-faced churches; at the irregular jagged roofs laced across and across with wires. Above was the dazzle of a watery but gleaming sky' (*TY* 119). She walks while the stream of cabs, vans and omnibuses is passing her. She walks on

---

[181] Azade Seyhan, 'Visual Citations: Walter Benjamin's Dialectic of Text and Image'. *Languages of Visuality: Crossings Between Science, Art, Politics and Literature.* Detroit: Wayne State University Press, 1996, p.231.

[182] Susan Buck-Morss, *The Dialectics of Seeing: Walter Benjamin and the Arcades Project.* 1989. Cambridge, MA: MIT, 1999, ix.

and stops at the entrance to Charing Cross station. People on foot, people in cabs – they keep passing her. At this moment she sees the word 'Death' in 'very large black' letters in the paper (*TY* 120). The dialectical image is a juxtaposition of the black colour in the Law Court, the watery sky of London and now Parnell's death in the newspaper in a very large black capitals. Eleanor walks slowly along towards Trafalgar Square, and suddenly the whole scene 'froze into immobility', like the stillness of Horatio Nelson's statue – 'A man was joined to a pillar; a lion was joined to a man; they seemed stilled, connected, as if they would never move again' (*TY* 121). Eleanor's camera eye again takes a snapshot of the image of masculinity, which is an outsider's snapshot with revolutionary power, making patriarchy a frozen moment.

Loss, Death, Desire: Delia's Surrealist London

It was back in 1913, on a snowy January day, that Eleanor had taken a last look at the dismantled house with the housekeeper Crosby, who had served the family there for forty years. The white light of the snow 'glared in on the walls. It showed up the marks on the walls where the furniture had stood, where the pictures had hung' (*TY* 231). Crosby follows Eleanor around 'like a dog' (*TY* 231), exchanging memories with her, on the point of tears, for it is the end of everything for her in that house in Abercorn Terrace (in St John's Wood district).

The drawing-room looks very empty. Crosby had

> known every cupboard, flagstone, chair and table in that large rambling house, not from five or six feet of distance as they had known it; but from her knees, as she scrubbed and polished; she had known every groove, stain, fork, knife, napkin and cupboard. They and their doings had made her entire world (*TY* 232).

Crosby is crying, because of her mixed emotions, her memories of this house and this family, including the night that the kettle would not boil – the night of the mother's death. Eleanor had been a little girl of fourteen, when Crosby came to them, 'looking so stiff and smart' (*TY* 233). The housekeeper Crosby's life in the Pargiters' house becomes an uncanny experience, something 'at once unexpected and oddly familiar',[183] after her moving out of the basement of the house, settling herself in a single room in Richmond. She is familiar with every corner of the Pargiters' house, for she knows it 'from her knees, as she scrubbed and polished' every inch of the house in a great detail, polishing silvers, knives, forks, chairs, and the handsome sideboard – 'all the solid objects' (*TY* 35 – 36). Crosby's photographic eye represents the 'optical unconscious',[184] for she had known the house 'not from five or six feet of distance' as any other Pargiters had. Crosby sees something that cannot be silenced, which remains 'real' even after she had left the Pargiters' house. It is a reality, at a point that in the immediacy of her realisation (the Pargiters and their doings 'had made her entire world'), after that long-past forty years; the future, so persuasively looks back. In that visual world of photography, it seems that Crosby had grown herself into the picture, the transformed world, during the long duration of a forty-year shot.

I would like to begin with the atmosphere of silence and emptiness of the Pargiters' house. But before that I will have to mention Benjamin's 'A Short History of Photography' (1931), in order to see how Woolf's photographic vision of London works in a surrealist way. Benjamin sees the historical tension between each stage of the 'rise and fall'[185] of photography. The first stage is 'the first decade' after Daguerre's silver plate is invented (it was in

---

[183] Peter Nicholls. *Modernisms: A Literary Guide*. London: Macmillan, 1995, p.279.

[184] Walter Benjamin, 'A Short History of Photography' (1931). It was originally published in *Die Literarische Welt* of 18 September, 25 September and 2 Oct, 1931. Reprinted in *Screen* 13.1 (1972): 5 – 26, p.7.

[185] Benjamin, 'A Short History of Photography', p.5.

1839, averaged twenty-five gold francs a plate, kept in cases like jewellery).[186] For Benjamin, the work of Hill, Cameron, Hugo and Nadar belong to this first stage. As Benjamin claims, Atget's Paris photos 'are the forerunners of surrealist photography; vanguard of the only really broad column which surrealism was able to set in motion'.[187] His photographs have been compared with 'those of a scene of action'.[188] Each corner of the city is staging a scene; each passerby can be a possible actor. For Benjamin, Atget is the person who liberates photography from conventional portrait photography, in which one can see the 'stuffy atmosphere'[189] spread in the photograph. The 'aura' is an atmosphere, creating by the silver plate, light and shadow, which reveals photography's here and now: a 'peculiar web of space and time: the unique manifestation of a distance, however near it may be'.[190] The emptiness of Atget's city scene creates possibilities for the viewer's imagination to 'act'.

For Benjamin, Atget's Paris is the forerunner of the French Surrealist movement. In 1926, Man Ray introduced into *La Révolution surréaliste* four images by Atget, in issue no. 7 in June 1926 and no. 8 in December. According to Man Ray, it was Atget who asked that the pictures should be used anonymously. As Ian Walker argues, Atget's work seems to form a bridge between nineteenth-century topographical photography and twentieth-century modernism. Atget's fame, as Benjamin claims, began to accumulate after his death in 1927.[191] Only in retrospect do these images stand out as 'being Atget'.[192] They are spectacles of an absolute reality. Atget's everyday directness, the simple documentary of Paris, becomes

---

[186] Benjamin, 'A Short History of Photography', p.6.

[187] Benjamin, 'A Short History of Photography', p.20.

[188] Benjamin, 'A Short History of Photography', p.25.

[189] Benjamin, 'A Short History of Photography', p.20.

[190] Benjamin, 'A Short History of Photography', p.20.

[191] Ian Walker. *City Gorged with Dreams: Surrealism and Documentary Photography in Interwar Paris*. Manchester: Manchester University Press, 2002, p.89.

[192] Walker, *City Gorged with Dreams*, p.89.

early Surrealists' practice of an Atgetian aesthetic (as what Man Ray considered, 'Atget's naivety'[193]), coming to see the haunted, somehow inexplicable, in its formality. I suggest that Atget's city scene represents a sense of emptiness, which is exactly Woolf depicts in *The Years*. The emptiness of Paris is not a ghost town, but a space in which 'act' is possible, filled with various possibilities, for 'every passerby' can be a possible actor. In this light, Atget's dismissal of the aura, for Benjamin, is a key which at a time 'when its development could not yet be foreseen'.[194]

Atget himself was an actor, according to Benjamin, who, 'repelled by his profession, tore off his mask and sought to strip reality of its camouflage. Poor and unknown, he lived in Paris, selling his photography for a song to amateurs'.[195] The contemporaries of Atget 'knew nothing of the man who hawked his pictures mainly round the art studios, throwing them away for a few pence, often for no more than the price of one of those picture postcards of around 1900'[196]. Benjamin suggests that Atget 'reached the pole of perfect mastery; but with the embittered mastery of a great craftsman who always lives in the shadows, he neglected to plant his flag there. Hence many others may imagine they have discovered the pole, when Atget had been there before them'.[197] Atget does not photograph the 'grand views and the so-called landmarks'.[198] The remarkable thing about Atget's pictures, Benjamin argues, is their 'emptiness' – 'the Porte d'Acceuil at the fortifications is empty, so too are the triumphal steps, the courtyards, the café terraces and, as is proper, the Place du Tertre. They are not lonely, but they lack atmosphere; the city in these pictures is empty in the manner of a flat which has not yet found a

---

[193] Walker, *City Gorged with Dreams*, p.92.
[194] Walter Benjamin, 'Surrealism: *The Last Snapshot of the European Intelligentsia*'. *Reflections*. Trans. Edmund Jephcott. New York: Schocken, 1978, p.178.
[195] Benjamin, 'A Short History of Photography', p.20.
[196] Benjamin, 'A Short History of Photography', p.20.
[197] Benjamin, 'A Short History of Photography', p.20.
[198] Benjamin, 'A Short History of Photography', p.21.

new occupant'.[199] The empty flat is a threshold, which allows images 'flooding back and forth', dialectically between 'waking and sleeping'.[200]

Atget's Westminster is suggestive. In that photograph, one cannot see the House of Parliament and Big Ben; rather, there is the Thames, the street light, the tree and the life buoy, which reads 'Westminster'. I would suggest that the 'empty space' is a situation of existence while withholding that existence itself – an ambiguous situation that is before meaning, also before the self, what Lacan regards as the 'imago', the 'imaginary'.[201] The emptiness allows imagination to step in and out, welcoming its 'new occupant' to step inside and outside the domain of intoxication – the dream – in a Surrealist sense.

It is interesting to see how Atget comes surprisingly close to Woolf in terms of the concept of emptiness. The death of the mother indicates exactly the situation of an empty house. The emptiness is the starting point, in which the self can imagine a scene before the self, where the imaginary is the world. The beginning of *The Years* does not have this 'aura'. The tea-kettle will not boil. The Pargiters's house in Abercorn Terrace is grey, silent and empty, as the city scene in Atget's photographs. Over the fireplace, there is a picture of a red-haired young woman in white muslin, holding a basket of flowers on her lap, smiling (*TY* 9). This young woman is the mother of the Pargiters, for later one can see that family members, such as Martin, who has the same red hair.

This young woman is not young anymore. She is dying in Abercorn Terrace. There she is, lying in her bed, looking so 'soft, decayed but everlasting, lying in the cleft of the pillows, and obstacle, a prevention, an impediment of life' (*TY* 22). Delia notices the detail of her mother's funeral. The black funeral horses are pawing the ground, they are scraping little pits with their hooves in the yellow gravel. To her they look 'vicious' (*TY* 91). The coffin looks 'too new to be buried for ever' (*TY* 92).

---

[199] Benjamin, 'A Short History of Photography', p.21.
[200] Benjamin, 'Surrealism', p.178.
[201] Lacan, *The Four Fundamental Concepts of Psychoanalysis*, p.279.

Delia stares down into the grave, and feels an excitement, an intoxication through the visual, which comes close to Barthes's experience, when he watched Fellini's *Casanova*, embracing the intense emotion when life mixes with death, 'painful and delicious' as Barthes puts it, which makes her pass beyond the 'unreality' of the thing represented (as the coffin looks too new to bury). In the funeral,

> There lay [Delia's] mother; in that coffin – the woman she had loved and hated so. Her eyes dazzled. She was afraid that she might faint; but she must look; she must feel; it was the last chance that was left her. Earth dropped on the coffin; three pebbles fell on the hard shiny surface; and as they dropped she was possessed by a sense of something everlasting; of life mixing with death, of death becoming life. For as she looked she heard the sparrows chirp quicker and quicker, she heard wheels in the distance sound louder and louder; life came closer and closer .... (*TY* 92)

Delia's intense feeling of life and death challenges the obvious aspect of reality – the death of her mother. The life-death intensity cannot exist without pushing death beyond its absolute horizon, inspiring the self to see his own desire. It is, for Barthes, a desire, a depth and a root which he does not know; and yet, while he is looking at Charles Clifford's *The Alhambra (Grenada)*, 1854 – 1856, he has a feeling that the landscape and the house is '*habitable*'.[202] The old house, the shadowy porch with Arab decoration, a man sitting against the wall, a deserted street, a Mediterranean tree: this old photograph touches Barthes, bearing on him with a dialectical intensity of life and death, as one pole forwards him to a 'utopian time', while the other is carrying him 'back to somewhere in [himself]'.[203]

---

[202] Barthes, *Camera Lucida*, p.38.
[203] Barthes, *Camera Lucida*, p.40.

A voyage back to the scene before the birth of one's self, while his mother was a little girl (Barthes's utopian time, the imaginary), is also a journey which carries one to somewhere in one's own present self. The picture shows a landscape of predilection, as if Barthes was '*certain* of having been there or of going there'.[204] A simple act of 'looking' at the old photograph of that particular landscape, reveals the dialectic – it is such a journey, a voyage to the end (death), but also a voyage of the beginning (life), which goes to 'a place' where one has been there: the maternal body,[205] the mother's womb. The old photograph Barthes looks at is a symbol of the maternal body, the essential landscape in one's self. Barthes's look comes close to Delia's, referring to a journey of searching for a self – an existence of the everlasting dialectic of dream and reality, life and death, the conscious and the unconscious – a journey one has been and is going to. Death and life are all in her.

'heimlich, awakening in me the Mother':[206] Sally

Barthes's looking at the old photograph awakes him to a journey in himself, between 'has been there' and 'is going to', a dialectic of being and nothingness, life and death, the conscious and the unconscious, reality and dream. It is an inner journey, revealing the psychological phenomenon of uncanny strangeness. As Kristeva points out, it is Freud's *Das Unheimliche* (1919) that begins by searching for the meaning of the very word *heimlich*. In that word, the 'familiar intimate' are reversed into their opposites, brought together with the contrary meaning of 'uncanny strangeness' harbored in *unheimlich*.[207] The immanence of the strange within the familiar indicates

---

[204] Barthes, *Camera Lucida*, p.40.

[205] Barthes, *Camera Lucida*, p.40.

[206] Barthes, *Camera Lucida*, p.40.

[207] Julia Kristeva, *Strangers to Ourselves*. Trans. Leon S. Roudiez. New York:

the secret that 'ought to have remained' hidden but which 'has come to light', which, as far Freud was concernd, was confirmed by Schelling.[208]

Consequently, the strangeness of the uncanny would be that which *was* familiar, as when Barthes looks at his mother's picture, finding out that the dead person in the picture is his mother, with whom he is familiar. Barthes's dialectical journey begins with removing the uncanny strangeness from the external world (a fact, the reality, the death of his mother), relocating it inside, as the familiarity tainted with strangeness and linked to the past, an anxiety, a double, and the unconscious. According to Kristeva, the past refers to the eye and the castration anxiety, which was repressed but surfaced again 'on the occasion of a state of love'.[209] The return of the repressed love.

The uncanny strangeness is an intensity of anxiety (for instance, the painful and delightful intensity, experienced by Barthes), a defence put up by a distraught self. It is the psychic evidence of an absolute repression, and the return of the repressed in the guise of anxiety. The uncanny strangeness appears as a metaphor of the psychic function of the self – 'the builder of the *other*', of 'the *strange*',[210] of 'the *death*',[211] of 'the *feminine*'[212] – elaborated by repression and one's experience of it. The uncanny 'reveal[s] the circumstances that are favorable to go through repression, making possible the confrontation with *death*', 'for our unconscious refuses the fatality of death'.[213] The image of death, in this respect, is this uncanny place – the entrance to the place 'where each one of us lived once upon a time and in the beginning'.[214] It

---

Harvester, 1991, p.182.

[208] Kristeva, *Strangers to Ourselves*, p.183.

[209] Kristeva, *Strangers to Ourselves*, p.183.

[210] Kristeva, *Strangers to Ourselves*, p.184.

[211] Kristeva, *Strangers to Ourselves*, p.185.

[212] Kristeva, *Strangers to Ourselves*, p.185.

[213] Kristeva, *Strangers to Ourselves*, p.185.

[214] Sigmund Freud. "The 'Uncanny'" (1919). *The Standard Edition of the Complete Psychological Works of Sigmund Freud: Volume XVII (1917 – 1919): An Infantile Neurosis and Other Works*. Trans. James Strachey in collaboration with Anna

is Barthes's dialectical journey – a voyage from where one has been and to where one is going to.

The uncanny is a symbolic process of the working of the unconscious, which is itself dependant on repression. This process, as Kristeva points out, is 'awakening of the value of signs as such and of their specific logic'.[215] The sign has a real importance, for it crumbles away from the material reality to which it was commonly supposed to point, to the benefit of imagination, referring to the over-accentuation of psychical reality, a fantasy, for Freud which means an 'intra-uterine existence',[216] in comparison with material reality. To worry or to smile, as Kristeva puts it, 'such is the choice when we are assailed by the strange; our decision depends on how familiar we are with our own ghosts'.[217] The 'foreigner'[218] is within us, as Freud discovered, in 'a sense of depersonalisation', 'one's infantile desires, fears of the other' – 'the other of death, the other of woman, the other of uncontrollable drive'.[219]

In *The Years*, the uncanny is evoked through Sally's ghosts: the meaning of the soul. The eldest Pargiter son, Sir Digby, lives in the house on Browne Street, Westminster, with his half French wife, Eugenie, and their two daughters, Maggie and Sally. Sally, alone in her top back room on a summer night, is reading, thinking, and from time to time looking out on the moon-lit back gardens, into which a party is overflowing. She leans her elbow on the sill and watches the party through the window frame. The iron staircase is marked out with blue and yellow lamps dotted along the wall. Sally cannot hear the talking and laughing, because it is too far. The garden of their own house is empty and silent. She is reading *Antigone*, which was

---

Freud. London: Hogarth Press and the Institute of Psycho-Analysis, 1955, p.245.

[215] Kristeva, *Strangers to Ourselves*, p.186.

[216] Freud, "The 'Uncanny'", p.244.

[217] Kristeva, *Strangers to Ourselves*, p.191.

[218] Kristeva, *Strangers to Ourselves*, p.191.

[219] Kristeva, *Strangers to Ourselves*, p.191.

translated by her cousin Edward. Her inner reflection on *Antigone* in this moonlit night mingles with the garden scene outside:

> 'the world is nothing but ...' She paused. What did he say? Nothing
> but thought, was it? she asked herself as if she had already forgotten.
> Well, since it was impossible to read and impossible to sleep, she
> would let herself *be* thought. It was easier to act things than to think
> them. Legs, body, hands, the whole of her must be laid out passively
> to take part in this universal process of thinking which the man said
> was the world living (*TY* 142).

Sally cannot sleep. She feels intense and melancholic. As Judith Butler points out, Antigone's legacy can be read as an example of anti-authoritarianism, as a certain feminist impulse.[220] Although there is the 'Antigone' of Sophocles' play by that name, and there is also, for Judith Butler, the Antigone who is made into a historical figure and an identity for women, standing for the principle of kinship, the ethical order, the state's law and authority in crisis. Antigone, as Butler argues, has been thought to represent kinship as the sphere of laws and norms '*that conditions the possibility of politics without ever entering into it*'.[221] Kinship has been seen as producing the social, the symbolic and the norm. The politicalisation of kinship as a feminist claim is essential for Butler. And yet, in *The Years*, Woolf's use of Antigone in Sally's reading Edward's translation, thinking about the meaning of the 'soul', comes close to the idea of bodilessness in *A Room of One's Own*. A female writer should not be limited by her own body: she can explore and create a literary landscape of her own, where no one has been there. Sally is reading *Antigone* (in her cousin's translation). Sally falls asleep. Her body becomes lighter and lighter; she cannot think about her legs, her hands, her

---

[220] Judith Butler, *Antigone's Claim: Kinship Between Life & Death*. New York: Columbia University Press, 2000, p.1.

[221] Butler, *Antigone's Claim*, p.2.

whole body. Sally's process of reading *Antigone* and falling asleep is symbolic. Her body and consciousness withdraw from the physical world, from her room, her house, and the people dancing in her neighbour's garden. Her self enters into an imaginary world, becoming an 'outsider' to the external world, the norm, the law, order, kinship, the blood-line (family). Her body 'dropped suddenly; then reached ground' (*TY* 146), as Antigone's dead buried body did. The imaginary world is like a 'dark wing brush[ing] her mind, leaving a pause; a blank space' (*TY* 146). The night, the imaginary space of darkness and emptiness, appears as in one's intra-uterine existence. Everything in that space 'stretched and generalised' as she was asleep. The book *Antigone* 'fell on the floor' (*TY* 146).

The Outsider's Snapshots: *Three Guineas*

By the end of 1930s, Woolf had come to realise the connection between *The Years* (1937) and *Three Guineas* (1938), for 'the public and the private worlds are inseparably connected; that the tyrannies and servilities of the one are the tyrannies and servilities of the other'.[222] As Woolf herself claims in her diary, *The Years* and *Three Guineas* should be read together 'as one book – as indeed they are'.[223] In *The Years*, Woolf objectifies figures of patriarchal power (the Judge, the statue of Nelson) into Eleanor's snapshots via an outsider's subversive point of view, as her way of depicting photographic vision. In *Three Guineas*, Woolf shows her readers an even more radical way of using and analysing photographic images of figures of male authority. In this section, I aim to show the way in which Woolf uses the outsider's snapshots, to have subversive power for social transformation by politicising art.

---

[222] Jeri Johnson, 'Literary Geography: Joyce, Woolf and the City'. *City* 4.2 (2000): 199 – 214, p.208.

[223] Woolf, *D* V, p.148.

At the end of his essay, 'The Work of Art in the Age of Mechanical Reproduction' (1935), Benjamin makes a distinction between the aestheticisation of politics under fascism, which 'inevitably culminates in the aestheticized spectacle of war, and the politicization of art – communism's possible antidote to that spectacle'.[224] The shock effects of the image, in this light, are exploitable to varying political ends, in which '[w]ar is beautiful because it enriches a flowering meadow with the fiery orchids of machine guns'. [225] Fascism, as Benjamin argues, will manipulate the crowd by providing propaganda. Politicising art, on the other hand, will make demystification possible, make sure a path to the goal of social transformation.

Woolf does not show the fragmented female bodies of the Spanish War for 'shock effects' in *Three Guineas*, because she does not want to objectify women first by the war and second by the gaze. If she did, that would be 'too constructed', 'too intentional'.[226] Instead, she shows five photographs of male authority figures: 'A General', 'Heralds', 'A University Procession', 'A Judge', and 'An Archbishop', to make one see where the 'horror' of the war actually originates. Barthes's view of the shock effects comes close to Woolf's purpose in using photographs of male authority. As Barthes claims in 'Shock-Photos', the horror of looking at a picture comes from 'the fact that *we are looking at it*', not from 'the photographer to *signify* the horrible for us to experience it'.[227] The figures of male authority are the 'horror' that Woolf is constructing and suggesting in *Three Guineas*, adding intentional

---

[224] Karen Jacobs, *The Eye's Mind: Literary Modernism and Visual Culture*. Ithaca: Cornell University Press, 2001, p.203.

[225] Walter Benjamin, 'The Work of Art in the Age of Mechanical Reproductions' (1935), *Illuminations*. Trans. Harry Zohn. Ed. Hannah Arendt. New York: Schocken, 1969, p.241.

[226] Roland Barthes, *The Eiffel Tower.* Trans. Richard Howard. New York: Hill and Wang, 1979, p.72.

[227] Barthes, *The Eiffel Tower*, p.71.

facts of horror. These photographs, for example, signify the horror, as Woolf looks at the visible world (the cityscape of London: Waterloo Bridge over the Thames, the river flowing beneath, Westminster and the Houses of Parliament, *TG* 110), thinking about the 'horror':

> There they go, our brothers who have been educated at public schools and universities, mounting those steps, passing in and out of those doors, ascending those pulpits, preaching, teaching, administering justice, practising medicine, transacting business, making money. It is a solemn sight always – a procession, like a caravanserai crossing a desert. Great-grandfathers, grandfathers, fathers, uncles – they all went that way, wearing their gowns, wearing their wigs, some with ribbons across their breasts, others without. One was a bishop. Another a judge. One was an admiral. Another a general. One was a professor. Another a doctor (*TG* 111).

Instead of showing the dead bodies of women and children, these photographs are rather suggestive, leaving the viewer a space to imagine the workings of patriarchy and the cruel war. Woolf uses these photographs in a highly suggestive way, which Barthes called 'the *numen*'.[228] It is unstable, with its own way – ambiguity, the 'delay of a destiny',[229] which 'adds to the reading of the sign a kind of disturbing challenge'.[230] Woolf demystified patriarchy by her analysis of a series of images of male authority, leading to a conclusion that she must elaborate herself, without being encumbered by the directness of a pure sign – the photograph of 'ruined houses and dead bodies' (*TG* 39). And yet, the phantom that haunts the narrator throughout the work, constituting the metaphoric counterpart to the photograph, is the dead bodies of women and child in the Spanish War.

---

[228] Barthes, *The Eiffel Tower*, p.72.

[229] Barthes, *The Eiffel Tower*, p.73.

[230] Barthes, *The Eiffel Tower*, p.72.

The image of the dead is an invisible presence in both Barthes's *Camera Lucida* and Woolf's *Three Guineas*. Male authority's figures/bodies are the punctum, associated with the dead body of women and children in Spanish War, just as the erotic dancer's body evokes Barthes's painful and intense response in Fellini's *Casanova*.

Woolf questions the role of women in a patriarchal society. A woman is an outsider, because she is outside of the gender line which represents authority. She cannot be a bishop, a judge, a lawyer, a doctor or a general, because she is not one of great-grandfathers, grandfathers, fathers, and uncles. A woman cannot wear the symbolic splendour of a general's uniform. A woman is excluded by patriarchy; and yet, for Woolf, it is an opportunity to see this gender line through a curved looking glass, from an outsider's point of view. The outsider's snapshot subverts the phallocentric vision. As Hélène Cixous points out in her essay 'The Laugh of the Medusa', a '[w]oman must write her self'.[231] By writing her self, as Cixous suggests, a woman can bring other women to writing, from which they have been driven away 'from their bodies'.[232] Cixous's concept comes surprisingly close to Woolf's bodilessness, as one can see in *A Room of One's Own*, *The Years* and *Three Guineas*. A woman puts her 'self' into the text – as 'into the world and into history' – making one see the possibility of a woman's creativity, and foreseeing 'the unforeseeable'.[233] When Cixous writes 'as a woman, toward women',[234] she is speaking of woman, as Woolf does, 'in her inevitable struggle against conventional man',[235] in order to bring women's senses and meaning in history, instead of repressing them in the darkness. Woolf's use of photographs from an outsider's point of view subverts the sanctuary

---

[231] Hélène Cixous, 'The Laugh of the Medusa'. Trans. Keith Cohen and Paula Cohen. *Signs: Journal of Women in Culture and Society* 1.4 (1976): 875 – 893, p.875.

[232] Cixous, 'The Laugh of the Medusa', p.875.

[233] Cixous, 'The Laugh of the Medusa', p.875.

[234] Cixous, 'The Laugh of the Medusa', p.875.

[235] Cixous, 'The Laugh of the Medusa', p.875.

of the phallus. This outsider's point of view is critical, subverting the masculine view, considering a woman not as men's lack or an unexplorable dark continent, but the subject – the affirmation of the feminine.

'A Sketch of the Past'

Photography had had a significant role in Virginia Woolf's world since she was fifteen. For instance, she wrote about photography in her diary, about taking Leonard Woolf's photograph in Asheham;[236] in her letters, about sending Vanessa Bell films she developed;[237] and last but not the least, in her essays, about her anxious experience of developing a film.[238] As Maggie Humm points out, photography 'was a continuous part of the Woolfs' lives'.[239] Virginia Woolf also uses photography in her fictional writings. For example, her mock biography *Orlando*, contains not only three photos of Vita Sackville-West, but also a photograph of her niece Angelica costumed as the Russian princess which, according to Diane F. Gillespie, 'kept Virginia close to Vanessa, who took least ten pictures of her daughter assuming different poses in different headdresses and robes'.[240]

The Monk's House album five contains one of the Woolf's favourite armchair (with Vanessa Bell and Duncan Grant's design), in which Dorothy Bussy was sitting with her daughter Janie under a triangular geometrical shaped object in the house (it may be a roof or a stair). The triangular pattern reminds me of Lily's painterly vision in *To the Lighthouse*. The relation between the past (for me, the moment when Dorothy's picture was taken, for Lily her memory of Mrs Ramsay), the present (my present gaze at

---

[236] Virginia Woolf, *D I*, p.54.

[237] Virginia Woolf, *L II*, p.187.

[238] Virginia Woolf, *E III*, p.139.

[239] Humm, *Modernist Women and Visual Cultures*, p.40.

[240] Gillespic, 'Virginia Woolf and Photography', *Multiple Muses of Virginia Woolf*, p.136.

the picture, Lily's moment of picture making) and the future (Dorothy and Lily's future are my present; my future will be whose present?) forms a meditation and an imaginative journey that goes across generations, between mothers and daughters. Woolf fictionalises this mother-child relation, just as Cameron photographed eternity in her aesthetic representations of Madonna and child: *Goodness, from the series Fruits of the Spirit* (1864), *The Day Spring* (1865), *The Holy Family* (1867), *Mary Mother* (1867).

Virginia Woolf had a passion for taking pictures. For her, photographs are a visual language, rather than a historical representation of facts. As Humm claims, the Woolf albums are "not chronologically ordered. For example, the cover of Monk's House album 4 bears the date '1939', yet the album begins with a *News Chronicle* cutting of Lady Baldwin dated 1938, followed by photographs taken at Ottoline Morrell's in 1923".[241] The Monk's House albums demonstrate Woolf's personal way of mapping her own memory, as a practice of 'matrixial' recordings of experience, which suggests new symbols, new awareness of 'a feminine dimension in subjectivity' between 'memory and oblivion', between 'what has already been created and what has been lost'.[242] I am particularly interested in mother-daughter relations in Woolf's verbal imagery, such as that in 'A Sketch of the Past' (1939), in which one can see how Woolf metamorphosises her mother Julia Jackson, Cameron's favourite model, giving meaning to the unthinkable, unnoticed and unrecognised in matrixial encounters.

The loss of such a central figure, her mother, in Woolf's life, in time, grew in time into a painful struggle between the pull of her talent and the behavior expected from an 'Angel in the House', the Victorian idealisation of a woman's role as a tender and caring angel in her family.[243] Woolf uses her talent, having her own 'visual way' of depicting her moments of being;

---

[241] Humm, *Modernist Women and Visual Cultures*, pp.69 – 70.

[242] Humm, *Modernist Women and Visual Cultures*, p.79.

[243] Vanessa Curtis, *Virginia Woolf's Women*. 2002. Phoenix Mill: Sutton, 2003, p.45.

in that respect, she comes to think of life as something of 'extreme reality',[244] as something that can be represented through 'snapshot'[245] scenes. By so doing, Woolf can feel her own independence, and also in relation to other people, for that relation is a force to overcome her mother's death, in which she makes what is real (the image of her Mother), what is unreal (loss, death) and what is surreal (her double vision of her Mother's personality).

Let me start with the image of Virginia Woolf's mother in 'A Sketch of the Past'. In this work, one can see how Woolf's mother shapes her inner life, in which emotion and sensibility can be expressed through visual forms. It is an essay-memoir, which has got the date, the month and the year of Woolf's present moment. According to Woolf, the present, for her, serves as 'platform to stand upon'.[246] Based on Woolf's present date, month and year; say, May 15th 1939, one can see how her past breaks into the daily life of the present, like the wave breaks on the shore. On this particular day, the memory of her mother's death forty-four years ago, came back to her. Recalling the past, Woolf writes as she thinks about her much loved and long dead half-sister, Stella, that it is the moments when the past emerges in the smoothly flowing present that give her one of her 'greatest satisfactions', not because she is thinking of the past, but because it is then that she is living in the present fully. Woolf found that 'the present when backed by the past is a thousand times deeper than the present when it presses so close that you can feel nothing else, when the film on the camera reaches only the eye'.[247] The moment when the film on the camera reaches deeper than the eye, the moment when the past breaks into the present, brings strong emotions and feelings, as if one was fully alive again.

---

[244] Virginia Woolf, 'A Sketch of the Past', p.118.
[245] Woolf, 'A Sketch of the Past', p.115.
[246] Woolf, 'A Sketch of the Past', p.75.
[247] Woolf, 'A Sketch of the Past', p.98.

And yet, Woolf also wonders,

> For what reality can remain real of a person who died forty-four
> years ago at the ago of forty-nine, without leaving a book, or a
> picture, or any piece of work – apart from the three children who
> now survive and the memory of her that remains in their minds?
> There is the memory; but there is nothing to check that memory by;
> nothing to bring it to ground with.[248]

Woolf's memory gives her mother a spiritual rebirth via photographic vision.
It shows a number of visual patterns connected with her, such as a black
empty centre (as the space underneath the table cloth in Talland House),
black and white patterns (her two dresses, two marriages, two contradictory
characters, the black sandhill and white lighthouse in St Ives). Woolf's
unique visual patterns construct her stream of thought, bringing her mother's
life back to her as if through photography, as if Woolf could 'snapshot' what
she meant by exposing this memory to 'some invisible ray'[249] – a moment of
intensity, a moment of sudden 'revelation'[250] that connects her inner and
outer worlds. Woolf's photographic vision (her moments of sudden
revelation) is indeed essential for her to achieve the unique moment of being.

Woolf had faced her absolute loss. And yet, she went through the
process of mourning not by looking at the image of her mother that was
caught in any existing pictures. Woolf has her voyage 'in' – into the depth
of her memory, to visualise colours and shapes which, for her, define the
image of her mother. Woolf's intense emotion about her mother brings her
matriarchal creativity. She sees it as the 'space beneath the nursery table',[251]
the great black space with the table-cloth hanging down in folds on the

---

[248] Woolf, 'A Sketch of the Past', p.85.

[249] Woolf, 'A Sketch of the Past', p.115.

[250] Woolf, 'A Sketch of the Past', p.72.

[251] Woolf, 'A Sketch of the Past', p.78.

outskirts in the distance'.[252] In Woolf's childhood memory, it is a 'vast space'[253] that she and her sister Vanessa Bell could roam and meet. This black empty space can also be metaphorical. It is a symbolic womb of Woolf's imagination, with the force of life 'which turns a baby, who can just distinguish a great blot of blue and purple on a black background, into the child who thirteenth years later can feel all that [she] felt on May 5th 1895'[254] – when her mother died.

For Barthes, photography produces Death while trying to preserve Life. Life and Death are like two sides of one coin (*Life / Death*).[255] By looking at a photograph, one literally dives into Death. Woolf does not use any photograph of her mother as any "nature witness of 'what has been'";[256] rather, she sees herself as a fish in the stream, describing the 'stream' – the very 'subject',[257] the invisible presence of her mother in this memoir. However, Woolf has a dual photographic vision of her mother, which on the one hand, contains her mother's general and natural quality: her beauty and virtue as a mother, her keeping of what Woolf describes as their 'panoply of life' – that children all 'live in common – in being';[258] on the other hand, her own contradictory personality. Woolf has three still photographic vision of her mother, in terms of her mother's virtue and beauty. Firstly, Woolf saw her mother 'knitting on the hall step'[259] of Talland House in St Ives while children were playing cricket. Secondly, she saw her mother 'writing at her table in London (22 Hyde Park Gate) and the silver candlesticks, and the high carved chair with the claws and the pink seat; and the three-cornered

---

[252] Woolf, 'A Sketch of the Past', p.78.
[253] Woolf, 'A Sketch of the Past', p.78.
[254] Woolf, 'A Sketch of the Past', p.79.
[255] Barthes, *Camera Lucida*, p.92.
[256] Barthes, *Camera Lucida*, p.93.
[257] Woolf, 'A Sketch of the Past', p.80.
[258] Woolf, 'A Sketch of the Past', p.83.
[259] Woolf, 'A Sketch of the Past', p.84.

brass ink pot'.[260] The first two images, according to Woolf, are in the centre of her childhood. She somehow encloses those two images, constructing her own world with her own temperament. Julia Stephen's knitting image becomes Mrs Ramsay in Woolf's *To the Lighthouse* (1926); again, her writing image becomes 'the woman writing'[261] in *The Waves* (1931). And the third image, Woolf's last sight of her mother dying on her bed,[262] makes her feel very deadly, calm, cold and still, as if 'everything had come to an end'.[263]

Woolf also has another dual photographic view of her mother, in which she sees a contradiction in the personality in her mother. Julia Stephen was 'central', a ray of light; she was '[v]ery quick; very definite; very upright; and behind the active, the sad, the silent'.[264] Woolf sees her mother as 'Julia Jackson the real person'[265] because of her complexity. Her two marriages explain it best; according to Woolf, they are two 'incongruous choices':[266] Herbert Duckworth and Leslie Stephen. Duckworth was genial, loveable and simple; he was also the ordinary type of man that Julia Jackson loves. However, it was always 'the queer, the uncouth artistic and the intellectual'[267] who wants to marry her. Julia Jackson combines great simplicity and

---

[260] Woolf, 'A Sketch of the Past', p.84.

[261] As Diane F. Gillespie points out, Julia Stephen wrote essays, but more frequently she invented her own stories, told her children, wrote them down and reworked them. See *Julia Duckworth Stephen: Stories for Children, Essays for Adults*. Eds. Diane F. Gillespie and Elizabeth Steele. New York: Syracuse University Press, 1987, p.2.

[262] In *Hyde Park Gate News* entry, Monday 11th March 1895, it was recorded that Julia Stephen was hoping to get well, so she could be out in to the Park in a carriage; but the weather was so stormy, windy and rainy. See *Hyde Park Gate News: the Stephen Family Newspaper*. By Virginia Woolf, Vanessa Bell with Thoby Stephen. Ed. Gill Lowe. London: Hesperus, 2005, p.189.

[263] Woolf, 'A Sketch of the Past', p.84.

[264] Woolf, 'A Sketch of the Past', p.83.

[265] Woolf, 'A Sketch of the Past', p.88.

[266] Woolf, 'A Sketch of the Past', p.90.

[267] Woolf, 'A Sketch of the Past', p.90.

directness with a sceptical, a serious spirit.[268] It is the combination that makes
a positive impression on the viewer. At the very moment, as I look at G. F.
Watts's sketch, *Julia Jackson*,[269] I find her character is shown very vividly
by the mixture of 'simplicity and scepticism' in her eyes which creates the
depth in her – 'a mixture of the Madonna and a woman of the world'.[270]

A Sketch of the Past offers Woolf's most intense reflection on her
past and the image of her mother. The creation of cinematic (as I have
demonstrated in my chapter three) and photographic visions both
construct a 'hybrid form', which allows her sketches of the past to break
into Woolf's present, as happens in her writing on *Roger Fry* (1940),
which cuts 'across boundaries of genre' that usually separate memoir from
fiction and essay; and 'essay and criticism from biography and
autobiography'.[271] The hybrid form allows Woolf to demonstrate her
vision – a mixture of literary genres in visual forms.

'Her face, as if bathed in inner light, ...':[272] Conclusion

For Woolf, a novelist's task is to give permanence not to the external
facts of existence, but to express complex emotions and thoughts,
visualising them with ever-changing images, memories and signs, by which
to combine both inner and outer realities. Woolf's appearence, as Gisèle
Freund observes, expressing an inner light of her own. Freund recalls their
meeting in October 1938, that

---

[268] Woolf, 'A Sketch of the Past', p.90.

[269] See Elizabeth P.Richardson, *A Bloomsbury Iconography*. Winchester: St Paul's
Bibliographies, 1989, Plate 1, next to p.148.

[270] Woolf, 'A Sketch of the Past', p.90.

[271] Elena Gualtieri, *Virginia Woolf's Essays: Sketching the Past*. London: Macmillan,
2000, p.94.

[272] Gisèle Freund. 'Virginia Woolf'. *The World in My Camera*. Trans. June
Guicharnaud. New York: Dial, 1974, p.130.

> She was fifty-eight when I met her. Her hair was turning gray. She
> was tall and slender, and her features, at once sensual and ascetic,
> were astonishingly beautiful. Her protruding eyebrows jutted out
> over large serious eyes in deep sockets. Her full and tender mouth
> was touching in its sadness. Her very straight, delicate nose
> seemed fleshless.[273]

Like Henry James,[274] Virginia Woolf has a horror of anything that might
expose her private life. The exhibition of her own body, or posing, makes
her anxious, because photography in itself is an exposure of both the
external and the psychological. For Freund, Woolf's face reflected both 'a
visionary sensibility and great sincerity'.[275] Woolf is indeed, a 'very
reserved woman [who] generated a captivating atmosphere'.[276] Freund's
portrait of Woolf reveals her psychological significance – a state of mind
which is losing hope, because of Fascism cannot be arrested without
resorting to violence. Ruth Gruber, in her *Virginia Woolf: The Will to
Create as a Woman*, also points out that in her meeting with Virginia Woolf
in 1935, Woolf depicted Hitler as the ultimate patriarchal power –
'Terrifying', for 'There is such horror in the world'.[277]

   I met Ruth in the International Conference for Virginia Woolf in
University of Birmingham, 2005. Looking at Ruth's eyes, I was in shock:
her eyes had seen Virginia Woolf!

---

[273] Freund, 'Virginia Woolf', p.130.

[274] Julie Grossman points out that Henry James dislike the situation, when he was
photographed in a suit 'with a single row of brass buttons' as a small boy. See
"'It's the Real Thing': Henry James, Photography, and *The Golden Bowl*". *Henry
James Review* 15 (1994): 309 – 328, p.309.

[275] Freund, 'Virginia Woolf', p.131.

[276] Freund, 'Virginia Woolf', p.131.

[277] Ruth Gruber. *Virginia Woolf: The Will to Create as a Woman*. New York: Carroll
& Graf, 2005, p.5.

Epilogue

The Bodiless and the Invisible: Woolf's Psychological London

Virginia Woolf's androgyny goes through a dialectical process, from gender identity to a narrative form of textual hybridity. Female writer's body has been transformed into bodilessness, coming out with words and texts. The hybrid textual form evokes the inner and the outer worlds, reality (visible) and dream images (invisible), verbal and visual arts. Her writing goes beyond Victorian aesthetics, creating her own aesthetic vision with the techniques of painting, photography and film, in which emotion, feeling, desire and the process of thinking can be visualised through literary expression. Woolf's visibility reveals invisibility. In her work, invisible emotion and desire can be visualised in verbal colours and shapes.

Woolf's shapes and colours are signs. It is important, because they refer to psychological reality. Woolf's signs reveal her psychological London. In *Night and Day*, London is shown as a map of emotions. The streets of London can be read as the characters' walking, thinking and emotional paths. By walking through the London streets, Katharine recognises what she really wants, what to do with her own life, and finally finds her own way out by figuring out her own emotion: love. Moreover, emotions are seen through Woolf's use of colours. External colours – red, pink, grey, green, silver, gold and blue make the inner life visible; shapes – heart shape, ovel shape, square shape combine the outer and the inner realities. Using colours and shapes, Woolf takes the painter's eye in literature to a different stage. The aesthetics of Woolf's narraitive form shows a development from Henry James's Impressionist Paris/London, to her own Post-Impressionist London.

In *Mrs Dalloway*, Woolf juxtaposes different shots in Cubist way, creating a cinematic montage by juxtaposing the characters' gazes, throughout different parts of London at different hours on a fine June day. Woolf's time-image shows in the form of *la durée*. The past comes to live a life in the present. Clarissa's London is a mixture of her memories and her present. Peter Walsh's walk in Piccadilly reveals his cinematic vision: a mixture of looking, desire, and thinking. Septimus's vision expresses Woolf's connection to the film, *The Cabinet of Dr Caligari*. The visual is symbolic, emotional and allegorical.

Peter Walsh's visual intoxication with Clarissa's image at the end of the novel reinforces photographic vision in Woolf's writing. Particularly in *The Years*, London becomes a scene which is filled with Surreal experiences – the imaginary is twisted with reality, the unconscious with the conscious, pain and intensity, death and life. Through the mixture of the real and the unreal, Woolf finds her significant form. In *Three Guineas*, Woolf uses photographs of male figures to demonstrate an outsider's photographic vision. By doing so, Woolf hopes to subvert a phallocentric point of view – like Lacan's seeing the skull as the anamorphosis.

BIBLIOGRAPHY

Abbs, Carolyn. 'Virginia Woolf and Gilles Deleuze: Cinematic E-motion and the Mobile Subject'. *Interactive Media* 1 (2005): 1 – 20.

Antliff, Mark. *Inventing Bergson: Cultural Politics and the Parisian Avant-Garde.* Princeton, NJ: Princeton University Press, 1993.

Banfield, Ann. *The Phantom Table: Woolf, Fry, Russell and the Epistemology of Modernism.* Cambridge: Cambridge University Press, 2000.

Barrett, Eileen and Patricia Cramer, eds. *Re: Reading, Re: Writing, Re: Teaching Virginia Woolf.* New York: Pace University Press, 1995.

Barrett, Michèle, ed. *Women and Writing.* New York: Harcourt Brace, 1979.

Barthes, Roland. *Image-Music-Text.* New York: Hill and Wang, 1977.

---. *The Eiffel Tower and Other Mythologies.* Trans. Richard Howard. New York: Hill and Wang, 1979.

---. *Camera Lucida: Reflections on Photography.* Trans. Richard Howard. 1980. London: Vintage, 1993.

Baudelaire, Charles. *The Painter of Modern Life and Other Essays.* Trans. Jonathan Mayne. London: Phaidon, 1995.

Bell, Clive. 'Art and the Cinema' (1922). *Vanity Fair* November 1922, 39 – 41.

---. 'Duncan Grant'. *Since Cézanne.* 1922. London: Chatto and Windus, 1929.

---. *Proust.* London: Hogarth Press, 1928.

---. *Art.* 1914. London: Chatto and Windus, 1947.

---. *Old Friends: Personal Recollections.* London: Cassell, 1956.

Bell, Quentin. *Bloomsbury.* London: Weidenfeld and Nicolson, 1968.

Benjamin, Walter. 'The Return of the *Flâneur*' (1929). *Walter Benjamin: Selected Writings, Volume 2, 1927-1934.* Ed. Michael W. Jennings, et al. Trans. Rodney Livingstone, et al. Cambridge, MA: Harvard University Press, 1999.

---. 'Surrealism: *The Last Snapshot of the European Intelligentsia*' (1929).

---. *Reflections*. Trans. Edmund Jephcott. New York: Schocken, 1978.

---. 'A Short History of Photography' (1931). *Die Literarische Welt* 18 September, 25 September and 2 Oct, 1931. Reprinted in *Screen* 13.1 (1972): 5 – 26.

---. 'Paris, Capital of the Nineteenth Century' (1934). *Reflections*. Ed. Peter Demetz. Trans. Edmund Jephcott. New York: Schocken, 1978.

---. 'The Formula in Which the Dialectical Structure of Film Finds Expression' (1935). *Walter Benjamin: Selected Writings, Volume 3: 1935 – 1938*. Trans. Edmund Jephcott, Howard Eiland, and Others. Eds. Howard Eiland and Michael W. Jennings. Cambridge, MA: Belknap of Harvard University Press, 2002.

---. 'The Work of Art in the Age of Mechanical Reproduction' (1935). *Illuminations*. Trans. Harry Zohn. Ed. Hannah Arendt. New York: Schocken, 1969.

---. 'On Some Motifs in Baudelaire' (1939). *Illuminations*. Trans. Harry Zohn. Ed. Hannah Arendt. New York: Schocken, 1969.

---. 'Theses on the Philosophy of History' (1940). *Illuminations*. Trans. Harry Zohn. New York: Schocken, 1969.

---. Charles Baudelaire: A Lyric Poet in the Era of High Capitalism. Trans. Harry Zohn. London: NLB, 1973.

---. *Berlin Childhood Around 1990*. Trans. Howard Eiland. Cambridge, MA: Harvard University Press, 2006.

Berger, John. *Ways of Seeing*. London: Penguin, 1972.

Bergson, Henri. *Time and Free Will* (1889). Trans. F. L. Pogson. New York: Dover, 2001.

---. *Matter and Memory* (1896). Trans. Nancy Margaret Paul and W. Scott Palmer. New York: Zone Books, 1991.

---. *An Introduction to Metaphysics* (1903). Trans. T. E. Hulme. Indianapolis: Hackett, 1999.

---. *Creative Evolution* (1907). Trans. Arthur Mitchell. New York: Dover, 1998.

Bowlby, Rachel. *Feminist Destinations and Further Essays on Virginia Woolf* Edinburgh: Edinburgh University Press, 1997.

Brennan, Teresa and Martin Jay, eds. *Vision in Context: Historical and Contemporary Perspectives on Sight.* London: Routledge, 1996.

Brewster, Dorothy. *Virginia Woolf's London.* London: Ruskin House, 1959.

Briggs, Julia. *Virginia Woolf: An Inner Life.* London: Allen Lane, 2005.

Bru, Sascha and Gunther Martens, eds. *The Invention of Politics in the European Avant-Garde.* Amsterdam: Rodopi, 2006.

Buck-Morss, Susan. 'The Flâneur, the Sandwichman and the Whore: The Politics of Loitering'. *New German Critique* 39 (1986): 99-138.

Cameron, Julia Margaret. 'Annals of My Glass House' (1875). Heron and Williams 8 – 13.

---. 'On A Portrait' (September 1875). *Macmillan's Magazine*, February 1876. Gernsheim 73.

---. *The Herschel Album: An Album of Photographs by Julia Margaret Cameron, Presented to Sir John Herschel.* London: National Portrait Gallery, 1975.

Chapman, Wayne K. and Janet M. Manson, Eds. *Women in the Milieu of Leonard and Virginia Woolf: Peace, Politics, and Education.* New York: Pace University Press, 1998.

Church, Margaret. *Time and Reality: Studies in Contemporary Fiction.* ChapelHill: University of North Carolina Press, 1949.

Cixous, Hélène. 'The Laugh of the Medusa'. Trans. Keith Cohen and Paula Cohen. *Signs: Journal of Women in Culture and Society* 1.4 (1976): 875 – 893.

Clair, René. 'Foreword'. *Caligari's Cabinet and Other Grand Illusions: A History of Film Design.* Léon Barsacq. Ed. Elliott Stein. Boston: New York Graphic Society, 1976.

Cox, Julian and Colin Ford. *Julia Margaret Cameron: The Complete Photographs.* London: Thames & Hudson, 2003.

Dalgarno, Emily. *Virginia Woolf and the Visible World*. Cambridge: Cambridge University Press, 2001.

D'Aquila, Ulysses L. *Bloomsbury and Modernism*. New York: Peter Lang, 1989.

Davis, Laura and Jeanette McVicker, eds. *Virginia Woolf and Her Influences: Selected Papers from the Seventh Annual Conference on Virginia Woolf*. New York: Pace University Press, 1998.

De Beauvoir, Simone. 'D. H. Lawrence or Phallic Pride'. *The Second Sex*. Trans. H. M. Parshley. New York: Vintage, 1989.

Deleuze, Gilles. *Bergsonism* (1966). New York: Zone Books, 1991.

---. *Cinema 1: The Movement-Image* (1983). Trans. Hugh Tomlinson and Barbara Habberjam. London: Continuum, 2005.

---. *Cinema 2: The Time-Image* (1985). Trans. Hugh Tomlinson and Robert Galeta. London: Continuum, 2005.

--- and Pierre-Félix Guattari. *What is Philosophy*. London: Verso, 1994.

Descartes, René. 'Optics'. *The Philosophical Writings of Descartes, Volume I*. Trans. John Cottingham. Cambridge: Cambridge University Press, 1998.

Detloff, Madelyn. "Imagined Communities of Criticism: 'Wounded Attachments' to the Icons of H. D., Gertrude Stein, and Virginia Woolf'. Mcvicker and Davis 50 – 64.

Dowling, David. *Bloomsbury Aesthetics and the Novels of Forster and Woolf*. London: Macmillan, 1985.

Eagleton, Terry. *Literary Theory*. 1983. Oxford: Blackwell, 1995.

Edel, Leon. *The Psychological Novel 1900 – 1950*. London: Rupert Hart-Davis, 1955.

Eisenstein, Sergei. 'The Eighth Art. On Expressionism, America and, of course, Chaplin' (1922). *S. M. Eisenstein: Selected Works, Volume I, Writings, 1922 – 34*. Ed./Trans. Ricahrd Taylor. London: BFI, 1988.

---. *Film Form: Essays in Film Theory*. Eds./Trans. Jay Leyda. New York: Harcourt, Brace and Company, 1949.

---. 'In Close-Up' (1945). *S. M. Eisenstein: Selected Works, Volume III, Writings, 1934 – 47*. Ed. Richard Taylor. Trans. William Powell. London: BFI, 1996.

---. *Notes of a Film Director*. London: Lawrence & Wishart, 1959.

Falkenheim, Jacqueline V. *Roger Fry and the Beginnings of Formalist Art Criticism.* Ann Arbor: UMI, 1980.

Fishman, Solomon. *The Interpretation of Art: Essays on the Art Criticism of John Ruskin, Walter Pater, Clive Bell, Roger Fry and Herbert Read*. Berkeley: University of California Press, 1963.

Flaxman, Gregory. *The Brain Is the Screen: Deleuze and the Philosophy of Cinema*. Minneapolis: University of Minnesota Press, 2000.

Ford, Madox Ford. *The Soul of London: A Survey of a Modern City*. 1905. Ed. Alan G. Hill. London: Everyman, 1995.

---. 'Henry James'. *Mightier Than the Sword: Memories and Criticisms*. London: George Allen & Unwin, 1838.

Forster, E. M. 'Visions'. *Daily News* 31 July 1919. Majumdar and McLaurin, 68 – 70.

---. 'The Novels of Virginia Woolf'. *New Criterion,* April 1926, 277 – 286. Majumdar and McLaurin, 171 – 178.

---. *Virginia Woolf*. Cambridge: Cambridge University Press, 1942.

Freund, Gisèle. 'Virginia Woolf'. *The World in My Camera*. Trans. June Guicharnaud. New York: Dial, 1974.

Friedberg, Anne. *Window Shopping: Cinema and the Postmodern*. Berkeley: University of California Press, 1993.

Frisby, David. *Cityscapes of Modernity: Critical Explorations*. Cambridge: Polity, 2001.

Fry, Roger. 'The Last Phase of Impressionism' (1908). *The Burlington Magazine*, March 1908, 374 – 375.

---. 'The Post-Impressionists' (1910). Exhibition catalogue: *Manet & the Post-Impressionists*, London, 1910 – 11, 7 – 13. Hyman Kreitman Research Centre for the Tate Library and Archive, Tate Britain, London.

---. "Introductory Note to Maurice Denis, 'Cézanne'" (1910). *The Burlington Magazine*, January 1910, 207 – 219.

---. 'Mrs. Cameron's Photographs' (1926). Powell 23 – 28.

---. 'The Double Nature of Painting' (1933). *Apollo*, May 1969, 362 – 371.

---. *Vision and Design*. Mineola: Dover, 1981.

Gillespie, Diane Filby and Elizabeth Steele, eds. *Julia Duckworth Stephen: Stories for Children, Essays for Adults*. New York: Syracuse University Press, 1987.

---. *The Sisters' Arts: The Writing and Painting of Virginia Woolf and Vanessa Bell*. New York: Syracuse University Press, 1988.

---. "'Her Kodak Pointed at His Head': Virginia Woolf and Photography." *The Multiple Muses of Virginia Woolf*. Ed. Diane F. Gillespie. Columbia: University of Missouri Press, 1993.

--- and Leslie K. Hankins, eds. *Virginia Woolf and the Arts: Selected Papers from the Sixth Annual Conference on Virginia Woolf*. New York: Pace University Press, 1997.

Gillies, Mary Ann. *Henri Bergson and British Modernism*. Montreal: McGill-Queen's University Press, 1996.

Girard, Xavier. *Matisse: The Sensuality of Colour*. Trans. I. Mark Paris. London: Thames and Hudson, 1994.

Goldman, Jane. *The Feminist Aesthetics of Virginia Woolf: Modernism, Post-Impressionism and the Politics of the Visual*. Cambridge: Cambridge University Press, 1998.

---. *The Cambridge Introduction to Virginia Woolf*. Cambridge: Cambridge University Press, 2006.

Gould, Veronica Franklin. *G. F. Watts: The Last Great Victorian*. New Haven: Yale University Press, 2004.

Grinley, Charles. 'A Plea for the Cinema'. *The London Mercury* XIII, 73, November 1925.

Gruber, Ruth. *Virginia Woolf: The Will to Create as a Woman*. New York: Carroll & Graf, 2005.

Guiguet, Jean. *Virginia Woolf and her Works*. Trans. Jean Stewart. London: The Hogarth Press, 1965.

Heron, Liz and Val Williams, eds. *Illuminations: Women Writing on Photography from the 1850s to the Present*. Eds. Liz Heron and Val Williams. London: I. B. Tauris, 1996.

Hind, C. Lewis. *The Post-Impressionists*. London: Methuen, 1911.

Holmes, C. J. 'Notes on the Post-Impressionist Painters: Grafton Galleries, 1910 – 11'. Exhibition catalogue: *Manet & the Post-Impressionists*, London, 1910 – 11, 7 – 17. Hyman Kreitman Research Centre for the Tate Library and Archive, Tate Britain, London.

Hueffer, Ford Madox. '"Novel' and 'Romance'" *Piccadilly Review* 23 October 1919. Majumdar and McLaurin 72 – 75.

Humm, Maggie. *Modernist Women and Visual Cultures: Virginia Woolf, Vanessa Bell, Photography and Cinema*. Edinburgh: Edinburgh University Press, 2002.

Irigaray, Luce. *This Sex Which Is Not One*. Trans. Catherine Porter with Carolyne Burke. Ithaca: Cornell University Press, 1985.

---. *Speculum of the Other Woman*. Trans. Gillian C. Gill. Ithaca: Cornell University Press, 1985.

---. *The Irigaray Reader*. Ed. Margaret Whitford. Oxford: Blackwell, 1991.

James, William. *The Principles of Psychology*. 1890. Cambridge, MA: Harvard University Press, 1981.

James, Henry. 'An English Easter' (1877). *Collected Travel Writings: Great Britain and America.* New York: The Library of America, 1993.

---. 'The Art of Fiction' (1884). *The Art of Fiction and Other Essays by Henry James.* New York: Oxford University Press, 1948.

---. *English Hours.* 1905. London: Heinemann, 1960.

---. *The Art of the Novel: Critical Prefaces by Henry James.* 1934. New York: Charles Scribner's Sons, 1962.

---. *The Painter's Eye.* London: Rupert Hart-Davis, 1956.

Jay, Martin. *Downcast Eyes: The Denigration of Vision in Twentieth-Century French Thought.* 1993. Berkeley: University of California Press, 1994.

---. *Vision in Context: Historical and Contemporary Perspectives on Sight.* Eds. Teresa Brennan and Martin Jay. London: Routledge, 1996.

Johnson, Jeri. Introduction. *The Years.* London: Penguin, 1998.

---. 'Literary Geography: Joyce, Woolf and the City'. *City* 4.2 (2000): 199 – 214.

Kolakowski, Leszek. *Bergson.* Oxford: Oxford University Press, 1985.

Kristeva, Julia. *Desire in Language: A Semiotic Approach to Literature and Art.* Ed. Leon S. Roudiez. Trans. Thomas Gora, Alice Jardine, and Leon S. Roudiez. 1977. New York: Columbia University Press, 1980.

---. *Strangers to Ourselves.* Trans. Leon S. Roudiez. New York: Harvester, 1991.

Kuenzli, Rudolf E. 'Introduction'. *Dada and Surrealist Film.* 1987. Ed. Rudolf E. Kuenzli. Cambridge, MA: MIT, 1996.

Lacan, Jacques. *The Four Fundamental Concepts of Psycho-Analysis.* Ed. Jacques-Alain Miller. Trans. Alan Sheridan. 1973. London: Penguin, 1994.

Lawder, Standish D. *The Cubist Cinema.* New York: New York University Press, 1975.

Lee, Hermione. *The Novels of Virginia Woolf.* London: Methuen, 1977.

Lewis, Wyndham. *Time and Western Man.* 1927. Santa Rosa: Black Sparrow, 1993.

MacCarthy, Desmond. 'The Post-Impressionist Exhibition of 1910'. *The Bloomsbury Group: A Collection of Memoirs, Commentary and Criticism.* Ed. S. P. Rosenbaum. London: University of Toronto Press, 1975.

Majumdar, Robin and Allen McLaurin, eds. *Virginia Woolf: The Critical Heritage.* London: Routledge and Kegan Paul, 1975.

Marcus, Laura. *Virginia Woolf.* 1997. Devon: Northcote House, 2004.

---. *The Tenth Muse: Writing About Cinema in the Modernist Period.* Oxford: Oxford University Press, 2007.

McLaurin, Allen. *Virginia Woolf: The Echoes Enslaved.* Cambridge: Cambridge University Press, 1973.

McNeillie, Andrew, ed. *The Essays of Virginia Woolf.* London: Hogarth, 1986 – 1994, 4 volumes.

Mcvicker, Jeanette and Laura Davis, eds. *Virginia Woolf and Communities: Selected Papers from the Eighth Annual Conference on Virginia Woolf.* New York: Pace University Press, 1999.

Meisel, Perry. *The Absent Father: Virginia Woolf and Walter Pater.* New Haven: Yale University Press, 1980.

Mendilow, A. A. *Time and the Novel.* New York: Humanities, 1972.

Mepham, John. *Virginia Woolf: A Literary Life.* London: Macmillan, 1981.

Minow-Pinkney, Makiko. *Virginia Woolf & The Problem of the Subject.* New Brunswick: Rutgers University Press, 1987.

Mitchell, W. J. T. *Picture Theory: Essays on Verbal and Visual Representations.* Chicago: University of Chicago Press, 1994.

Moi, Toril. *Sexual/Textual Politics: Feminist Literary Theory.* London: Routledge, 1985.

Mullarkey, John, ed. *The New Bergson.* Manchester: Manchester University Press, 1999.

Mulvey, Laura. *Visual and Other Pleasures.* London: Macmillan, 1989.

---. *Fetishism and Curiosity.* Indianapolis: Indiana University Press, 1996.

---. 'Cinematic Space: Desiring and Deciphering'. *Desiring Practices: Architecture, Gender and the Interdisciplinary*. Eds. Katerina Rüedi, Sarah Wigglesworth, and Duncan McCorquodale. London: Black Dog, 1996.

---. *Death 24 x a Second: Stillness and the Moving Image*. London: Reaktion, 2006.

Onega, Susana and John A. Stotesbury. Introduction. *London in Literature: Visionary Mappings of the Metropolis*. Heidelberg: University of C. Winter Heidelberg Press, 2002.

Parsons, Deborah L. *Streetwalking the Metropolis: Women, the City, and Modernity*. Oxford: Oxford University Press, 2000.

Picasso, Pablo. *Picasso on Art*. Ed. Dore Ashton. New York: Da Capo, 1972.

Pollock, Griselda. *Vision and Difference: Femininity, Feminism and Histories of Art*. London: Routledge, 1988.

Powell, Tristram, ed. *Victorian Photographs of Famous Men & Fair Women by Julia Margaret Cameron*. 1926. London: Hogarth Press, 1973.

Reed, Christopher, ed. *A Roger Fry Reader*. Chicago: University of Chicago Press, 1996.

Richter, Harvena. *Virginia Woolf: The Inward Voyage*. Princeton: Princeton University Press, 1970.

Rose, Jacqueline. *Sexuality in the Field of Vision*. 1986. London: Verso, 1991.

Rosenbaum, S. P., ed. *The Bloomsbury Group: A Collection of Memoirs, Commentary and Criticism*. Toronto: University of Toronto Press, 1977.

Sartre, Jean-Paul. *The Imaginary: A Phenomenological Psychology of the Imaginarion*. Trans. Jonathan Webber. 1940. London: Routledge, 2004.

---. *Being and Nothingness: An Essay on Phenomenological Ontology*. Trans. Hazel E. Barnes. 1943. London: Routledge, 1993.

---. *The Philosophy of Existentialism*. Ed. Wade Baskin. New York: Philosophical Library, 1965.

---. *Truth and Existence*. Trans. Adrian van den Hoven. 1989. Chicago: Chicago University Press, 1992.

Seldes, Gilbert. 'The Abstract Movie', *New Republic* 15 September 1926, 95 – 96.

Shone, Richard. *Duncan Grant and Bloomsbury*. Edinburgh: The Fine Arts Society, 1975.

---. *Bloomsbury Portraits: Vanessa Bell, Duncan Grant and Their Circle*. 1976. London: Phaidon, 1999.

---. *The Art of Bloomsbury: Roger Fry, Vanessa Bell and Duncan Grant*. London: Tate Gallery, 1999.

Showalter, Elaine. *A Literature of Their Own: British Women Novelists from Brontë to Lessing*. 1977. Princeton, NJ: Princeton University Press, 1999.

---. Introduction. *Mrs Dalloway* (1925). London: Penguin, 2000.

Simmel, Georg. 'The Metropolis and Mental Life' (1905). *The Sociology of Georg Simmel*. Ed. Kurt H. Wolff. New York: Free Press, 1950.

Snaith, Anna. *Virginia Woolf: Public and Private Negotiations*. London: Macmillan, 2000.

---, ed. *Palgrave Advances in Virginia Woolf Studies*. London: Macmillan, 2007.

Spalding, Frances. *Duncan Grant: A Biography*. London: Pimlico, 1998.

Squier, Susan. *Virginia Woolf and London: the Sexual Politics of the City*. Chapel Hill: University of North Carolina Press, 1985.

Terry, Ellen. *Four Lecturers on Shakespeare*. Ed. Christopher St. John. London: Martin Hopkinson, 1932.

Torgovnick, Marianna. *The Visual Arts, Pictorialism, and the Novel: James, Lawrence and Woolf.* Princeton: Princeton University Press, 1985.

Twitchell, Beverly H. *Cézanne and Formalism in Bloomsbury*. Ann Arbor, Mich: UMI Research Press, 1987.

Walker, Ian. *City Gorged with Dreams: Surrealism and Documentary Photography in Interwar Paris*. Manchester: Manchester University Press, 2002.

Watney, Simon. *English Post-Impressionism*. London: Studio Vista, 1980.

Weinstein, Arnold L. *Vision and Response in Modern Fiction*. Ithaca: Cornell University Press, 1974.

Williams, Linda. *Figures of Desire: A Theory and Analysis of Surrealist Film.* Berkeley: University of California Press, 1981.

Williams, Raymond. "The Significance of 'Bloomsbury' as a Social and Cultural Group". *Keynes and the Bloomsbury Group.* Eds. Derek Crabtree and A. P. Thirlwall. London: Macmillian, 1980.

---. Introduction. *Vision and Blueprints: Avant-Garde Culture and Radical Politics in Early Twentieth-Century Europe.* Eds. Edward Timms and Peter Collier. Manchester: Manchester University Press, 1988.

Wilson, Elizabeth. 'The Invisible Flâneur'. *New Left Review* 191 (1992): 90 – 110.

Wilson, Jean Moorcroft. *Virginia Woolf's London: A Guide to Bloomsbury and Beyond.* 1988. London: Tauris, 2000.

Woolf, Virginia. 'Mr Henry James's Latest Novel' (1905). McNeillie 1986, 22 – 24.

---. "A Mark on the Wall' (1917). *Selected Short Stories by Virginia Woolf.* Ed. Sandra Kemp. 1993. London: Penguin, 2000.

---. 'Movie Novel' (1918). *Contemporary Writers.* London: Hogarth Press, 1965.

---. 'Kew Gardens'. London: Hogarth Press, 1919.

---. *Night and Day* (1919). Ed. J. H. Stape. Oxford: Blackwell, 1994.

---. 'Modern Fiction' (1919). *Collected Essays by Virginia Woolf: Volume Two.* London: Hogarth, 1966.

---. 'Old Bloomsbury' (1922). *Moments of Being.* Ed. Jeanne Schulkind. Sussex: Sussex University Press, 1976.

---. *Jacob's Room.* 1922. London: Hogarth Press, 1965.

---. *Mrs Dalloway's Party: A Short Story Sequence* (1923). Ed. Stella McNichol. London: Hogarth Press, 1973.

---. 'Pictures' (1925). *The Essays of Virginia Woolf: Volumn IV, 1925-1928.* Ed. Andrew McNeillie. London: Hogarth Press, 1994.

---. *Mrs Dalloway.* 1925. London: Penguin, 1992.

---. 'Julia Margaret Cameron' (1926). Powell 13 – 19.

---. 'The Cinema' (1926). *The Essays of Virginia Woolf: Volume IV, 1925-1928.* Ed. Andrew McNeillie. London: Hogarth Press, 1994.

---. 'The Art of Fiction' (1927). *Collected Essays by Virginia Woolf: Volume Two.* London: Hogarth Press, 1966.

---. 'Street Haunting: A London Adventure' (1927). *The Essays of Virginia Woolf, Volume IV, 1925 – 1928.* Ed. Andrew McNeillie. London: Hogarth Press, 1994.

---. 'An Introduction to *Mrs Dalloway*' (1928). *The Essays of Virginia Woolf, Volume IV: 1925 – 1928.* Ed. Andrew McNeillie. London: Hogarth Press, 1994.

---. 'Phases of Fiction' (1929). *Collected Essays by Virginia Woolf: Volume Two.* London: Hogarth Press, 1966.

---. 'Speech Before the London / National Society for Women's Service' (1931). *The Pargiters: The Novel-Essay Portion of THE YEARS'.* Ed. Mitchell A. Leaska. London: Hogarth Press, 1978.

---. 'Great Men's House' (1931-2). *The London Scenes.* London: Snowbooks, 1988.

---. *Walter Sickert: A Conversation.* London: Hogarth Press, 1934.

---. *Freshwater: A Comedy* (1935). Ed. Lucio P. Ruotolo. London: Hogarth Press, 1976.

---. *The Years* (1937). London: Hogarth Press, 1965.

---. *Three Guineas.* London: Hogarth Press, 1938.

---. 'A Sketch of the Past' (1939). *Moments of Being: Unpublished Autobiographical Writings.* Ed. Jeanne Schulkind. Sussex: University of Sussex Press, 1976.

---. *Roger Fry: A Series of Impressions.* Ed. Diane Gillespie. London: Cecil Woolf, 1994.

---. *Roger Fry: A Biography.* 1940. London: Vintage, 2003.

---. 'Ellen Terry' (1941). *Collected Essays by Virginia Woolf, Volume Four.* London: Hogarth Press, 1967.

---. *The Moment and Other Essays.* London: Hogarth Press, 1947.

---. 'Evening over Sussex: Reflections in a Motor-car' (1942). *Collected Essays by Virginia Woolf: Volume Two*. London: Hogarth Press, 1966.

---. *A Writer's Diary*. Ed. Leonard Woolf. 1953. London: Hogarth Press, 1975.

---. *A Room of One's Own and Three Guineas*. Oxford: Oxford University Press, 2000.

---, Vanessa Bell with Thoby Stephen. *Hyde Park Gate News: the Stephen Family Newspaper*. Ed. Gill Lowe. London: Hesperus, 2005.

Zwerdling, Alex. *Virginia Woolf and the Real World*. Berkeley: University of California Press, 1986.

The Film Society Programmes, 1925 – 1939. New York: Arno, 1972.

語言文學類　AG0105

Virginia Woolf and the European Avant-Garde:
London, Painting, Film and Photography

作　　者 ╱ Allison Tzu Yu Lin（林孜郁）
發 行 人 ╱ 宋政坤
執行編輯 ╱ 賴敬暉
圖文排版 ╱ 姚宜婷
封面設計 ╱ 陳佩蓉
數位轉譯 ╱ 徐真玉　沈裕閔
圖書銷售 ╱ 林怡君
法律顧問 ╱ 毛國樑　律師
出版印製 ╱ 秀威資訊科技股份有限公司
　　　　　　台北市內湖區瑞光路 583 巷 25 號 1 樓
　　　　　　電話：02-2657-9211　　　傳真：02-2657-9106
　　　　　　E-mail：service@showwe.com.tw
經 銷 商 ╱ 紅螞蟻圖書有限公司
　　　　　　台北市內湖區舊宗路二段 121 巷 28、32 號 4 樓
　　　　　　電話：02-2795-3656　　　傳真：02-2795-4100
　　　　　　http://www.e-redant.com

2009 年 01 月　BOD 一版
定價：350 元

讀 者 回 函 卡

感謝您購買本書，為提升服務品質，煩請填寫以下問卷，收到您的寶貴意見後，我們會仔細收藏記錄並回贈紀念品，謝謝！

1.您購買的書名：＿＿＿＿＿＿＿＿＿＿＿＿＿＿＿＿＿＿＿＿

2.您從何得知本書的消息？

　　□網路書店　□部落格　□資料庫搜尋　□書訊　□電子報　□書店

　　□平面媒體　□ 朋友推薦　□網站推薦 □其他＿＿＿＿＿＿

3.您對本書的評價：(請填代號　1.非常滿意 2.滿意 3.尚可 4.再改進)

　　封面設計＿＿＿　版面編排＿＿＿　內容＿＿＿　文/譯筆＿＿＿　價格＿＿＿

4.讀完書後您覺得：

　　□很有收獲　□有收獲　□收獲不多　□沒收獲

5.您會推薦本書給朋友嗎？

　　□會　□不會，為什麼？＿＿＿＿＿＿＿＿＿＿＿＿＿＿＿＿＿

6.其他寶貴的意見：＿＿＿＿＿＿＿＿＿＿＿＿＿＿＿＿＿＿＿＿

＿＿＿＿＿＿＿＿＿＿＿＿＿＿＿＿＿＿＿＿＿＿＿＿＿＿＿＿＿＿

＿＿＿＿＿＿＿＿＿＿＿＿＿＿＿＿＿＿＿＿＿＿＿＿＿＿＿＿＿＿

＿＿＿＿＿＿＿＿＿＿＿＿＿＿＿＿＿＿＿＿＿＿＿＿＿＿＿＿＿＿

讀者基本資料

姓名：＿＿＿＿＿＿＿＿＿＿　年齡：＿＿＿＿　性別：□女 □男

聯絡電話：＿＿＿＿＿＿＿＿　E-mail：＿＿＿＿＿＿＿＿＿＿

地址：＿＿＿＿＿＿＿＿＿＿＿＿＿＿＿＿＿＿＿＿＿＿＿＿＿＿

學歷：□高中(含)以下　　□高中　　□專科學校　　□大學

　　　□研究所(含)以上 □其他＿＿＿＿＿＿＿＿

職業：□製造業 □金融業 □資訊業 □軍警 □傳播業 □自由業

　　　□服務業 □公務員 □教職　　□學生 □其他＿＿＿＿＿＿

To：114

　　台北市內湖區瑞光路 583 巷 25 號 1 樓

　　秀威資訊科技股份有限公司　　　收

寄件人姓名：

寄件人地址：□□□

秀威與 BOD

BOD（Books On Demand）是數位出版的大趨勢，秀威資訊率先運用 POD 數位印刷設備來生產書籍，並提供作者全程數位出版服務，致使書籍產銷零庫存，知識傳承不絕版，目前已開闢以下書系：

一、BOD 學術著作—專業論述的閱讀延伸
二、BOD 個人著作—分享生命的心路歷程
三、BOD 旅遊著作—個人深度旅遊文學創作
四、BOD 大陸學者—大陸專業學者學術出版
五、POD 獨家經銷—數位產製的代發行書籍

BOD 秀威網路書店：www.showwe.com.tw
政府出版品網路書店：www.govbooks.com.tw

　　永不絕版的故事・自己寫・永不休止的音符・自己唱